CW01091158

FAERYDAE

GEORGIE DeLAINE

Printed in Australia

Cover and internal design by Shawline Publishing Group Pty Ltd

Illustrations within this book are copyright approved for Shawline Publishing Group Pty Ltd

First printing: July 2024

Shawline Publishing Group Pty Ltd

www.shawlinepublishing.com.au

Paperback ISBN 978-1-9231-7130-5

eBook ISBN 978-1-9231-7142-8

Hardback ISBN 978-1-9231-7154-1

Distributed by Shawline Distribution and Lightning Source Global

Shawline Publishing Group acknowledges the traditional owners of the land and pays respects to the Elders, past, present and future.

A catalogue record for this work is available from the National Library of Australia

FAERYDAE

GEORGIE DeLAINE

For Violet, my little wonder-child

1

Woman of the Woods

Isolated on the farthest edge of the Winding Woods, a woman stared through her window to watch the approaching storm.

'The rain cannot hide that blinding olde moon,' she murmured almost lyrically, rolling a piece of rabbit jerky between her tongue and teeth. 'Sailing over the trees for another long night. Froalla will grow my crops strong tonight, and the wild grasses will glisten wet, like glass.'

A sentimental pause.

She glanced down at the pumpkin sitting on the floor beside her feet and swallowed the slimy piece of jerky. 'Let me tell you something ridiculous, Mr Pumpkin, about those common folk in their cities and towns and villages. They'll say that the moon has a sharper glow than anywhere else when it hovers over these woods. They'll say that you can *hear* its glow as a slicing sound across the sky, like two cleavers sliding against one another's surface, carving the night into pieces. They'll say that these woods make it so.' And the woman began to laugh so lifelessly that she did not even make a sound.

The huge pumpkin did not reply, it just seemed to stare at her. It looked alive as the crackling fire reflected a wave of orange ripples across the room.

Meanwhile, thin particles of water danced lightly upon the wind outside, floating, as if lost.

She sometimes felt lost.

Such rain was called *froalla* to those who lived in the woods. Froalla meant wispy.

The water made a delicate sound as it tickled the window and roof above, audible only because her homestead was so quiet and still. Sometimes the rain was heavy and fuller: *invierno*. Or it could be that kind of rain that was angry and unrelenting: *olvido*.

Though, no matter how it rained, it was always somehow quiet. For everything was quiet out past the woods – nobody wanted to live on that side of the trees. In that terrible badness.

'This is no place for moons to be watching over,' the woman went on. 'I tell that pasty dome every evening to go somewhere else. The night is a home for shadows. A home for death.'

She sought out and flicked one particularly sinewy piece of jerky from her jar and into the fire. She then used two fat fingers to fiddle with a needle and thread. The needle forced its head through the piece of material between her hands, which created a slow stitch. The material was almost too coarse.

She sat upon a crimson suede armchair as she worked, jammed in like a mushroom in a teacup. Her creation was taking shape now; a long coat for one of the new scarecrows to wear, made from the skin of a man who came wandering too close. The woman could tell, even now when the scarecrow was not assembled, that this was going to be a feisty one. 'Albie' had been that wandering man's name, as far as the woman had understood. It was the only piece of information she'd acquired from the stranger before lacing a bowl of pumpkin soup with poison and serving it to him. A clean way to go out.

Last week's news.

If Albie had showed up on her doorstep *this* week, the woman might just have been tired enough to simply give him the directions he sought back to Dainmerry. She probably would have sent him on his way and grumbled to herself about how useless people are from Dainmerry – because if one is going to live in the Winding Woods, one ought to know more about them.

The fire suddenly blazed brightly, as if stoked.

'Hush!' the woman hissed.

In the ensuing lull, she reminisced about everything that was going on in the world; circumstances playing out here and afar – she believed it would take *many* years for this dreadful mess to sort itself out. *Oh yes.* She shook her head.

The woman tied her thread into a knot. The pumpkin was silent but attentive (pumpkins are the smartest of vegetables, after all).

'A little girl, I think,' the woman mumbled. 'The child will be a girl, Mr Pumpkin.' She stroked the pumpkin and brought it up into her lap, twirling her forefinger around and growing long black claws from her nailbeds. Green spirals of magic departed her claws and circled in front of her face like a river of incandescent pea soup. 'Oh, but the girl will grow up,' the woman added. 'And she will learn of this world, that is for sure.'

Seeing poorly through her bloodshot eyes of emerald green, the woman looked at the steep hill outside of her lounge room window, towards the trees. Somewhere on the other side of the vast woodland, near a bustling village perhaps, a baby was taking its first strange breaths.

The woman clutched the pumpkin between her fingers, creating green veins beneath the vegetable's skin that throbbed brightly.

'I'll be here little one,' she whispered towards the icy window. 'Grow your webs and woes. I'll be here still, wondering how this all will end.'

2

The Troll from Manjarta

Winter ice was not far away. Frost was curling its long powdery fingers around flowers and insects, and birds had fled the naked grey skies. An eerie wind made the few orange leaves left turn into brittle sheets that would soon disintegrate from their perches and become parchment upon the earth. All of life was awaiting some warmth to grace another autumn morning in the lagoon.

Sleeping in the centre of such wildness, snoring and farting in her own graceless slumber, was a creature who looked the same as a common human girl. Although this child was, in fact, quite different; she was only really *half* a girl, on account of the strange condition affecting her. For her own beating heart had grown outside of her body.

This girl's name was Faerydae Nóvalie.

Faerydae yawned herself awake, just like she did every morning, inhaling without any difficulty into her hollow chest. The wooden boards beneath her feet rocked and the nearby sea sang a melodic tune as she licked the sleepy morning film off of her lips.

Faerydae's bed of straw clung to her sides as she lifted herself up to sitting. She heard some movement as she rubbed her eyelids: Euphraxia, Faerydae's dear mother, was twisting over and moaning from somewhere in the soft shadows of morning, still deep in slumber, dreaming up a storm. Faerydae scratched her rear and yawned again as Euphraxia murmured sweet nothings into the dark.

Euphraxia Nóvalie had always tried to be a good mother, in her own special way. At the very least, she had not been upset that her daughter was born so... *unique.*

At Faerydae's birth, all alone despite the cockroaches surrounding her, Euphraxia had carried her child's beating organ like a hot pie and stowed it inside a crystallite jar. She balanced the jar on top of a barrel of malt whisky where it was to stay for four monotonous years.

The little heart gave lively beats day in and day out as alcohol sloshed around inside the barrel to the rhythm of the rocking ship the two lived upon.

The heart gave a strong beat. And yet, anybody could see, it was all so utterly wrong: to birth a child with her heart separate to her body. Any parent would worry about the future of such a child. However, Euphraxia, strange and whimsical herself, did not find it at all that compelling. How could she, when so much strangeness had befallen her already?

Euphraxia Nóvalie had endured more than most women of thirty years old; the gruesome death of her husband had been awful, and she swore she'd never marry again. When her parents were eaten alive by serpent monsters on a doomed voyage across the sea, she cried for many days. When a devious illness consumed her mind and turned her quite mad... well, she didn't think much of anything after that.

But the bad luck would not let up.

Four years after Faerydae's birth, the poor girl's bottled-up heart was stolen from their ship in the delusion of night-time, without any evidence to suggest that somebody had even come or gone. Worse still, Euphraxia had become so mad by that point that she merely laughed and laughed and laughed about it.

Faerydae had not laughed along with her, old enough by that point to understand loss.

The child was, firstly, saddened that her heart had been taken away by a stranger (saddened also that her mother should find it so hilarious) but then optimistic that the heart might actually be somewhere even safer, most likely, she thought, in the protection of heavenly angels who sung gentle lullabies to it every night.

Euphraxia began to snore, painting over the sounds of the ocean with a thick, cloggy brush.

Cocooned by willows, boulders and a small pine forest on one side, the Nóvalie's dilapidated Herring Buss floated stoically. It was frozen in a long-lost time of simplicity, a time of modest fishermen. Nowadays, the only blemish upon the lagoon was the ship itself, steadily sinking and decaying evermore since its prime, lodged forever by a sunken anchor deep below.

A precarious wooden boardwalk stretched out from the bank and into the centre of the lagoon where the ship  lingered. Through the huge broken boards in the ship's flank, and within the vast cabin inside, Faerydae and Euphraxia slept soundly apart from one another every night, hearing all those forest sounds and monster calls one might imagine from the dark.

The pair had lived there, just like that, for all of Faerydae's thirteen years of life.

Euphraxia's sleepy voice came out in a croak. 'You look filthy,' she said and waggled a bony finger. Faerydae could see frail sunlight creeping in through the deck above and shining over her mama's pallid face. 'You look filthy and rotten. Are you sick, little girl?'

If Faerydae looked sick, then Euphraxia looked even worse. Perhaps Euphraxia was referring to what the girl was wearing rather than the dirt caking it. It was a messy assortment of found garments: a loose button-down shirt with frills near the buttons, too large for her, of course. A man's shirt, a sailor's shirt. The sheer material showed the slightest hint of her tiny nipples, and Faerydae wondered if she should be more curious about that. Her pants were brown and covered in sewn patches, but at least they fit her better than the shirt. They were actually becoming slightly too small by now. They were a child's set of pants. And Faerydae would not be a child for much longer.

She dragged her body out of the straw and stretched.

She was a scrawny girl with long black hair as thick as the night. Her eyes were a deep brown hue and her skin was like dark honeycomb, both the same as Euphraxia's – although Euphraxia's skin had lost its radiant glow some time ago. They did not look much more alike than that though. Euphraxia had a long crooked nose, narrow oval face and gaunt cheeks.

'I'm not sick, Mama,' Faerydae said, dusting herself off. 'I'm just the same as I always am. Perhaps my heart is sick. Perhaps it is lonely.'

Her mama rolled her eyes then threw straw from her bed back onto Faerydae's clothes and into the air like confetti.

'Please.' Faerydae gritted her teeth. 'Please stop. Don't – Mama! I need to make a start for breakfast.'

Euphraxia stopped at the suggestion of food.

Breakfast would consist of raw fish, as per usual, which needed to be caught first. And if Faerydae could not snare a lizard or plump jubilee toad during this late autumn time, it would be fish again for lunch and dinner too. How the poor Nóvalie's did hate fish after so much of it.

Faerydae's mama patted the straw poking out from underneath her bottom, beckoning the child to come and sit with her for a moment.

When Faerydae plopped down beside her, Euphraxia started to brush through the girl's hair with her fingertips, yanking the thick strands in any other direction but down. As they sat together in silence, Faerydae craned her head from the grooming to see the possessions her mother kept close by her bedside. There was not much. Three items: a strand of Faerydae's matted black hair; a voodoo doll that Euphraxia had been given by her late parents that used to sit in her baby cot; and a featherbone slipper made from the feathers of a rare silver peasparrow – only *one* slipper though, not a pair.

Faerydae had always liked that silver shoe. It was so silky that she often enjoyed stroking it and imagining it was a wisp of fallen cloud or a sleeping fairy. *Where did you get it?* Faerydae would ask her mama, and Euphraxia would always say the same thing: *When I kissed the fire omen, he made me a beautiful gown, braided my long hair and prepared a carriage made of glass. And on my feet, he knitted me two gorgeous slippers out of peasparrow featherbones. That is how I got those shoes, Ferrihead.*

Shoe, Faerydae corrected her. *Yes*, Mama would reply, *shoe*.

But that was years ago.

'My precious little pumpkin,' Euphraxia whispered into Faerydae's ear. 'Let me tell you a story about that heart of yours. I'll tell you about how it disappeared.'

Faerydae peered over her shoulder at the woman. 'You won't tell me the truth though, Mama. I'm getting too old for stories.'

'You don't know what is truth and what is not, young lady.'

Faerydae shrugged.

'A hideous bitch stole it!' Euphraxia growled, proving Faerydae's point immediately. Faerydae rolled her eyes. 'An evil woman with a bounty on her head! Your father gathered up thousands and thousands of young boys to hunt down the vile hag and bring back her skull!' Euphraxia was flailing her arms around crazily at this point. '*Bring back that bitch*, he said! Such dangerous things those little boys faced for you, Ferrihead, following the bitch's trail deep into the perils of the Western Province, where the Winding Woods seduced them all. None succeeded.'

Euphraxia suddenly slapped Faerydae's back, making the poor girl jolt upright.

'Murderers lurk in those woods,' Euphraxia went on. 'And all manner of unnatural things take place, cannibalism, necrophilia, *murder*. Many boys lost their lives in that treacherous quest, but how they longed to marry the little, heartless girl. They wanted to be your husband, Ferrihead! They wanted to marry you and have ten daughters and seventeen sons.'

'Those are all lies,' Faerydae laughed. 'All of it. Papa was just a fisherman; he could never have rallied up a thousand little boys. He was… he was dead then, Mama. Remember?'

'Yes, that is true. A fisherman of the deep blue. That man was a wonderful fool,' Euphraxia sang. 'A fool to be so drunk! Dancing up and down the boardwalk like a whore until he fell right into the lagoon – deserved it, if you ask me. A rock split his head open like a coconut, turning my afternoon all red.' She let go of Faerydae's hair and pushed the girl away with so much force that she stumbled. 'That's the end of the story, little girl. No questions.'

Faerydae pondered about her papa's dire fate for a moment; the reason why this lagoon was abandoned when it used to bustle so vibrantly with merchants and sea pirates. It had been said, years ago, before Faerydae's time, a man was pulled into the water by the *bad* will of the lagoon and drowned. Some folks said that the water had gripped him around the throat like a noose, whereas others told of the man's drunkenness. Either way, the only ship remaining now was that which Faerydae and Euphraxia lived on – her papa's olde ship, filled with darkness and bad luck no doubt.

'You are safe with me, Mama, you *know* that,' Faerydae mumbled. 'I love you.'

She reached over to hug Euphraxia for no other reason than it seemed the right thing to do. Faerydae Nóvalie had a strange feeling that perhaps she did not know what love was yet.

3

Faerydae collected her bucket and line from the front cabin of the ship. Once outside, she dug for blue sludge worms beside the lagoon rocks as the tide was out. They were the best kind of bait. But the worms lived down in the dense sand and arose only to eat shell debris once every morning.

Faerydae smelled the air; it was salty and fresh. A worm wiggled into her hand and she snatched it up quickly. She drove the huge blue thing onto the end of the hook and found her spot along the boardwalk where she liked to cast her first line. *Plop*. The hook sunk down into the depths where her papa lived a deathly afterlife.

It was still bitingly chilly, but a peaceful stillness sat over the green water. The wind had eased off with the sun's arrival and there were no black warbler birds harking as per usual at this time.

'Where is the world?' Faerydae mumbled and landed her finger on a distant cloud. 'There you are. Yep. One day I might visit for a while.'

She gripped the woven string of her makeshift fishing rod tighter, feeling a niggling on the end. The niggling became a firm bite in less than a second. The jolt of it brought her gaze back to her line. Her instincts hauled her up to standing. She steadied her feet, taking a balanced stance. Whatever kind it was, this fish was stronger than her usual morning catch, determined to get away, wrestling with the hook, which only burrowed deeper as it struggled.

The line jarred around in little circles, pulling Faerydae closer to the drop off over the boardwalk. Faerydae really did not want to take a swim this morning. She retired to her bottom and was able to heave the string up from that position, slowly, all the way out of the depths. Seaweed and moss came out slumped over the line first, until, eventually, there appeared a mutant mudfish the size of her head, with four pulsating green tentacles and gnawing, razor-sharp teeth.

Faerydae screamed, jumping back up to her feet in horror. She'd never caught a creature *so* hideous and vulgar that it made her want to vomit. Sometimes she would catch strange crabs or serpent fish, but *never* this.

She dragged the fish out of the water without making eye contact with it. The frazzled line promptly snapped right where the fish was chomping away with hundreds of spiny teeth, and the creature fell onto the boardwalk with a heavy thud. Wood chips splintered into its scales and the open air made it gasp, but neither seemed to deter the thing from attacking. It squirmed and closed in on Faerydae's heels. She skipped backwards, causing the fish to take chase. Faerydae considered kicking it right back into the water, but restrained herself.

'I'm going to eat you if it kills me!'

With another scream, Faerydae leapt atop the creature's head. A slippery *crunch* erupted from its shattering body. Faerydae's legs stomped down with immaculate force, pushing harder and harder into its flat-headed skull and bulbous eyes. Something squirted gas into the atmosphere, most likely a deflating orifice. Beneath her feet, the fish's body was incaved inside a sloppy sack of scaly skin. It twitched, only once, before becoming perpetually still. Thick blood dribbled out from the creature's broken head and gaping mouth, through the boardwalk planks and then back into the lagoon like red syrup.

'Bloody hell!' Faerydae huffed. 'Anyone? Anyone at all to see such a thing? Oh! It's all in a morning's work.'

She began wiping blood spatter off of her cheeks, before she noticed something shiny residing deep within the fish's broken jaws. Perhaps a shard of tooth? Or her hook. Faerydae knelt down into the puddle of blood. She peered inside the fish's bloody maw. A sparkle enticed her closer. She reached inside to grab at the hard object, which was slightly wedged between bone and flesh. She pried it out of the corpse with her fingernails.

'I'll be damned,' Faerydae mumbled.

It was a gem about the size of a tomato, ruby-red and sparkling in the sun as if it were made of molten glitter. Faerydae examined the gem's surface, tracing the edges hypnotically.

'Good mornin', Faerydae,' the gem said suddenly. Or Faerydae *thought* the gem must have said that. *'What a righteous girl you are for saving me! Listen up and I'll do you a good turn.'*

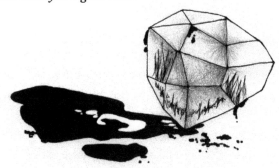

The child dismissed such a remark and held onto the peculiar object with both hands.

Faerydae ran to her mother's bedside in the gloomy corner of the ship-hold, screaming 'Mama! Ma! Holy heck. Mama!'

Euphraxia Nóvalie rose up to sitting. She'd fallen back into a light doze. Now that she was awake again, she screamed for her daughter to shut up. But then she spied the gem within Faerydae's shaking hands. Euphraxia watched the object sparkle, blinking rapidly. Faerydae pushed the gem closer towards her mother's long nose, as if the woman might have wanted to sniff it. Euphraxia's skinny fingers slid across its surface, feeling its smoothness and realising its beauteousness. Faerydae too realised how truly peculiar the thing was. It looked as if it had human-like features because of the moving streams of fire inside its lucid core. Two collections of sparkling flames formed a pair of button-like eyes and a ripple of faint sparkles created a wonky mouth; a mouth that perhaps was smiling up at them both.

'My child,' Euphraxia breathed. 'You found *Lume*.'

Faerydae frowned. 'Lume?'

Her mama nodded slowly.

'It said hello to me, Mama. *Lume* did,' Faerydae said. 'It thanked me for rescuing it from the lagoon. Why was it in the lagoon, Mama?'

Faerydae watched with concern as Euphraxia abruptly lost her train of thought and pointed a finger at Faerydae's face.

'You naughty little wench, take this far away from me!' Euphraxia ordered. 'Get rid of it! Go to the nearest trader's shop, take whatever price you can for it and come right on home with a sack of gold. Don't speak with another soul. I don't want you getting kidnapped nor fiddled with, ya hear? Listen to your mother, dear, she is a wise mother.'

Faerydae forced a smile. Euphraxia's fingers wobbled out towards her daughter's un-beating chest and she held the girl's gaze for longer than usual, smiling. It was an affectionate gesture; manufactured a closeness that did not exist.

Between them, Lume shone with silent rage.

4

Faerydae flew out of the ship, across the boardwalk and past the fish's corpse, which she side-kicked excitedly over the edge. Her wild hair danced upon the wind like a piece of material. She scurried into the tall pines as they made the slightest sounds of *woooosh woooosh woooosh*. A winding sand track through the forest meandered upwards, then dipped over a crest. The girl followed the path scrupulously as she always did and stumbled down the other side of the hill. She burst out of the trees that bordered olde Brindille Village in a plume of leaves.

The village was quiet – quieter than normal, more deserted than normal. It was the first week of the last month of autumn and the great Festival of Spirits was being prepared in the western quarry to run throughout the evening and into nightfall; a riotous party full of violent drunkards and debauchery. It was not the best time to come into town.

Flood Lane's shops were closed for such preparations, and although it left the village totally susceptible to looters, the whole place sat uncharacteristically ghostly. No pirates nor feral children were causing havoc in the streets. Voices that usually swore blasphemy across one side of the village to the other were gone.

'*Faerydae... Faerydae... Faerydae...*'

The little gem was calling her name like a song.

'You'd better be quiet,' Faerydae said. 'I have to sell you off to somebody right away, so we shan't get too familiar.'

' *I am not some diseased whore, you know.*'

'Shut up! I won't hear it,' Faerydae barked. 'I have to listen to my mama; I *have* to do as she says. She is a wise mother.'

'*...Her intellect truly knows no bounds.*'

Faerydae struggled to read the long names of passing streets and lanes as she walked, hoping to find somewhere promising to go. Though she had studied the language used by her mother and the various villagers she happened to encounter, she'd not had the discipline to truly master the art.

'Lam-minton Alley? Op-prurm Street? Devonite Way?'

Nothing inspired her just so.

'*What about a nice trip to the woods?*' came the voice. '*Do you know much about them? The Winding Woods, I mean. Oh! They're full of rainbows and flowers, handsome boys and fairies and whatever else a little imp might enjoy.*'

'Nope,' Faerydae concluded, ignoring the gem. 'Nope. Nope. Nope – Dear Lord, I am so sorry, sire!'

Faerydae bowed her head in apology to a hunched gentleman whom she had collided with. Where did he come from? The stranger, a wide-eyed middle-aged man with peculiarly sharp teeth, had dropped his striped hat full of silver and bronze coins all over the road. Faerydae frowned, apologising again. The man had materialised out of nowhere, him and a younger bald lady behind him. They stood affront one of the village's vast stone towers with no streets nor alleys hiding anywhere beside it. Faerydae wondered if these people had climbed out from beneath the road itself.

Faerydae swept all the man's coins into a pile, even the ones he had already collected in his gnarly, arthritic hand. She spied his unblinking glass eye watching her from above. The man grinned and allowed Faerydae to put the coins back into the hat, which he immediately replaced on top of his head. The coins jingled against his balding scalp.

'Thank you so very much, pretty girl,' he said in a voice that was almost too faint to hear. 'What a good and decent girl you are to help me out.'

The younger lady in netted stockings stepped up beside him and pressed her petite hand upon his shoulder. Her nails traced the edges of his coat's golden embroidery.

'What'cha got there, sweety-pie?' she asked Faerydae. 'Behind your back?'

Faerydae stepped away.

'Sorry,' she replied. 'Nothing. I didn't mean to make you drop your stuff. I've got voices in my head.'

The older girl made an intrigued *huh* sound and scratched her legs where the tight netted stockings seemed to be irritating her. An extensive cigarette holder protruded out of her left hand and she took a drag.

'Huh,' the lady said again. 'Show me what you've stolen. I'd love to take a peek.'

'No, I don't think I...' Faerydae started. 'It's... private. It's... gross. You wouldn't want to see. I accidently ripped off all my mama's toes in a bloody fishing accident. They could not be reattached. So, I'm taking them to the cemetery... To bury.'

'Oh dear,' the man gasped. 'Surely you will take us adults to your poor mama and we might endeavour to help her–'

Faerydae's body tensed as the man reached for her. His touch was ice-cold. He stroked Faerydae's arm for a moment before gripping it a little tighter. A strange reflex moved the girl's legs into motion, and all too quickly she had thrust her foot between the man's undercoat and into his groin. He squealed in a high-pitched crescendo, grappling for his manhood lest it should fall right off onto the street. Faerydae tensed again, watching the man turn red and sweaty on the road.

He moaned helplessly, 'Little bitch, little whore, aw god, I'll kill ya!'

'Run off!' the young lady hissed, creeping by the man's side and stifling a grin as she stroked his cheek. She glared at Faerydae, who still wasn't moving. 'Run off, little imp, for goodness' sakes! Do you want him to tear you in two?'

'No.'

Faerydae finally turned and ran. Her throat became so tight that she spluttered. Her heart would have been pounding if she had one to feel. After five minutes of sprinting, Faerydae stopped abruptly and rested her body up against the side of a villa, hidden away between walls. She felt dirty. The man's touch remained on her skin like a rash. She pulled Lume into the light, checked him over, then tucked him underneath her shirt to keep him safe.

'*Hello!*' he cooed. '*Nudity in the morning. That could have gone awfully, but what a jolly good time that it didn't! Good for you. Come on, Faerydae, let's go to the woods—*'

'Shut up!'

Faerydae could hear the glass-eyed man swearing back on Flood Lane, but his voice was growing more distant. Faerydae's eyes were drawn to reading a poster across the street as she waited to catch her breath. 'Happy Haunted Moon,' it read. 'And a jolly Spirit Festival. Party through the streets and alleyways until morning light. Purge yourself of all your urges while the Gods are feeling lenient!'

Faerydae felt a sickness gurgling deep in her gut, like warm vomit bubbling.

'The world has a lot of bad ideas, Lume,' she said.

'*Indeed,*' Lume replied. '*The world is attempting to kill us all, and life is merely a length of time that we allude it.*'

The gem's laughter sounded like a crackling fire.

5

Galadriel's Shop of Comings and Goings; the rambunctious title was painted in stilted swirls upon three wooden planks above Faerydae's head. The breeze jiggled the sign's rusty chains back and forth. 'Open seven days a week,' the sign informed in smaller scrawl below the first. 'And we **never** close, not even for floods, tornadoes or festivals.'

Faerydae sighed in relief. She'd found her trader! She blessed herself for spotting the creaking sign way up there, hiding behind a veil of orange leaves, otherwise she'd never have thought a shop lingered down here. Ha, ha, Faerydae thought, ain't nothing can hide from olde me. Little, olde, wise and special Faerydae.

'*I am* not *entering that establishment,*' Lume protested. '*I swear I will have to steal your fertility Faerydae if you do this. I'll make you a barren hermit. I–*'

Faerydae sighed extravagantly. 'You're so rude, has anybody ever told you that?'

Here in Worble's Place, the high walls on either side of the courtyard clearing blocked out the light of day almost completely. Faerydae rubbed her eyes with her hand until they adjusted. An arrow painted on bricks directed Faerydae towards a narrower side street, encroached by more heavy brick walls on both sides.

Faerydae stepped towards the alley's dark opening and peeked in at the emptiness. Lume remained silent. She moved into the tight alleyway without a sound, searching for the entrance to the shop. Mist laced the air, making Faerydae wave her hands about to try and clear a path to see. She was feeling her way along the walls when a phantom breeze tore apart the white fog. The mist dispersed for just a moment. Faerydae leapt towards what appeared to be a pokey green door concealed within an indent of bricks. She gripped its handle, not wanting to lose sight of it once the fog returned.

'Open', the door read. Faerydae thought, is the shop open? or does the door itself want to be opened up?

'Come on then, Lume,' Faerydae teased. 'Your new proprietor awaits.'

'*Do NOT–*'

Lume erupted into a voice louder than ever before and Faerydae almost dropped him onto the stone ground. She was frankly shocked as Lume persisted to hiss and growl.

'*I warn you only once more! I WILL MAKE ALL THE BLOOD IN YOUR BODY SIMMER AND GUSH OUT OF YOUR ARSE AND EYES UNTIL YOU DIE STANDING.*'

The gem had an apparently violent imagination.

Faerydae went inside anyway, and Lume did not utter another word.

The door swung shut behind her with a bang. Inside, the place was full of an unending horde of *things*. Faerydae peered at the faraway ceiling and at the walls of shelves laden with items to buy. Some items were even hammered to the walls or balanced endlessly atop one another. It smelt old inside the shop, like stale age and memories becoming stagnant within each object. The single dirty chandelier that dangled like an insect hive above was dull and brown, making the room look smoky. Perhaps all the fog in the alley was only excess from this strange place.

Faerydae left a trail of small shoe-scuffs along the oily floor as she moved closer to the centre of the spiraling octagonal room. She stopped moving to listen to the sounds of the shop. There was a faint shuffling and then a mumbling sound coming from behind a counter that lay in the middle of the mess ahead.

A green troll appeared from below it, stepping up from behind the rectangular counter. He crossed his endless lanky arms across his contrastingly podgy chest. It grunted. The creature's face displayed a sincere disinterest and he even left his eyes shut with apparent boredom.

Faerydae had never seen a troll before. He had the bulbous head of a wrinkled-up toad, and skinny arms that almost dangled to the floor. He was lightly covered in fuzz all over and smelt of ripe fruit. The troll wore a leather waistcoat and a ripped blue button-down shirt underneath. Thicker hairs sprouted out of the troll's ears and warts, and his neck folds looked like a multitude of leather necklaces. On top of his head, liver spots and black moles teetered in between wrinkles, suggesting that the creature was of a great age and perhaps not in great health. He started talking with a flat and gravelly voice, displaying two rows of gapped fangs.

'Welcome to Galadriel's Shop of Comings and Goings, valued customer. I am sire Galadriel–'

He stopped, eyes flittering open. They were red and small. He leant over the marble teal counter to squint at the young girl below him. And then he started to smile. Faerydae stepped up to the counter on the tips of her toes, unafraid of his glowing eyes and hideous grin that was now stretched from ear to ear.

'What a pleasant surprise,' he groaned. 'Are you here all alone, little girl? 'Tis a dangerous thing for an unaccompanied lady to wander into a man's keep.'

Faerydae clenched her teeth.

'Well,' he continued. 'You are lucky I am not a mean creature, only a warm and benevolent troll. What brings you to this part of Brindille, miss?'

Faerydae immediately dropped her gem onto the counter. A second passed, one more, before the troll could not stop himself from snapping the gem up into his greedy claws. Just to hold it seemed to give him great pleasure. He momentarily lost focus on the child and scratched the gem with his huge claws.

'Why are you hurting it?' Faerydae asked, then added, '*Sire*. It has feelings, you know.'

He grunted as if his windpipe were slightly too short to function properly. 'I'm assessing it. I *am* a puddle-troll after all – this is what I do. Trading is a troll's business.'

'Sorry,' Faerydae frowned. 'But I did never hear of a puddle-troll before.'

'Well, what a shame is that. We are ancient creatures, descendants of the olde toad giants of the bog lands who would thieve upon unsuspecting travellers. Ah, good times. Nowadays, we puddle-trolls are regarded as the best in the business when it comes to the matter of *true* or *false* treasures.'

'Treasures?' Faerydae whispered.

'Treasures. Now shut up for a moment so I can focus.' The girl bit down on her lip and fiddled with her fingers. '*Hmmm*,' the troll said. 'Strange… how incredibly odd is this…'

'What's wrong with it?' Faerydae asked. 'Is it *special?*'

He shrugged.

'Perhaps. Perhaps, very much so,' Galadriel spoke. 'This material is certainly... rare. Could it possibly be–'

'Be what? Be what!'

Galadriel could not control his sudden irritation and slapped the girl across her flushed cheek. Faerydae repelled instantly. It was not the first time she had been struck. Her mama used to beat her a lot when she was younger, using her fists or even her teeth, like some wild animal. But it had been many years. Faerydae believed that it was usually her own fault. She drove the adults to it with her nonsense. Calm down, she thought. You're not a little kid. Act your age.

'Dear girl,' Galadriel started soothingly. 'See here, just leave me to study this artefact, my dear, precious flower. Go and stand over there, why don't you?'

Faerydae stepped back as Galadriel continued to poke and prod the poor gem. He was terribly rough with it. Faerydae did not like the way his claws dug into its delicate, glassy surface. But it was better the gem than her face. Galadriel placed some spectacles upon his enormous nose as Faerydae turned away.

Steeling her gaze, Faerydae looked at the items strung upon the walls in their frantic, spiraling formation. She counted on her fingers. One bloodied harpoon. One gnarled wizard's stave. Three magical cloaks that had long since lost their zest. Four dilapidated books of spellchemistry that lay open to random pages – one was about turning people inside out.

Faerydae moved two pieces of a chess set made out of stuffed warbler birds. The birds were somehow warm to the touch, as if they were merely sleeping. A lonely giant's boot lay shoved underneath the chess set. Faerydae hadn't noticed it until now, but the boot was playing the role of a table. She felt along the old leather, trying to disturb it from out of its stagnant position. Black spiders and roaches scurried out from beneath it, making Faerydae lurch back.

The troll grunted at her to keep quiet.

A cockroach the size of Faerydae's hand made its way towards the nearest corner of the shop to try to hide behind another object, legs moving like hairs in the wind. Crammed in between boxes and dead creatures that had perished inside cages of smashed baskets, Faerydae could see a shrivelled-up piece of blackened flesh. She had discovered the giant's leg.

Her stomach lurched. She gagged, corrected herself, and twirled in the other direction. There was so much crap in this shop. Faerydae imagined herself falling inside the huge boot. In some sort of abstract way, she imagined disappearing inside the stench that was thick like wax.

'FAERYDAE! YOU VILE CRAB-PUSSY! YOU TRAITOR!'

Lume had finally begun screaming again. He'd not been able to remain silent for very long at all. Faerydae let her body become slack against a mirror propped against the wall. And sighed.

'Oy!' the puddle-troll snapped. 'No leaning on that, girl. You'll fall right through.'

Faerydae cringed. 'Well then' – she cleared her throat – 'you must be nearly done. Give me your best offer. I will only accept a fair amount for such a rare item. Twenty shillings. Two thousand dimes. A million and one cents–'

'Shut up, little girl. Don't you know who you're talking to?' He picked at his fangs and chuckled with dry smoker's lungs.

Faerydae shrugged. 'I don't really know anybody, sire. I live in the abandoned docks just out of town where I have never seen another soul to know of.'

'My name is Galadriel. I am a troll from the vanishing city of Manjarta. Have you even heard of Manjarta? A *magical* place. 'Twas where I was first breathed.'

'You are a magical puddle-troll?' Faerydae asked, examining his features. 'But you're so tiny and so ugly.'

'Magic ain't pretty, girl. It is, in fact, slithery and small.' He wiped his nostril and licked whatever had been smeared away. 'Do you know what puddle-trolls used to do to travellers when they caught one on their way to find the vanishing city?'

'No.'

'Well, okay.' Galadriel chuckled. 'You've twisted my wrist, I'll tell you. We would lie in wait within the deepest puddles along the dirtiest of trails. Lonely and quiet, those roads are not easy for a tired mind to endure. Weary travellers were perfect for the taking. First, we would pounce out of the puddle and onto their ankles. Rip out their weak knee joints like an imbedded splinter. Take their wallets and bags, let those things sink down to a place where they cannot ever be recovered. So stunned that they would collapse, screaming, inhaling water, we could make our final move. Crawl inside their mouths, squeeze down their skinny throats, inside their stomach, then grab their insides, an organ in each hand, and twist around and around in a bloody tornado.'

The troll's grin widened further than it seemed his jaw should allow and brought the child to thinking back on her crazy mother's few words of warning. *Listen to your mother... She is a wise mother...*

'I...' Faerydae spoke. 'My mother told me to get whatever money I could for that gem there, and not to speak of anything else.'

'Well.' Galadriel grinned. 'Fine, if you want to talk about *money*, I can certainly oblige. Shallow little girl. Don't you know I can offer more than money for such a rare prize as this? I am, as I said, a magical troll after all.'

Galadriel twisted his long fingers around and around in graphic circles. Faerydae was a curious girl; she had been born that way, and she needed no encouragement to become *more* curious. She slid her tongue across her teeth with intrigue.

'Wouldn't you like to know your future, little flower?' Galadriel asked. 'What awaits you in the beyond? I'm sure a poorer such as yourself thinks about her future often. Whether you shall be married off to a wealthy man soon enough. Whether your man will be handsome and stout, green and well-aged. Good in bed too.'

Faerydae touched her chest as he winked. It was all true – well, the parts about her wanting to know her future were true. Galadriel had embarked on a different tangent after that. But Faerydae was more than curious to know what the future would hold for herself and her mama. She hoped that there might be some happiness awaiting them both, someday. Mostly, she expected the worst. And the worst possible thing of all was that this life might never change. Galadriel was watching her, his beady eyes flittering almost spasmodically.

'You are a decent troll, aren't you?' Faerydae asked, eyeing Galadriel down. She was trying to convince herself more than anything. 'How would you show me my future, Galadriel?'

Galadriel waved his leathery hand and gestured towards the purple velvet curtain behind him that led deeper into his workshop's depths.

So, this was how it was going to be. Faerydae inhaled deeply.

She shuffled in behind the crowded counter where heavy boxes covered in dust held the benchtop up. Galadriel came down from the stool he had been standing on with a grunt. He was certainly a tiny thing. He had to waddle just to keep his arms from dragging. Galadriel pulled the curtain across with one arthritic hand and held it open so as Faerydae could walk through.

'Thank you,' she said with a nod.

'My pleasure, little flower.'

And the girl disappeared into the dark. Lume, it seemed, had been forgotten about; he sat quietly with that knowledge, ignoring the girl with the utmost abhorrence. The gem was, in fact, stowed safely inside Galadriel's sweaty pocket by that point.

Tricks and treasures, Galadriel thought, patting his pocket slyly. Tricks and treasures. Galadriel had acted out this scheme many a good time before. Deviations in his mood sometimes led to various outcomes, but he always knew where to begin.

He flicked a long claw back towards the shopfront door and followed after the girl. There was a soft clanking before the lock sealed itself with a *click*.

The paint on the outside of the door rewrote itself within seconds: 'Galadriel's Shop of Comings and Goings is now CLOSED until further notice.'

6

Galadriel followed very closely behind Faerydae as they walked down a long passageway. She could hear the troll's steps pattering at a rapid pace; so much exertion for so little groundcover. The top of his bald head only reached up to the girl's neck.

Galadriel watched Faerydae's body, analysing how her legs and arms moved in rhythm. Such graceful physicality was something he had trouble coordinating for himself. His body was a difficult specimen to arrange.

As they neared the end of the passage, Galadriel pushed ahead, swiping his wrinkled hand across Faerydae's thigh. He fumbled around in his pants' pocket for a tiny silver key and unlocked a door at the end of the expanse. It creaked inwards. They stepped through another curtain that surrounded a low arch, and found themselves in a storeroom filled with mops, cleaning products and buckets.

Faerydae clenched her teeth when she noticed an orb sitting on a black draped table. Two long pews were arranged on either side. The orb was dormant at first, but with the presence of visitors it lit up in a hue of starry purples and blues, making the tablecloth and walls glow. The troll took Faerydae's hand. She swallowed a repulsed gasp. And then he led her towards the heavy pews beside the table, encouraging her to lie flat. He intermittently stroked the orb's surface and dangled his claws around its aura.

'You speak the language of fortune orbs?' Faerydae asked as she tried to get comfortable upon the harsh wooden pew. 'Where did you get it, Galadriel?'

'Never mind that. A girl of your age should be asking more intelligent questions.' He peeked at Faerydae's legs. 'What is your age?'

'Thirteen, sire.' Faerydae curled herself up and away from the troll and he retreated back to the orb.

'I am the cleverest in Brindille Shire with these magical objects.' Another grin. It seemed he could not control the curling of his lips. 'Now, pray tell me your name, little princess.'

'Faerydae Nóvalie,' said she.

'Faerydae!' he exclaimed, sitting down on the adjacent pew. 'Pretty name, that one. Hold it close, don't ever let anyone steal it.' His finger ticked back and forth as if to tell her off, and she nodded. Galadriel closed his puny eyes.

'Greetings, dearest orb of fortune. How have you been? How are the children? Is life treating you well–' He cackled momentarily then waved a hand. 'I'm kidding,' he said. 'Huh hm. I cometh to you, Orb of Fortune, seeking knowledge from the future.'

He winked at the object almost tantalisingly. The orb grew bright with a thousand different colours, listening obediently to the troll.

'Quickly, child, do as I say,' Galadriel said. 'Touch your hand upon the orb's surface and she may show you all that is not visible to your mortal eyes.'

'She?'

'Of course – you think I would let a *male* Orb of Fortune inside this shopkeep?'

The troll was freakishly wide-eyed. He was possibly channelling some kind of innate magical force that flowed through his bloodstream and made his eyes bulge. Or, possibly, he was just trying too hard.

Faerydae did as she was told, feeling over the smoothness of the orb with one hand from where she lay, petting it almost. It was awkward to do whilst remaining lying down. So she began to sit up, only to be forcibly pushed back down by Galadriel's weedy four-fingered hand. The starry lights departing the orb grew linear from Faerydae's touch, like rainbows snaking around the room. Faerydae gasped, watching the lights tickle the ceiling and walls around her. The colours were soothing. Faerydae was only too quick to become hypnotised by their slow, sympathetic movements.

'That's it,' Galadriel assured. 'Sleep, my princess.'

Faerydae drifted into the existence of the orb as if in a rowboat down a steady stream. Great channels of riveting lights swirled around and around in the liquid that she floated through. The room turned into a dreamscape full of colours and distant stars. Galadriel's eyes were still huge and bulging to the point of almost bursting, as Faerydae dissipated away into a state of oblivion.

7

Faerydae sank down. She was falling off of an almighty cliff and into obscurity. At some point, she began to wonder if she were really falling or simply floating. Reality caught her either way, so as she did not vanish into limbo.

A sudden jolt made her realise that she was standing upon solid ground again. Her feet recognised their gravity. The wooden pews and table were gone, as was Galadriel. It was as if the orb had devoured Faerydae right up, sucking her into its thick, glassy exterior and placing her in an alternate dimension. She stood atop glossy navy-blue floorboards in the middle of a wide lobby. The room looked like a normal hallway that had been stretched out and bloated into a tunnel.

Faerydae whimpered quietly.

Was this part of a hotel? Or some sort of enormous house? Where on earth *was* she?

A gaping window sat bare on her right side, huge and black and empty. So empty. The vast room was capped by a high ceiling with decadent ceiling roses around three chandelier lights. It felt to Faerydae like she had entered this structure somewhere in the middle, instead of wherever it began; that the way in or out of this place was a long way away, if it was anywhere at all.

A thick artesian carpet ran across the polished blue floorboards, and a tall side-table supported an array of indulgently over-sprinkled biscuits. An urn of water stood on its own three feet beside a sign saying *complimentary.*

Standing insouciantly beside the table, and rather alarming in its appearance, was a huge black spider. It stood upon its lowest six legs and wore a top hat with a stripy shirt and suspenders. The creature was motionless and silent. It would have looked fake, dead or stuffed, if it were not blinking its numerous eyeballs intermittently. Its eyeballs were so wet that you could almost swim around inside the huge glassy orbs. He had a sadness about him, as he clung to a silver tray of brown eggs with his other two spare legs. He seemed to be waiting for her.

Faerydae bowed her head to the peculiar animal. He then opened his mouth and spoke with such a high-pitched voice that Faerydae clenched her teeth in shock.

'Good day, tiny miss!' he said. 'Welcome home. Welcome!'

Reluctant to move any closer to the spider creature, Faerydae glanced back over her shoulder. She had nowhere to run. The tip of her nose was met by a giant wall of solid ice and fog. Through the translucent surface, a smiling Galadriel loomed back at the table in his Shop of Comings and Goings. He blew her a kiss from the other side. Faerydae's own reflection misted just over Galadriel's loose features, warping them both into a grotesque facade. The more Faerydae stared at her own reflection though, the clearer it became. The wall was a window and a mirror at the same time.

'Wormhole,' the butler spider's voice hissed, as if having overheard her lingering thoughts in the air. Faerydae flinched and turned back to face him. 'That's a wormhole. It pulls you out of one place and puts you back down in another.' He ticked a hairy limb back and forth to demonstrate. *From one place... to another.*

'Wormhole?' Faerydae reminisced.

She tried to understand what exactly had happened to herself; any time that had been lost, worlds since changed. She wondered how it was at all possible to be in one place for a moment and then apparently somewhere else. She looked up at the glorious high ceiling, and thought, *this place is ancient.* It was struggling to remain majestic though, becoming more dilapidated than anything. If one inspected the details closer, extensive cobwebs clung to the corners of the ceiling and laced all over the dusty chandelier lights. Black smudges of mould and damp were developing in the crevices of the wall's cracks. What had first appeared grandiose and decadent, sparkly clean, was fading into darkness. Outside the vast window was only that horrible pitch-blackness – not merely a night-time darkness but an overshadowing darkness, a sort of *hiding* darkness.

'Complimentary chilli bomb, miss?'

Faerydae hesitated.

The spider had scuttled over to her and was offering one of those peppered brown eggs so eagerly. She could see the creature's long wispy hairs and the small blue flecks around his fuzzy arms – legs. The smell of the eggs was overpowering so close up, like sour fruit mixed with storm clouds.

'I laid them just this morning,' he said. 'They're still warm. Have you ever laid an egg, little girl? It's almost… arousing.'

'No. No, thank you,' Faerydae said, holding back the mounting waves of nausea.

Graciously, the little spider bowed and tipped its top hat at the front.

'No bother, miss. Welcome to the Home of Badness and Mess. Take your pick of one our shows and enjoy your time in The Ivory Mountain's finest absurd destination.'

'Shows?' Faerydae said. 'This place is… like a circus?'

'We are performers,' the spider said with earnest.

Gaining composure, Faerydae bowed back at him.

'Oh!' the spider chimed again. 'I must advise you; theatre twenty-five is for adults only. It is full of naked mole rats and that is not a night you can easily forget – believe me.'

The spider went back to its position against the wall, urging the girl forwards and further inside. *Pick a show!* he gestured.

Faerydae walked through the tunnelling lobby for about thirty seconds before it adjoined a smaller corridor that left most of the light behind in the previous room. It was so quiet. Flittering moths and butterflies raced past Faerydae's vision. Were they real?

Arrowhead arches began appearing on the left wall, bordering closed doors. Anything that lay deeper along the corridor was too abstract to wonder about. The further Faerydae walked, the dimmer it became. How many distant flights of stairs and unending doors might there be in this place?

The heavy timber doors along the wall spoke to her. She listened to them, leaning an ear against the closest. Faint voices murmured and flute music played within, almost too faint to even distinguish from the flapping of moth wings that had now congregated over Faerydae's head. On this door, it stated in calligraphy scrawl: **Theatre 11: Hoot Toot's See Voyage.** Faerydae moved along to the next door: **Theatre 10: The Hog Hilarity.** And the next: **Theatre 9: Pray for Prey!**

'Strange,' Faerydae whispered, coming to a stop. 'All these names. Which door is the one for me?'

'I cannot say!' yelled the spider from the lobby, though Faerydae had surely not been talking loud enough for it to overhear. 'Look for a guiding sign.'

Faerydae squinted back at him. He was the size of a normal spider in comparison now. The creature's front pincers rose at the tips, creating the impression of a grin.

A guiding sign? she thought.

Theatre nine beheld a rosy glow beneath the crack under the door. The redness pooled out like a liquid shadow. It looked like blood had oozed from the framework, the only colour leftover in a world full of night.

Faerydae stalked towards the door, feeling too small for the interminable tunnel.

'Why so scared, little girl?' she asked herself. 'This is a beautiful olde palace, and I am its regal princess. I feel totally at home! Why, I could just die of excitement right here on the carpet–'

Faerydae choked on her words. A man with a long-entangled moustache strolled out from the shadows further along, moving with determined steps that were muffled by the moth-eaten carpet. He smoked a pipe through clenched teeth; his slim frame encased in a cloud of smoke. He stared at Faerydae with flittering eyes as he moved past her and Faerydae saw a spider's egg in his hand. The man looked squeamish. He was slightly pallid, and his eyes were bloodshot. He burped.

'Don't eat it,' his husky voice murmured to Faerydae before he stumbled into theatre ten.

Faerydae shuddered. She strained to look inside the open theatre as the sickly man walked inside. The light was a pale blue and made it hard to see much at all. But Faerydae surmised that there was a small stage playing host to a nude pirouetting piglet...

Faerydae entered into theatre nine.

8

The theatre was set up to look like a dining room. It beheld a silver backdrop that acted as a reflector for the bloody red lights drawn above. There were other sections of the stage further along, not yet lit-up, like a chain of different scenarios waiting to be acted out.

Faerydae absorbed the scene, looking over the tall cabinets and various cupboards around the edges of the first stage, a maze of haphazardly placed furniture. A huge rectangular dining table lay in the centre of it all, laid out with plates and cutlery. There was not a single other person inside this theatre. All the available chairs along the wall, meant to seat an audience, were devoid of attendees – unless they were all invisible ghouls.

'By fate's celestial hand…' Faerydae spoke in a daze. 'There was but one lonesome guest.'

She observed a prominent oak wardrobe for a moment. It had a cracked mirror at its front and tiny curved feet at its base. It did not fit with the rest of the furniture in the room, which looked as if it had been made of paper. As her fingers began tapping behind her back against the theatre door, the wardrobe began to rattle on its feet. A yellow spotlight found its way towards the wardrobe's doors. Thudding sounds came from within, a splintery rapping.

'Hello?' Faerydae said warily. 'Is there somebody in there? I… I have been sent here by Galadriel to learn of my future… *Hello?*'

She stepped towards the wardrobe in intervals.

When she was close enough to distinguish her own reflection in the cracked mirror, the thudding ceased. She watched herself. The spotlight was creating dark shadows underneath her eyes, making her look warped. And then the shadows became alive and started to drip further down her face, drooping grotesquely, until she was looking at the visage of a much older woman, one with huge undereye bags and deeply wrinkled skin. Faerydae touched her cheeks. Her skin felt soft and young to the touch but appeared ancient in the mirror. Olde eyes watched her back.

'Are you me?' she asked. 'Is this what I am to become?' The reflection's mouth moved just as her own did.

The wardrobe rattled again.

The olde lady's reflection vanished.

Faerydae looped her fingers through the wardrobe's peculiar brass handles and pulled the doors towards her. The spotlight immediately crept inside, revealing a deeper interior than what there had appeared to be from the outside. The wardrobe must have been very deep, very *huge*, for she could see no end to it. Faerydae could hear breathing sounds coming from within the depths, then a gentle sniffling sound. The shadows started to reveal a huddled figure. It appeared to have a fuzzy body covered with grey fur, and its face exhibited a pair of stitched eyes that could not see. It was a huge rabbit, the size of a full-grown man.

The strange creature grew in size as it seemed to swing towards the

open door. It wore a fine black suit with white gloves over its stubby hands. A badge stated that the creature's name was Rainier.

Faerydae stared into Rainier's vacant face, up to his huge ears and to where a collection of thin coiled strings protruded out of the top of his head and vanished into the roof of the wardrobe. She chewed on her nails. A puppet, perhaps? And yet it *was* breathing – something like that could not be faked.

Faerydae swept her fingers against Rainier's downy cheek and over his sharp whiskers, feeling the warmth in his fur. That was when the rabbit suddenly burst into almighty life, cowering in the wardrobe as it tangled up all those delicate strings.

Faerydae screamed.

The rabbit screamed as well, and a drizzle of urine darkened the fur on his legs.

'Who are you?!' he cried, white stuffing flying out of his mouth. 'What are you doing in my dressing room? The show will begin *soon*. Please, take a seat.'

He clutched his heaving chest and took a peek around the side of the wardrobe to see the rest of the audience. But he saw only unoccupied seats. His mouth wobbled as if he were going to cry, then he composed himself. For, he was an actor, and the show must go on!

Faerydae struggled to control her laboured breathing as the rabbit buttoned his cufflinks. He forced his floppy arms out in an all-encompassing gesture from within his wardrobe. The thing moved and spoke like a living sack of potatoes.

'WELCOME!' he cried. 'Welcome one and only, odd, daft and deranged! The show has begun. I beg of you now, Pray for Prey.'

He cleared his throat as a symphony of flutes consumed the air.

'Imagine a world where you aren't who you are,' he said with such rhythm that it could have been a song. 'For in this world, a rabbit fears for its last breath; not a moment goes by that we don't wait for death. I am the prey of the world! Take a slice, I shan't mind. Have a rib, a leg, an eye. My teeth are not numerous, my jaws cannot rip you apart. Take the juiciest parts of me at your leisure. After all, the night is a blanket that covers all violence, and tomorrow I shall be a pile of bones. No one will know when I'm replaced by rabbit clones.'

Faerydae found herself clapping as Rainier slumped into a bow. The poor rabbit wanted to cry, to run away and cry inside his dressing room about how his talent was so wasted here. But something compelled him in his empty theatre, to lunge forth and grip that strange girl around her shoulders. He looked to see that no one was watching. No one at all.

'Don't tell anyone this…' he whispered, 'but the stars are giving me a message, and they *insist* that I tell you. They're going to set my insides on FIRE unless I get this message out.'

'Stars?' Faerydae said, straining against his firm grip. 'You must have good hearing.'

Rainier spluttered for a second. 'You're being watched by a *vicious* darkness!' he blabbed, as if in a sneeze, holding the girl tight. He twitched, forcing more words out. 'Your heart must guide you... The bonds of Alalia WILL break... The darkness is coming.' He paused, calming down. 'There, that's better.'

Faerydae considered it. 'Do you often give people messages from the stars?'

'No,' Rainier wilted, releasing her. 'Stars are very particular.' He bobbled back into the wardrobe and let himself hang limply. The rabbit waved a hand at Faerydae one final time.

'You've got a lot to do,' he finished.

Faerydae stumbled aside as Rainier grasped the doors of his wardrobe and locked himself inside.

The theatre lulled into darkness and the flute music faded away. A moment later, the yellow spotlight once again appeared. This time, it settled over the dining room table, where a group of five rabbits sat huddled in seats. The rabbits wore frilly dresses and velvet coats as they waited in tableaus to proceed with their act.

Faerydae felt dizzy, she held her breath, trying not to be noticed by them, trying not to disturb them into motion. But the rabbits already knew she was there. Their one and only guest. They turned to look at her and smiled wide enough to reveal long fangs inside their mouths – another unexpected revelation.

'Good morning,' said the tallest rabbit, turning back to address the littlest rabbit. 'I see you did not get murdered last night on your way home from foraging.'

'On the contrary,' the little one replied. 'I only lost a foot.'

'How delightful!' said another. 'Only a foot! Let's take a look. If they only eat you one limb at a time, you'll be around for some time yet!'

Upon gazing at the rabbit's missing foot, they all smiled. They passed around cups of tea and spoons of sugar and jugs of milk.

'But let me pose this to you, dear family,' the tall rabbit said jovially. 'With the prospect of being eaten alive, should we possibly change our nature, create weapons or armour, dig deeper burrows, plant traps or trip wire. Oh, no, no, no… Tell me to shut up, all these silly ideas.' They all laughed.

Faerydae peered at the rabbit's missing foot, the bone jutting out in a gory mess. It looked so real. She leaned closer, reaching out a curious hand.

'Get back from those actors!'

9

The ominous voice dissipated as quickly as it had appeared, out of nowhere and without warning. It came from none of the rabbits, who sat timidly like statues, but somehow from all around her, like it was the house itself telling her off. She lurched backwards towards the chairs, swaying nervously. A breeze ruffled her hair, then a sudden gush tangled her locks around her head like a blinding scarf. She scrambled to tug her face free. Her eyes trained themselves on a dark formation standing before her.

A woman had materialised in the centre of the stage, her black silken gown swirling in the remnants of the sudden draught. The woman glared at Faerydae, hands upon her hips, one finger tapping relentlessly.

The woman's grey hair quivered like snakes, long and straw-like. Her eyes were like tunnels, for she had no eyes at all, just hollow, empty sockets. She was tall and primal looking, with gnarly hands that ended in lengthy curling nails. Her face was hard to understand, hard to *notice,* next to the tunnelling sockets in the middle that seemed to endure forever.

'What do we have here?' the woman spat. 'A troublemaker? I'm afraid you are not allowed to touch the actors little girl.'

'Sorry,' Faerydae replied hastily. 'So sorry… I…'

Her voice trailed off as she stared over the woman's ghastly appearance. It was so horrendous, and Faerydae, who had never observed so many creatures of this rare sort in one day, was frankly perplexed.

'My goodness,' Faerydae went on. 'What huge fingernails you have. What a shocking charcoal smile. Why do you have tunnels of cobwebs where your eyes should be, madame?'

'Because,' sighed the woman as she went and stroked one of the rabbit's faces. 'I ate a truffilo spider and it made its web inside of me. Truffilo spiders do that, you know, it's common knowledge really.'

'I did not know that,' Faerydae admitted.

'Well, if you are close to dying a most gruesome death, and a truffilo spider happens upon your path, it might just save your life to let him build a nest inside your brain.' The woman slapped her hand against the dining table and Faerydae's back arched straight. 'But I am not here to chat. You aren't to talk with my rabbits, girl. You aren't to *touch* them, it's part of their contract. Oh, my poor rabbits, they're such stupid animals. You will have to pay for touching them; it confuses their tiny minds.'

Faerydae didn't know what she could pay this woman with. She peered over at the rabbits again and saw that they had each fallen onto all fours and were now eating the rug and intermittently fornicating under the table. Ferocious squeaks came from the one-legged female as she tried to clean her wound.

'Payment for the show!' The woman barked Faerydae back into focus. 'Everybody's gotta pay, even little girls, *especially* little girls, so make it quick.'

'I do not have any money, madame,' Faerydae said.

The woman lolled her head backwards. 'Then something else! Use your imagination. How about your hair? It's long and thick, and will suffice just fine. I'm offering you a generous trade here, child.'

'You want my hair?' Faerydae asked. 'You want to *wear* it?'

'Don't make me laugh. Of course not, I want to *eat* it. It will revitalise me and keep me looking my best.'

'You want to *eat* my hair. Well, I suppose I do not have anything else to offer–'

'DEAL!'

Before Faerydae could finish her sentence, the woman had grabbed her arm, pulled her close, and started slashing wildly at her head. Faerydae clamped her eyes shut. The woman used her razor-like fingernails to graze over the surface of Faerydae's scalp, making sure to cut the stubble down to nothing. She nicked the skin in a few places. When she was finished, the woman felt Faerydae's bald head over with her palms as the girl began to groan. It was not one of her better jobs, tufts of hair remained along with some nasty cuts, but she had the bulk of it.

'Mmm,' the woman exclaimed. 'That's okay. That's not too bad.'

'My chest...' Faerydae winced. 'It's aching... I think I'm going to die from all this shock! I think I'm having some sort of stroke!' She gripped her ribs as some glassy tears snaked down her cheeks. Her scalp burned and stung.

The woman scrunched up her nose and sniffed Faerydae's body. She lingered her nose over the girl's chest and gasped. With one hand, she lifted Faerydae up by her baggy shirt and into the air with such abnormal ease that Faerydae briefly fainted.

'I don't think your chest aches–' said the woman. Faerydae tried to lift her head up. 'You have no heartbeat?' the woman mused. 'Just a silent ribcage, and yet you stand before me living and breathing all the same. You must be of very strong magic.'

After a moment of consideration, the woman placed Faerydae back on the ground.

'Cheer up, child,' the woman said. 'I think a heartless girl like you would fit in nicely here. I have a soft spot for the abnormal. We got off on the wrong foot. Let me introduce myself. My name is Messy. I am the madame who runs this establishment.'

An odd name for an odd creature. Messy shook the girl's hand.

'Thanks for noticing,' Faerydae muttered. 'Most people cannot tell how truly abnormal I am. But I am neither strange enough nor normal enough to fit in anywhere.'

'Anybody can fit in here. Here, there is magic in the very air we breathe. It is in the shadows we cast and hiding around corners where nobody ever walks. If you can catch the magic, hold it inside, you can be very powerful. You can become whatever you feel you should be. Change your future. But you already knew that.'

Did I? thought Faerydae. Yes. Yes, I did. Lume told me…

Messy strolled around the table, stroking her rabbits like only she was allowed to. 'Melt the skin off a stranger by brewing a wicked potion, perhaps? Levitate sacks of gold out of a moving cart or spare change from a passer-by's pockets. Destroy your worst enemies by stabbing an enchanted voodoo doll with a pin!'

'Stop!' Faerydae shouted. 'I'm not that kind of person. I don't use *badness*.'

'But you could,' Messy pointed out.

Faerydae bowed her bleeding head. 'I only came here because I thought somebody was going to tell me my future. I thought I was going to find out if anything good was ever going to happen to me!'

'Is that what Galadriel told you?' the woman asked. 'So many people get sent here by that awful troll. So many have been killed in these walls. I really should barricade up that damned wormhole. Listen to me, magical girl, no one can tell the future. The future is like rain. It can be powerful or light or elusive to find. It is erratic, I mean. They have words for rain in magical places, you know, because rain *is* magic. You just have to trust in whatever your path may be.'

Faerydae gritted her teeth. She'd been sent here to die.

'I have to get back, Messy,' Faerydae realised. 'I have to get out of The Shop of Comings and Goings.'

'Through the wormhole,' Messy replied. 'I hope we'll meet again someday, heartless girl.'

Faerydae managed one more smile. The rabbits were waving at her from where they lingered on the carpet.

Through the wormhole…

Faerydae's fists clenched up into little balls of anger, as she stormed back out into the hallway. The mere thought of Galadriel, the troll of Manjarta, made her brain become clouded by hot rage. Theatre eleven's door came crashing open just as she was passing by. A huge crowd of tall, long-necked people appeared around her, chatting, bustling, and all rushing to get out of the place along with Faerydae.

'Awful! Just awful,' they cried.

Faerydae flowed into the stream of slender people drifting in varying directions. She made an attempt to flow along the wall and found herself making headway soon enough. When Faerydae made it back into the crowded lobby where the spider butler was busily scurrying around and collecting complaint cards, she could barely see the wormhole at all.

Clambering through slim masses, trying not to get trampled by rubbery legs and feet, Faerydae came to see the foggy mirror between torsos. She scooted towards it as best she could. The rubbermen were closing in on her all around. She made a hopeful dive through the air towards her only escape.

Something cracked. It was glass.

Faerydae became smeared into the wall like a spattered bug or a paint blob being smoothed out into the rest of a picture. The initial solidity of the wormhole was broken by the momentum of Faerydae's body until it just felt like she was being devoured by a lake of frozen lily pads. That falling sensation consumed her body again; an endless fall into time.

The bustling crowd continued to prattle and devour the truffilo spider's offerings in the meantime. They did not even notice the little girl who disappeared inside the walls.

10

'Well, well, well!' Galadriel's voice came. 'You are still alive, brave princess.'

Faerydae was a paralysed dead weight, she could only manage to groan about the sickly feeling in her gut. It felt like she was spinning, still falling, but drawing closer to stillness. Her head hurt and there was dry blood crusted in the corners of her ears. Her hands slid over her back and neck; enduring the waves of nausea that had become quite familiar to her.

She found her way onto her feet from where she had been sitting. Familiar with the grim surroundings of the shop, Faerydae observed the orb of fortune, which sat seemingly untouched and undisturbed on the table. The room was as silent and somehow as peaceful as when she had left it. Her horrible escapade could all have been a dream, if not for the coolness of her bald head. *That* was definitely real. The close shave was raw and weeping.

She looked around the room for Galadriel. He was hiding somewhere; she could feel his little eyes watching her in that violating way of his. Faerydae clocked movement near the purple curtain leading out to the storeroom doorway. It was Galadriel's small silhouette, standing too still. A stroke of fear consumed Faerydae as the troll sniggered coldly.

Galadriel's sniggers grew louder, before he lunged out from behind the curtain like the violent fish Faerydae had caught that same morning.

'Boo, I gotcha! I'm gonna rip you into strips! I'm gonna skin ya little bald head until you're nothing but bones!'

Faerydae screamed, dashing past the troll's little looming figure, his disgusting potbelly wobbling around from laughter. She ran through the curtain, down the passage and over the piles of clutter that seemed to be trying to hold her back from escape.

Just as she felt she was gaining ground, she became tangled up in the velvet curtain at the other end of the passage. She wailed and screamed, pulling the material away from the railing above in a panic. The heavy rod landed on her oozing head and stung so badly that she bit her tongue. Blinded and running circles madly, Faerydae tore the curtain away from her eyes and chucked it to the side where it plumed into a soft pile beside the various boxes and crates.

Faerydae found her balance, holding her nerve. The front door was closer than she'd thought. Just metres from escape, and yet she could not bear to run away, like a coward, like some scared little girl.

She looked back and tried to focus on the green figure coming into view, but it was so hard to keep her eyes from drifting. Galadriel scowled down at Faerydae from where he stood, grotesquely stationed on top of the counter like the proud chauvinist that he was.

'My, that is not a good look, little princess!' He laughed about Faerydae's messy shave. 'Once so pretty, and now, such a pity. Let this be a warning to you, little poorer: never bargain with a puddle-troll, because we will out-wit you every time. Common folk like you are so ignorant, you just haven't seen the world for what it really is: *a fucking mess!* Now go and never return, or you shall lose more than your hair.'

Faerydae stood, feeling exposed. She stared into his beady eyes. Galadriel was watching her with a similar disposition, trying to see inside her plotting mind and figure her out. He expected her to run at any moment. But she waited.

*'FAERYDAE. IF YOU LEAVE THIS PLACE WITHOUT ME, YOU'LL DIE! I'LL DIE! And you'll never ever find that heart after all. You **need** me, Faerydae!'*

Faerydae sucked in a tight breath.

Lume… She glanced around the shop. He was not on the counter. Galadriel had literally stolen the gem right out from under her nose. *Stupid girl.* The emanating red glow around Galadriel's torso pocket was enough to ruin the illusion of Lume's miraculous disappearance. And little did the troll know that the gem could speak only to her.

'*Lume, where are you hiding? What do I do?*'

'*The troll,*' Lume replied. '*Tricks and treasures. Give him what he wants, give him what he craves, what he hungers for, girl.*'

Faerydae considered tackling the little green devil instead, then: '*Well, what does he crave from me?*'

'*Do not fight with force. The troll is of flesh and blood. A kiss on the cheek or a dance in his lap will be enough to mislead him. You can play the same games as he can. See what power you have, my child. We can all perform the art of deception.*'

Faerydae gulped. She'd never kissed anybody before, not even her dear mother.

'Galadriel!' Faerydae found herself screaming, then, softer, '*Galadriel…*' Her voice broke into an uncharacteristically nervous whine. The troll, too, was just as surprised to hear her girlish cadence. '… You were right,' she said and let go of the doorknob she had been clutching. 'I should not have bargained with you.' She stepped towards him. 'I should not have entered into your shop all by myself. I was asking for trouble, wasn't I, Galadriel? I was trying to tempt you.' Faerydae leisurely clambered on top of the counter to be by his side without breaking her gaze. 'Thank you for teaching me a lesson, Galadriel. Now that I've survived it, I'll be the best-behaved girl forever now, better off than before. Smarter. You are the most magical troll I ever did meet. You're the handsomest troll I have ever seen.'

The troll's smell was eye-watering.

Faerydae persisted through the troll's intense odour and puckered her chapped lips in anticipation. Galadriel let himself melt a little. She stroked her hand against the coarse hide of the green creature's face and moved in closer and closer until she was pressed tightly up against his round belly. She touched her lips against his grotesque cheek. The troll was swooning. He was enjoying himself much more than Faerydae would have expected. After all, it was *just* a kiss. Surely he had been kissed before.

Faerydae's little hand curled inside Galadriel's unbuttoned waistcoat as his smell became palatable. She could not kiss him forever though; he would soon want more. She started to lick him a little to mix things up. Galadriel twitched. And his fingers suddenly found Faerydae's probing hand. The firmness of his hold made Faerydae assured that she would be thrown to the floor immediately, and yet the troll's body only undulated with an incipit laughter.

'Ooh,' he cooed. 'Feisty.'

Repulsive. Faerydae wanted to curl a lip, to shiver and possibly vomit, but resisted all of those things. She let her hand slip deeper around the vulgar creature's body. The harsh lump of what could only be Lume (she hoped) stuck out of Galadriel's ribs. Faerydae found her preferred grip on it.

'Steady,' the troll whispered, then made a purring sort of pleasure sound. 'I gotta build up to these things nowadays. Why don't you slowly take off my–'

Faerydae pulled Lume free of the troll's tiny pocket in one fast swipe. She spat in the troll's face and accidentally headbutted him as she did so. Her smooth assault worked better than expected. Galadriel stumbled backwards just as Faerydae was propelled towards the door. She reached for her throbbing forehead but held tightly onto Lume, who might shatter if he were dropped.

With a high-pitched scream, Galadriel toppled off of the counter in a flailing backflip. A loud crunch and snapping sound erupted from behind the obstacles blocking Faerydae's view. Then there was nothing.

'RUN!' Lume laughed. 'Let the troll rot!'

Faerydae crawled to the side of the counter and peered around the gapped end to see what damage had been done to her foe. There, Galadriel lay in a pile of limbs that pointed in all the wrong directions. He was wheezing; gurgling in wet breaths. His right arm had broken at the elbow joint and now jutted backwards towards his ear. His legs were warped underneath his body like a jack-in-the-box. A rack of apparently sharp mannequin hands had impaled the back of his neck, not deeply but messily, leaving jagged pieces of flesh around their finger-sized wounds – such were the hazards of owning a shop full of useless things.

Faerydae's mind was blank as she watched him. What's wrong with me? she thought, I feel nothing for this creature, dying on the floor. Perhaps I am *bad* after all.

'Righty oh,' came Lume. '*A sickly pleasure to see such a mess of life, Faerydae. Now, let us return home. Euphraxia will be waiting.*'

Faerydae walked to the front of the shop and turned the doorknob that opened up the little door. The cold air outside gushed in through the narrow opening. It was dusk now light was leaving the world, and Warble's Place was not a place to remain in at night. She jumped skittishly away from an indistinct shadow at her side but chuckled anxiously when it followed her every move.

A boom erupted over head then. Fireworks, red and gold, raced into the sky some twenty miles away; so, the Festival of Spirits had begun. The villagers would soon be heading back into the streets to drink and dance and laugh and screw one another until dawn.

Faerydae sprinted in the direction of the lagoon, following the moon's creamy glow. Galadriel's Shop of Comings and Goings was left to become an indistinct memory behind her. But Lume, her new and vile companion, with knowledge of things unbeknownst to her, would never let her forget the horrors she'd discovered there.

11

A Girl Made of Stars

It was misty when they arrived back home. The world only went as far as Faerydae's eyes could see – as far as she could imagine. Her floating ship was covered in green moss and spiders from hull to rudder, its sails were black and decrepit. The entire lagoon had turned red and syrupy, like an ocean of olde blood. The forest was bigger now.

She walked over the crackling leaves, when the trees started to move around her and warp into rabbit shaped figures that walked closer and closer, Faerydae absently noted that she was inside a nightmare.

The trees began to bend inwards towards her, making her sink into the thirsty ground. Into a *wormhole* – this one was full of clawed hands poking out of the sides, surrounding her in an entombing well. They grabbed hold of her neck, and she willed herself to disappear as the hands clamped down tight. *Wake up!* She wanted to grow taller but only began to melt into the dark wormhole like candle wax.

'Get up and dress up,' a voice sung energetically over the dreamworld. *'Get up and dress up. Get up and dress up. We can all perform the art of deception.'*

Faerydae's eyes opened in a desperate surge. Her fists unclenched. Gashes were leftover in the skin where her jagged nails had squeezed half-moon shapes into her palm.

She rubbed away the sweat on her brow and took in a deep pull of cold night air. The wind blew in a blizzard through the open wall of the ship. Faerydae only wished that daybreak would come soon. This night seemed endless. She had arrived back home hours ago, and yet time seemed not to have moved at all.

Lume assured her everything was as it should be, in his own careless way, comforting her through his indifference. He was becoming quite the voice of reason and a grounding sort of energy to have around.

Faerydae turned to look at the sparkling red gem, sitting in a pile of straw that she had been instructed to create for him.

'Why won't the morning come, Lume?' Faerydae asked, rubbing her watery, red eyes. 'I've drifted in and out of nightmares for hours.'

The gem twinkled of its own accord, creating refractions of an unknowable light source. *'Tonight is magical and wicked because of you. The night will hold us for as long as it can, so do not fall asleep, Faerydae, I keep telling you. Stay awake and the sun will rise to break the spell.'*

'Galadriel cast this spell on me?' Faerydae asked, very nearly too tired to care.

'Of course not. The magic *did. And magic does not merely exist in people and things, girl, it merely hides in them. Magic floats within particles of the air. I should know, for I too am a part of the air, and by extension, the universe itself.'*

Faerydae stretched onto her stomach across the straw-covered cabin. Euphraxia was, and had been since she and Lume returned to the isolated lagoon, sound asleep. Faerydae rested her head on her elbows in an attempt to rest but not doze, and looked within Lume's glistening core.

'You are a part of the air, huh?' the girl murmured, raising an eyebrow. 'What a load of tripe. But seeing's as I am stuck with you for at least another day, we might as well get to know one another – or get to know the parts of one another we're willing to share.'

Lume seemed unenthused.

'I'll ask you something first, shall I?' Faerydae suggested. 'Why did my mother want me to get rid of you so badly? I know she can think up some strange things at times, but her repulse towards you seemed so genuine. Why?'

'Your mother is a whore,' the gem uttered in reply.

'You do not even know my mother!'

'And you do?' Lume's twinkling smile curled with pleasure.

'Why did you say that I would die without you?' Faerydae spat next. 'Or were you just trying to make sure I would help you?'

'I said we would both die without each other, because you were planning on leaving me with that sweaty troll without even a little bit of a fight.'

'So, that's all?'

The gem's colour fluttered between crimson red and orange, moods of his. *'No. Not entirely. We are certainly...* connected, *you and I. Though I am assuredly the wiser one.'*

Faerydae crawled closer. 'What makes *you* so wise?'

'Perhaps I should tell you a story,' Lume said. *'A story about Faerydae—'*

'I know the story of Faerydae Nóvalie. Why do you think you know anything about such a sad story?'

'I...' Lume started. *'Was born over three centuries ago in the clock tower of a great kingdom. There were five of us then...'*

Faerydae lifted her eyebrows slightly, as if to display her slight interest.

'And there still are five of us today,' Lume said. *'Although I have not seen my brothers and sisters for many breaths. We were born out of the earth. My father tried to bring us together and harness our mystical powers for himself, but we could not be tamed. Let me ask you, Faerydae, do you know about the origins of magic?'*

Faerydae had not been able to learn anything more than what her mother spoke about in her dreams, not like other children her age, who had already attended the village school for at least three years. But Faerydae was unaware whether those children had been taught anything about *badness*. People did not really speak about such awful things as magic.

'You're saying that you helped bring magic into the world, Lume. That there are other objects just like you?'

'As for why you and I are connected,' Lume went on, ignoring her. *'I cannot yet say, for there are disturbing forces at work which, if I dare speak of them, might overwhelm your young mind. You can hear me because you understand my nature, and apparently, I trust you. Magic does what it pleases. The divine forces can sometimes be vague.'*

Faerydae became impatient. 'I have lived just as any adult for many years now. I deserve to know more than that.'

'But tonight was your first real day,' Lume pointed out. *'You are still a child. Tonight has only awakened you to the real world. I feel it would be unwise to divulge too much to you now, Faerydae, for I do not want your mind to implode. That is how people go mad.'*

Lume's fiery eyes darted towards the sleeping lump that was Euphraxia, watching her carefully. Faerydae did not know if he was suggesting that her mama had gone mad due to something awful she'd learnt or whether he was just trying to ward her off of asking anymore questions.

'Fine,' Faerydae spoke in a yawn. 'Do what you wish and say what you will. The fact is, when Mama finds you, she will ask for me to get rid of you again and, presently, I see no reason to keep you around. Perhaps the prospect of abandonment will loosen your tongue.'

As the night wore on, Lume persisted to wake the child up just before restless slumber until the morning was finally allowed to arrive.

Faerydae's eyes were the same ones that she had possessed yesterday, but they saw a different world in the light of a new day. Lume was right, she had been awakened to the real world.

'Mama.'

Faerydae felt a sense of urgency as she sat before her mother's body, not entirely sure if the woman was awake to the sound of her voice and not sure if she wanted her to be.

She spoke in a whisper, 'I wish to attend the Brindille Shire school for a term, Mama. It is free for that amount of time for a child of my age, after which it will cost a shilling until I turn sixteen. Of course, we cannot afford the full practice, but I feel I would do well to take my free term now rather than later. The world, after all, is changing so much right now. It is getting darker.'

'What are you on about, Feriihead. The world hasn't changed in decades. They'll simply fill your head with smoke and you'll be even more dazed than you already are, dreaming about the world beyond and the past that has left us all behind.'

Faerydae slumped slightly.

If her mama had been awake, she was sure that her reply would not be far removed from that. There was really no point asking. But it occurred to Faerydae then, in her newfound state of wanderlust, that she did not necessarily need her mama's permission to attend her allocated term of schooling. It was her right. She would not be breaking any rules or offending anyone at all if she were to show up at the school and learn what she was entitled to learn. Before yesterday, the thirteen-year-olde had never desired to spend even a single day at school. She had never desired more knowledge of the world – until she was shown how little she really knew and how much was really out there. Knowledge could prove powerful.

'*School has not always been offered to young girls,*' Lume was mumbling, still sitting upon the nest of straw Faerydae had made for him. '*Learning things was deemed a man's business. I have always been indifferent to the preferences of the sexes, for I believe a self-sufficient body of all parts is best; reproducing through imagining. I really must suggest, Faerydae, that we head to the Winding Woods today. The magic lives in there comfortably, it would really be the best place for us.*'

'I am not your slave.' Faerydae spoke as she went to the corner of the ship where she kept her only pair of scuffed shoes. 'Grow some legs if you want to go somewhere.'

'*You're not going back to that village today, are you?*' Lume said. '*After everything that has happened? You've barely slept a wink!*'

'No time like the present, isn't that what they say?'

'*Well!*' Lume started. '*Take me with you. I can't sit here all day. What if Euphraxia finds me and throws me back into the lagoon?!*'

Faerydae sighed and absentmindedly forced Lume inside her trouser pocket. Then she left the ship to its silence.

Faerydae did not know exactly where the village school sat within the tangled mess of streets in Brindille, but she had a rough idea because, once or twice, she had spied groups of children milling out of the corner of her eye. She just had to remember where. It was possibly near the olde town mill, or in the new district courtyard. Somewhere Faerydae rarely went.

She wondered what day it was today, understanding the concept of weekdays being the time when most people worked or attended school. Faerydae had never needed to know the name of the days; they were all the same to her. Whatever happened within them, and whatever season it was, was the only reminder she needed of time's moving hand.

'*You won't be let into school* today *if that is what you're hoping,*' Lume said from within her pocket as the girl moved across the sandy slope towards the village.

'You never know,' she said. 'They might have a free space; it might be my lucky day. You have to be optimistic sometimes, Lume. You should try it.'

'*Optimism is but another word for ignorance. I strive to remain in the light of knowledge, if you don't mind.*'

'Suit yourself.'

Faerydae was nearing Flood Lane, pondering which route to take. She had never really been in the village this early before, with all the villagers milling briskly away at their various trades.

A man stood affront one shopkeep, chubby fingers smeared with blood as he skinned various creatures for sale. Fur skins had been hung to dry around the border of his small shop terrace. Faerydae suddenly felt hungry. She had not caught anything to eat. She was not concerned for herself so much, for she believed she could manage to find something during her travels, but her mother was a different matter.

Faerydae recalled why she never tried doing anything new. It was because of Euphraxia. She needed to be looked after continuously. It was either bathe and feed the woman or slack off and let her starve or freeze. Faerydae would have to return home as soon as possible, she knew. But it was like trying to keep a job that she desperately wanted to quit. It was hard to force herself sometimes. The urge to be independent of her mother was getting worse. Whenever Faerydae's mind wandered to those turbulent thoughts, she ran from them, literally.

After asking random strangers for directions and then for scraps of food if she felt brazen enough, Faerydae eventually came to find the building hiding within a bushy area of the new district courtyard. There was a dilapidated mill by happenstance, like she'd first thought, but it had long since been closed down. The school building itself did not like a school. It was a was an olde church with a wooden cross erupting out of the shingled roof and a lathering of flaking white sand-paint separated it from the rocky ground.

Faerydae hovered next to the little fence that ran around the front yard and watched whatever she could spy through the building's tall windows. She crept closer when a woman appeared in the window. Faerydae hid lower, sliding deep into the weeds behind the fence. After a moment, she peeked up again. The woman had appeared coming down the huge front steps of the school towards her. She was tall and slim but solid too, like a giant, with huge round spectacles and grey hair. The lady reminded her of Messy, and for some reason that was comforting to her. Faerydae crept out from behind the fence like a feral cat.

'Hello there,' said the stranger placidly. 'Would you like to come inside?'

'I…' Faerydae hesitated.

'*Don't do it, girl,*' Lume hissed. '*There are better things to do, I promise you, just think of your poor mother.*'

'I am *always* thinking of my poor mother. But I have a life of my very own and I must follow my path.'

'What was that?' asked the woman.

'My name is Faerydae, ma'am,' said she, walking up to the woman and, by extension, the school itself. 'I am thirteen years olde and wish to study here for one term.'

The woman led Faerydae inside with one hand behind her back.

Two dozen tiny pairs of eyes stared up at Faerydae from behind desks as the schoolmarm made a spectacle of her affront the only classroom in the entire school. Faerydae did not see a reflection of her own wild spirit in any of them. They all looked bored if anything. They looked hideous and dirty, their dull features making Faerydae's nose curl slightly.

'*At least you're not here to make friends, Faerydae,*' Lume said.

Faerydae had almost forgotten he was there, her blatant voice of reason. And he was quite right, of course. She had no intention of making friends.

Faerydae would attend the little Brindille Shire school for all of twelve days before an inconspicuous day altered her path forever.

12

It was a summery day for late autumn, impossible to imagine that a frozen winter storm would be upon Brindille by the end of the week. Faerydae inhaled the morning breeze. The fine stubble upon her head had grown into an inch of thick black strands within only a matter of days, as if the magical way in which it had been cut affected the way in which it grew. The wind tussled it into fluttering waves.

Faerydae held one hand over her stomach as she walked to school, cringing behind a casual smile. She would be expected to smile – it was a beautiful day, after all. She was not hungry. No. Those were the worries of a simpler time. Her body endured through knots of unyielding cramps that only a walk and fresh air seemed capable of numbing slightly. Faerydae often wondered about how it must be for boys to become men, what they had to endure behind smiles, pretending that they were not changing when they most definitely were. The girl really did not care much for boys. Physically. Thoughtfully. Carnally. She thought they were immature and ultimately uninteresting, they were all pretty much the same.

The huge cross of the school came into view. Children laughed and squealed with delight as they played games in the courtyard before class began. Some of them threw rocks through the olde windows of the dilapidated mill. Those kids aren't the same as me, Faerydae thought. I am different; I *know* things. She had already been christened a nickname, and would forever beknown as 'Faygay' by the other children in her class. So it was. She had been ranked as low as the rats who ran beneath the hooves of other animals in the mud.

'Out of my way!' a boy named Julien screamed. 'I ain't slowing down for a Faygay in my way!' Julien's shoelaces were dancing around in the air, daring him to try them, and his huge pants were so loose that they were almost falling off of his hips and revealing whatever laid beneath. 'I'll explode on ya! Jizm that'll blow your mind right out of your head!' His voice broke back and forth on the verge of adolescence.

'Don't trip over the rod dangling out of your ass!' Faerydae called back. Then, 'Or the shoelaces twirlin' around your ankles.'

Too late, the boy went skidding.

Faerydae Nóvalie had realised, apart from numeracy classes and the writing of tales, that school was mostly just a rugged bombardment of dirty faces and cruel words; it was where children learnt their place in the world.

Faerydae walked up the front steps of the school where bodies thickened in front of her; the front doors were not yet open.

Tillber Gargbuttle was a fisherman's daughter. She had sharp eyesight, and that was about all she had. The squat girl was trying to count the coins that her papa had given her from his sales of the week. She kept forgetting what number she was up to though. Poor Tillber was as simple as she looked. For as little time as Faerydae Nóvalie had been attending the same classes as Tillber, Faerydae had already overtaken her in the schoolmarm's eyes. It was infuriating in the most tiresome way to Tillber. Her intellect had firm boundaries. But Tillber strongly believed there was something evil about Faygay. All the kids did.

'Watch your back, Faygay!' Tillber called out, flicking dirt out from under her nails like some brute. 'Don't wanna be standing out in the open for too long, someone might suck ya up into another orb of fortune.'

Tillber laughed, a gargling sound.

'Magical orbs are not funny things,' Faerydae replied. 'And it was a *wormhole*, actually. A *wormhole*, dear.'

'Right, a *warthole*. You are *such* a liar, Faerydae Nóvalie.'

Faerydae rolled her eyes. Poor, simple Tilly. Granted, it must have been hard for Tillber to be so well-off and have no capacity to make anything of herself.

In that instance, the bell rang across the yard and the front doors of the school magically opened with a grinding wooden echo. Everybody blocked their ears against the screeching bell and ran for the sanctity that the classroom's walls provided.

Every day, the roll was called. Faerydae had learnt her number on the list; number sixteen. After roll call, the children would begin practicing their cursive letters before a demonstration of at least twelve new words was drawn on the board by the schoolmarm. After that, mathematical problems began much to everyone's dismay. When they had been endured, the children knew the routine allocated them a class break. And nobody ever preferred to stay inside during class break.

Faerydae always sat on a secluded bench chair on the boundary of the yard during break time. Being alone with her own good company was best for her – minus Lume, of course. It was safe from the other children, sitting right there on that perfect sunbathed seat. She had nothing against spying on her classmates during that time. And it was hard to escape the smell of their fresh food even on her distant bench, when she had nothing at all. Faerydae had learnt the power of a delicious smell.

'It is a strange day today, Flea,' said Lume, who had demanded to be taken along with Faerydae wherever she went from now on.

He had also begun calling Faerydae *Flea*, for some reason or other. No doubt it was a criticism, something akin to scum, which he found hilarious. Lume also managed to find something – *anything* – to say whenever the girl had a single moment alone. All in all, it felt as if she had acquired a devilish kind of guardian angel. And poor Faerydae, lonesome and misunderstood, had not had the heart, *literally*, to dispose of her one and only friend.

Euphraxia remained ignorant to Lume's presence. It wasn't hard to keep the gem hidden, and only Faerydae could hear him speak. In fact, Faerydae's mama had not asked a single question about the gem since the day she'd found him in the lagoon and been told to sell him. She never asked for the money. She never spoke of him again.

'Just look at the weather, so very abnormal,' Lume went on.

'It is a strange day,' Faerydae agreed. 'As if the sun wants to have a final say before the storm clouds steal the show.'

Lume sounded uncharacteristically worried. *Just keep your eyes open, Faerydae... Faerydae? Are you listening to me?'*

Faerydae shushed him vigorously with her hand. 'Who is *that*, Lume?'

'Who is who?'

Faerydae pointed to the front doors of the school. A girl with red hair stood upon the concrete steps, the schoolmarm beside her, looking out across the yard with such an air of grace that she might have been royalty.

'Do you see her?' Faerydae pried. 'I haven't seen that girl before, have you?'

'Nor had any of these *students seen you before you arrived. It is just a new student, Faerydae. Calm down, for goodness' sakes, you act like you've spotted the king.'*

Faeydae rose to her feet. The whole world seemed to have gone away at that moment. Faerydae, hypnotised, wondered if anybody else saw what she did. This girl. She was mystifying.

'Let's get closer...' Faerydae heard herself mumble.

If Lume was protesting, she could no longer hear him.

Her hair hung in tight curls, glowing red in the sunlight. Faerydae could see the more golden parts as she grew closer to the girl. She wore a pair of red, featherbone slippers upon her small feet and light pink stockings around her legs. A dress the colour of the pale blue sky cocooned her agile frame, the same colour as her stupefying eyes. Her dress looked handmade because of the fraying ends and uneven sleeves. Her skin was the colour of milk, so different to Faerydae's, which was like caramel. Freckles teetered across her pale porcelain face and her cheeks were painted with a vibrant, sun-kissed blush.

'She's kind of' – Faerydae frowned – 'beautiful. Don't you think, Lume? Not in the way that she looks, so much as in the way that her eyes smile. I've never seen eyes do that.'

She possessed the beauty of a storybook princess. Faerydae had read about a princess once upon a time, in some random novella that she'd stolen from the village bookshop. Princesses had to be kind but strong and beautiful, but wise too.

The redhead peered over her shoulder as the schoolmarm beckoned her back inside the building. The girl paused, her blue eyes surveying the schoolyard. Her curious gaze panned across every detail. She craved knowledge; she craved an understanding of her surroundings. Her eyes landed on Faerydae. Faygay. Inside of her almond-shaped blue eyes lived a universe of inquisition. Faerydae felt as if she were being sucked up into them, that they were deep and wandering. She could see a reflection of herself in this girl, could sense a piece of the stranger's soul that was exactly the same as her own, belonged to Faerydae, and only Faerydae.

Faerydae felt a pleasant kind of nausea as the heat from her cheeks spread to her palms and armpits. The other girl held her gaze, even as the schoolmarm's impatient hands tugged her towards the classroom.

Did she feel it too?

A sharp pain shot through Faerydae's arm and she jolted to the side. She felt short of breath, as a burning heat coursed up the veins in her neck. Or, perhaps, it was a burning coldness. I'm having a stroke again! She thought. I am going to die right here on the grass! My heart is finally giving out on me.

Faerydae pressed one hand against her chest and waited. Could she feel something in there? It couldn't possibly be so. How could it be possible that there was something moving inside of her? The unmistakable rhythm of life in her chest:

Bud-ump! Bud-ump! Bud-ump! Bud-ump! Bud-ump! Bud-ump! Bud-ump!

Her heart beat with an infinite power, the likes of which Faerydae had never experienced before. She could feel it – her heart beating with strength and life. It was almost ticklish. She broke into such riotous cackling laughter that her classmates could only stare. The girl on the steps could not help but smirk as Faerydae made such a scene. The redheaded girl's smile only made Faerydae's heart beat faster.

The schoolmarm finally coaxed the new girl inside the school building and away from the growing commotion outside. Faerydae's heartbeats left along with her, slowly dispersing into slow and distant thuds, and then nothing at all. Her heart had gone, *she* had gone. Lume's dulcet tones crescendoed into booms that were undeniable.

'*WHAT ON EARTH ARE YOU DOING, YOU STUPID IMP! You're an embarrassment to the Brindille community. You call yourself a lady?*'

'Lume!' Faerydae beamed.

She pulled him out of her pocket and twirled herself around to shield him from the other children. 'Lume, did you hear it? My heart! That girl was like a wormhole that connected me to my heart!'

'*How romantic.*'

Faerydae paused. 'That's it. I think I'm in love, Lume.'

The gem grimaced. '*Perfect.*'

During the remaining two hours of the school day, Faerydae could not stop staring at the back of the new student's head. She knew she was being annoying. She knew the girl could sense her. But Faerydae could not stop herself. The redhead was so beautiful that to look at anything else was pointless.

Faerydae had learnt nothing of the new student, only that she knew a lot about mathematics and spoke like an eloquent olde woman when she answered questions with the utmost politeness. Faerydae considered that the girl was slightly older than she was. Perhaps even by a couple of years.

When classes ended and the children were set free, Faerydae found her on the steps of the school building, but she was not alone. A buzzing horde of inquisitive students surrounded her, wanting to steal her away for a few minutes and size her up. Faerydae had undergone the same treatment on her first day. By the look on the girl's face, she was unfazed by all the attention, possibly even bored by it. The pack thinned out just enough for the girl to make a break through the front fence and sprint away down the alleyway towards the westside woodlands. She was fast.

'Oh bullocks!' Faerydae sprung up from where she was crouched in the weeds where she often liked to hide.

'*Ah well!*' Lume laughed. '*There is always tomorrow—*'

Faerydae bolted after her, but by now she had already vanished down the trail. Faerydae ran up the inclining alleyway until it turned into a dirt road. She looked to the ground. The other girl's footprints were almost too faint in the earth to see, but Faerydae decided to follow them anyway. Again, she could not stop herself. And she, least of all, wanted to return home.

The dirt road became a small path. It winded into the woodlands like a river. The terrain became rugged, and the path did not deviate around tricky obstacles such as dry riverbeds, boulders nor drop-offs. Twigs zigzagged across Faerydae's face as she struggled to stay on the overgrown path. In the near distance, there came a soft humming melody. A pretty tune with an angelic tone. The other girl was singing to herself as she walked, and she was close. Faerydae started to run again.

'Hey!' she called out. 'Please wait!'

'Who's there?' the girl's tense voice came back from behind a gathering of branches that divided them. 'I'm warning you, I am armed.'

'Please,' Faerydae muttered as she spat out a bug. She scurried down the slope until she stood before the redheaded girl down the path. A gaudy slingshot was aimed at Faerydae's face. The slingshot was loaded with a small pebble from the woodland ground and did not wane from its position.

'Sorry,' Faerydae said, suddenly aware of how dirty her face was, how unkept her hair looked and how baggy her clothes were. 'I did not mean to frighten you.'

'*Leave now, Flea,*' Lume said. '*The girl is bad news. The girl is going to* kill *you.*'

'Shh,' Faerydae spat, and the redheaded girl snarled.

'Do not tell *me* to shush. I promise you, I have shot people with this thing before.'

Faerydae smiled, her legs carrying her closer, though the redhead warned her back.

'Sorry–'

'Stop saying sorry and tell me what you want, creep.'

The word *creep* cut Faerydae deeper than she would have expected. This meeting was going so badly, Faerydae only longed to start all over again.

'I just wanted to say,' she gulped. 'I... I am Faerydae Nóvalie. I'm in your class and just... I truly am sorry. But you're so... Let me get the right word. Magical.'

This stumped the redhead, and her slingshot eased off just slightly.

'Magical?' The girl frowned in reply, as if she heard more in that sentence than was meant. 'What a weird thing to say.'

Faerydae was nudging closer again, unable to stop her own legs from walking.

'Stay back!'

'Sorry.'

The redhead pushed a stray hair out of her eyes. 'Don't you want to know what I think of *you?*' she asked tersely.

'Not with this haircut. Perhaps a homeless man who stole an outfit from another homeless man?'

The girl grinned. 'For the record, I think your hair has grown an inch since the moment I first saw you sitting on that bench all by yourself at lunch. But I was going to say beautiful… I think you're quite beautiful.'

Faerydae froze. Nobody, *ever*, in her whole life, had referred to her as anything remotely synonymous with beautiful – except Galadriel, who did not at all count. The heartless girl was going to faint if she did not change the subject immediately.

Faerydae heard herself ask, 'What is your name?'

The other girl thought for a second then decided she'd allow it. 'Alalia. My name is Alalia Riviera–'

'NO! FAERYDAE, IT'S THE GIRL! IT'S THE DEVIL THAT THE STARS WARNED US ABOUT!' Lume's voice was so loud in Faerydae's mind that she had to grip the sides of her head and wail at the sudden migraine.

'What's wrong?!' Alalia gasped.

Faerydae clutched Lume from where he lay inside her pocket and tried to shut him out. His voice, still screaming, faded by her will and she returned to look at Alalia.

'Headache,' she admitted. 'Sorry. I get… sudden onset migraines… it's a real thing, I'm pretty sure.'

'So.' Faerydae inhaled. 'Alalia. What a beautiful name. I have heard it before, actually.'

The slingshot was dangling by the girl's side now. 'Really. When?'

'Oh… In a dream. But it wasn't really a dream, more like another world entirely.'

'Well, what are the odds? I've been to other worlds too. So, Miss Faerydae, you followed me out here to tell me I was magical and then what were you going to do?'

'Well' – Faerydae bit her lip – 'I was going to ask if you wanted to be friends.'

Alalia seemed to mull the suggestion over in her mind. Faerydae rolled her eyes before she could stop herself.

'Huh,' Alalia declared. 'I don't see why not. I don't have to sign anything, do I?'

Faerydae grinned. 'Seeing's as you mentioned it.'

The pair stared at one another for a peculiarly long time, in complete silence; not even the nagging screams of Lume proved strong enough to break the sanctity of their gaze.

'Would you like to come visit my home, Miss Nóvalie?' Alalia asked, each word rolling out of her mouth before she could dare reconsider it. 'I only just moved to the North from Eastlea, with my father. My childhood home is now two days' ride from here, or an overnight voyage around the cove. It might as well be an eternity away, don't you think? Have you heard of Eastlea, Faerydae?'

Faerydae smiled dumbly back. 'No.'

'Well then… Maybe I can tell you about it.'

Faerydae walked along beside Alalia towards her house in the trees. When it came into view, although Faerydae could hardly break her gaze from Alalia's eyes to see it, the house was actually just a small mudbrick structure that clung to the ground like a bloated leech. It was not far from where the pair had just spoken, nestled in between the trees and scattered boulders of the woodland. It was a dome-like formation of mud with a straw roof and only one small window at the front.

Alalia tugged at the crooked front door, which was tilted to the right, and Faerydae went inside first.

'Papa, I've come home!' Alalia sung out. 'I have a visitor.'

'You are sure that your papa won't mind me being here?' Faerydae asked.

'Excuse the clutter, we have only just started unpacking.'

Faerydae nodded. It was perplexing to see so much wealth scattered carelessly amongst the mess of the ramshackle home. There were gold watches, rings, tailored suits and tiaras. But despite Alalia's glamorous featherbone slippers, she did not look otherwise wealthy.

The girls walked through a short corridor and into the small, messy kitchen where Alalia grabbed a yellow scone and started inhaling it. She gestured for Faerydae to take one out of the mouldy basket sitting upon a pile of dirty dishes as well, which the girl did happily.

'Papa is a little quiet,' Alalia said to Faerydae through bites. 'He is not in good health and can appear frightening at first. But do not be afraid. He is a solitary man; just doesn't want to say the wrong thing nor upset anybody.'

Alalia was not exaggerating.

Faerydae almost gagged on her scone when the olde man, so much older than she had expected, found the way towards their company. His skin was sickeningly pale, almost to the point of being grey. No person should look like this man did, as if he'd been sewn together by daemons. His eyes were empty, blue, but not at all like Alalia's. They were a doll's eyes. His arms were like long noodles dangling by the side of his unhealthy gut,

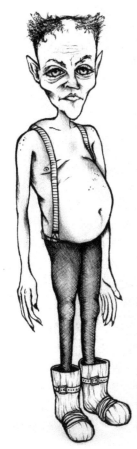

swinging against his knobbly knees. And the man's head was somehow too large for his stature, teetered with fuzzy ginger hair. This man looked as if he had been dead for a century. He wore no shirt, only a pair of suspenders attached to his yellow pants and two heavy boots upon his large feet. The man was tall, hunched slightly, but terrifyingly imposing as he crept closer.

'Papa,' said Alalia. 'This is my friend, Faerydae Nóvalie. She is attending Brindille Shire school as well.'

The man, the nameless man, turned his glassy eyes on Faerydae. She felt a chill.

'How do you do?' Faerydae did not know what else to say.

'Oh, my dear sweet Alalia.' The man spoke with a slow, eloquent tonality, shaking his head. 'You are as vibrant as your dear mother was when she was fifteen. Before she changed, of course – people just cannot stay away from you apparently. Just look, making friends already.'

Faerydae laughed quietly as the man pulled Alalia into his cold embrace.

'And where do you hail from, Miss Faerydae?' He went on.

'Brindille,' Faerydae said. 'Just Brindille. I have never been out of the Northern province, sire.'

'A home body.' It sounded like a criticism until the olde man smiled. 'And Alalia has invited you here for supper, I presume?'

'Actually,' Alalia said. 'I did not invite Faerydae so much as she followed me most of the way… declaring I was *magical*, of all things.'

Faerydae laughed with embarrassment. She could tell that Alalia was teasing her, but there was little she could do to bid her longing to seem somehow impressive towards the girl.

'She is joking, of course,' Faerydae smiled. 'And what is your name, sire?'

'Well, I do not detest to Mr Riviera, if you don't mind. My name is Alejandro, but I don't believe I have been called that in many breaths.'

A silence.

'Come on then, Faerydae!' Alalia sighed, grabbing her hand. 'I have so much to show you – all the time in the world could not help you to learn everything about me.'

Alalia dragged Faerydae through the narrow mudbrick passages of the house and down an unsuspecting flight of stairs that opened into an underground room. There were still piles of unpacked boxes strewn everywhere, but this room also had some degree of personality. The blankets upon the little bed in the corner were all either purple or blue. The white pillows were frilly but stained with blotches of oldness.

This was Alalia's bedroom.

As she lingered inside the small hidden space, Faerydae felt a strong sense of intimacy cast over her. She wandered around the room to keep herself from blushing, fiddling with various possessions and trying to breathe steadily through her nerves.

A broomstick with a ridiculously thick handle stood propped against the damp wall near Alalia's bed. It looked impossibly heavy and the wiry flecks of twigs protruding out of the end did not look as if they could collect much dust at all.

'It's dark balsa wood,' Alalia said as Faerydae turned to meet her eyes. 'Incredibly light, actually. It kind of looks like a tree, doesn't it?'

Faerydae hadn't initially thought of that, but now that Alalia mentioned it, the broomstick did indeed look like a strange sort of stubby tree trunk.

'It was my mama's,' the redhead went on, sitting on her bed with her legs crossed. 'It was the only possession of hers that I brought with me when we left Amaryllis – that's the town where I grew up, in Eastlea.'

Faerydae sat on a collection of rugged wooden crates, wondering what was inside of all the boxes if not the rest of Alalia's possessions, and attempted to cross her legs gracefully. 'Your mama gave you a broomstick?'

'Well.' Alalia grinned. 'I kind of stole it. But I'm sure she'll be glad I have it now. My brother and I used to fly around on it to make deliveries for my mama's bakery business.'

Faerydae grinned and Alalia laughed. Faerydae was so intrigued about every part of this girl's life that she wished she could simply dive inside of her head and understand it all in one split second. But alas, getting to know someone would take more time. And Faerydae had never been a patient girl, nor had she ever had the opportunity to get to know another human being in her life.

'Why did you have to leave Amaryllis and the rest of your family behind?' Faerydae asked. 'Did something happen? Something between your parents?'

Alalia grinned again, this time slightly less enigmatically. She picked up a small doll from a box below her bed and pulled thick strands of black hair over the blank, featureless face. 'It's complicated.'

'Sorry,' Faerydae started. 'It's just. What your papa said earlier, about your mama changing?'

'That is the most complicated part of all,' Alalia said. 'I suppose my parents do not see eye to eye anymore, though I do not truly think they ever did. You see, my parents do not love one another, like most parents, they never have. It has always been more of an obligation. Even a *privilege* for my mother.'

'Why?'

'My brother and I used to wonder about that, until it all seemed rather pointless, and other things became more important to wonder about.' The redhead sighed. 'Faerydae, my father and I have come to Brindille because Mama no longer wishes to work with him. Jákob, my little brother, a naïve and harmless boy, was left with her. And Papa took me. It is only fair, I suppose.'

'That's' – Faerydae did not know how to feel – 'horrible.'

'Too right it is.'

They sat in silence for almost a minute. Faerydae skimmed over the contents of the room one more time, although she was barely concerned with what her eyes could see. Her mind was rolling over and over in thought.

'My papa died before I was born,' Faerydae found herself saying. 'And when I was born, my heart was not inside my chest. It was beside me. I could actually watch it beating even though it was not physically connected to me. Can you imagine that?'

'Very bizarre.'

Faerydae did not want to bother the beautiful girl, but she couldn't stop herself from venting now that she had started. It was so glorious to talk to another human being.

'I have to look after my mama now because she is sick in the head – probably because of everything awful that's happened to her. We live in an olde ship that belonged to my papa. Ma used to be quite smart apparently, was studying Arachnid Language before she met my papa and joined his crew as a translator.'

'Remarkable,' Alalia replied.

'Your papa,' Faerydae added. 'He is sick too. What exactly is wrong with him though–'

'Oh, let's not get into all of that!' Alalia leapt up off of the bed. 'Grab that broomstick and I'll take you for a ride?'

Faerydae laughed. 'You're not serious? What are you, some kind of sorcerer?'

'I'm a wiccan, Faerydae!' the girl corrected. 'Now come along and I'll tell you about the day I learnt to fly!'

13

Amaryllis

Alalia

Amaryllis was a huge city compared to Olde Brindille Village. Children who grew up within its towering buildings and steep streets learnt about the unreliable nature of other people fairly quickly. And magic was not so easy to ignore in a city that resided under a near constant shadow of cloud.

Alalia was born as Alalia Miseria. The Riviera title would not be endowed upon her until much later on.

She lived with her mother Blanchefleur and brother Jákob on the outskirts of the smoggy Amaryllis city in a slanted cottage at the base of the Ivory Mountains. The Cottage of Dancing Sweets, it was called; a family of bakers of the most unusual kind. Every family in Amaryllis knew about the cottage, and that it dwelt in the forgotten field of an unknown woody-stemmed crop. A crop that never grew nor died. It just existed and, sometimes, it protected.

Alalia's mother had baked sweet pastries for as long as she could remember, deserts that came alive and danced and sung like little human dolls. When Alalia turned five years olde and eventually her little brother too, they were recruited to help work for the business, mainly assisting with the baking and deliveries. There was a certain method to making the delicacies come alive though, which Alalia would not understand until she was much older. As far as she understood it, her mama would put a spell on them, which only worked after the ingredients were baked into one another, creating some kind of functioning body.

Alalia had always been a happy enough child. And she would not meet her papa until the night he was to steal her away to Brindille Shire at the age of fifteen. After that night, things would be different. But for the time being, at thirteen years olde, she knew her place in the world well enough. She did not have many friends; she attended school sometimes; and her brother, although completely dissimilar to herself, sufficed for somebody to talk to.

Jákob Miseria was two years younger than Alalia. He had been a chubby boy, until the age of eight when he started to grow a little taller. The boy had pasty white skin and jet-black hair that always managed to be oily and dangle over his left eye due to the swirling cowlick above his right eye. Jake spent his days practicing his own trade: warlock hunting – the role had been decided on when he was much younger. He and Alalia had *both* had to make their decision. And it wasn't so much about what one was good at, so much as what one *wanted* to be good at. It was a choice. Jake chose warlock hunting. Alalia chose to become a wiccan.

'ALALIA!!!' Blanchefleur's voice managed to fill the three-story cottage to its brim. Her voice, though airy and sweet, became incredibly powerful when she was angry enough. The middle-aged woman was short and round, with wiry red hair and freckles across her broad face. She had tiny lips, but they were full and pouty, so made her look as if she had been stung by an insect. Blanchefleur was often amazed at how attractive her offspring had turned out, especially when their father was not a whole lot nicer to look at than she was.

'Coming, Mama!'

Alalia was in her room at the top of the house, but it would take her less than ten seconds to reach the ground floor because she was so practiced at levitating. Straight down the spiraling staircase was the most direct route. That was the only skill that Jákob was truly jealous of. He did not understand the true intricacies of the wiccan lifestyle. The girl wore a dress made by her mother out of black silk. It was a traditional gown. It covered most of her pale skin with long embroidered sleeves and an expansive skirt. A white shirt showed through at the cuffs and around the bow at her neckline.

It was her uniform. It had become a part of who she was. The dress helped her remember her vows and to keep herself in line. Sometimes she slipped up though. She was still a child, after all.

Blanchefleur knew why Alalia spent most of her days sitting up in that room. It was so she could look out of her window at the Ivory Mountains and watch them sway in the wind. A girl like that could stare all day and imagine a whole story up in her head. A girl like *that* needed to be pulled back down to reality with some good olde-fashioned hard work.

'I'ma count to ten and you'd better be at my heels when I turn round with this batch of neighing marshmallow unicorns... One... Two... Three...'

'Here, Mama,' Alalia said, standing dutifully behind her already. 'These are for the Vermonts, aren't they? They have that pumpkin throwing festival at their manor this afternoon.'

'Indeed, child.' Blanchefleur let her unicorns jump off of the steaming hot tray and into the basket her daughter held open. 'Where is Jákob? I want you to take him and pick up two dozen bags of flour on your way home.'

'He's gone to the beach, Ma, remember? Somebody sent for a cleansing of the Sanwhich Cemetery. There's a ghoul problem, apparently.'

Blanche nodded agreeably. 'Of course, of course. Well, all right then, just pick up one dozen. And if you're going by the Daltry grounds, I'd like you to give this potion to Mrs Daltry. It's for Freya.'

'Freya?' Alalia looked down at her featherbone shoes. 'You want *me* to give it to them? Can't it wait until Jákob is free? You know that I don't like going to the Daltry's.'

'Of course I *know* that you don't like to. But the Daltrys are in need of the vial today. There's a full moon tonight and their daughter will require it as a matter of urgency. You like Freya, Alalia, don't you? You're friends?'

'We were.'

'Good, then it's settled,' Blanchefleur said as she dusted off her floury hands. 'But remember to be inside the house and out of the field before sundown. I don't want another incident with those perverted night hands.'

'Nor do I,' Alalia nodded, recalling the incident when she'd arrived after sundown and the field that they lived in started to grab her and pull her down into the dirt. If it wasn't for Blanchefluer, the field would have eaten Alalia alive that night. Security measures, of course. *Extreme* security measures.

'In fact,' Blanchefleur added. 'Take my broom. I think you're quite olde enough now. Add the saddlebags and you'll be able to carry the two dozen flour bags all by yourself.'

'The broom!' Alalia screeched, making Blanche jump. 'Are you sure? I can honestly fly the broom all on my own?!'

'Well, not if you're going to behave like that. A wiccan needs to be mature and focused to ride a broom tree.'

'Sorry.' Alalia simmered down. 'I'm mature. I'm calm. I can do it, Mama.'

'Good, I'm glad.' Blanche started to move over to the cauldron where another recipe was bubbling intensely. 'You have read how to control said brooms, I presume? Or do you need me to give you a lesson?'

'No,' Alalia muttered. 'I know what I'm doing.'

The child levitated upwards towards her mother's bedroom where the olde broomstick lived for safe keeping. Alalia had read precisely four articles in her wiccan bibles about flying on broomstick trees, not as much as she let on to her mother, but enough. She pushed the bedroom door open and gazed in at the almighty flying stick beside her mother's dresser. The deep and rotund indentations of Blanchefleur's buttock's cheeks in the splitting wood made the broom forever hers, no matter who flew it. But Alalia was related to it by blood. It would warm to her, for sure.

She grabbed the object by its frazzled twigs and dragged it towards the second-story window, considering that the median height out her mother's window was a good compromise. She hung the basket of unicorns upon the stumpy hook jutting out of the broom's blunt end and pulled it to make sure it was secure. Alalia wondered how to begin, how best to get acquainted with the corpulent object. Before she could think of something to say though, she had mounted the object and drawn the windows wide open.

'There's no better way to get to know someone than to be thrust into a deadly situation together. No?'

Her grin could not have grown wider as the stormy breeze fanned her soft curls.

'Grip, aim, believe, push.' She closed her eyes, daring herself to jump. 'I can just levitate if it doesn't work... Though, the broom might be damaged by the fall...' She tried to imagine a more logical sequence of action, but could not push aside her innate instinct towards magical objects; the belief that they would either like her or hate her. All the study in the world could not prepare a person for the unpredictability of magic particles.

'Grip, aim, believe, push. Grip, aim, believe, push!'

Alalia leapt out of the window and free-fell towards the impending field below.

The broom seemed to be considering her, wavering slightly during its descent, before it supposed that the girl had proven herself valiant enough. Together, Alalia and the broom eclipsed the sky with their almighty arrival and raced towards the overhead clouds. The broom was fast despite its size and girth. And although its wood was olde and weathered, it was still pliable enough to be comfortable for the girl to sit on. They became one with the sky, one with each other, moving instinctually towards their destination, sharing thoughts and intentions.

'We did it! You magnificent creation!' Alalia hooted as the wind tore across her face. 'You're incredible! Just look at us soar!'

The broom wavered for a moment before steadying itself like a gliding bird, almost hovering in the air; the land below was a distant memory now, the worries amongst its hills no longer felt within reach.

Alalia considered she might never walk again.

14

Faerydae

Huge birds capped the mountains surrounding Faerydae. The air was the colour of sweet oranges and tasted of bugs and exhilaration. Her arms were enclosed tightly around Alalia's taut waist as the redhead sat so stoically that Faerydae could not imagine doubting her abilities. They were above Brindille, *somewhere*. The ocean line was sparkling in the distance ahead.

Alalia had done this many times, she could tell.

She leant lower into the wood of the broom, egging it to go faster, and Faerydae found herself laughing with excitement, though not daring to loosen her grip. She was terrified, of course, but it was the kind of terror that could feed a person. The courage radiating from Alalia's body transferred through her skin and became enough for both of them. Faerydae now felt so comfortable with the girl in front of her it was as if she had known Alalia for an impossibly long amount of time.

'I'M GOING TO LAND DOWN THERE!' Alalia screamed back to Faerydae, pointing at a beach in the distance. 'THAT'S THE NICEST SPOT I'VE FOUND SO FAR!'

The broom took a dive downward so suddenly and steeply, with Alalia's legs wafting out to the sides like a ballerina, that Faerydae's stomach backflipped. Faerydae was screaming now, but she couldn't even hear it as they descended. The wind was howling too loudly. She was going to vomit, she was sure of it. The little scone she'd just eaten was going to end up all in Alalia's hair. And then the broom straightened just before impact; her nausea evaporated. The howling wind became a pleasant swirl. Faerydae realised that her eyes were clamped shut and she had to climb the waves of nausea just to open them.

They were above the ocean now, surfing the mere thirty centimetres of air between water and sky at least a mile out from shore. Twinkling afternoon light was almost audible as it moved with the impenetrable sea tide.

'THIS IS IMPOSSIBLE!' Faerydae squealed. 'ABSOLUTELY RIDICULOUS!'

'YOU, OF ALL PEOPLE, SHOULD KNOW THAT MAGIC HIDES IN EVERYTHING, FAERYDAE!'

The broom veered to the left and slightly upwards again, coasting towards the shoreline at a reasonable altitude. They plopped onto the sand in a jolting motion and Faerydae would have propelled onto her stomach if not for Alalia's steadying hand. They ran for a few paces before coming to a stop. Alalia held the gigantic broom in her hands and smiled expectantly at Faerydae. When she could gather her thoughts, Faerydae leapt into the air, pumping her fists with excitement.

'That was… incredible!' Faerydae said. 'Where are we?'

Alalia walked towards the nearby caves that lingered in the recesses of the cliff. 'I've named it Freya Cove. I don't know its real name and who really cares, anyway?'

'Freya Cove. I like it.'

'There's never anybody else here; I don't think they can get down from the cliff's edge. So, it's all ours because *we* have a broomstick!'

Faerydae blushed. A beach all to themselves.

Just then, Alalia sank to her knees and then to her back, sprawling out beautifully along the sand and staring up at the orange sky. Faerydae kneeled beside her and did the same. It was the most peaceful moment in Faerydae's life. Nothing seemed quite real enough; everything was light and numb to the touch.

'Give me your hand, Faerydae,' spoke Alalia, resting on her elbows. 'Do people call you Fae?'

'Um.' Faerydae thought back through all the names she had ever been called. *Ferrihead. Faygay. Flea.* 'Yes, I think they would.'

Alalia held Faerydae's calloused hand in her own and started to twirl her forefinger in a spiraling motion towards the centre of Faerydae's palm. Faerydae let out a giggle at the ticklish impression, immediately coughing to conceal her own immaturity. Alalia did not look up, but grinned beneath her hair. A sparkling amber aura departed Faerydae's palm before a small sunflower followed it, growing from the spot where Alalia had touched her. The flower disappeared within seconds of having materialised. Alalia sighed.

'Stunted,' she said. 'I need to keep practising or I'll just keep going backwards. It's all the travelling around, I've lost my concentration.'

'That was incredible!' Faerydae assured her. 'I can positively say that I have never grown a flower out of somebody else's hand.'

The redhead was looking at the sky again, lost in an entirely different thought. 'You really don't know where your heart is, do you?'

Faerydae frowned. 'No.' And she lay beside the girl again.

'I can tell. You're full of magic.'

'Yes. I suppose I am.'

'There's no difference between you and I, you know,' Alalia said. 'Or a person in the street and a practiced wiccan. Magic doesn't discriminate, doesn't prefer certain vessels. Not really. The only difference is that I've *practised* how to use it. But even if I stop practising, I lose my abilities too. I'm not special, if that's what you're thinking.'

Faerydae opened her mouth to blurt out something rather brash, but closed it again. There was something in the way that Alalia talked that made Faerydae think there was no changing her mind.

'Well,' Faerydae started. 'Using my mother as a vessel would've taken the magic right off of that cliff by now. So, if I was Mr or Mrs Magic, I'd probably prefer to live in you.'

Alalia laughed lightly and her fingers crawled inside of Faerydae's hand. It was then that Faerydae realised how truly lonely this girl was. She'd been taken away from her brother and mother, her home and everything she knew. If Faerydae could have known how it felt to have a family, she was sure that she'd miss them terribly.

'Okay, now give me *your* hand,' Faerydae promptly ordered, scurrying to sit up straight.

Alalia raised an eyebrow, daring Faerydae to try to top her mesmerising flower trick. The redhead was competitive.

'You're not going to bite it, are you?' Alalia asked randomly. 'The other kids were only too eager to warn me about you, Miss Faerydae. They told me your stories about venturing into orbs, meeting paedophilic trolls and getting all your hair cut off. They tell me you're pretty crazy. They say you were molested by the troll and have major issues now.'

Faerydae broke out into cackles of laughter. 'Molested? I suppose in a way. I can't recall ever having had so much physical contact in one afternoon.'

Alalia shook her head in amazement at the uncanny girl. Faerydae, still laughing, took everything she'd just said as some kind of a joke. Such immunity was unthinkable to a girl like Alalia, who was so easily affected by the words and thoughts of others. Faerydae took Alalia's hand in hers and placed their palms flat against one another, pointing up towards the sky. Faerydae wiped away tears of laughter.

'Now.' Faerydae grinned. 'Watch. I'll twist my hand around, like this… And poke this through here… And then… See!'

Alalia examined the creation with which their hands had created. Scepticism beheld her face.

'It's a wiener!' Faerydae informed, wiggling the finger she had slid between Alalia's. Alalia remained motionless, frowning at the protruding worm of a finger.

'I thought it might be funny,' Faerydae mumbled. She immediately pulled her hand free, judging herself harshly upon the blank reaction. 'It's stupid, sorry. I'm not really used to having conversations with people who aren't me.'

There was a beat of unsureness before Alalia averted her gaze back to Faerydae, having been staring at her dangling hand in wonderment. The redhead let a smirk crack at the sides of her mouth. And then she eased forward and pecked Faerydae on her sunburnt lips, mixing the suppleness of her own skin with the weathered harshness of Faerydae's. It was not powerful, more fragile than anything. But Faerydae froze up all over again anyway.

Alalia broke away with a chuckle. She stared into Faerydae's perplexed eyes and hugged her.

'Do you ever wonder where your heart is?' Alalia asked, holding the other girl close.

'Ah.' Faerydae's voice sounded parched. 'Yes. All the time.'

'Well.' Alalia leant back. 'Why haven't you ever tried to find it? No! Why don't *we* go find it? Together, right now?'

She leapt to her feet in a surprisingly lithe manoeuvre, grasping the broom in her hand from where it had sat beside them both.

'What?' Faerydae asked, getting to her feet. 'You can't be serious. I haven't a clue where it could be, who took it, why they took it, or if it's even still, well, *mine*, I suppose. It was lost over eight years ago, Alalia.'

'Have faith!' The girl beamed. 'Of all the places a magical object could be, which your stolen heart surely is – the Winding Woods holds them all safe.'

'Winding Woods?' Faerydae grew distant.

Have you ever been to the Winding Woods? They're full of rainbows and flowers, handsome boys and fairies and whatever else a little imp might enjoy.

The girl became aware of who was still sitting in her pocket then, inconspicuously, like he always did, listening and watching, waiting to say what he thought of everything when the time was right. If Lume wanted to go to the Winding Woods, then Faerydae was naturally wary of satisfying his desire. Faerydae *believed* the gem was somehow indebted to her, and therefore lenient towards her wellbeing, but he also had motives of his own, intentions that Faerydae could not imagine, the nature of which she could not truly understand.

The Winding Woods were akin to blasphemy in Brindille Shire. Nobody ever spoke of them. Perhaps it had something to do with the fact that the quiet community resided only miles from the Wood's darkened border. People needed to watch what they said and who might be listening. *Things* from inside the woods did not stray outside of the darkness often, but if they so wished it, they could corrupt the goodness of the shire with their arrival. It was best not to tempt them.

Something waited in there. Something sinister was always waiting.

'Don't you want to understand yourself?' Alalia was saying, realising Faerydae's hesitation. 'There is a wizard in the woods by the name of Eggnorphixeus–'

'Hang on,' Faerydae smiled. 'Eggnorphixeus? The wizard from the stories?'

'The same.'

'You cannot truly believe such a creature exists outside of cotton pages, Alalia.'

'I can. Because I *believe* my papa, and Papa says that he has seen the wizard with his own eyes. Of all the famous story creatures within the woods, Eggnorphixeus knows more than most. He is a watcher and shepherd to the shadows. He would know what happened to a bottled human heart if it passed him by. He remembers.'

'Maybe so, if he did not steal it himself.'

'Exactly, so it will be beneficial to seek him out either way.'

Faerydae frowned. 'I'm not sure if I follow your logic, my dear.'

'That is because there *is* no logic, Fae. I follow my heart. And, not to be facetious, but so should you.'

'Facetious, ay?' Faerydae assumed it meant something ironic.

Faerydae sighed and strolled past Alalia to look at the waves crashing onto the shore. The thundering nobility of water continued to roll in and out, even when nobody was there to notice or to hear it. To Faerydae, it was hard to believe that a world existed even in places where she was not, had never been before. As if, behind her back, a place she could not see, nothing at all existed. Only emptiness. Alalia was not real. The caves were not real. The broomstick. It was all in her head.

Alalia's hand slid inside of her own... That confused Faerydae's theory for a moment.

'Let's just go,' Alalia said.

'What about my mother?' Faerydae mumbled. 'What about school?'

'That's the thing about life. If you worry about keeping the pieces of it in order, it will never take its true course. You have to learn to let go, Faerydae.'

She had an answer for everything. It was as if all the doubts and worries Faerydae was facing, Alalia had already overcome. As for why Faerydae even *wanted* to protest against running away with this beautiful girl, she could not say. She needed to be told that it was okay to leave her mama behind – *or had she actually been looking for a reason to run all along?*

'Why do I feel like I know you?' Faerydae asked.

'Because we are soulmates!' Alalia replied. 'Now, we can't take the broom into the Winding Woods. It's a ground job, that. A *walking* job. We'll have to take Lolanthie.'

'Lolanthie?'

Alalia began mounting the broomstick and gesturing for Faerydae to do the same.

'Papa's horse. He's friendly, but quite frankly, a nuisance when compared to a broomstick – has too much of a mind of his own.'

Faerydae found her preferred seating behind Alalia and held on tightly as the broom shuddered. They blasted off of the ground in a sparkling burst of power and were almost immediately back in the sky, leaving Freya Cove below them.

It felt like a changing kind of time to Faerydae, the dawn of a new way of life; that nothing would be the same as it had been after that day. She was aware of her hollow chest as they soared across the clouds. Could somebody else care about finding its lost contents just as much as she did? There had to be more to it than compassion. Alalia, and all that she had brought into Faerydae's life with her sudden presence, was all too sweet and perfect.

15

Possession of the Daltry Girl

Alalia

The Daltry's Manor was encased in black iron gates and thorny hedges. It was the epitome of nightmarish castles, but Alalia had never feared its presence, only what lingered inside.

Freya Daltry was a girl of Alalia's age, and they had known one another since the birth of Jákob when it was agreed that the two would marry when they came of age.

Alalia carried the cumbersome broom in the crook of her elbow as she winched open the eroded gate. Walking up the gentle slope towards the front door, Alalia considered what she might say depending on whom happened to open the door. The house was a huge granite construction with two stories and an infinite porch around the bottom level. You never knew exactly how many people were hiding inside. Alalia's two dozen bags of flour dragged along with the broom, straddled over its circumference, and the basket of unicorns had been delivered, much to the delight of the Vermonts.

She knocked on the door without hesitation, abruptly remembering that there was a doorbell to the side, which she rattled for good measure. The sound of the gold bell was whimsical. The air was humid and warm, but it could rain at any given moment in precarious waves of mist. Alalia held the flask of potion in both hands, positioned forthrightly in front of her thighs. She could hear approaching footsteps inside the mansion. The doorknob rattled around for a moment before Alalia smiled briefly at the appearing form of Mr Daltry in the doorway. He smiled back with crooked, yellow teeth bordered by a black goatee and moustache.

His smile vanished as rapidly as Alalia's did. This visit was not a pleasant house-call, after all.

'Good day, Mr Daltry.'

'Alalia,' he replied in a wealthy man's English. 'It has been too long; I feel as if I haven't seen you since you were only this high.' He gestured to his knees, and Alalia smiled again.

'I do apologise, sire. I've been… rather busy.'

He nodded. 'Ah, yes. Your *studies*.' And winked.

Alalia's studies were indeed taking up much of her time these days, not that they were something that one went around talking openly about – due to their 'bad' nature. But they were not the reason she hadn't made a house-call to the Daltrys in at least a year.

'Aye, sire,' Alalia agreed anyway. 'I have the potion you ordered. Mother insisted its delivery was of the utmost importance today.'

He took the flask in his manicured hands, grimaced. 'Important. Indeed. Freya has been gradually succumbing to her illness, as I'm sure you are aware.'

'I,' Alalia hesitated. 'Yes, I'm so sorry to hear it. But the potion is still abating the symptoms somewhat?'

'For now.'

Alalia held her breath for a few moments. The air was tense between the pair. She exhaled slowly.

'Well, I best be off, sire–'

'Alalia?'

She stopped and met Mr Daltry's hazel-eyed gaze.

'Yes, sire?' she said.

'Won't you stay a while longer? I know it would mean the world for Freya to see you again. You two used to be so close. And, well, we don't exactly know how long she has left.'

Alalia cringed with her head bowed. She knew this would happened. She knew she shouldn't have come. But when she lifted her head back to look at Mr Daltry, a pleased smile had appeared and she nodded her head eagerly.

Alalia followed Mr Daltry through the day-lit rooms of his great manor.

The curtains draping every passing window fell to the slate ground in sweeps. Everything was brown or red, or patterned in both. Alalia remembered fondly the days she had once spent running through the hallways of this labyrinthine house. Jákob and Freya had both been there, both answered to her, but it only ever felt as if the world belonged to her and Freya. They were the first friends.

A drab dining hall came upon them, when Mr Daltry poured himself a glass of rum at the little bar. He gestured for Alalia to make her own way to the dining table, which was dressed for a main meal. She walked quietly over the slate until she found herself sitting opposite to Mrs Daltry who suddenly rose out of her crowned chair at the girl's appearance.

'Alalia Miseria!' the thin blonde-haired woman said. 'My goodness, what a wonderful surprise. Are you joining us for dinner?'

Alalia shuffled the lavish chair under her. 'I would be delighted to, Mrs Daltry. It has… It has been a long time. It is good to see you again.'

'Oh, my dear, it certainly is good to see you. TEA!' she screamed to the maid. 'Now tell me all about your mother, is she well? And what of young Jákob? He is becoming quite well known around the city, I've heard?'

'He's certainly making a name for himself. As for his methods,' Alalia grinned. 'There is room for improvement.'

Alalia was always picking up the pieces of the messes her younger brother made. Of course, all the daydreaming boy cared about doing was helping people, no matter what destruction to buildings or religious temples it caused. Even now, Alalia could not help wondering what Jake might be doing to the ancient church that sat upon the cliffs of Beach Cemetery. A poltergeist was supposedly terrorising the area, and who better than a young warlock hunter, with his handmade crossbows and numerous gadgets, to save everybody? People preferred heroes they could understand. Anybody with a brain for technology could create underworld weapons that worked, but not everybody could bear letting *the magic* inside of them to have free rein. It might just kill them.

'Blanchefleur is expanding her trade area,' Mr Daltry said as he came to the table with a second glass of iced rum. 'Now that you and young Jákob are getting older you can help out more, isn't that true?'

'Yes, sire,' Alalia replied. 'I hope to be of much help to my mother now that she has entrusted me with her broomstick.'

'What an honour,' Mrs Daltry started.

'Where is Freya?' Alalia cut in. 'Will she be joining us?'

Mr Daltry shared a tense glance with his wife. 'The maid is administering the potion your mother made. She may need a few minutes to feel the effects.'

'I see. Of course. I was just.' Alalia paused. 'Wondering.'

The Daltry couple watched and smiled down on Alalia similarly from across the vast table, with expressions verging on awe and pity. The little girl gave a crooked smirk and looked around the dining room as another maid arrived with a pot of tea, three ceramic teacups, sugar, milk and biscuits. People hiding everywhere in this house.

Alalia took a biscuit and allowed the maid to pour her a cup of tea, when she suddenly wondered about the growing hour. The shadows were expanding. The forgotten field would try to murder her if she returned home later than sundown. Nevertheless, she ate her biscuit and sipped her tea with apparent patience. It had been so long since she and Freya had seen one another, and the thought that this may be the last time was something Alalia could not truly comprehend.

'She will be down soon, won't she?' Alalia heard herself asking again.

Just as Mrs Daltry inhaled to reply, a violent scream erupted from the upstairs part of the house. It dripped with gore and fear, a mixing of two kinds of emotions.

Alalia and the Daltry couple craned their necks in horror to watch the empty stairway. Mrs Daltry's hands were shaking as she stalked towards Alalia who could not move her eyes from the stairs, the empty scene, the scream that continued on. Flustered, Mrs Daltry gripped Alalia's elbow, beckoning her to her feet. The scream stopped.

'Alalia,' Mrs Daltry whispered. 'Why don't you come with me into the garden for a breath of air? Dinner shan't be long.'

'But–'

'*Now*, dear.'

The pair went to the front door just as Mr Daltry ventured up the staircase. Alalia struggled for only a moment before accepting the reprieve. The air outside had begun to cool off quite drastically. There was an icy breeze blowing just hard enough to creep inside loose clothing. Alalia shivered though she felt clammy and hot and pushed her short hair behind her ears.

'Was that Freya?' she asked.

Mrs Daltry's eyes were strained with worry, red and glassy. She looped her arm through Alalia's and they walked into a gathering of hedged animal shapes.

'My dear,' the woman spoke. 'How much do you know of Freya's illness?'

Alalia thought deeply about what she thought she knew. 'Only that her body is dying, being devoured by darkness. She has… inhuman symptoms. The potion stops the darkness from spreading into her heart. But it won't work forever.'

The woman was nodding with each added piece of information.

'It is the night. The moon. It brings forth the evil within her and we all have to take precautions because of *it*.'

'What sort of illness would do that, Mrs Daltry?' Alalia said.

'Freya becomes something at night. Somebody else.'

'A possession?'

The woman nodded. 'It does not come every night. This gives her some reprieve, but most nights it does, and it is becoming more violent. The spirit calls itself Daneya. We… We do not know what she wants.'

'How long has Freya been affected by this spirit?'

'A season. Since the death of her black cat.'

Alalia shrugged. 'Black cats can be very sensitive; however, they do seldom manage to possess another entity in their passing.'

'Please help her,' Mrs Daltry was pleading in her own proud way now. 'You're the only person I can console in. She would be rejected by any witchdoctor. You *know* her, you're her *friend*.'

'An exorcism,' Alalia spoke agreeably. 'It is the only way. Do not worry, I know what must be done. I think it would be best if I stay the night. Have your hand travel to the Cottage of Dancing Sweets and ask for my mother's potions kit, before nightfall'

Mrs Daltry smiled. 'Are you sure you can do this alone, my child? The daemon does not usually show itself until midnight – there is still time.'

Mrs Daltry began to sniffle, so Alalia hugged her awkwardly and nodded. 'I can do it.'

Alalia looked towards the road to Amaryllis. It was laced with muddy potholes full of water that the narrow wheels of an appearing carriage struggled through as it headed off for Alalia's home. Mud sloshed up onto the carriage's spotless sides. Alalia turned. The Daltry mansion was terribly startling from this angle, looking up at its imposing magnificence.

Alalia and Mrs Daltry retreated to the warmth of the indoors again to await the arrival of the girl's materials. They wandered into the dining room where the fire had been lit, and, to Alalia's startling surprise, a bright Freya Daltry now sat at the head of the grand table.

The girl had long black hair, straight as silk. Her pushed-up button nose was red from the cold and her dark green eyes were somehow tired, although they sparkled widely.

'Freya!' Mrs Daltry said it first.

The girl smiled bashfully. Mrs Daltry considered what to say next. 'Alalia Miseria is staying the night. A carriage has been sent for her things and might you be able to show her to her quarters, my dear, once they do arrive?'

Freya nodded gently. 'Of course. Alalia Miseria. It has been so long. Since the Amaryllis Pumpkin Throw, I believe, many seasons ago. It is on again this year I hear, always coinciding with the Grand Amaryllis Ball. Such a fun time of year I always thought, though I feel regrettably I will not be in attendance this time. How is Jákob?'

'Very well.' Alalia licked her lips. 'How have you been?' It was almost a cruel question.

Freya grinned. 'Just grand.'

Alalia returned the smile. 'Sorry. The potion is still helping, I see?'

'The darkness is growing stronger, but yes, the potion from your mother is still working for the most part.'

Alalia nodded. 'Good.'

Mr Daltry walked in through the doorway to the living room then, another glass of rum or scotch between his fingers. He swayed and placed his free hand upon Freya's bony shoulder. The man laughed in a rather goofy kind of way. He was clearly intoxicating himself.

'Here she is!' Mr Daltry boomed. 'The girl of the hour. Thought we might have had a bad turn there, but all is well again.' And he kissed Freya on the top of her head as if she were a rabbit in a pen.

Mr Daltry continued to talk about Freya in the third person and so Alalia took a seat to rest her legs.

'Your belongings ma'am.'

The house hand had already arrived back with Alalia's things and now stood behind her and the very resolute Mrs Daltry who hovered by the far wall.

'My goodness!' Alalia stood up. 'You are certainly punctual, sire.'

The man smiled. ''Tis a fast coach, ma'am. And I believe your mother may have already had your cases packed.'

'Really?' the redhead frowned. Blanchefleur always had a sense for those sorts of things. Perhaps she had packed them as soon as Alalia left this morning.

'Well then,' said Mrs Daltry. 'Freya shall show you to the guest room and then we might finally be able to have that dinner. Edgar–' She looked to Mr Daltry. 'Why don't we have another cup of tea, Dear?'

Alalia, cases jangling, looked shyly to Freya and they walked up the stairs together. Dust could be seen flying around in slow motion swirls through the large corridor. The place was as silent as a catacomb.

'Keep up!' Freya's voice called. She was grinning from the end of the corridor, having moved there without a sound, as if she'd disappeared for a moment and then reappeared somewhere else.

'Your house is so huge!' Alalia called.

'It's terribly quiet!' She agreed. 'It is so nice to have a guest stay over.'

Alalia wondered if Freya was fully aware of what this visit entailed. She followed Freya into what would be her bedroom for the night. It was a simple room. Nothing decorated the space except for the bed and its faded grey sheets and the wardrobe beside the window. Alalia placed her things on the bed.

Freya remained in the doorway, so Alalia said: 'Thank you. I'll unpack now, see what my mother has left over in her case.'

Freya nodded. 'Thank you, I'm just in the next room.'

When she left, Alalia watched the place where she had been standing, listening to hear where her footsteps went. They did not go far and were followed by a closing door; it seemed Freya had gone into her own room next door. Alalia felt the weight of her undertaking finally fall flat against her stomach. She could not shake the adoration she held for Freya, but she could not let it become a distraction, either. Alalia stroked her dress. The uniform was her reminder. She unpacked her equipment before making sure that the bow below her chin was centred. The mirror on the wardrobe was foggy but allowed her to fix her hair somewhat too. She continued to check her flasks obsessively until being summoned for dinner. She went back downstairs and found the Daltrys, all of them, once again waiting to eat. It was dark by now.

'I'm late,' Alalia said.

'Nonsense.' Mr Daltry smiled. 'Come and sit. I hope you like roast; Ms Fickle makes a wonderful cranberry sauce.'

Alalia suddenly felt uncomfortable. She went to her seat beside Freya who was eying her brightly. The roast turkey came out promptly, and a very youthful Ms Fickle served their dishes one by one. There was wine available but Alalia declined.

'How do you like it?' Mrs Daltry asked.

'The turkey is amazing,' Alalia said.

'Jasper caught the thing,' Mrs Daltry replied. 'Our hand. You met him earlier.'

Mr Daltry added, 'It was a determined creature, but I have traps all over this residence.'

'Is Jákob's training going well?' Freya asked.

'I doubt my brother is ever unwell.' Alalia poured some more thick sauce on her plate.

Freya grinned. 'The last time I spent any time with the both of you, he and I were forced to dance together. He was terribly quiet. I believed he was somewhat offended.'

'That is highly unlikely.' Alalia decided she might have some wine after all, considering where this conversation was heading. Freya, seeing the redhead take such huge sips, dropped the subject and took up another.

'I do love autumn,' Freya reminisced. 'I love the way the world changes; it's like there's something coming to get us. Winter.'

There was a beat.

'Freya showed you to the room, Alalia?' asked Mrs Daltry.

'Yes. Thank you.'

'After dinner you two can head upstairs and talk for a time until bed. Freya goes to bed at eight. Eight-thirty the latest.'

Dinner was mostly quiet after that, until Ms Fickle cleared the plates. Alalia thanked her, and she asked if anybody wanted tea and biscuits for dessert. The younger girls declined, but the adults stayed back. Heading upstairs together again, not terribly close this time, Alalia and Freya wondered what to talk about. And as much as Freya tried not to, she brought up Jákob again.

'Your brother is becoming rather famous these days,' she said. 'As for you, we rarely hear a word spoken—'

'Perhaps that is how I prefer it,' Alalia blurted. 'Fame is not for everyone.'

'I'm sorry, Alalia.'

Freya's soft footsteps stopped sounding from behind Alalia and she turned to see the girl gazing up at her. Freya's expression was of irritation and also frustration, not towards Alalia but internally towards herself.

'I don't know what to talk to you about anymore,' Freya admitted softly. 'I don't even care to talk about Jake, really.' She stepped closer to Alalia. Freya was shorter than Alalia now, when she had always been the taller one. 'We haven't even spoken since... Well, since the day I think I might have broken your heart. The day I had to spend with Jákob instead of with you.'

Alalia shrivelled into herself. 'Honestly, it is okay, I would prefer not to talk about it—'

'I am sorry, Alalia. But I rarely have a choice in my life. It was decided I would marry Jákob before he was even born. The fact I might love another had never been a factor. But now that I might not live to see many more mornings, I feel there is little to lose. I fell in love with *you*, Alalia.'

'We should get to bed,' Alalia said. 'You are unwell. Please do not get yourself all worked up.'

Freya raised her eyebrows. 'Isn't it funny that the ones who are apparently the weakest are actually the strongest of all.'

'I didn't mean…'

'If you need anything during the night, I am just next door. But do knock as my door will be deadlocked from the outside. Something my parents insist on.'

Alalia nodded along with the sudden change of topic. 'Thank you,' she said. 'And Freya, everything is going to be okay, I promise.'

Freya's expression did not waver. She passed Alalia up the stairwell and went into her own bedroom without another word, only the firm closing of her door.

Of all the things Alalia could have thought to say, *that* was the most condescending to the stoic girl. Alalia wished she could say what she meant for once in her life.

16

Faerydae

By the following morning, Faerydae awoke in the lagoon to find that her hair had grown down to her shoulders overnight. It curled around her ears in soft new tresses, reflecting up at her from the lagoon's green water. The olde ship moaned behind her as she stroked the new hair. The water bobbed the ship up and down with its tiny ripples.

Faerydae went back inside wearing a dumbfounded expression, wondering if her hair would continue to grow at such a rapid speed for the rest of her life.

'So bizarre, Lume.'

Silence.

Lume was refusing to talk with Faerydae after yesterday's events.

The gem sat upon his throne of straw like some sort of arrogant king, his sparkling features as blurred and indistinct as his mood. Faerydae wondered if the gem had found himself conflicted. After his screaming declaration of Alalia's wickedness, perhaps her suggestion to travel into the Winding Woods had swayed him to reconsider her. Her suggestion was to become more than a suggestion though. By tonight, she and Faerydae were to make their escape. *Escape?* It definitely felt like an escape. And maybe Lume finally did not know his own mind on the matter.

Euphraxia lay splayed out on her bed of straw, murmuring in her dreams as she always did. The woman lived a whole intricate life inside of her head, and spent more time there than in the real world. Euphraxia twitched her fingers sporadically and Faerydae found herself unable to stop watching the poor woman.

The girl had already pondered what to do with her. What to tell her. What would be *best* for her. The morbid thought had occurred to Faerydae already that perhaps Euphraxia was better off left to fade. However, unexperienced in the process of death, Faerydae could not fully believe that being dead was any better than this. Whatever *this* was to Euphraxia. Maybe Faerydae could simply walk away from it all and find everything exactly the same when she returned. The village would continue to function even without her being there to see it. And so too could Euphraxia.

Faerydae would be reunited with this dreary life before she even knew she'd left it.

Faerydae sighed, flopping down in a mess of buckets that she had no motivation to fill with fish today. How strange it was to have met a person like Alalia Riviera amidst all of the darkness in her life.

And what of that kiss?

Did a kiss mean different things to different people? Perhaps it was more like a handshake to Alalia. Of course, Faerydae knew how lonesome the girl was. But Faerydae was a lonesome girl too, and she had never kissed a stranger to ebb the desire for interaction.

She could broach the subject later that evening. Maybe… How Faerydae was so curious about the night soon to unfold.

'It's just all a bit too good to be true, don't you think?'

Faerydae turned to look at Lume, her hair bouncing in soft rings.

'Well, well, well. Hello again. I thought you might have become a normal piece of stone after all.'

The gem had little to no jest within his voice.

'That redheaded girl,' he went on. *'I cannot place her, but I believe something rather shadowy is approaching, Flea.'*

'You are probably quite right. She and I are going to find my heart, together tonight. I thought you'd be happy. Haven't you said all along that you wanted to go to the Winding Woods?'

'Indeed. But why is this girl so eager to help you?'

'This isn't her home,' Faerydae explained. 'She is lonely. She wants an escape, as do I. It's almost like, we're connected in that way.'

'I suggest you tread with caution, my child. Do you expect to be home before Euphraxia has the chance to kill herself?'

Faerydae grimaced. 'I expect I will be home before that, yes. I will make it my business to be home before too long, even if circumstances try to sway me to do otherwise. I will not abandon my mother.'

'Really?' Lume said. *'If you have an opportunity to follow your heart, you will not take it?'*

Faerydae faltered – she wasn't *lying*, she just wasn't sure if she was telling the truth either.

'I won't.'

'That is your decision. I am of no opinion on that matter.'

'Of course you are not. All you care about is yourself.' Faerydae crawled towards him. 'I don't know what you're planning, but if I take you into the woods with me, I want your word that you will not do anything to harm me or Alalia.'

Lume watched her indecisively.

'Your word,' Faerydae persisted. 'Or I swear I will leave you sitting here in the company of the screeching birds and my hungry mother.'

'You have my word,' Lume said. *'If the word of an inanimate object means anything to you.'*

'It does. I believe you will keep it.'

'Very well.' Lume smiled. *'What now?'*

Faerydae returned to sitting on her pile of buckets. 'Now we wait. For nightfall. Alalia believes it will be our best chance to escape without her papa discovering us. She insists we will be back home before morning's light arrives, and nobody will suspect a thing if we can pull it off. We are to travel to this so-called *wizard's* house and find out what we can about my heart's whereabouts. I suspect it will be the first of many trips. I do not expect to learn much this time around, even if we do find the wizard.'

'I see.' The gem sounded more like himself now, a hint of drollness. *'You have got it all figured out then.'*

'Quite right,' Faerydae hissed back at him.

They were silent for a while and Faerydae even dozed off. When her eyes flittered open again, Lume was still staring at her but he was no longer glowing. Euphraxia was awake.

'Mama.' Faerydae got to her feet and discreetly placed Lume inside the pocket that was fast becoming his own little pouch. 'How are you feeling today?'

'Ferrihead,' Euphraxia said in a yawn. 'I was having the strangest of dreams.'

'Did you want to tell me about it?' Faerydae heard herself saying as she crouched down beside her. If there was but one thing they could talk about, it was the dream world.

'You were running through a field,' Euphraxia laughed. 'A tribe of walking scarecrows chasing you with pitchforks and fiery stakes. There was somebody else with you. Another girl running ahead. Her hair... *Ferrihead...* it was a blazing mess of flames. And she was screaming.'

Faerydae gulped. She tried to think if she had mentioned Alalia at all during the last day and if her mother might have overheard her saying 'a girl with red curls'. It was a frightful depiction nonetheless, one that made Faerydae wish she hadn't asked about it.

'How interesting.' Faerydae paused thoughtfully. 'Mama, I want you to know something. I don't always say it, but I want you to be happy. I want the best thing for you. Whatever that may be.'

Euphraxia frowned, a deep wrinkled expression too olde for her years. 'What on earth are you talking about, Ferrihead?' she said. 'I haven't got the time to listen to your babble, darling.'

Faerydae bowed her head so her mama would not see the tear sliding down the corner of her eye and onto her chin. Faerydae told herself she was being stupid. She wiped the tear away and smiled at her mother's expectant gaze. The girl did not fully understand why she felt so upset. It was as if this was to become some sort of memento between them, what Faerydae would take with her as she went out into the world, a child becoming an adult. How would she remember her mama on the days when they were apart? As a woman who was too distant to reach, even when close enough to touch.

'Sorry Mama,' Faerydae said. 'I shall start fishing and leave what I catch in the front cabin for you. I might be late tonight. I might not be home until very late.'

Euphraxia waved a hand. 'I have too much to do today. Can't you take care of yourself?'

'I'll certainly try.'

The irony was not lost on Faerydae, who grabbed her roll of fishing line and headed outside to try and catch enough fish or frogs to last her mama a couple of days.

17

Alalia

There was not a sound in the dark house apart from the hounding winds outside. Alalia Miseria lay atop her white sheets upon the cold hard mattress, reading over notes that had been written many breaths ago by a much younger Blanchefleur. Her candlelight flickered intermittently over olde sketches of potions and ingredients, and the young girl's spectacles glimmered. She pulled the glasses away from her face to rub her tired eyes.

'So late,' Alalia whispered. 'And not a sound anywhere.'

Her mother's book had been good reading for some time, good to keep her occupied and awake, though it had not informed her much on the subject of spiritual possession. Such disorders were more suited to a demonologist than a wiccan, or even a warlock hunter. Like Jákob. And yet here Alalia was, swearing she could help the dying Freya.

She sighed, rubbing her eyes once more.

She dozed off for only a moment then, but a dream came to her fully formed and with intent. A girl with dark black hair stood before her. Alalia, in her mind, assumed it was Freya. Only this girl was wearing boy's clothes and had more deeply set features. The dream girl reached a hand out towards Alalia's mind's eye, disappearing there. The girl's arm wavered for a moment. When it was drawn back into view, a heart sat beating upon the dream girl's weathered palm. Alalia felt herself want to smile. But the feeling faded. For a monster with a featureless face loomed behind this stranger's shoulders. The monstrous shape began creeping closer, nearly at the dream girl's back, reaching for her with a gargantuan claw. And the heart beat. Beat. BEAT–

A gentle rapping woke her.

It felt as if a minute had passed, but it had surely been longer than that. The rapping was coming from the wall opposite the bed. Alalia cleared her head. It sounded like the noise was *inside* the wall. Alalia considered that it must have been some kind of rodent or even a possum. She watched the length of wall, motionless, from her bed. Again – a scratching in the wall between herself and Freya's bedroom. Something small was trying to get out. *A mouse? Maybe a rat?*

A flickering of candlelight caught in the corner of Alalia's peripheral vision and she darted her head to the side. It came from the darkened hallway. Her door was open just a crack, just enough to see onto the landing. She tried to recall if the candles had been lit in the hallway all night or not. It could have easily been her imagination, but such a coincidence was worth following up under these circumstances. There was not much else to steal her attention, after all.

She slid off of the bed and pulled the sheet away from her shoulders that had been keeping her warm. She glanced at her watch. 11:46. She was still dressed and her shoes were still tied. The girl approached her mother's potions kit and placed various flasks into her pockets that were the size of her pinkie finger and a necklace of rosery beads in her hand. She approached the open doorway quietly. Alalia felt a prickling of chills run up her arms and legs once the coldness of the hallway consumed her. A sound lingered in the air, but it was currently just an undertone. Too distant to hear or too unique to recognise, like a faint humming. The house wasn't sleeping anymore. Something had awoken.

Alalia picked a lantern out of a hallway mount and held it affront her nose as she moved towards Freya's room down the hallway. Freya's door was still closed. But Alalia rattled the doorknob just to be sure. It was locked. Freya had to be inside still.

'Go hide!'

Alalia twirled around, her lantern rattling in her grip. Nobody behind her…

She had heard the airy voice almost in her ear. The girl glanced from every dark corner of the hallway to every inch of candlelit wall, but could not see anyone. Childish giggles and whispers floated in the air around Alalia. She moved away from Freya's doorway and closer to the stairs. She believed she could hear two separate voices now, kids, female. They were so far away. She watched the ceiling, trying to follow the trail of murmurs as they moved, echoing through the whole house.

Alalia retrieved a certain murky purple flask out of her pocket and pulled at the tiny cork with her teeth. It popped open with a bubbling fizz. As she walked closer to the stairs, she let the flask tip until it was leaving a trail of drips beside her. The drips drew attention towards another substance on the floorboards, the reaction causing whatever it was to glow like fiery ashes. A track of small footprints appeared, headed down the stairs, burning hot embers in the shape of little feet. Daemon footprints, invisible to the naked eye. Alalia clenched her teeth. She returned to Freya's room before committing herself to the ghoulish trail and leant down to peer under her door.

'Freya?' she whispered.

The crack under the door was too narrow to let Alalia see onto the bed. If Freya was in there and merely asleep, she was as silent as a corpse. Laughter swirled around the house again and lifted the shadows on the walls, making them grow. *Go hide! Go hide and we'll seek!*

Alalia wrenched her head away from the floor and sat kneeling for a moment. She blinked rapidly. Her eyes were suddenly cloudy and burning hot. They itched as if something from the floor had gotten inside of them. *Shadows.* She rubbed her face with her palms and webs of black sinewy shadows came away from her cheeks and out of her eyes. It was like sticky ink that wouldn't let go. The black threads spooled into a knot and dribbled onto the ground. Alalia tried to breathe steadily. The stuff was out of her eyes… it was crawling back to the walls. She was okay.

With the same purple flask, Alalia dripped exactly thirteen droplets onto the space of floor where she had just been kneeling, just at the base of Freya's door. The boards lit up with patches of ashes again. And Alalia's throat clenched. She swallowed a moan. The footsteps were coming directly out of Freya's bedroom. It was certain. One of the footprints even lingered halfway between both rooms.

'Freya!' Alalia cried loudly.

A hiss of laughter sounded from underneath her, in the parlour below the stairs. *Hide and Seek! Hide and we'll seek!* Alalia eyed the trail of footprints heading downstairs and stood. 'Freya…'

She followed the trail.

'What was it that Mother always said?' Alalia arrived on the ground floor and walked towards the dining room with her lantern. 'Courage is only a by-product of fear. And *everybody* is afraid of something… That should be more comforting.'

She found herself in the parlour all too soon, a room at the back of the household with various disused armchairs, relics and forgotten paintings. Silence had overcome it again. It was even colder down there than upstairs despite the mild temperature outside.

The thrashing sound of a windstorm crashed in through the swinging back door, which hung on the remnants of its shattered hinges. Alalia hadn't even heard the door being broken; hadn't heard the howling wind through the house until now. She sucked in a deep breath and walked outside.

The wind was actually comforting. It whistled inside her ears as she tried to see around the huge bushes in the shapes of animals. A crashing of metal barked in the near distance, around the side of the house facing the hills. The girl walked hurriedly towards the sound and found an open cellar leading under the house. She sighed. The cellar was a black square in the ground surrounded by a wooden frame and the two open doors that sat jutting out at either side, banging in the wind. Concrete stairs led down into the darkness below. Just to be sure, Alalia dripped the last of her purple potion over the first step and, sure enough, perfectly formed ashy footprints lit the way down.

'Freya?' Alalia called lightly as she entered the cold clamminess that was the cellar.

The sound of girlish laughter filled the space.

'I'm here,' Freya's voice came from out of the dark.

Alalia was surprised. She waved the lantern about the air and rounded a huge pile of chopped wood that enveloped almost the entire space between floor and ceiling. Only to be blocked by another pile of hacked-up wood behind it. Alalia soon found herself weaving through the seemingly endless cellar at a loss. Stacks of pickled fruit jars and various vegetable containers filled the gaps where the chopped wood did not. The Daltrys kept themselves well stocked. Upon reaching the cobbled back wall, Alalia spied a shadowy form. Freya was staring at the stones in the wall in a hunched position.

'Freya,' Alalia said. 'What are you doing down here in the middle of the night? How did you get out of your room?'

'Playing.'

The girl did not turn to face Alalia.

'Playing by yourself?' Alalia asked. 'Or is there someone else down here with you?'

'I'm playing with Freya. But she's a sissy, afraid of the night.'

Alalia stepped closer. 'So you're *not* Freya?'

'We're both here,' the girl replied.

'But I'm not currently talking with Freya, am I? Might I ask who you are? Is your name *Daneya*?'

'You don't know?' the girl asked. 'I know who you are. Your name is Alalia.'

'Daneya–'

Suddenly, Daneya twirled to the side in a frighteningly limber movement, her body not quite at one with her mind, and disappeared behind a row of piled jars.

'Hey!' Alalia ran after her, trying to keep the lantern steady.

The girl hadn't run far. Alalia found Daneya standing at the end of a makeshift corridor created by the piles of wood and jars. Daneya was facing Alalia now, straight on, her eyes just white orbs that had rolled into the back of her head. She held a splitting axe in one hand, which dangled by her side. Alalia instinctively held her hands up, submitting herself.

'May I talk with Freya?' Alalia asked.

Daneya's mouth curled into a grin as she let her axe swing passively in her grip. It was a warning. Alalia felt around her hip where a larger flask of holy water sat ready in her pocket. If she could get it into Freya's eyes, she would be able to sedate her at least.

'*I* own the night-time,' Daneya said. 'I come out to play now. This is my time.'

'How did you get out of Freya's bedroom? The door was deadlocked. I checked.'

'I crawled under the door.'

'Under the door? That *tiny* gap.'

The girl was still smiling. Alalia stepped closer, her gaze sternly fixed on Daneya's hands. Alalia's features hardened.

'What do you want, spirit?' she asked. 'Tell me why you have possessed Freya Daltry.'

'You're giving me the giggles.' Daneya started to laugh and swing the axe in a bizarre rhythm, to and fro and in tiny circles.

Alalia pressed on, approaching the girl with tentative steps and with one hand still clutching her pocket anxiously.

'By the all-consuming powers of the omen Maxia,' Alalia chanted. 'And the winds of sorcery at my back, we of this household wish you gone. Desterrar! Desterrar!'

Daneya hissed, growled, and tilted her head sideways. 'If you can catch me, you win the game!' She looked up to the cellar's ceiling. Her head continued to turn around as she began to mount the stone wall and climb it with her bare hands and feet.

Alalia found herself backing away, watching the grotesque event absently. Daneya made a scuttling sound as her hands dug somehow into the crevices of olde masonry. She was still holding onto the dangling axe as she made it onto the ceiling, holding her body up like an insect. Her scuttling limbs proceeded to make haste and she looped her way back towards Alalia's direction. It took Alalia a moment to realise that Daneya was gaining on her, a sharpened axe at the ready. She backed away, back towards the woodpiles. One step. Two steps. Daneya escalated into a sprinting sort of scurrying that chilled Alalia to the core. She finally found the courage to turn her back and sprinted in retreat, dropping the lantern as she made her escape.

'Run, run, run,' came Daneya's sickly taunt. 'Ready or not, here I come, Alalia.'

Alalia skidded into a tight gap between the piled-up wood and jars. It was so dark in there. She crouched down and tried to steady her hands enough to pull the cork out of her holy water vial. Her hands wouldn't stop shaking.

'Blast.'

She gripped the little vial as tightly as she could, praying not to shatter it, and held it close to her chest. She peered back towards the edge of the woodpile.

'It's time for you to leave this family in peace Daneya!' she belted. 'They have been through enough.'

'*They?*' Daneya's parched voice came echoing around the cellar. Alalia had no idea where she was now. 'What about me? I am a part of this family too. Don't you remember me? Freya and I are *sisters*, Alalia.'

Alalia sat in silent wonderment for a moment. She considered that it might be a lie, or some kind of imagined fantasy, but so far the origin of Freya's possession was just too hazy to rule anything out.

'I died at age two,' Daneya moaned. 'You don't remember, Alalia? Whooping cough. I suppose Freya's the only one you have ever really been interested in.' Daneya sounded as if she was growing farther away, but Alalia was reluctant to trust the echoing resonances of the room.

'The black kitten was sitting beside me on the windowsill that day; the day that I died. It started raining outside when I couldn't inhale another breath,' Daneya said sweetly. 'And Freya was holding my paw when the cat died of olde age. I move onto the closest soul to me. So you see, I do belong here, with *my* family.'

Alalia's hands were shaking again. She started to crawl further into the crevice she was basically trapped in, trying to reach the other end, although it was too dark to know if anything else existed there.

'If you love Freya,' Alalia said. 'If you are her sister and you love her, you will release her from this curse. You will give her back her life, so she can live without you.'

'*I* don't love Freya,' said Daneya, almost too distant to hear. 'You're the one who loves Freya. That's why you're here, isn't it? Because you love her. No one else would be stupid enough to try and stop me, except that pathetic potion maker; it is like giving the girl lollies to treat the Black Plague.'

Alalia found herself in yet another darkened corridor of woodpiles and jars that led all the way back around to the moonlit cellar steps.

'Freya is a kind girl,' Alalia whispered as she started towards the light of the cellar's opening. 'It is easy to love her. But to earn her love in return is a gift... I'll do my best though—'

The whooshing sound of the axe blade missing Alalia's neck by a centimetre pierced the air. The axe crashed into the wood pile and crumbled it like a tower of cards. Daneya appeared scurrying on top of the logs, hissing and growling, spit drooling into Alalia's hair as she tried to gain purchase. Alalia ricocheted away from the tumbling wood.

A gap in the pile allowed her to crawl into the adjacent row and run. Smashing jars and falling wood trailed her every step. The whole cellar sounded as if it were crumbling into shards. Alalia dove into a different row. Daneya appeared on top of the woodpile to her left and scuttled down the side, reaching to swing her axe again. Alalia grasped the girl's slim forearm and heaved her off of the mound. She fell to the concrete ground, where they both skidded onto their sides.

Daneya writhed for a moment, as if she were a cockroach stuck on its back, and Alalia took the opportunity to get to her own feet. Daneya was quick though. She leapt up once she caught sight of Alalia's form holding a mysterious vial. Daneya lunged at her. Alalia darted aside and grabbed onto Daneya's forearm to pin herself across her neck. Daneya was forced up against the splintering wood where Alalia crisscrossed her elbows over her neck and strung her up by her own limbs. An almighty strength exuded from the wiccan girl. Daneya snapped. Alalia reached for her vial and sprayed drips of holy water into the girl's eyes, ears and mouth. She drenched Freya without relent. Even when the water appeared to be melting into her skin, sizzling and steaming, Alalia did not stop until the bottle was empty.

'Desterrar!' Alalia screamed breathlessly. 'By the will of ungodly sorcery, to the devil's lair I pardon thee, the gates of heaven shall open, and thou shalt never return to these living realms. Desterrar! *Desterrar!* DESTERRAR!'

Daneya laughed bitterly before the entirety of her weight fell into the hands of Alalia. They both crumpled again. Alalia fell below Freya's unmoving and soundless body. Thick red ooze dribbled out of the girl's head, her mouth, eyes, ears and nose. Alalia shoved the body delicately off of her to rest on the concrete, then she gripped Freya's saturated head in her hands. Alalia was saturated too, too frantic to feel the dampness though.

'Freya?!' she urged, feeling the girl's icy cheeks. She leant down to Freya's chest and listened for a heartbeat. There was none. 'No! No, come on Freya.'

Alalia forced air from her own lungs into Freya's but got little response. The girl's eyes were wide open and still totally white. Alalia pressed up and down on her chest before forcing more air into Freya's motionless body. Suddenly, miraculously, Freya's eyes rolled around to face the world and her head flew up to headbutt Alalia. A stream of dark blood erupted from her mouth. Daneya seeped out of all the crevices of Freya's mind. Her ears and nose dripped endlessly with a dark poisoned blood.

Alalia collapsed backwards. Relief took hold of her in a cloud of subconsciousness for all but a second.

'Daneya?!' Freya screamed in disorientation.

'No,' Alalia comforted, crawling back to her side. 'It's just me. You're okay, Freya. Truly. You're safe.'

Alalia grabbed Freya's hand and squeezed it.

Freya's terrified features settled, and ever so slowly, relief began to wash over her as well. Her slim arms, covered in blood and holy water, fell over Alalia's shoulders and tightened. Alalia hugged her just as tightly back. They laughed, overwhelmed.

Freya pulled away, then retreated back into Alalia's embrace almost immediately. She was crying.

'There, there,' Alalia whispered. 'My strong Freya. You have nothing to fear. All is well. The game is finally over; I think you have won.'

Freya stared hopefully into her saviour's blue eyes, *wanting* to believe, and then believing completely. She cupped Alalia's flushed cheeks in her hands. Alalia pressed her own hand over Freya's, which was cold and shaky. She tried to steady it by squeezing it again. It was so cold. The girl needed to dry off and warm her body or else she would catch a fever.

The mere touch of their skin though, the presence of their bodies so close to one another, was a sensation all too real to even consider thinking about what might happen afterwards. This is what kept Freya alive for so long, Alalia found herself thinking. This love. This love had saved her.

Freya's lips tasted of coppery blood, but Alalia had never cared less about anything.

'I'm sorry,' Alalia cried delicately. 'I'm so sorry that I left you alone for so long. I was a coward. I never want to lose you, Freya. To anything. To any illness. Or *anyone.*'

Freya forced herself against Alalia and the redhead pressed amorously back. She took a breath and whispered, 'you never will.'

Alalia felt unleashed. Her hands slid down to Freya's waist and held her tight enough to make the fear go away. Freya ran her fingers through Alalia's wet curls. She left a trail of kisses down Alalia's neck and chest. Alalia opened her eyes to the dark, hearing Freya's breath. Alalia's hand slipped under the Daltry girl's petticoat and Freya moaned, finding Alalia's lips all over again.

'I love you,' Alalia whispered desperately.

'I love you too.'

18

Faerydae

A soggy basket of mudfish and lagoon eels writhed beside Euphraxia. Faerydae walked alone towards Alalia Riviera's house. It was already nightfall, but the day was only just beginning really. Faerydae and Alalia had agreed that neither would attend school that day, which they hadn't, as far as Faerydae knew. Alalia apparently had 'some things' to take care of and she suggested that Faerydae get some rest in the meantime. Alalia was not afraid to speak her mind; she was fearless. Faerydae hadn't rested though. She had been up since sunrise, thinking, then fishing, worrying and wondering. Finally, the cover of a clear night sky had arrived.

She carried nothing with her, just as Alalia had instructed. However, she did conceal Lume within her little pocket and decided that Alalia need not know about his presence for the time being. Faerydae would not let him off of a tight leash once they arrived in the woods. He could prove to be a nuisance, but if she was going to find her heart, or find answers at least, then the red gem who spoke of so much that was unknown would surely be of use.

Faerydae was, admittedly, fond of the horrid thing; perhaps it was because he was the first friend she had ever known. He was a temptation to most. Faerydae had learnt that well enough with the troll. If she could keep him safe, Faerydae hoped he would do the same in return.

Faerydae had never wandered the trail around the village at night before and everything became the same in the dark. Objects held no individuality anymore. Birds squawked at her from above, but she couldn't see them.

'*You know,*' Lume said. '*If this girl gets you into deep trouble, or does away with you, nobody will ever know what happened.*'

Faerydae twisted her lips. 'I'm more capable than you think.'

'*She's older than you are,*' he said.

'I'm taller.'

'*So, you* are *nervous?*'

'No.' Faerydae chuckled. 'I'm going to find my heart, and she knows the way.'

The gem made a sighing sound. '*Flea. Little Flea. So eager to find your heart, after all these years of not caring.*'

'It's not that I didn't care,' Faerydae said, trying to grasp what she meant. 'But so much has happened so quickly that I don't think I can pretend as if I'm normal anymore. I'm not. Nothing about my life has been normal. I need to know why... I suppose.'

'*You* suppose.'

The girl pressed ahead, sticking to the winding track at a steady pace. She passed an olde windmill surrounded by bleating goats before the path divided into two tracks. One led into the forest and the other continued to loop around the outskirts of the village before dissipating away to nothing. Faerydae followed the path into the forest that concealed Alalia's little house.

When she arrived at the Riviera's front door, the homestead sat in darkness and Faerydae hovered her fist over the handle. She wondered if she was not meant to knock. Had Alalia wanted her to wait outside for her? She drew back and veered towards the back garden where she knew a water fountain preceded a small stable.

'Alalia...?' Faerydae knew she was being too quiet for anyone to hear.

'*Just go back and knock on the door,*' Lume suggested. '*Climb in through a window if you must.*'

'I'm not breaking in, Lume,' she replied.

Faerydae walked towards the little wooden stable, treading over dried leaves that crackled like seashells. No sign of a horse. Not a sound. 'I wonder if she got caught up with something else,' mumbled Faerydae.

There was an immense crushing of leaves behind her before it felt like a pair of forks had been jabbed into her ribs. Faerydae squealed and spun around, punching out frantically.

Alalia dodged her blows by mere inches before breaking into startled giggles.

'Hey there!' She grinned. 'Who were you talking to, Faerydae Scaredyhead?'

Faerydae, regaining her composure, laughed lightly. 'No one.'

The redhead circled around to the other side of Faerydae and picked something up from out of the grass and leaves with a smile.

'You dropped this.'

Faerydae's breath caught in her throat. Alalia fumbled Lume around between her fingers, looking over his glassy exterior curiously.

'Didn't think you were going to bring anything,' Alalia said, giving the gem back to Faerydae slowly.

Faerydae took him from her hand and tried to inconspicuously stuff him back inside her pocket. 'Forgot that was in there, sorry. Just something I found this morning, in the lagoon.' She shrugged, and Alalia grinned again.

'So,' Alalia started. 'Papa's sleeping with the dead; I put a nightshade potion into his tea so he won't even realise Lolanthie is missing before we're long gone, at the edge of the woods at least.'

Faerydae nodded as she followed Alalia into the dark stable.

She felt over the silhouetted shapes of leather horse tack and various hay bales and buckets. A lamp sputtered into life and Faerydae saw Alalia waving a smoking match beside it. She was wearing a black dress that went down to her knees, Faerydae could see now. The sleeves were long and laced intricately in patterns of uneven swirls and flowers. Thick ribbon looped back and forth across her chest and tightened at the base of her neck. She wore a pair of delicate black heeled shoes that went up to just over her ankles.

Faerydae saw that the ground was covered in olde hay that could relish the ashes of even a small toothpick. She found herself wondering how strange it all was, for her to be standing there with that other mysterious girl, in the night. In the dark. Alone.

'Why are you doing this for me?' Faerydae asked, catching Alalia off guard. The redhead stopped fussing with a leather hackamore but did not turn to look at her.

'Doing what?' she asked.

'You know what,' Faerydae said. 'Helping me. Going into the woods with a girl you hardly know to help find the most bizarre thing of all' – a pause – 'my missing heart, for goodness' sakes.'

Alalia looked over her shoulder.

'Why not?' She stepped towards Faerydae. 'I am a wiccan, Faerydae. if I can help somebody, I will. And I have never met anybody quite like you before. There is something very dark inside of you – no, it's not bad,' Alalia assured her when Faerydae grimaced. 'We all have darkness in us. We all have *magic* in us. But whoever stole your heart has left a gap inside of you that can only be filled by something else. I want it to be filled with the right thing, that's all.'

Faerydae's grimace did not fade. 'I am not going to let anything change who I am,' she spoke sternly. 'If that is what you're worried about?... I know all the parts of myself that are important to know, and I also know exactly what I will *never* become. I have lived this strange life for thirteen years, Miss Riviera, and I have learnt my own strengths. I am not a weak person. Not at all.'

'Somebody else said that to me once...' Alalia's charming demeanour flattened as she seemed to retreat inside of herself for a moment. 'I know you are strong, Faerydae. You are my friend. All I have ever known in my life is to serve others, and I want to help you if I can. I *need* to help you. I want nothing in return.'

There was a beat.

Faerydae grinned. 'Alright then. I suppose we'd better get moving before anything can dare try to stop us.'

'Into the unknown, my darling.' Alalia held Faerydae's hand and kissed it chivalrously, almost dotingly.

Faerydae eyed her, taking the hackamore from her hand as if it were a token of exchanging leaderships. 'To welcome whatever storm the unknown may bring.'

19

Wizard of the Winding Woods

The world raced past them in a blustery haze – so open and yet endlessly undulating, with eternal views of a world that Faerydae had never seen before. They galloped towards the Western Province border without heed; Faerydae believed she had never felt quite so free as this, riding atop a wild beast, not even flying held quite the same quality for her.

The journey towards the woods had started over shallow hills and grassland, until they made it out of the Shire, where it continued through fields that overlooked a vast valley. There was nothing out there except for the few distant lights of mountain communities in the great beyond.

Lolanthie kicked his hind into the air and the girls held on for dear life. The charcoal stallion was huge and excitable; he hadn't run like this in years and was not showing any signs of stopping. Faerydae wondered if Alalia, who sat up front to steer, even *could* stop him with the few dangling straps of leather wrapped around his face. His gait was too wild and mad to be tamed. They were in his hold now. The stallion's legs bounded like uprooted tree trunks. He was tall, at least eighteen hands. If one of the girls were to fall from his sleek back and become trampled underneath his feathered hooves, they would surely be killed instantly.

'THERE IS A FENCE UP AHEAD!' Alalia screamed just as she had done on the broom yesterday.

Faerydae could not see a fence in the murky dark until it was suddenly upon them and Lolanthie disembarked the earth. He sailed over the barbed wire barricade, his legs tucked in close to his body, over the sign that read: '**!Danger! Winding Woods Dead Ahead!**'

Faerydae howled, spreading her arms wide with little care towards her own balance. She belonged on top of the world.

With the last defence between them and the danger they so willingly invited behind them, Faerydae and Alalia could see the tips of the woods appearing on the other side of the grassy hill. Faerydae stroked the muddy black fur over Lolanthie's rump as he ran.

The tips of the Wood turned into long branches as they drew closer, and then into whole trees that stretched into the night, at least a hundred feet tall; a disgusting black mass of shadow and mist. Faerydae scowled and felt her throat become dry with terror. She had seen this sort of a *hiding* darkness before – in the House of Mess and Horror, outside that endless window. She had never wanted to see it again. And yet here she was… walking straight into its grasp.

The air was growing cooler now. But it would be warmer once they were safely inside the woods, Faerydae thought.

Lolanthie slowed into a trot as the woods drew close enough to smell, wild and earthy. It was comforting to know that the stallion had brakes, but his trot was not as pleasant as his canter for the girls who were riding bareback with no padding at all. Alalia had, at least, worn jodhpurs beneath her black gown, and Faerydae's usual trousers were multipurpose anyway.

'We made it,' Alalia whispered to herself, jostling the reins in order to keep Lolanthie from bolting. 'I'm back.'

'What now?' Faerydae called over her shoulder. 'Do you know where you need to go from here, Alalia? The woods are huge – like an entire country in there. If we get lost…'

'The woods won't hurt us.'

The smell of wet leaves and pine tinged the cool air as they became engulfed by the shadows. The narrow roads through the trees were not signposted. There was really no way to navigate the place. But Alalia remained purposeful as she steered Lolanthie along the misty path that appeared to have no end other than a foggy deterioration. His hooves *clip-clopped, clip-clopped* against the hard ground. He was walking finally.

The trees were so tall that most of their branches only started protruding from their trunks five or ten metres above the road. It meant that the space below the canopy was actually quite open and protected. It was quiet apart from the songs of night birds, and Lolanthie's breath and stride.

'I know three things,' Alalia said. 'We must pass the Willow of Eyes. We must take the middle path of a three-way forked trail. And we must let Eggnorphixeus find *us*. You see, he only helps those who are lost.'

'So' – Faerydae frowned – 'you're saying that we have to get lost in order to find this man?'

She nodded. 'I never said this would be easy.'

'Then do what you have to.' Faerydae clenched her teeth.

It seemed the way to Eggnorphixeus' mansion was to be partly derived from a long-ago memory of Alalia's and partly up to pure chance. Alalia trusted these woods. She did not exactly *like* them, but she believed they held some respect for magically embraced beings.

Faerydae ruffled her windswept black hair, pushing it behind her ears. In that instance, she noticed that her hair now reached down to her collarbones and was seemingly blacker than it had ever been before – perhaps it was just the night. Her hands were frozen cold, so she rubbed them together and breathed hot air inside her palms.

'We're being followed… We're being followed… There is a creature who watches our every move,' Lume said. *'Keep your mind alert, Flea.'*

They soon moved past what seemed a more prominent tree than most: a willow in the middle of the woods, covered in a skin of sappy knots of bark that resembled a thousand prying eyes. From there, Lolanthie clambered down a narrow rocky track. They travelled around many more steep and twisted bends after that, eventually coming upon a forked trail where Alalia followed her gut down the middle path. That trail went on for some miles more, before Alalia slowed Lolanthie down with the reins.

'Keep quiet,' she said softly to the group, her voice nothing more than a dimple in the silence. She pressed a finger to her lips. 'We're getting close. Can't you hear it?'

Faerydae's eyes widened in anticipation. She listened, but she heard nothing but the trees in the wind. Or perhaps she *could* hear something, the sound of walking feet, of huge distant stomps. The encompassing trees started to taper away on either side of them. The area was becoming more sparse. A shimmer of light appeared through the intertwined trunks.

There was a house coming into view.

Faerydae couldn't believe that somebody actually did live in these woods, that somebody would willingly exist in a world so unlike her own.

'We... we're lost... aren't we, Alalia?'

Alalia grinned over her shoulder.

The haunting mansion of Eggnorphixeus sang a deep and horrifying tune as it drifted into the children's company. It was an ominous place, lurking where it was not expected, nor fathomed.

'This is not where I remember it,' Alalia murmured with a shrug.

Faerydae could not see all of the mansion from the angle they were approaching, because so much of it was covered in a thick, tangible shadow. There were two lit lanterns on either side of the tall and slender front door, like glowing orange eyes. Brickwork stretched into the sky, up between the gnarled trees, and balanced precariously along the building's skinny foundation. The mansion was crooked, and far longer than it was wide. It was like a piece of paper that seemed to disappear if you turned it at just the right angle.

Alalia gave the motion for Lolanthie to stop and let them down. He bowed his long black neck to the grass, and they slipped down its length onto solid ground. Faerydae stretched muscles she had never really used before. She almost crumpled in on herself because her legs were so numb. Alalia chuckled and placed a hand on the girl's shoulder to steady her.

'You're doing great,' she said. 'We're right on time.'

Faerydae nodded agreeably. She was a bottle of excitement, nerves and adrenaline. Birds gawked down at the girls from towering branches above, so curious to determine what these strangers were doing in here, for they did not belong. Faerydae could hear twigs snapping throughout the woodland, as if shadows were stalking the night air. The exasperated stallion snorted gentle whinnies as Alalia bound him to the trunk of a tree with his reins.

'Stay quiet, Lolanthie,' she said and kissed his velvety muzzle.

Faerydae darted across the grass, low down on her hands and feet, veering ever closer to the freakish building's lofty entrance. She was, funnily enough, enjoying the covertness of it all, being at one with the anonymous realm of the woods. But as the mansion loomed higher and higher above her, more alive than structural, Faerydae's excitement dissipated away to nothingness. This mansion could swallow her whole.

Alalia walked up to Faerydae's side and continued to the door without a care. Her heeled shoes made a gentle clicking sound as she stepped onto the tiled porch.

'It's certainly something,' Alalia said.

'How do you know that anybody even lives here?' Faerydae asked. Alalia shrugged and gestured to the flickering lanterns above.

'Somebody is always watching this place.'

Alalia teetered her hand over a golden button that must have been the doorbell. Faerydae held her breath, wondering how loud the bell would be. The air was, presently, as still as a mountain. It was peaceful. She hated the thought of being *found* by the woods, that they would know where they were and come for them.

Faerydae raised a hand. 'Wait–'

Alalia's finger depressed the golden orb into its tight cylinder, making a soft click. The deed was done. Faerydae swallowed a lump in her throat, peering back across the grass towards Lolanthie and the trees. Birds were already leaving the clearing… something was coming.

The ensuing sound was more profound than Faerydae could have even imagined. It shook the ground, the girls' feet and their minds. It was a deep hum that ricocheted up the oak door frame and erupted out the top of the chimney two stories high. *BOOM! BANG! DONG!* The bell died in its own pitiful belly, bottoming out and leaving a whine in the air.

Swarms of birds fled their perches, crowing in disgusting sounds of fear. Alalia blocked her ears. Lolanthie reared and pulled back against the tree as the birds seemed to morph into a crazed horde of buzzing flies around him.

'IT'S DONE!' Faerydae called to Alalia, holding her shoulder. 'THEY KNOW WE'RE HERE NOW. WE JUST HAVE TO WAIT!'

'*You fools!*' cried Lume. '*You stupid little children!!*'

The bell's reverberating hum faded into a distant moan and the little golden button expanded back out of the cylinder into its original position. *Click.*

Meanwhile.

There was a voice that could only be heard by the spiders who lived in the corners of the mansion; whomever the voice belonged to could not yet be seen by any with eyes or ears.

'Two children of the night have arrived at the door. A girl with dark hair like the night. And a girl with curls of fire. Anotheris concealed within their ensemble. But he doesn't **want** to be found.'

A wizard crept along the empty halls.

The spiders could hear his footsteps from somewhere deep within the silence of his home. Creaking floorboards groaned with each thoughtful step. The wizard scratched his smooth face and scraped a finger along the wallpaper. Eventually, when the doorbell's throng had become a memory, he came upon the door and clasped the knob with one spindly hand, hearing bickering voices just on the other side of the wood.

Visitors, he thought. Do come in. Visitors shall be taken **care** of in this house.

20

'We should leave,' Faerydae was saying. 'Nobody is coming–'

'You have to be patient, Fae. Please.'

'The place is deserted.'

Alalia held Faerydae's hand. 'Trust me…'

The doorknob jiggled. Faerydae's eyes darted sideways to watch it, wondering if it had been a draught, her imagination, *anything*. Alalia looked back at the door as well. The knob started to spin, turning itself round with a squeal. The heavy door made a dilapidated sound and then opened inwards like a gaping mouth into hell.

A tall figure waited inside the house. They stood too far inside to make out properly just yet, only a silhouette that could have been mistaken for a coat stand or cabinet. Faerydae stepped closer to the dark opening.

'Hello?' She balled her fists to stop them from shaking. 'Is somebody there? We are children of the night–' She looked to the sky and added, 'Moonwalkers.'

Alalia frowned, would have laughed, if not for the situation.

Scraping floorboards followed the figure as it stepped into the light of the doorway.

The – *thing* – did not say anything. On the contrary, it *was* a man, of strange sorts. He was tall and lean, just like the doorway. He wore a pair of black slacks with a grey waistcoat and jacket and a handsome bowtie too. Everything about him was perfectly in order. Perfectly normal. Apart from his head, which was rather absent. In its place sat a pale egg about the size of Lolanthie's head. The man's narrow shoulders did not look fit to balance such a craterous thing, but apparently the egg *was* his head. He had no mouth, no nose, nor eyes; just a beige sphere, totally empty of any emotional value.

He tilted his bulbous head with the visage of looking at the two adolescents upon his doorstep. Faerydae flinched at seeing the egg move like that.

'Hello,' Alalia said gently. 'Is this your home, sire?'

'Yes.'

The voice of the mouthless egg was unexpected to Faerydae, whose eyes bulged and stared for some time in horror. But Alalia took it all in her relaxed stride.

'I live here with the shadows and the webs,' the man added.

His voice was a muffled, husky sound, as if it was reverberating from deep within the huge eggshell. There was a twang of olde English quant about his invisible tones.

'Are you lost?' he asked with the upmost politeness. 'What would moonwalkers be doing lost out here when the moon itself sings so vibrantly? Could you not follow its tune, children?'

Alalia collected her thoughts. 'We are hunting,' she said. 'Something that was lost a long time ago has called us back to the woods. And you are the wizard of these woods, are you not?'

'I *own* these woods, girl. I am a Night Stalker; a Shepherd to the badness.'

Alalia glanced at Faerydae who was straining her eyes against the wizard's ghoulish façade. For this was not at all what Faerydae had expected. This was not the wizard she had envisioned to help guide her to her heart, nor the wizard from storybook tales. She glanced behind him, to see inside the mansion. It was too dark. Faerydae thought for a way out, a way that did not mean having to give herself over to the situation. Alalia might have trusted in these woods, but Faerydae was harder to collect. She could not trust this… thing.

Alalia frowned as Faerydae squeezed her hand for conviction.

'We're lost,' Faerydae said to the man. 'Even by the moon's song… we could not retrace our path. We were foraging for mushrooms on the border of the Wood when our stallion bolted, sire. All we seek is the path home. That's all. We came across your house and thought: there's a normal place where a normal person will be able to see us on our way. So, if you don't mind, we will be heading off.'

Alalia reeled in hesitation, then gestured needlessly to Lolanthie who looked up at her with grass flecks poking out of his mouth and mucus oozing from his nostrils.

'He's a mad horse,' Alalia said rather plainly. 'We have gone so deep into the woods now that we've no hope of getting out. Thank heavens we hath found a kind soul within these wretched shadows – might we take a moment's refuge in your house? We are so dreadfully weary.'

Faerydae tugged Alalia's hand right before it snaked out of her grip.

A kind soul, the wizard thought.

'If you seek refuge,' he said. 'I can certainly offer you a bed. I am Eggnorphixeus, after all, the wizard of wayward souls. Please, leave your inhibitions at the door, my children, and come into the *only* house in the woods, which is also a home for all. You are always *welcome*; you will always be taken care of.'

Eggnorphixeus teetered his fingertips together and stepped to the side of the doorway. The darkness inside the mansion was immediately disturbed by the sudden appearance of candlelight inside. The girls glanced at one another sceptically. Faerydae shook her head. And then Alalia went inside the mansion first.

21

Patches of light illuminated areas of the mansion, but these rooms were only dots in the corners of a much larger painting. Too many crevasses and cracks, empty tunnels and deep pits… no one could ever truly discover it all.

They congregated in the foyer as the wizard closed the front door ever so gently. Faerydae slid her hand along the wallpaper that masked the curve and dips of the old brick walls. Alalia looked to the ceiling, gaging the place's depth and complexity. It was such a big house for one lonely occupant.

The foyer sprouted off to both a left and right room. The girls waited to be shown the way as the wizard took a quiet moment to precariously straighten a mirror on the wall between paintings. Then they followed him into the room on the right.

'I am so pleased to hear that you found my home when you most needed it, girls,' Eggnorphixeus remarked as he walked beside Alalia. He looked like a slender giant and cast the most peculiarly spindly shadow upon the wallpaper. Faerydae flinched in hearing him talk again. 'It has been a while since lost souls found their way here, but folks will be taken *care* of in this house.'

Faerydae noticed how he expressed certain words with an important quality, as if they meant something entirely unique to him. *Care*. He found a long candle stick and spiked it into a golden dish. A snap of his reedy fingertips was enough to light the wick in an instant, casting a warm flicker over his face. Faerydae glanced at Alalia, who appeared pleased by the man's use of magic, almost comforted by it.

They all walked in unison and then circled around the room to sit among the small glow of Eggnorphixeus' flame light. Resting side by side upon a leather couch, the girls had a moment to take in the parlour. A tall rectangular window behind where they sat displayed Lolanthie tied up outside. The moonlight flooded in through the space and washed over their faces with a sick paleness. The room was tall but narrow and filled with paintings and a thick rug and various ornate furniture.

Eggnorphixeus sat down on an armchair all of his own, opposite them, and held the candle with one hand. There was a low glass table between them all, where a tray of cobwebby teacups and a floral kettle sat empty except for dust. Strange. The items were placed just so, as if the wizard had been entertaining guests not long ago, yet clearly it had been months if not years. The fireplace at their left lay empty – had possibly been empty forever, leaving a void-like coldness to settle on the room. A carpeted stairway leading to the topmost floors endured diagonally along the far wall of the parlour, right behind Eggnorphixeus' huge head.

'My name is Eggnorphixeus, but I *assume* you both know that. I am the wizard of the woods. You've probably heard of me in *tales*.' Again, he spoke with those strange inflections, and Faerydae couldn't help noticing the words he liked to say. 'But the woods are a dangerous place these days. Especially for children of your age, *young* girls on the brink of womanhood, what with all that's being offered to those who collect *bodies* like yours.'

'Bodies like ours?' Alalia repeated. 'What's being offered?'

'Money of course,' he replied. 'Money and gold and riches untold. What else could a king have to offer? Desperate times call for desperate means. I believe time is running out for all of us.' The wizard scratched his apparently itchy egg chin. 'It is time for us all to do what must be done.'

'The king is looking for... bodies?' Alalia mumbled. 'This is news to me.'

'Useless really,' Eggnorphixeus added. 'In a time like this.'

Faerydae heard him all too well. She agreed, for some reason, though she hadn't a clue what he was talking about. His advice seemed somehow relevant in other ways more pressing to her. For she had made it here, after all, to this house. She and Alalia had come all this way, into the woods and away from their homes. She couldn't leave now. *No.* That would be dumb; it would be a waste of every brave moment so far. Faerydae had to make the most of this moment, for there may never be another time to try.

'You are right,' Faerydae said. Alalia turned to look at her. 'We must do what has to be done.'

'Indeed.' Eggnorphixeus sat motionless, his slim legs and arms draped around the chair in an unreal way.

Faerydae tried to continue her line of thought but fell short and soon a deep silence thickened in the air. Eggnorphixeus seemed to have lost his words also; they'd fallen right out of his egg brain. Alalia looked down at her crossed hands in her lap, speechless for the first time since Faerydae had met her. The wizard eventually rose to the full stature of his long legs and hovered before them. Faerydae had an impulse to run from him. It had something to do with the way he towered so frightfully over their *bodies*.

'My guests,' he spoke suddenly. 'I'll go and put a pot of tea on, shall I?'

Eggnorphixeus grabbed the tea tray from the glass table and went back into the foyer with his candlelight. His footsteps then disappeared, and so the girls assumed he must have ventured into the other rooms.

'Now what do we do?' Alalia whispered to Faerydae in the moonlight. 'I want to ask him about the heart–'

'No,' Faerydae said. 'I don't trust him.'

'Then what?' Alalia asked. 'You seemed pretty sure before that you wanted to *do what must be done*.' She smirked.

Faerydae rolled her eyes. 'Do you know what he was talking about before? About the king wanting bodies?'

'I...' Alalia paused. 'No. The king is a long way from us. He is searching for something. But a lot of people are searching for things right now, Faerydae. We are searching for things.'

'Well,' Faerydae uttered. 'That's vague – I have an idea. If the wizard has my heart somewhere in this mansion then there is nothing to stop me looking for it right here and now. If he *doesn't* have it, then there's really no way he could know where it has ended up after all these years.'

Alalia pursed her lips. 'That's something that might have been good to think of *before* we rode out here.'

'No.' Faerydae smiled. 'This is good! Keep the wizard occupied and I'll search the floor above us.'

'You're going to leave me?' Alalia asked. 'What am I supposed to say to him?'

'Anything. Anything he wants to talk about.'

'Right,' Alalia breathed. '*Okay*... no problem. Easy done.' She knew this was all a very fatuous strategy, but she was not yet worried enough to protest.

'You'll do fine,' Faerydae said. The redhead gave her a sly look, nodded, and then glanced into the adjoining room.

'Good luck then.' Alalia shrugged. 'At least he won't be able to *see* that you've gone. I'll just pretend you're still there, maybe I'll do voices for both of us, like a play. I'm actually quite a good actor.'

Faerydae chuckled as she rose from the couch, but they both felt that the wizard would immediately know that Faerydae had disappeared. He would somehow *know*. Faerydae dashed over to the staircase, hovering close to the wall, and vanished. Alalia was left alone in darkness.

22

Alalia walked out into the empty foyer where lanterns flickered, dulled and revived themselves. She stood in the sanctity of her own company for a moment, looking at her reflection in the mirror. What *was* she doing here? Her eyes looked unknowable. Alalia sometimes found it hard to even know what she was up to. The only thing that seemed absolutely true, right now, to her, was that Faerydae tugged on a very innocent part of her soul.

She peered around the doorway to the other room. It was dark and quiet within, but the only other space to be seen; the only other way the wizard might have gone. Through the narrow archway and down a small step, Alalia found herself walking down a dome-shaped brick tunnel. Eventually, it spawned into a space at the end that looked like some sort of kitchen. Eggnorphixeus was inside, studying a brass kettle of boiling tea. He stood, hunched slightly, as he mixed the brew around with one bare finger through the kettle's scalding lid.

The roof was lower in there and rounded at the corners, claustrophobic even. Bathed in the feeble orange glow of hovering lanterns, the space was more akin to a boiler room than a kitchen, really. It housed three large stoves shoved up against the curving walls that whistled as they heated huge pales of water. There was not much else in the room except for that, only a small cauldron and firepit against the adjacent wall, three or four pots and pans hanging from hooks, and various shelves of herbs and spices above. Alalia did not think the emptiness of the kitchen to be odd. For what would a creature with only an egg for a head attempt to eat?

The girl coughed to announce her arrival and stepped closer towards the wizard.

'Your tea smells quite unique, sire,' Alalia remarked. 'Sorry to be impolite, Mr Eggnorphixeus, but my companion and I have had a disagreement. Faerydae has decided to wait outside with our horse rather than offend you with her ill-tempered disposition.' She spoke with such ease; every lie she'd ever told had been spoken with the exact same conviction. She tapped her fingernails across her stomach. 'You have such a beautiful home, just like in the stories. It is peaceful and well away from the hectic towns and cities of other provinces.'

The wizard did not turn to face her. Maybe he was disinterested.

'I have a rather rare opinion when it comes to the subject of impending doom,' she said. 'That was what you were talking about before? The darkness that is spreading around us? I believe it is all merely a cover for something we cannot possibly imagine. What we see is never what we *should* be seeing, if you know what I mean.'

The girl watched Eggnorphixeus' arachnid-like limbs and fingers dancing over the pot like twine.

'This *is* a peaceful mansion,' Eggnorphixeus said. 'If it were just *you* in here though, I am certain that you would become lost *forever*. Luckily, you have me – so how about I give you the *grand* tour?'

23

Faerydae pulled Lume out of her pocket, finally able to tell the gem to shut up directly to his face.

'What is the matter with you?' she hissed as his colour bloomed. 'You're acting like a child, Lume! Will you stop complaining all the time when I'm trying to focus.'

'*You are in over your head, Flea,*' he warned. '*This creature is created from night. And you're going to rob him?*'

'No–' Faerydae paused. 'I'm just going to see if he has stolen anything from *me*. A person with nothing to hide has nothing to fear.'

'*He does* not *fear you, Flea.*' Lume chuckled. '*Not at all.*'

Faerydae shoved the gem back in his pocket. 'Just try and keep your head.'

'*Oh… I'll try.*'

Expanding from the lantern-lit lobby where Faerydae now stood were two parallel corridors. They branched straight ahead of her and into the distance, like long roads. One went slightly to the left and the other went slightly to the right, but it seemed they were on such a minutely different angle that they would reach the same end eventually.

The carpet below Faerydae smelt of dust and mould. She looked to her immediate left. The same staircase from the ground headed further up along the wall and towards the third floor. Faerydae had been overly confident. It would be nearly impossible for her to find her heart if it was even hidden somewhere in these walls. But she refused to accept defeat.

Faerydae sidestepped towards the stairs and continued further up into the riddle of shadows beyond. Up where even Eggnorphixeus could get lost, up where ghosts and devils hid in their corners, where it was too far to run back down the stairs again.

The third floor mimicked the appearance of the one below it with precision. It was dizzying. The stairs opened out onto the same wide space with another set of parallel corridors veering ahead of her. Faerydae cringed, feeling depressed by the insanity of the mansion's design.

Upon coming to the departing of ways, Faerydae inhaled deeply and chanced on the right corridor. She walked in silence, in gloom. Lanterns appeared after some time, fluttering in an imagined breeze.

The corridor's floor soon dipped down three tiny steps, and Faerydae came to see a white door on her left. She paused. Her hand moved towards the wood and gripped the handle. Without thinking too much, she turned the nob and pulled the stark door open towards herself. She sighed, neither pleased nor disappointed by what she discovered. It was a bedroom. A lantern ignited itself from where it was wedged above the small bed. The sheets were covered in dust and two cabinets sat beside an empty fireplace in the corner.

Faerydae retreated, closed the door and continued on down the corridor.

Minutes passed. When she looked in the following room, she found a dark pantry. It was tiny and filled with junk, amongst other cleaning products. Faerydae fussed around in the collection of disused mops and brooms, knowing it was a useless effort, looking for her heart at the bottom of a cleaning bucket. Who knew how deep the mansion was and how many rooms therein existed.

She continued to the next room anyway.

It was entirely empty. As were the following four.

She kept going, deeper and farther. The quietude became infuriating. The walls began to bend and curve, maddening her completely. She imagined that she was running around and around in a spiraling circle. There were eventually less doors and more of the blank corridor, which was surely getting narrower with every step. Faerydae had been wondering how much farther she should go before turning back.

She decided to keep moving along the confining stretch, almost hypnotised by its infinity. Then the never-ending ground fell right out from under her feet.

She stumbled head over feet and pushed her hands out to catch herself, but there was no longer any floor. It was a sheer drop off. Actually, it was a staircase. She tumbled all the way down to the bottom of the sudden expanse. The stairs were heavy and hard where the carpet had peeled away to reveal splintering wood beneath. Faerydae screamed. Waiting for her at the bottom, little could she see as she fell though, was a mangled door covered in deep gouges and claw marks. It popped open just slightly when her body fell against it. Stagnant air plumed with dust.

A moment later, Faerydae stirred from unconsciousness . Her head throbbed with disorientation and her eyes flittered open and shut from the blunt pain in her temples. There was an insatiable aching in her neck, and her limbs felt all knotted like ropes. A burning sensation consumed her head when she stood with dizzying vertigo. She sniffed, her senses slowly returning.

Wherever she had ended up, it stunk like the devil's grave.

Faerydae spluttered against the horrifying stench and gripped a hand to her nose. The smell was of death, polluting the already sour air and making it barely breathable. The girl gazed back up at the horrifying flight of steps that she had fallen down. By the length of them, she figured she must have tumbled all the way back down to the second floor. She was lucky she hadn't broken her neck.

'You're getting in deep now, Flea,' said Lume with a grunt, as if he too had sustained some injuries from the fall.

'Where am I?' Faerydae asked pointlessly.

There was a space of light on the other side of the narrowly open door Faerydae had fallen against. She pushed the groaning wood fully open to reveal a moonlit scene. A vast ceiling rose above her, made out of a plethora of decadent glass sheets. The walls were made of creeping vines and brick. Lilies and cyclamens and other unknown wildflowers bloomed all around, a unicorn statue towered in the middle of the glowing greenhouse. A fountain of water spurted out of the statue's mouth in rainbows.

The night-time sky above was like a painting of perfection.

But Faerydae's smile was not to last. For the more Faerydae looked at the details sitting just out of sight, the more she noticed how terribly wrong everything was. That smell. Under bristles and azaleas and ferns the size of wagons, were dozens of gaping eyes watching her with a deathly stare. Animals. But they were not alive. And they had no bodies. Their severed heads had been planted in the garden like vegetables, raw windpipes like stems in the ground.

Faerydae wasn't sure if she was hallucinating after the fall she'd had.

But the dead eyes continued to watch her nonetheless. Buzzing flies congregated in hungry families and made a humming chorus.

Heads… Decapitated *heads!* Animals though, not people, not *children* – a fact that Faerydae found herself reasoning with.

Hogs and birds, horses and newts. A wolf and a coyote. Cut by a clean blade.

The grass below Faerydae's feet was sticky. It clung to her shoes when she tried to move. Moonlight had washed away the colour of this world, but Faerydae knew she was standing upon a pool of dried blood.

24

'We must venture further up, Miss Alalia,' Eggnorphixeus said. 'There is far more to discover up there.'

Alalia's cup of tea remained untouched in her hand. The wizard had given it to her when they left the boiler room and embarked along another brick tunnel. She had been shown at least eight different rooms since then, all varying between libraries, bars, a ballroom and bedrooms.

Alalia nodded agreeably.

She followed the wizard as he led her towards a staircase at the end of a wide carpeted room. They hadn't ventured up any stairs as yet, merely down the same long corridor and into intermingled rooms – so long had they travelled that winding corridor in fact that Alalia wondered how deep inside the mansion they were. She felt a jolt of rebellion inside. She could not bring herself to follow the wizard up those stairs, could she? She was not a stupid girl. It was as if traversing those planks would surely mean she was never coming back down them.

Alalia shivered as cold air seeped through her jodhpurs and into her flesh, eating at her. The safety of the ground floor disappeared quickly behind them as the darkness above drew closer. Alalia noticed how silent she was, her breath was low, and her steps were like a mouse's. Eggnorphixeus' feet left a trail of loud creaks like a giant spider. Alalia's made no sound at all. She could simply disappear, if she wanted to. She could retrace her steps back through the house and leave.

The girl paused on a step, watching her companion creep up further and further with his candle. She placed the ice-cold cup of tea on the step beside her feet and hovered. *But why would I do that?* she thought. *Why would I want to leave?* She wondered what Faerydae was up to. That girl was brave and strong, so much braver than Alalia considered she could ever be. In that way, Faerydae reminded her of Freya. *Freya.* How Alalia missed that human more than her wearisome emotions could ever express.

'Alalia? ALALIA!'

Eggnorphixeus' voice came out shrill with angst as he twirled his top-heavy body from side to side, dancing his candlelight away almost to extinction.

'Where have you *gone*, Alalia? Come **BACK**!'

There was almost a gasping sound between his grazing words. Alalia was somewhat surprised by Eggnorphixeus' desperation but, in another way, she expected nothing less.

'I am coming, sire.'

Alalia reappeared inside the wizard's candlelight and smiled up at his ghastly face of nothingness, reassuring his racing heart.

'You are a worry, girl, keep up, *won't* you?' Eggnorphixeus warned.

'Sorry.'

'What is wrong with you? Are you hurt?'

'No,' Alalia mumbled. 'I am perfectly well.'

Eggnorphixeus tilted his egg head. What would his face have displayed if he had a mouth and eyes, or even a set of hairy brown eyebrows to furrow? Alalia pondered if he would be handsome. Would he have an air of entitlement or of deprivation?

Eggnorphixeus leaned forwards and wrapped cold fingers around Alalia's hand, holding her tight so as she did not drift too far away.

'Please do not fret, sire,' Alalia said, smiling up at him reassuringly. 'There is no reason to be afraid.'

'Quite right,' he said and leaned closer, stroking her supple cheek. 'You are a *beautiful* girl, my dear. But there is something bad inside of you, isn't there, Alalia *Miseria*? The same something that lives in me too.'

Alalia became lost in thought as his huge blank face hypnotised her. 'You remember me.'

And then they continued up the stairs, hand in hand, the only sound being that of Eggnorphixeus' pitter-pattering spider legs. Eventually, they came upon a single door with scratches across its peeling white paint, bringing an end to the colossal journey below. Eggnorphixeus jiggled the handle and turned the olde knob with a rattling of metal, pushed it inwards. He ushered Alalia towards the light of the doorway, holding her for balance on the final step of the mountainous stairway.

An open sky, clearer now than it had been when they arrived, lingered through the glass ceiling above the repugnantly smelly room. Stars watched Alalia, like angels of the night, spying her way down there as she remained lost in the maze of the mansion. Lost in the maze of her own life. *They* knew the way out; the stars could see everything.

The wizard's sharp fingertips zapped Alalia's spine with impatience, until she was inside the room. The girl passively let herself traipse over the threshold. The smell of death and rot consumed her nostrils.

'You may be a Miseria,' Eggnophixeus whispered in her ear, sounding a million miles away inside his eggshell. 'But I cannot say no to a beautiful head when it asks so kindly to be taken *care* of.'

25

'Faerydae?' Alalia rubbed her head. There was blood on her hand. 'Wh... What happened?'

She had lost time.

Faerydae's eyes now stared into hers. They were both on the ground. Eggnorphixeus had thrust Alalia to the floor so forcibly that she momentarily blacked out as her head collided with the side of a concrete garden bed. Faerydae's arms now shook Alalia into reality.

'Alalia! Are you okay?!' Faerydae was screaming. 'He's a murderer, Alalia! He collects heads and souls, luring them into his web with promises of safety. He's had to make do with animals but... but within the garden there are skulls, Alalia! *Human* skulls!'

Faerydae had only ventured to the other side of the putrid greenhouse once she'd seen Alalia forced to the ground. Luckily. A minute or two later and Faerydae would have turned back to wander through the endless corridor of doom back to try and find the parlour.

Eggnorphixeus laughed. 'Well, now we're all here!'

Faerydae let go of Alalia and turned back to the door, she had almost forgotten the wizard was there, blocking them from escape on either side with his huge span of arms.

'You *told* me you sought refuge, my children, and refuge is what you *shall* get. An endless *refuge* in my beautiful garden.'

'Sire, please–' Faerydae started, but the wizard waved a hand affront his egg face, pulling the girl's words ferociously from her lips.

'Silence!' he bellowed. 'What would you have me do, when you walked willingly through *my* front door? But before I do what I must,' he added. 'Let me ask why you really came here on this night? You are two strangers of the woods, but not strangers of magic; your names have been whispered in the wind. It is no coincidence.'

'I told you the truth.' Alalia spoke as she climbed to her slippery feet. She glowered at the wizard without care. 'We were hunting.'

'Hunting a heart,' Faerydae added, glancing at Alalia, then back to the wizard. 'Eight years ago, somebody stole a bottled human heart from Brindille Shire. We want it back.'

Eggnorphixeus drew forth a sleek stiletto dagger from his coat's innards and twirled it in his palm as if to reply. The menacing blade was at least the length of Faerydae's forearm, and just as thick; as sharp as her tongue could sometimes be, but not right now.

'What a funny thing you should mention that,' Eggnorphixeus said, wiping the blade on his trousers. 'A human heart? Of all strange things... Bottled and stolen at midnight? Oh yes, I do remember it well, would not have thought it too enticing, except that I could hear the organ still beating throughout the woodland, and that *truly* was unique. Let me think now... yes. *She* came past here with it bundled in a hessian sack, carrying it in her pointed teeth. A woman of the woods. She was departing the Velvet Swamp when last I remember stalking her.'

'Where is she now?' Faerydae demanded. She stepped closer towards him. 'Where IS SHE?'

The wizard lunged forward in an instant and clutched Faerydae's petite frame in his hands, holding the blade against her pulsing throat, eager to peel away the layers of flesh. Faerydae's lips and the tip of her nose were pressed against his bulbous face. The egg felt cold and dead.

'You will never need to know,' he said to them both. 'You will sleep in my garden forever.'

Something came hurtling through the air then. There was a distant whistle of a breeze that alerted Eggnorphixeus to the approaching object before a scream escaped Alalia. Eggnorphixeus threw Faerydae aside so as he could attempt to deflect the approaching entity away from his delicate head.

Faerydae fell into the bloodied grass, glancing around the scene to try and understand it. Alalia panted from exertion. She had thrown a hog's head, which was quite a feat, just a dead weight of bones and pounds of flesh. The perfect weapon. It crashed into Eggnorphixeus' guarding elbows with a crunching blow and then ricocheted onto his impossibly thin stomach, making him crumple to one side.

Alalia grabbed Faerydae's hand and hauled her to her feet.

'Come on!' Alalia cried.

Eggnorphixeus snatched vainly at Alalia's heels from the ground as the redhead bolted back through the doorway behind him and down the stairs. Faerydae went for the doorway in the same frantic manner, when Eggnorphixeus' fingertips dug their way into her ankle, gripping her skin as if it were the corners of a blanket.

The wizard yanked Faerydae down to her knees, climbing up her calf with his maddened grip. Faerydae shrieked in pain. The stiletto dagger lay temptingly close to the wizard's other hand now, where he had dropped it as he fell. He stretched for it, fingers walking out across the floor like legs. Faerydae lunged with her foot and kicked the blade away as his other grip wiggled about inside her leg. The knife skidded across the tiles and under the leafy foliage of plants.

'Bitch!' Eggnorphixeus howled. 'Little whore!' He reached for Faerydae's face with his hands. 'I *own* your head; I'm going to skin you alive and wear your skull like a crown!'

He squeezed his hands around Faerydae's throat, turning his knuckles white. Faerydae kicked out with her legs as the wizard quaked with anger. She heard a crunching sound as her flailing arms lashed against his head. Tiny splintering cracks appeared, spreading across the shell of his face. Faerydae smiled through gags, her eyes bulging. She lunged out with her fists, trying to deepen the cracks. Her fingertips gouged inside the wounds of his shell and eggy goo started to dribble from them.

The wizard groaned. Faerydae felt his hands weaken. She dragged herself towards the stairs, holding his forearms to try and pry them off of her. Her eyesight faded, and the emptiness inside her lungs began to burn. She made it to the doorway, almost dead, but not quite, and tried one more time to pry his curled fingertips off of her throat as more goo raced down his face. He wailed. It seemed his fingers would not be removed unless broken off; so broken they surely were. Snap. Snap. Snap. Faerydae bit into them like carrots.

Eggnorphixues screamed desperately about his inconsolable fingers, staring at the mangled bones protruding from his hands. The pair hustled for a moment longer until Faerydae grabbed the wizard in company and threw herself over the edge of the stairs.

They fell, becoming departed from one another at some point.

Faerydae's brain rattled around and around the inside of her skull. She reeled for purchase and dug her nails into a split in one of the boards, catching her tumbling momentum. Eggnorphixeus was not so creative. He continued on his descent, like a flung rag doll, all the way down to the bottom of the stairs.

'AHHHHHHHHHHHHHHH!' he shrieked.

Right where the carpet met the olde wood of the first floor, Eggnorphixeus' giant head exploded. The yellow, mucous-like innards sprayed all over the walls and floor, and onto Alalia's back as she dodged his flailing limbs. The sound was like an echoing shatter, like the dropping of a ceramic bowl of soup. Brain goo drooled along the floor in a viscous puddle and surrounded the wizard's decapitated body.

Alalia backed away. She could see floating pieces of shell caught up in amongst the rosy mess and she could scarcely believe that *this* was the mind of a man she'd been conversing with all night.

'Are you okay, Alalia?' Faerydae's voice called down.

She looked up and nodded.

'Fine. You?'

Faerydae leapt down the stairs two at a time and clambered over the dead body as it twitched grossly.

'Not bad,' Faerydae said. 'Not dead. How about we get the hell out of this slaughterhouse?' She grabbed hold of Alalia's clammy hand and turned to run. But Alalia did not move, she was rooted to the carpet. Faerydae looked back into her eyes.

'I am so sorry, Faerydae,' Alalia said. 'I didn't know.'

'It's okay,' Faerydae replied with a smile. 'Come on. We have to go.'

Alalia nodded.

Not long after, the girls found themselves back in the wizard's kitchen, then the dark foyer. The front door, which stood tall and unassuming, was like finding the pot of gold at the end of the rainbow.

Birds chirped happily outside in the early morning darkness.

Lolanthie roared at the girls angrily when they appeared through the door, dawdling with tiredness. Alalia walked to his side and untangled the reins that he had looped into a tight mess around the tree.

'Good boy. There, there. What horrible frights have you endured in the night?' she said to the nervy stallion. He bowed before her and Alalia climbed onto his back, stretching a hand back for Faerydae.

Once they were both aboard, Lolanthie turned and walked into the thickening of trees ahead. Faerydae clung to her ankle with one hand. It was bleeding onto Lolanthie's charcoal fur. With a cringe, Faerydae curled her trouser leg back over the wound.

'We know one thing now,' Faerydae mumbled, and Alalia looked at her over her shoulder. 'The wizard *did* see my heart that night. It was stolen by a woman. A woman of the woods.'

26

Magicians Needed

Alalia

Jákob Miseria liked to play pretend. No wonder he had decided to study Warlock Hunting. The job essentially consisted of him locking himself away for days to create his own crazy inventions that would be used in the craziest of circumstances. Alalia thought he loved the attention he received from the work, but she was wrong.

Jákob felt his feet sinking out from under him with each step as he walked down the sandy bluff towards the ocean. He could see Alalia. She was wading in the shallows of the dark blue waves. Water lapped at her torso. She had been calmer than usual, since returning from her night stay at the Daltry's. Whatever could have happened to make his sister tame?

'ALALIA!' Jake called to her with his hands cupped. She turned for a moment and then moved deeper out to sea, ignoring him.

Alalia held a minuscule blue flask in her hand as the sand bed dipped away under her and she was left treading water. She dragged the flask through the water in a circular motion and the blue melted into the water. For a start, it was just fish who were attracted by the potion. They darted in between her feet and arms and around her stomach. The congregating marine life started to become larger species of fish, then turtles, sting rays joined them along with harmonious sharks; all spiraling around Alalia worshipfully in the same uniform pattern.

She grinned.

'Vida Marina,' Alalia breathed. 'Ven aqui. Marina. Mia. Vida Marina.'

Crabs scuttled over her skin as the fish enclosed around her and began jostling her. She no longer had to tread water; the sea dwellers held her full weight.

'ALALIA!'

The critters fled at the sound of her brother's eruptive voice.

'I'M COMING! Jeez.'

She turned and started kicking her legs again. The shore looked a thousand miles away from her now; she had been carried by the marine life with such ease and pace. Alalia paddled. She was a strong swimmer and made it back to shore within minutes where she found Jákob waiting beside the boulders.

He was lean, even for a twelve-year-olde boy. Alalia wondered when her brother would ever grow up, because she could not fathom this boy becoming a man.

'What is it, Jake?' Alalia asked as she grabbed her blanket and began drying herself off.

She was wearing nothing but a sheer white nightgown, something that she often wore when she slept, not really suitable for a morning swim. Jákob could see his sister's womanly figure beneath the material. She was not shy about it. And he did not really care. Sometimes, Jákob really felt like the more mature one of the pair, in his unique kind of impermeable way. Alalia was just a paper girl who would crumble whenever she needed to be vulnerable.

'We have to go to the Amaryllis Ball tonight... Together,' he said. 'Blanche believes somebody is going to try and raid it. Rebels. They'll be hunting.'

'I see,' Alalia replied.

Jake looked out to sea. 'How is that potion coming along?'

She shrugged. 'Fine.'

They remained silent for a moment.

'So,' Jake continued. 'Shall we fly? We can leave home by nightfall. That way, I mean, if there's time, we could catch the Woodchopping at the Pumpkin Throw.'

'Alright. Is that all then?'

Jákob bit his tongue. 'That's all.'

And he turned and left, back up the sloping hills towards Amaryllis and then home. He had no errands to run in town today; the boy only walked for half an hour all the way across Eastlea to tell his dear sister that one thing – *it had clearly been worth his effort.*

They left that night by broomstick. Jákob sat behind Alalia with his hands wound tightly around her waist despite himself. He hated heights; Alalia found it quite funny. Above the city, the moon guided the siblings towards their destination, glowing behind a diffusion of thick clouds. Lanterns could be seen from where they sailed through the sky. The Grand Amaryllis Ball looked like a glowing fire from so high above. But they would soon be much lower.

Alalia gripped the neck of the broom, forcing it downwards at a steep angle. Then they nose-dived through the air, headed straight for the centre of the raging party filled with music and cheer. Jákob held on tightly to his belt of gadgets with one hand, praying no flasks or variously intricate inventions broke away in the wind, never to be found again. They started to shudder in motion. The broom was sparking into flames at the head.

'SLOW DOWN!' Jákob cried.

He could hear the twigs behind him crackling with enticement. Alalia glared at him over her shoulder and straightened the broom. They coasted through the tables of the Ball and people dodged them as they went.

Alalia veered down a side street and leapt off of the broom as she halted. Jákob flung himself sideway once he saw the impending stone wall ahead, but he did not land as graciously as Alalia had.

'Right then,' Alalia said. 'Let's start securing this place.'

Jákob gasped, leaning on his knees for balance as his sister made her way into the party without him. He had little breath to call her back. He had no voice at all to ask what their plan was.

27

The music along the rambunctious street drowned out all the voices of the dancing people. It was a bombardment of happiness. The Ball coincided with the Pumpkin Throw and so it was easiest to wander through both in order to make sure there were no hiccups. Lantern lights danced around on their string tethers in the night air and the clouds were holding off for now. Jákob gently forced his way through the crowds of chatty people, past the games of pumpkin toss and apple bobbing, to find the arena of axe man. The boy considered he would be safe to wait around there for the time being. He cased the area, looking for anything alarmingly unusual, as the axe men started on their logs with unrelenting power. He wondered if there really was a threat of rebelling tonight, or if Blanche merely wanted her children to work together for once. After all, it was only the siblings to keep the events safe, which was a big task for two children.

Look at those arms, Jákob thought, watching the axe men. Then he looked at his own: thin and scrawny and pale. He wished he could become more impressive soon, to look more like a man. He wanted to hold his own in the family instead of feeling useless most of the time. Sure, he did well as a Warlock Hunter, and always received thankful letters for an unending number of jobs that kept him occupied. He was well liked. But not by the people that mattered.

'Jákob! Jákob Miseria?'

The boy turned to meet the emerald eyes of Freya Daltry. He smiled without bounds and hugged the girl.

'Freya,' he replied in a weedy voice, pushing black oily strands to the other side of his cowlick. 'I can't believe it is you, Miss Daltry; you look absolutely beautiful! How long has it been since your recovery?'

Freya smirked. 'It has been a month since Alalia exorcised me.' The girl paused. 'I have a long way to go, but all is looking up for a change. I am even back to studying Blood Species. I found an interest in the subject for obvious reasons. Is Alalia with you?'

'Indeed,' He glanced around the ball, noticing abruptly how much taller Freya was than him. 'I think she would have gone to the darkest corner available. Look in the shadows, would be my suggestion. We've been alerted of a possible threat tonight. Keep safe, Freya.'

Jákob kissed her hand and she waved to him as she went in search of the aloof wiccan who had saved her.

Alalia had, in fact, travelled to the line of banquet tables, and was now stuffing herself silly with scones and pumpkin pie – a drop of brandy here and there too. As the girl devoured a slice of meringue in one depressed mouthful, she willed herself not to think about the failed potion of the previous week. She always seemed to remember her failures rather than her achievements.

A shadowy man with an eyeglass averted his gaze. He'd been staring at her for a while now, she'd noted. He strode into the crowd.

Alalia Miseria knew of most people within the Amaryllis and greater Eastlea community; she was used to gatherings such as these and could often predict the guest list without even knowing the occasion. She had never seen this man before.

Alalia peered around the party, looking for Jákob. A scone fell from her overstuffed hands and who should pick it up but Freya Daltry herself.

Freya brushed the object off and placed it on top of the pile Alalia had created in the crooks of her elbows.

'Are you alright?' Freya smiled at the redhead.

'Of course.' Alalia swallowed a mouthful of a concoction of brandy, scone and meringue. 'Perfectly fine. I am now anyway.'

Freya bit her lip. She was wearing a green gown that plumed out to just over her knees. A lacey purple too-too bloomed from the edges of its hem and she wore a pair of classic green heals on her feet. Her straight black hair was tied back, and a violet stone glistened around her neck, just above where the stitching of her dress revealed a considerable amount of her bare chest.

'I haven't seen you for weeks,' Freya said. 'You truly saved me, you know. We have not heard a single whisper of Daneya anywhere in the household. And my parents wanted to apologise to you, Alalia. They did not tell you about my twin sister because they thought it might have led you to be one sided. They were not sure if the spirit was *truly* Danyea or merely using her name.'

'I understand,' Alalia said. She blinked rapidly, feeling light and pleasant now that the brandy was absorbing nicely into her bloodstream.

'Do you want to dance?' Alalia asked.

Freya glanced at the other people around them. 'I'm not sure if it is rather appropriate.'

'I see,' Alalia teased. 'Now that you're not dying, you've started to give a damn what other people think?'

Freya laughed as Alalia grabbed her hand, dropping her obscene collection of scones onto the road, and dragging the Daltry girl into the centre of the Ball. They flew into a jiggling waltz that went with the clapping rhythm of the song. Freya held onto Alalia as she twirled her around. They swayed, arm in arm, in time and in unison, each remembering the night they had shared. If Alalia had not caught a glimpse of that same eyeglass man on the edges of the crowd, watching her with a deep-set stare, she might have had a wonderful night.

Alalia slowed her twirling body and rested against Freya as she peered around the crowd. The man had disappeared again. Every time she glanced him, he ran. There was shuffling in the audience. People were moving back and forth, some sort of commotion parting them. Alalia pulled Freya off to the side.

'What's wrong?' Freya said.

'Stay close,' Alalia said. 'Something's happening.'

She looked around. 'What?'

Alalia squinted into the crowd, moving Freya behind herself. 'I'm not sure.'

The redhead briefly caught sight of Jákob, running with a bow and arrow in hand. His face was stricken and Alalia immediately prepared a vial of Purchancë and poured it over her hands. The potion was orange and coated her hands in a pungent goo, like a layer of decomposing skin.

A short lady with a frill of lizard-like skin around her neck came towards Alalia from out of the singing crowd. The lady was holding something. Jákob was on her tail, but the eyeglass man was on his and there was little time for Alalia to decide who was the prime target. Others were closing in around the Ball. *Rebels.*

'Alalia!' Jake's voice boomed. 'It's you! The target is you!'

There was a crashing sound; something was departing an item held in the frilled-neck girl's hands. Jákob tackled the half-breed to the ground just as it fired. A pistol. The girl had fired a pistol. It was all happening so quickly. The bullet spurted into a thousand tiny shards as it came Alalia's way with a whistle of momentum. Alalia flattened her palms and elongated her arms, lifting into the air slightly as she channelled her own *badness.* An orange glow surrounded her. She was impervious to the bullet as it collided with her, evaporating into dust, as if someone had thrown sand at a raging fire.

The eyeglass man aimed a second pistol and fired it as well. She should have been paying more attention to him all night, following him, apprehending him! She should have known he was up to something. Stupid. Alalia sunk back to the ground. The bullet became a thousand tiny shards in the air again. Jákob cried out to her. But there was no time.

Alalia closed her eyes.

28

Somebody screamed. Then everybody started to scream.

Seconds later, when Alalia reopened her eyes, she came to discover that she was not bleeding, she felt no pain. Her vision was still blurry from the brandy. Jákob was firing his crossbow at the rebels as they ran and headed for the dark cover of the city streets. Watchmen appeared at Jake's short sides, assisting with the evacuation of the Ball's civilians.

A body was sputtering at Alalia's feet. The redhead couldn't see well and had to crouch down to fully understand what was happening.

Freya's mouth was full of blood again. But this time, the blood was not poisoned; it was not *meant* to be departing her. She looked scared. Her green eyes were wide with a cavernous realisation of her own mortality. The girl had jumped in front of the bullet, Alalia realised, to save her from this exact fate.

Freya gagged as her drowning lungs tried to inhale air. Searing pinpricks had left a dozen holes in her stomach and bare chest, going all the way through her. They streamed with redness, her blood, her life force, draining away into the dirt.

Alalia pulled Freya into her arms and stroked her cheek. Alalia was still so delirious that she wasn't fully aware of the situation.

'Freya? Freya?' she kept saying, her mouth a wobbling stutter.

The next thing Alalia knew, Jákob was crouched down beside her, his hands covered in the blood of other rebels. He was holding back tears as he looked down upon Freya Daltry.

Alalia hadn't realised it, but she was screaming now, screaming Freya's name out. She was crying and heaving sobs. When had she started to cry? Freya was dead. Her emerald eyes were now set in a wide stare of ghostly silence. Jake pried Alalia away from her body. But it was too cruel to leave Freya lying there alone in her own blood and the dirt.

Eventually, Alalia became too weak to fight Jákob off and she fell to the side, leaving Freya to roll wherever gravity took her. Watchmen, finally arriving now that it was all too late, formed a line around the alleyways of the Amaryllis Ball and the Pumpkin Throw Fences and marched a collection of captured rebels towards the dungeons in the Eastlea Tower. The eyeglass man was dead in the grass beside the pumpkin toss rink, but the half-breed girl was in iron shackles, grinning with pointed teeth.

Alalia trained her eyes. It took much effort to get to her feet. When she was up, she grabbed a knife from the sheath in Jákob's belt. He attempted to tackle it out of her hand, but she heaved him away with a wind-bound shove that sent him flying three metres back.

Alalia approached the girl who was now grinning wider, poking out her forked, lizard-like tongue with a flicker. Alalia cut it off before the watchmen could realise her intention. The half-breed girl shrieked and fell to the ground, but she was also laughing as blood dribbled down her chin. Alalia scrimmaged through the feet of the captured towards her with the bloody knife.

The girl slithered out of her shackles, out of the watchmen's wrestle, and ran for the winding alleys screaming, 'Remember my name! Remember I cut the Family into pieces! Wendolyn, the lizard lady from Autumn town!'

29

Worms and Wounds

Faerydae

Black skies had lightened to a smooth gradient of purples and pinks. Dawn was already arriving, but they hadn't yet reached the hills that could lead them home.

Faerydae and Alalia were asleep.

Morning's mist was snaking through the trees in channels all around them, frosting up fallen leaves and even the clothes upon the girl's bodies. Tiny dots of light broke through the canopy, like the same twinkling stars of night that had since vanished.

They had slept on top of Lolanthie, and Lolanthie had eventually come to a stop somewhere along the road just past the Willow of Eyes and slept on his feet for some hours. He was walking again now that the sun was rising, just slowly dawdling, and occasionally grazing on frosty lengths of grass.

Faerydae blinked herself awake to the sounds of Lolanthie's munching teeth. She stretched down to pull up her trouser leg and examine the deep gash she had received from Eggnorphixeus' claws last night. To her surprise, the wound was almost non-existent. Her bruised neck too felt strong and supple, like she could climb a mountain and back.

'*Sorcery.*'

Faerydae drew Lume out into her hand. 'Was this Eggnorphixeus' magic?' she asked him.

He stifled a laugh. '*Of course not, Flea. Why would he want to heal you? It was the* wiccan… *I'd keep an eye on her. While you were sleeping, she did things. I've been watching her.*'

Alalia stirred into consciousness in front of Faerydae. Faerydae flinched and returned Lume to his pocket.

'Everything okay?' The redhead yawned.

Faerydae shrugged slightly, her voice just a morning crackle. 'I suppose. I thought I'd hardly be able to walk, but…'

She showed Alalia her ankle where the dried blood had gathered around a tiny scratch, and the girl grinned pleasantly.

'What a miracle,' Alalia mumbled.

Faerydae frowned suspiciously at her and let her bloodied trouser fall against her dangling feet. Lolanthie stopped to leave a pile of steaming manure along the road and then pawed at the ground with his humongous hoof. Alalia slid down from his body; Faerydae followed her. The ground was too hard all of a sudden, so sturdy that Faerydae buckled down to her knees with a weak shriek.

'We're still here,' Alalia reminisced.

Faerydae grappled at the air for stability, still feeling the motion of Lolanthie under her. 'Did you think we'd have found our way out by now?'

Alalia went to Faerydae's side and outstretched a hand. 'Here,' she yanked the girl up straight.

They soon came to stand side by side, looking out at the morning woods with a different perspective than the previous night. Alalia shook her head in wonderment.

'I thought Lolanthie might have… Horses, you know, they sometimes have a sense?'

Faerydae bit her lip. 'We can't go home yet,' she said. 'Not when we have learnt so much. We have a *clue* Alalia–'

'A clue?' Alalia frowned. 'Faerydae, the wizard said your heart was taken by a woman, he did not say where to, and he did not say her name, if he even knew who she was. That is not a clue.'

'It's more than anything I've ever had before.'

Alalia sighed and collected Lolanthie's reins in her hand. She started walking down the road and Faerydae followed as she trailed ahead.

'Where are you going?' Faerydae called.

Alalia shrugged. 'Nowhere probably. I haven't a clue where we are anymore. This is the *Winding Woods*, Faerydae. Once you're in here for longer than a night you are truly, *truly* lost, my dear friend.'

Faerydae let that sink in.

'You mean,' Faerydae started. 'You cannot get us out of here? Honestly, you can't?'

'I could try,' Alalia replied with a wave of her hand. 'But it would be up to the trees to decide if they wanted to let us go.'

A moment passed and they walked in utter silence. Then, out of the apparent tranquillity, Faerydae shoved Alalia from behind, hard enough to make the redhead stumble and twirl round in alarm. Lolanthie shied away from them both, but Alalia managed to hold onto his tethers.

'What was that for?!' Alalia cried.

'Home in a couple of days, huh?' Faerydae squealed. 'You told me you knew the way, Alalia Riviera! You said that we would be home in no time–'

'You didn't *need* any encouragement to agree with my plan, Faerydae! I was trying to help. And, please remember, my dear, I am not the one who has something to gain from this trip–'

'Then why?' Faerydae demanded. 'Why would you do this, Alalia, without wanting anything in return?! Why would you risk your life in this violent place that you seem so at home in? I should have known there was something in it for you – What? Are you going to sell me? Hand me over to the king?'

'Maybe I wanted to get lost,' Alalia said softly. 'And maybe I never wanted to be found.'

She pulled Lolanthie by her side and continued to walk down the road again. Faerydae did not give in. She ran up to meet the redhead and held her shoulder so tightly that she could not deflect her away.

'Why?' Faerydae asked again, softer this time. 'You can trust me, Alalia. You have nothing to fear from me.'

'I don't know what I should do,' Alalia said, frustrated. 'My destiny is but a blur. There is so much I cannot seem to understand about myself. The barrier between good and evil is always shifting. Sometimes it is just easier to… run away.'

Faerydae hugged her. 'You are a good person, Alalia. Whatever is going on back in Brindille, or Eastlea, with your family, is nothing that cannot be fixed. Family, although I have never had one, is the most important thing in the world.'

Alalia chuckled and wiped away a tear. 'I think you mean love, Fae. Love is the most important thing in the world.'

A peculiar sound consumed the woodland then. The girls craned their heads into the air with confusion, and even Lolanthie's ears twitched with curiosity. It was too bizarre a sound within such a place as this. It was the voice of a cheerily yodelling man.

'Yod'l, yod'l, yod'le-hi-hoo!'

The girls stared at one another, then raced after it.

Lolanthie followed the running girls over the rocks and overgrown mushrooms towards the singing. They leapt over an erupted root and then stopped abruptly, falling in behind a boulder where, through the wood, they could see a clearing ahead. In the centre of the clearing, there appeared to be some sort of vastly oversized and perfectly deranged red flowerpot sitting in plain sight with tiers of spirals leading to the top. It was bordered by shoots of grass at its base and a fabulous arrangement of humongous petalled flowers sprouted from where clayey soil had formed a solid roof. Two curtained windows watched the front of the home, wide open but dim, and a small wooden door lingered in the centre. It was like a doll's house.

'What in all hell...' Faerydae stared at the thing. 'It's a house?'

Alalia inclined her head. 'Technically, it's a flowerpot. I'd not be surprised to find some rather unusual tenants living there.'

Faerydae examined the colourful display. 'Should we?'

'Definitely not.' She could see the curiosity in Faerydae's brown eyes. 'But you're the boss now.'

Faerydae liked the way that sounded. 'Well, they might know more about this 'woman of the woods'. If we're stuck here for now, we need to gather information.'

'Alright then.' Alalia smirked, and Faerydae could not help but melt a little.

A trail of half-buried boulders ushered them out of the shadows and towards the front door. There was a picketed fence bordering the far end of the clearing, but it only went halfway around the property, and the sound of rushing water was close by, making the girls realise how thirsty they were. Lolanthie clopped his hooves against the paved boulders as the girls floundered towards the small pond at the side of the flowerpot house for a drink. The water was clean and icy cool against their throats. Lolanthie decided to insert his whole body into the clear depths.

The girls backtracked towards the front of the flowerpot and haltered. The yodelling song had suddenly left the woods.

'*Greetings, strangers.*'

The girls screeched in unison and leapt closer to one another. Faerydae searched the scenery, her wide eyes lingering over the small garden at her left where tomatoes and pearly cauliflowers grew. Alalia suddenly spotted a resident down in the undergrowth, all covered in dirt, and pointed a wary finger for Faerydae to train her eyeline.

A puffy pink worm the size of a young child looked up at Faerydae from where it sat crouched in the vegetable patch. The creature had stringy pink arms and legs and wore a straw hat upon its domed head with green gardening gloves over its little hands. The thing smiled a toothless smile, then rose up as tall as it could manage without the need for its two back legs, which apparently hung useless on the ground.

'Ya'll folks alright?' the worm added in a feminine southern drawl.

Lolanthie snorted in disapproval, still seated in the pond behind them. Faerydae felt a bug crawl inside of her gaping mouth and began to choke. Alalia merely rolled her eyes at both of them. They were not yet becoming accustomed to the oddities of these woods.

'Hello, ma'am,' Alalia said. 'We are children of the night and stumbled upon your property by chance. Please do not fear us; we mean you no harm.'

The worm smiled at her with that gummy mouth, her soft features suggesting a placid enough nature.

'I am Alalia,' the girl continued. 'And this is Faerydae and Lolanthie. We are Northeners.'

The worm chuckled. 'Northerners? Well, how 'bout that.'

She slimed over to Faerydae, who reeled slightly back in horror until the worm shook her hand. The creature's grip was squishy and soft.

'How do you do?' Faerydae said through gritted teeth.

The worm smiled, moved on to Lolanthie, bowing her head calculatedly at him. He tilted his dripping head. Then she shook Alalia's hand last and the redhead bowed in return.

'Can I help y'all out with anything?' the worm asked. 'I must say, this is quite the surprise. I think I may have had one or two visitors in all my time of livin' here.'

Alalia nodded with interest. 'Really? You don't have neighbours nearby, or family elsewhere in the woods?'

'Oh no! We do not venture *into* the woods, good heavens. We stay here, in the clearing, and in our nice humid home. Worm folk do not fare well in the perils between the trees, and, if we stay close, then the house never goes missing either!'

Faerydae frowned. 'Missing?'

'Oh aye,' beamed the worm and waved her hand around carelessly, dirt flying everywhere from her floppy gloves. There were definitely fewer than five fingers in there.

'I am so surprised, sorry!' the worm wailed. 'You're so *young*. This is a dangerous time for little girls to get lost in these woods; *bad* things are going on these days. Terrible things. And there are plenty of awful folk around this place. Now, just let me–' She turned toward the flowerpot house and screamed. 'DONALD! Come on out here, we've got ourselves a couple of little guests.'

The worm winked at Alalia.

'*Guests?*'

A deeper voice approached, no less riddled with a southerner's accent. It belonged to the one who had been singing that cheerful song.

Another pink worm appeared slithering out from behind the flowerpot house, a clichéd sprig of wheat poking between his lips, though Faerydae could see no room for a field. This male worm moved so irregularly, so slowly, as if he had a limp in his slither. His vulnerable pink flesh appeared to be quivering against the obstacles below him. He gave a welcoming yodel to the girls, and then persisted to whistle another melody, unable to remain quiet for even a moment. His squishy hands fiddled around, clicking and slapping against his body in rhythm. He was a fidgety thing.

'This here is my husband, Donald, and I am Bobbie Jo.' The lady worm placed her thin, boneless arm around him and kissed his dome-shaped head. 'We would like to formally welcome you to the Wolseley's Ranch.' She gestured around the clearing. 'This is the ranch, and we're the Wolseleys, not the other way around, of course!'

The two creatures looked at one another before bursting into laughter. Faerydae and Alalia smiled, glancing sideways at each other. *These worms are insane,* Alalia mouthed. Faerydae nodded. The Wolseleys certainly seemed like a full-on couple, but they could not be any worse than their last host.

'We heard your yodelling from in the woods, sire,' Faerydae said to Donald. 'It was quite a pleasantly unexpected sound.'

Donald shushed her humbly with his hand. 'I am a true Southerner at heart, 'tis the song of the deep South.'

'How did you come to reside in the western province?' Alalia asked. 'If you don't mind my asking.'

'Official business,' Donald whispered. 'Very hush, hush. *Royal* business.'

Faerydae scratched her chin. She thought it seemed more likely that these worms had been royally *exiled* here, like so many other magical folks before them.

'You wouldn't happen to have a map of any sort?' Faerydae asked then. This stumped the worms. 'We are looking for a certain 'woman of the woods'. Perhaps there is a town nearby where she might reside? We have business with her, see. But there is apparently no way to locate anything within these trees.'

'You cannot map that which is always changing,' Donald said, as if it were common sense. 'The only town in here is Dainmeree, and even that can be a finicky place to find.'

'Dainmeree,' Faerydae replied.

'Anyway,' Bobbie finished. 'We don't talk about the woods; it seems only to encourage its ego. Come inside girls and we'll have ourselves a fresh lunch. It would be an honour to accommodate you before you must head off in search of your grandmother or aunty or whomever you said you were seeking—'

'Woman of the woods,' Alalia said.

'Right, right!' Bobbie Jo agreed. 'How *peculiar*!'

Alalia beckoned Lolantie to her and slipped off his hackamore to allow the stallion to graze about freely for some time whilst they followed Donald and Bobbie Jo into their flowerpot.

The first thing the girls noticed once inside was the pungent odour. It was like being inside a hot humid greenhouse in summer – though not nearly as horrific as Eggnorphixeus' garden. The walls of dirt, floor of dirt, and ceiling of dirt all worked together to create a mouldy smell and hot atmosphere that was almost palatable. Roots from the giant flowers up above dove all the way down from the ceiling, along the walls and into the earth below, creating a sturdy frame and pillars. Although the smell of the place was hard to overcome, the worms' decor was adorably crafty. The home was really quite neat.

Faerydae touched a wall, crumbling granules into her hand and sniffing them. It smelt like cocoa and rain.

'Don't mind if we do,' Donald said as Faerydae retracted her hand from her nose. She frowned, not sure what he meant.

The worms then burrowed their faces into their dirt walls with shocking wildness and began munching on the soil with an animalistic hunger. Faerydae struggled not to scream. Alalia gasped just from the shocking speed with which the docile creatures had moved. Bobbie Jo pulled her head out of the wall. Her straw hat was now crumpled and brown, her beady eyes flittering between each motionless girl.

'Lunch?' Bobbie said.

'Oh,' Alalia muttered. 'No, thank you.'

Bobbie Jo wiped the sides of her mouth and tapped at the ravenous Donald, who came out with a brown mouthful.

'I am sorry,' Donald said softly, dusting off his chin. 'Is this not good? Do you not wish to eat with us?'

Faerydae stuttered. 'No, I mean, *yes*. We just eat *normal* sorts of things. Human sorts of things? Fish. Frogs… Scones?' Alalia grimaced.

'I see,' Donald said, turning to Bobbie. 'These girls do not eat dirt.'

Bobbie looked around cluelessly before saying, 'Vegetables?'

Alalia nodded as if it were the most amazing suggestion ever. 'Please!'

Bobbie Jo slimed to the kitchen bench and assembled a bowl of her freshly picked vegetables; brought them over to the two girls.

'We make mulch with these,' she said. 'It fertilises our flowers, keeping our home warm and our soil rich. Would you like to eat these as they are, or shallI dice them for you?'

Faerydae took the bowl as a few small bugs crawled over the various zucchinis, bruised tomatoes and deformed carrots.

'This will be wonderful, thank you.'

As they all ate together, assembled about the round kitchen table, Donald and Bobbie Jo sung merry country tunes for the girls' amusement. Donald slapped his hand against his knee for a beat and Bobbie Jo came in with her harmonica in various parts.

Faerydae settled in slightly, relaxing her shoulders. She prayed for the peace to remain, that she could enjoy a moment of safety and regain her strength. She hoped they all could, for how long would they have to endure the frightening unknown of the woods?

Thump, thump, thump.

The muffled noises came softly from behind a closed basement door under the worm's dirt stairs. It had gone unnoticed by everyone else. Faerydae peered at the door. Had it been there all along? The noise was very faint, like an open window caught in a breeze. And then it came again, louder this time. Alalia heard it too now. She and Faerydae glared at the basement door as the thumping sound came twice more, then disappeared.

'Never mind that, children,' Bobbie Jo grimaced. 'That is just the snail, running around and causing a riot down there.'

A silence.

'Do snails really run, though?' Alalia pointed out.

Donald laughed hysterically. 'He's a funny thing, invisible except for his shell. But don't you ask us any more questions about him – or we might just *have* to kill you.'

The worms hooted morbidly before returning to their tunes, singing so wantonly now that it seemed they were truly insane.

30

It was not at all Faerydae's concern, nor her business, to uncover what these worms kept locked away below their house. But if she had to act ignorant for the remained of their stay, then she preferred to get away from this place sooner rather than later. Alalia sat with the chatty worms beside the basement door that had not made another sound for at least half an hour. Alalia was telling a joke but the worms did not seem to understand the punchline.

Faerydae opened the two wooden doors of a cabinet, looking for a place to spit out her pumpkin pips. She had discovered much bizarreness during her hunt for a wastebasket. There were decaying beetle corpses under the sink, a gumboot by the pantry and a steel wool sponge in a bucket that the worms apparently used to descale their skin.

In the end, Faerydae spat her pips into the bucket.

'Whom might I ask is this, Wolseleys?'

Faerydae turned around to see Alalia holding a woven picture frame made from weeds and dried flowers. The redhead was pointing at a charcoal illustration in the frame of a wide-eyed girl with an orange frill of loose skin around her neck and a sharp black bob.

Bobbie Jo's rose sullenly from her dirty seat and gazed at the image.

'That was Wendolyn,' she said. 'Our dear sweet Wendolyn.'

'Wendolyn?' Alalia repeated, staring at the girl.

'She went missing not long after Donald sketched that one of her,' Bobbie said. 'Oh, what a great day of beetle bashing that was! Wendolyn had travelled from the east, Autumn Town I believe, after we sent a dove requesting farm hands. She was a quiet country girl. We struggle to keep the ranch going all by ourselves now. Wendolyn helped with the gardening, the pests and keeping our… possessions safe.'

'What happened to her?' Alalia asked sternly.

'Well,' Bobbie said, wiping her eyes. 'No doubt the trees probably devoured her right up.'

'Awful. How long has she been gone?' Alalia pressed further. Faerydae wondered why Alalia was so interested in this girl, and it was even more frustrating because Faerydae only longed to make headway down the road.

'A month,' said Donald. 'She often went into the woods to find other food. She preferred 'human' food also. We told her that it was dangerous to venture into the shadows so often, but she was a free spirit.'

Alalia seemed confused. 'You have not gone looking for her? Are you serious, she could have returned to Autumn Town for all you know.'

'Alalia,' Faerydae cut in. 'It is not really your place to pry. And I believe we should start heading off soon.'

'She is right,' Donald sighed. 'It is not your concern. We will most likely be dead all too soon anyway. We cannot go looking for Wendolyn because the house might go missing, and we cannot persist here for long as the water supply has become dangerously low- something Wendolyn would have sorted out for us if she were still here. Oh, ever since Wendolyn went missing it is as though we have been cursed!'

Donald pointed through the window to the small pond that watered their garden and kept their home humid. It was fed by a trickling pipe. He started to cry.

'Why is the water disappearing?' Alalia asked in a daze.

'We cannot fathom it!' Bobbie Jo wailed.

Alalia eyed Faerydae through tight slits. Faerydae shook her head. *No, we cannot help them – we have to LEAVE.* Alalia did not look away. Her eyes were like fireballs of intensity. Then Bobbie Jo began bawling and screaming, which became all too much for Faerydae.

'Fine!' Faerydae shrieked. 'We'll go see what is stopping the water! But then we are leaving.'

They plodded outside without delay.

'Many thanks for doing such a thing, children,' Donald said, his tune changing so easily, willing them now to go into the woods and save him. He smiled gingerly, noticing Faerydae's demeanour, but following them only as far as the pond's edge. 'You must be quick though. Be back before the darkness comes. Stick to the drain children. Stick. To. That. Drain.'

He pointed his deflated finger ominously and they both nodded. Alalia clambered on top of the tunnelling drain to prove their compliance, then helped Faerydae up behind her. The darkness called to them with a sinister lure. Lolanthie neighed as they went within, he was now leisurely grazing on the worm's cauliflowers.

'Be a good boy,' Alalia called back to him.

Stagnating mould and moss made the path along the pipe slippery, but it felt safer walking up there than on the ground. Alalia was leading the way, of course, not daring to look behind and see Faerydae's discerning gaze.

'So,' Faerydae mumbled, her voice strained with terseness. 'Here we are. I hope you are quite pleased with yourself.'

'Indeed.' Alalia did not turn, she just kept her pace quick and sure. She seemed to know where she wanted to go but Faerydae could tell it was all just a rouge; the redhead's confidant persona had come out to protect her.

'What are you up to?' Faerydae asked quietly.

No reply. A minute passed.

'We should split up,' Alalia said and Faerydae shook her head emphatically.

'What?!' Faerydae demanded. 'You heard the worms, stick to the drain, there is only *one* drain, Alalia.'

'Fine,' the redhead slid off of the cold, metal side and crumpled to the ground, staring back up at the girl over the huge circumference of the drain. 'You follow this thing and I'll search the perimeter for clues.'

'Clues?' Faerydae laughed. 'Why are you so determined to help these worms?'

'They have been kind to us,' Alalia shrugged. 'The woods expect us to repay their kindness. It's just how it works in here, Faerydae. I do not want to get on the bad side of the woods, do you?'

She turned and walked off into the clustered leaves ahead.

Faerydae simmered in frustration for a moment. 'I didn't know there was a *good* side to them.'

Alalia examined the trees with her eyes as she walked, looking for anything out of the ordinary, although nothing was ordinary around here – the yodelling worms and egg-headed wizard could attest to that. She walked for some time, stopping only when the leaves appeared more crumpled, possibly disturbed by footfalls. The huge trees were watching her as she went, surrounding her with their towering indifference. Her eyes lingered on a rocky formation across the way, over a slight ditch in the earth ahead. Alalia ran to the structure, weaving through the crusty bark fallen from trees and jumping the ditch like a hurdle. She found that the pile of rocks was actually stacked together to create a rustic well. The hole stretched deep into the ground in blackness.

'This must be it,' Alalia whispered. 'The drain must weave back around, under the earth, and end up at the bottom of this well.'

She turned around to see if she could spy Faerydae or the drain through the shadows, or if she could hear anything in the near distance. Everything was still and motionless. Alalia poked her head inside the murky hole. It was dark and damp in there and hard to see anything at all past the first few hands. Her fingernails tapped against the mossy stones that she leant on, sending gentle echoes down the tunnelling depths of the well.

A hoard of black birds suddenly fled from the pit of the well, pecking at one another with chattering beaks as they flew towards the canopy. Alalia screamed and dove aside to protect her eyes from their beating wings and grating talons.

A fragile voice came next. It trailed out of the well like a ghostly song, making Alalia lurch back to the side of the rocks at attention.

'I-Is somebody out there?' the voice said. 'Please help me, I've fallen quite rightly down the olde well. My arms are broken, and I can't feel my legs.'

Alalia clamped her jaw, her neck veins pulsating against her skin. 'Wendolyn?' Alalia called. 'The Lizard Lady from Autumn Town?'

A silence was followed by a distant sloshing of water.

'Who are you?' the voice asked.

'Alalia Miseria.'

The girl in the well moaned a laugh. 'Alalia Miseria… Of all the awful people in the world to have found me dying down here.'

Alalia had to stop herself from throwing a boulder down the dark pit.

'What have you done to the water, Wendolyn?' she asked too calmly. 'You're trying to kill the Wolseleys. Why?'

Wendolyn snickered. 'They have something I want. But look at me now, I've doomed myself. I was so close. Your father would be pleased.'

Alalia's strained expression twitched. 'You are a coward, Wendolyn. A traitor. Everyone must pick a side. You are not an island.'

Wendolyn waited before her voice came back much softer, much more defeated. 'I'm not anything now.'

'And you deserve nothing less.' Alalia spat into the well before she could control herself. Wendolyn giggled.

Alalia strode around the stones, examining the perimeter of the well. She circled the gaudy obstacle three times before noticing a wooden stick poking out from the edge of the well. She'd thought it was just a branch or a tree root, but it was too uniform now that she was paying more attention to it. It was a lever. Alalia rubbed away grime to reveal small golden letters painted on the wood, one side said *Flow* and the other said *Halt*. The level resided in the heated position as it was. Alalia knelt down and examined a patch of scuffed dirt beside the large rocks that created the base of the well, mostly camouflaged by tall reeds.

'You tripped…' Alalia whispered to herself. 'How stupid could you be?' She looked inside the well again and called: 'You tripped, didn't you, Wendolyn? When you turned this lever to stop the flow of water to the ranch, you fell right in!' It was almost too *stupid* to have actually occurred.

'Laugh if you must,' Wendolyn called back. 'You win, Miss Miseria. I hope you're happy–' Her voice darkened. 'But when the final eve is nigh, I will be laughing from my own restful place in hell.'

Alalia pulled the lever with all her might. The stiff lever eventually jolted into motion and slid over to flow position. It moved so suddenly that it almost flung Alalia inside the well to meet Wendolyn's fate. Alalia shrieked, catching herself upon the ledges of the well.

The thundering sound of water rushing through a smaller pipe in the earth approached them. It gushed into the well and rained down to the fill the huge pipe that fed the Wolseley's pond. Wendolyn could be heard laughing, all the while. But as the water became too high, Wendolyn's laughter became nothing more than a gurgling plea. Then nothing at all.

Alalia stepped away from the well, her face expressionless.

She turned and walked away.

31

The drain continued on for a good long while, winding through the grisly trees like a river. Faerydae walked without purpose.

'Why do I feel as though I'm always missing something with that girl?' she asked Lume.

'*Because you are an idiot who cannot possibly see the truth to anything,*' he replied.

'Thanks, Lume.'

Faerydae looked ahead to where the drain disappeared into the trees beyond, possibly unending for all Faerydae knew. No sign of Alalia either.

'This is hopeless,' Faerydae muttered. 'Maybe we should turn back.'

'*By all means,*' said Lume.

There was a stomping sound then, like an approaching stampede of some kind. Alalia suddenly appeared from the shadows to Faerydae's right, her face stricken and distraught.

'Alalia!' Faerydae squealed leaping down to the girl. 'Are you okay? What happened?'

'It's her!' Alalia replied. '*Wendolyn,* she's chasing me. I fixed the pipe, but we must get back to the ranch quickly. She will eat us alive, Fae!'

Alalia wrenched Faerydae's hand in her own and they sprinted crazily beside the pipeline back in the direction of the ranch.

Faerydae's fingers squeezed dangerously tight around Alalia's hand, feeling the palpable danger, turning the girl's fingertips blue. Faerydae would not dare let anyone hurt her, not again. They flew over logs and huge tree roots with ease. Faerydae could imagine Wendolyn's screeches echoing out through the vast woodland as she chased after them. She could imagine her gaining on them, that thirsty expression from the charcoal drawing was enough to bring her presence to life.

Donald was singing again.

'I see it, I see the ranch,' Alalia breathed, soft light flooding in through the clearing ahead.

The pond was raging; it sounded like a waterfall, and Lolanthie was neighing with delight.

The girls made it past the pond when they collapsed in a mess on the sloping grass. Faerydae stroked Alalia's head. She gasped in air. They were alright. They were safe.

'Are you hurt?!' Faerydae examined Alalia for damage. 'Did she hurt you, Alalia?'

'No,' Alalia assured her, holding her cheek. 'I'm fine, Fae. I'm perfectly fine.'

'Girls!' Bobbie Jo's voice lit the air with frightening determination. The creature herself then appeared sliming out through the front door with a grin, gesturing graphically to her raging pond. 'You did it!' she screeched. 'I didn't actually think – oh, thank you! Thank you!'

Donald came out of the front door behind her and gave the girls a single, resolute nod of appreciation.

'Did you come across any sign of our dearest Wendolyn in there?' asked Bobbie Jo, her hands pressed tightly together. 'Anything that might indicate her fate? Whether it was a quick and painless ending for her?'

Faerydae said nothing as Alalia helped her up. The redhead bowed her head. 'Wendolyn has lost her mind to the woods, ma'am. You must move on without her. You will be okay, though. You are brave worms.'

The worms shed their final tears for the lost farm hand but appeared to recover rather quickly from the dire news. Bobbi sighed.

'Will you be leaving us now, children of the night?' Donald asked. 'It will be eve all too soon.'

Faerydae helped untangle Lolanthie 's hackamore from where he had nuzzled it over to and relentlessly around a nearby tree trunk. The stallion remained unhelpfully log-like all the while, munching gingerly at the grass beside the tree as if he hadn't had enough time for such things. Alalia gave him a shove and yanked him by her side.

'We must be on our way, Wolseleys,' said Alalia.

Bobbie Jo chuckled at the seemingly adventurous pair. 'Well, don't be strangers now, you hear? A fine eve to you both!'

Bobbie and Donald waved the two children off and the girls waved briefly back. The worms then slithered into their flowerpot house, holding one another close. The pond now held a gathering of small birds and croaking frogs.

Faerydae watched the worms go. She wanted to remember this moment, that it was real. But Lolanthie and Alalia were trailing swiftly out of sight, and so Faerydae chased after them. As she left the flowerpot house behind her, Faerydae found herself wondering if her time at the Wolseleys' Ranch had all been but a fantastical dream. She peeked over her shoulder one last time, one last inkling of delusion keeping her from letting go – and what did she see there?

Nothing at all.

The flowerpot house, the clearing and even the pond had all disappeared. It was as Bobbie Jo had suggested sometimes happened around these parts. Faerydae dared not madden herself by wondering any further. She turned resolutely and followed Alalia who was walking rapidly out of sight.

For maybe some things are better left in the unknown.

32

The Guest at Dinner

Alalia

Blanchefleur settled the gravy until it sat in a thick line across the top of the jug. She wiped her sweaty hands on her apron. In one hand, she took the floral-patterned jug of gravy and in the other she held a plate of unicorn pasty scrolls. The unicorns neighed.

She waddled precariously across the room and placed the dishes amongst the other plates in a fiesta assortment on the little round table in her kitchen. She had used her best tablecloth this evening. The kids were getting dressed in their best clothes. She had picked what they would wear; neither had been pleased by the fact.

Alalia came down the stairs first. She floated down actually, landing with a click of her featherbone slippers. The girl wore a blue, handmade dress that only covered the skin to her elbows and knees. It was a surprising colour choice from Blanchefleur, all wiccan customs considered.

'This is unnecessary,' Alalia mumbled, taking food from the pantry and sitting upon a bench near the kitchen stove.

Blanchefleur whacked her away with an old scroll and the girl skittered to the side.

'What's gotten into you?' Alalia reeled.

The woman dusted the bench where Alalia had sat and dropped crumbs off a little corn cookie. 'This is an important dinner, Alalia,' her mother replied. 'I don't want you messing it up. And give me that–' Blanche swiped the cookie out of the girl's hands. 'You'll spoil your appetite.'

Jákob appeared at the bottom of the stairs then. He was wearing a red velvet suit with a grey waistcoat and bowtie. If Alalia had the emotional energy for it, she would have laughed at him. But, as it was, she felt very little of anything towards anybody anymore.

The boy circled around the table, noticing Alalia distancing herself from the situation, and sat down on a chair. Alalia went into the other room.

There was a silence then; Jákob and Blanchefleur had never been the types to talk about their emotions with one another. They had more of a friendly understanding, and got along very well because they rarely spoke of anything with much substance.

Jake bowed his head and watched his hands. 'I'm worried Alalia will never recover from this.'

Blanchefleur heard him. She briefly stopped what she was doing, only to begin fussing almost immediately and even more frenziedly. 'She will. She must. There is too much at stake.'

'She will never be the *same* again, Ma.'

'The same as what, Jákob? Your sister has never warmed to you in the way that you would like.'

'It's because of Freya. It has always been because of her.'

Blanche sighed. 'And now the poor girl is dead, after everything I did for the Daltrys. I should never have trusted the pair of you with such a task. It is clear, you need to be separated for the good of the Family.'

Jákob nodded. 'I suppose so.'

A knock pounded on the other side of the front door, making them both jump. Alalia, in the other room, rose to attention from where she had been reading by the fire.

Jake peered through the split in the front window curtains but only saw the darkness of night outside. He sat down in one of the polished chairs at the kitchen table, pondering. *Who could get to the house at this hour through the forbidden field?*

Blanchefleur stared at the door, its old swirling pattern of wood hypnotising her. She pointed at Jake and snapped her fingers.

'Get it,' she mumbled, almost in a daze. 'Now, Jákob.'

The boy stood, his grey pointed shoes clacking against the wooden floor. When he opened the door, a man appeared standing on the other side, too tall to even be seen fully within the short frame. His skinny legs were covered in black slacks, his pot-bellied torso and lengthy noddle-like arms in a black suit. The man crouched down and stepped inside the Miseria's house, like a spider entering its burrow, slowly and precisely. When his head became visible, Jake noticed how empty his eyes were. They were like a googly pair of doll's eyes stuck onto his face unevenly. They were blue. His hair was a fuzzy red coating. The man smiled; his teeth were huge and stained, pointier than one's teeth should be.

'Hello there,' the man said to Jake, bending down to the twelve-year-old's height. 'You must be Jákob?'

'Yes,' the boy replied, wanting to clutch his belt of gadgets but knowing it wasn't there. 'Do I know you?' Jákob stepped back, clenching his jaw.

'You will.' He grinned. 'Where is the other half? Where is Miss Alalia?'

Alalia appeared in the archway to the other room at the sound of her name, holding her paperback by her side. She stared at the tall stranger. 'Should I know you?'

The man seemed pleased to see her, more pleased than he was to meet Jákob. He stepped closer towards Alalia and reached for her hand. Alalia allowed him to kiss it gently. 'Hello, my dear daughter. You have become a beautiful girl.'

She leaned away at that. 'I do not know you, sire.'

'Not yet,' he agreed. 'But I am indeed your father and I have returned to collect one of you. The time is upon us.'

He went to Blanche and the woman submissively bowed before him; the mere presence of his gaze led her to avert her eyes. Alalia frowned at Jake. They both knew their mother was not the meek type.

'I have travelled far, Blanche,' the man said. 'I must rest.'

She nodded, looked at the children. 'Take your seats, please. Dinner is ready.'

They slowly assembled themselves around the little table and waited as Blanchefleur laid out a selection of plates. Alalia stared at the man at her table. He said he was her father. She had no reason to protest, no evidence to suggest otherwise. But although Alalia knew very little about her father, she felt so surely that this man could not possibly be him.

'So,' Alalia started with Jákob watching after her like the little brother he was. 'What is your name? And why have you come here?'

'All in good time,' he replied, straightening his black tie. 'Nobody likes a spoilsport.'

'I will not sit here with a man who will not even tell me his name.'

The man's lip twitched. His fingers shook, possibly with the desire to tighten around Alalia's throat. 'Now… now. Let us all relax.'

Blanche's hands were shaking too as she took her seat. Alalia could not move her face from the tight despising expression she held.

'I want to know too,' Jake said.

The man considered it. 'Very well. My name is Alejandro Miseria. I am your father, as I said, and I would appreciate it if you treated me as such.'

'Why?' Alalia blurted. 'How do we know that you're really who you say you are–'

'It is true.' Blanche cleared her throat before repeating. 'He *is* your father.'

Alalia thought of how best to respond. 'Why have you come now?'

Alejandro smiled. 'Because you are both getting older. You are both growing stronger. As are the rebelling forces that seek to destroy us.'

'Rebels?' Jákob looked his father in the eye for the first time. 'At the ball, you mean? Their target wasn't the civilians. It was Alalia.'

Alalia remained unblinking as she stared through Alejandro.

'Yes, Jákob,' Alejandro spoke. 'They are trying to destroy my followers, my collection, my *Family*. These rebels were previously a part of my Family. However, they became selfish. They have decided to create their own group, seeking prosperity only for themselves. One of the main leaders,a half-breed with no distinct lineage–'

'Wendolyn,' Alalia spat.

He agreed. 'She has gone rogue, plotted numerous attacks, including the Amaryllis Ball, which saw the death of multiple civilians, including a close friend of yours, I am aware. Such incidents have stirred me out of my work in the Underground.'

'*Wendolyn*.' Alalia had become teary. 'She escaped. She got away because of me. We need to hunt her down.'

'She has gone off of our radar,' Alejandro said. 'Possibly, she has retreated to the safety of the Winding Woods. In that case, she would have immunity if the woods see fit to grant her life.'

'She has to be brought to justice!' Alalia demanded, slamming a fist against the table. 'We cannot let her escape simply because the woods have granted her passage. We should *hunt* her down.'

'It won't bring Freya back,' Jákob mumbled. 'Nothing will. You can't hope to rid yourself of the pain simply by killing those who hurt you.'

Alalia crunched her teeth together, trying to stop herself from screaming at the stupid little boy. She had been, and still was, enduring through a strain of emptiness that made her cry all the time. It had been a season since Freya died and Alalia hadn't spoken about it at all. This was the first time somebody had even said her name. She tried to calm herself down. She *tried* so hard. But tears, hot and burning on her cheeks, brought with them heaves of hopelessness. The emptiness felt as if it was sucking out anything of her soul left; it was the deepest nothingness she'd ever seen. A sorrow from which there was no real return.

'Don't say her name,' Alalia whispered. '*You* don't get to.'

'Me?!' Jake squealed. 'If you weren't so difficult to work with, we could have devised a plan. We could have *found* the rebels before they attacked, and Freya and the others would still be alive!'

'We wouldn't have been able to predict the number of rebels that were going to be there that day! You're such a stupid little boy!'

'Please, children!' Alejandro bellowed. 'This is precisely why I am here. We need to work together. One of you is going to be the heir to my duties and you cannot possibly have a healthy battle in such close quarter.'

'Battle?' Blanchefluer spoke up. 'It is not a *battle*. Both of my children are disciples.'

The man took a beat of silence and everybody settled down. Jake picked at his food with a fork, and Alalia sat in silence.

When Alejandro spoke again, his voice was placid and smooth. 'One of you will come with me to the North, to a quiet village by the name of Brindille. By the time we can collect what *needs* collecting, one of you will be chosen to lead the Family. It has always been so.'

Alalia looked up, staring at her little brother but seeing nothing in his furious eyes. Looking to her mother, she found no solace either. Her father then, monstrous and strange. It didn't matter anymore. The whole world was a stranger now. She was alone. She would do whatever she had to.

And that, apparently, was that.

33

Deeper into the Woods

Faerydae

They were exhausted by the early hours of another morning, struggling to escape the clutches of their own separate nightmares, twisting and turning on the grassy earth below a towering tree.

Faerydae had been running away from the headless corpse of Eggnorphixeus, moving as fast as she could and yet being unable to elude him – in the way of dreams. Alalia felt at war, torn between blatantly ripping Wendolyn's throat out with her bare hands or leaving her to die, slow and alone.

Faerydae and Alalia had each woken early, when it was still dark, and found that the tree they had so adamantly sought refuge under had apparently wandered off during the night. They set off once more but fell asleep again when they were on top of Lolanthie, just as the sun was rising.

Faerydae was roused by the sounds of birds chirping first, then the scurrying of leaves, but the pleasure of a mindless rest kept her in a state of ambiguity. It was not until Lolanthie reared that Faerydae lurched forwards. She snatched at Alalia's back for purchase, but she too was sliding. Lolanthie roared in the way that stallions sometimes do when they are threatened. He kicked out and skidded sideways. Faerydae and Alalia tumbled from his back as he flung himself into a bucking frenzy.

'Lolanthie!' Alalia screamed as she hit the dust, her voice croaky. 'Calm down, you silly horse!'

Her stallion curled his top lip to reveal a row of yellowing teeth. Alalia grabbed for his reins, but the spooked horse only continued to rear against her fruitless efforts. Faerydae dusted her knees off while they fought. She attempted to stand but only managed to stagger, so retired to sitting on the ground. She felt exhausted, and stared up at the sky above the canopy as Lolanthie shuffled backwards. Alalia refused to let go of his reins, which resulted in her being dragged on her hands and knees across the dirt.

'Brooms really are less opinionated than horses,' Lume snapped.

Faerydae assumed he was only relieved not to have fallen or been broken during the stallion's frenzy. The darkening rain-filled clouds made Faerydae feel so tiny as they swooned with fullness. A storm was brewing up there. Faerydae felt the weight of her ambiguity. They had no idea where they were going. Lost. Lost below the storm.

'Oh fine then!' Alalia screamed at Lolanthie, letting his reins go finally. 'Go on then and bugger off, see how far you get, you dumb animal! Don't you know that we're all lost–'

'Lost?'

Another new voice came out of the congested tension in the air. Lolantie reared again. Faerydae scurried to standing, looking around the undergrowth by the sides of the road. She wondered if it would be more worms.

'Who's there?' Faerydae called, steadying herself against a tree trunk.

There was a scrimmaging. Then a large creature slunk out of the bushes with its orange body all frizzy from fright. It was a bizarre-looking fox. Faerydae stepped back. The animal had long, spidery black legs and ears as lengthy as its snout. Its lanky limbs were almost as long as Faerydae's legs and its black snout was pointed to precision as were its huge black ears and the almond-shaped edges of its emerald green eyes.

'Lost?' the animal said again with a delicate voice inflected by the sharp white teeth jutting from its mouth. 'Did I hear you speak that dreaded word? Oh, I hath heard it far too many times in these here woods.'

Alalia dove for Lolanthie's reins. He did not evade her this time as she lunged him around in a tight circle.

'Our horse doesn't like you,' Faerydae heard herself saying. 'Not at all.'

Lolanthie whinnied as if to agree with her and the fox eyed him with a wrinkled scowl of its snout.

'That beast ran right over the top of me! The way it carries on, you'd think it had seen a ghost.' The fox shook its head. 'Might I suggest some training for him, girls.'

And then the furry red creature started to turn and head on its way. Faerydae staggered after it with a bemused frown. She saw that the fox was carrying a little brown satchel around its neck. The bag swayed back and forth with the fox's graceful loping stride. Faerydae turned around and looked at Alalia, who had also noticed the fox's little satchel.

'Do you have food in there?' Alalia called to the animal.

The fox abruptly stopped and turned back to watch them both. Alalia licked her lips, and added. 'My apologies, but it is rather unusual to see a wild animal carrying a purse. I can't imagine what else you would need to use it for.'

The fox considered her for a moment, looking over her clothes, Faerydae's too. 'I carry my own meat, yes; small mammals that I catch. Humans aren't the only ones who can accessorise.'

Alalia nodded. 'So you catch more food than you need? To store for a later time. That is very smart.'

'For a wild animal.' The fox added, she tilted her head. 'Are you hungry?'

The fox nudged its head into the satchel and threw a collection of shiny red apples out of the bag with its mouth and towards the girls. 'No need for these really. I had imagined I might make an apple pie ... But perhaps not...'

Faerydae smirked as Alalia snatched up the apples, Lolanthie too. She crossed her hands over her chest. 'Where are you heading to this morning, Misses Fox?'

The animal chuckled. 'I am not a fox, girl. I am a *wolf*. A maned wolf of the Winding Woods.' The creature stood proudly.

'Really? Huh,' Alalia said. 'I have never heard of such an animal.'

The wolf walked back towards the girls. 'Well, you are quite an odd sight too. Two humans and a stallion. You look a little worse for wear if you don't mind my saying so. Can I *help* you at all?'

Alalia started on another apple as Faerydae's eyes veered down the dirt road ahead. 'Does this road actually lead anywhere?' Faerydae asked. 'It feels almost impossible to get where you want to go in this place, if you're planning on going anywhere at all.'

'I was merely wandering,' the wolf replied. 'I had plans to visit the ocean and camp out at the Point of No Return, but I am not set on that.'

'You can navigate the woods?' Alalia asked.

'In a manner.'

'What is your name?' Faerydae asked.

'Temperance.'

Faerydae stepped towards the creature. 'Do you have a home somewhere in the woods, Temperance? A family too, maybe? A family of tiny wolven-fox children?'

The wolf sat down and curled her tail around her long legs. 'Oh no, my family and I are not at all close… I imagine the two of you would be dearly missed by whomever you have left behind though?'

'Of course,' Alalia assured. 'We…' She sighed. 'We are lost. I thought I would be able to get us out of here by now. But I was a fool.'

Faerydae shook her head. 'It's *my* fault. We came in here for me. You see, somebody stole a human heart from Brindille Shire some years back. As far as we have learnt, the culprit was an older woman a 'woman of the woods'. Have you heard anything at all about such a woman?'

Temperance seemed to think about it, then shook her head. 'These woods are so diabolical, so full of *magic*.' She chuckled. 'Some people think that magic is only spells and bewitching, but it is not so rare as that. It likes to crawl inside forgotten places, like a disease. Magic is in everything, it is even in *you*, in the very air we breathe. Such a dreadful country this is, cursed since the very beginning… Brindille shire, you say? Yes, I believe I have heard of the place. Granted, I do lack knowledge of the outside world, of the lands beyond the Ivory Mountains. The North is a foreign land to me.'

Her tail was lifted high, curling around thin air in a pulsating rhythm.

'I could take you home. If you wished it,' she offered. 'Would that be good? Would you like to go home?'

'How could you promise that?' Alalia said. 'That's impossible, the woods are inexplicable.' The wolf grinned at Alalia who did not appear amused.

'In order to know that which is unknowable,' said Temperance. 'You must listen to the wind, for the wind moves through all the trees and knows everything all at once. I have large ears, as I'm sure you have noticed, and therefore can hear that which you cannot.'

Faerydae seemed enthralled. 'That's incredible, Temperance.'

'Perhaps you might like to know more about the woods,' Temperance asked Faerydae. 'You might like to know more about what *I* know?'

Alalia dropped Lolanthie's reins into a heap and stomped towards the wolf, forcing her arms by her sides. Temperance rose up from where she had been sitting and stepped back slightly.

'You know what?' Alalia said. 'I don't trust you. I don't know what you *want*, and that is a dangerous thing not to know. So, I'll ask you, plain and simple, and I do hope you'll be honest, what do you want from *us*? Why would you offer to help?'

'Companionship perhaps,' Temperance suggested, clawing at her satchel with one paw. 'Why should two groups who are both travelling somewhere not help one another out. Do you think I have a lot to do? I am a wolf, for goodness' sakes. Honestly, it would be nice to use my vast knowledge for once.'

Alalia laughed dramatically. 'You want to take us home because you're bored?' Alalia looked to Faerydae, her eyebrows raised.

Faerydae looked intermittently between the wolf's polite countenance and Alalia's expectant glower.

She shuffled on the spot, her fists clenched with indecision. 'One moment,' she mumbled and ran into the trees at the side of the road until she was out of sight.

'FAERYDAE!' Alalia called after her.

'One second!' she called back. 'Uh… peeing.'

Alalia shrugged, making a point not to look the wolf in the eye.

Faerydae crouched down in the shadows and reached into her pocket, where Lume was glowing brightly under the material of her trousers. His sparkling eyes blinked into awareness once she had him sitting in her palms.

'Were you sleeping?' Faerydae whispered.

'*So what if I was?*' he replied in a crackling voice. '*I am a rock, Flea, it is not as if I have a lot to do other than dream.*'

'You dream?'

'*I see everything, Flea. My dreams are the future.*'

'Right,' Faerydae replied. 'Lume, I need your advice. I don't know what the right thing to do is. I don't know where to turn, who to follow. Where am I supposed to go from here?'

'*Mmm,*' Lume yawned. '*That wolf has lived many years in these shadows. It is curious that I cannot hear much of the animal's innermost thoughts. You know, only magical beings can hide their secrets from me. Should you be concerned about that? Probably. So, follow the wolf, or don't follow the wolf. My advice is: you will end up at the same place either way.*'

'That's it?' Faerydae said.

'*Indeed.*' Lume closed his sparkling eyes. '*You are in over your head either way, Flea. I would love to help, but there is a future that needs to be imaged by me... So much darkness... So much blood.*'

And then his vibrant glow dissipated and Faerydae knew he would not be awoken again.

'Seriously?' She couldn't believe it. 'The one opportunity I give you, the *one* time I come to you for advice, and that's it?'

Nothing.

The girl reappeared out of the trees and pretended to fuss with her trouser belt, smiling as she passed Lolanthie.

'Okay,' Faerydae said not daring to watch Alalia's expression sour further. 'Take us home.'

Lolanthie was reluctant to follow when Alalia and Faerydae started after the scuttling orange creature.

'Now, now,' Alalia told her horse. 'I cannot go anywhere without my brave stallion. Who's my big brave stallion?'

Lolanthie whinnied. *Me – I am your brave stallion.* And he podded along behind them all with obvious disapproval.

Temperance led them down that same road for a while without comment, the only sounds being that of their trailing steps. Then she diverted off into the unwritten land of trees at the side and the young girls only hesitated for a moment before following her.

The skies whistled eerily from above. That storm, creeping ever closer.

They walked through the land of shadows like a line of mice. It would soon rain down upon them all with relentless gusto.

'Invierno,' Temperance murmured at hearing the thundering clouds.

'Invierno will trap us all unless we find shelter.' She turned to look at the almost silhouetted girls behind her. 'What are your names, children?'

There was a beat of silence before Alalia told the wolf her name and then Faerydae too.

Temperance nodded. 'Do not fret. All will be well, soon enough, Faerydae and Alalia.'

34

And so they travelled together for the night that followed. The girls were heading *somewhere* now, at the very least, which was more than Alalia could say of her own leadership. There would be no going mad from disorientation. Faerydae considered that Lume was quite right too. No matter who they followed or where they planned to go from here, they would end up wherever the woods wanted them to be.

The darkness barely seemed to change from afternoon to nightfall, back to morning and then to another night again. Temperance allowed them to stop and sleep under the protection of umbrella-like trees that she explained only grew in certain areas of the woods, where mushrooms grew like sunflowers. The *invierno* washed away layers of loose dirt upon the ground as it thundered down with unyielding force. But it came and went quickly, leaving avenues of flooded road and swamps.

The following night, after a whole day spent in the company of Temperance, Faerydae had a strange feeling in her gut when she retired to sleep upon a pillow of wildflowers. She and Alalia had not spoken much since the expedition with Temperance had begun. And the simmering animosity between the pair was becoming stagnant and toxic. She scuttled further around the side of the large tree they all lay under so as she would not be too close to her. Of all the people in the world; Faerydae couldn't believe she wanted to get as far away from Alalia as she could. It was the most bizarre and rapid change of heart Faerydae had ever experienced. As if a cog inside Faerydae's brain had broken and stopped fuelling her growing adoration for the girl.

As for Alalia, well she felt quite the same way towards Faerydae, curled up on her own patch of grass and ignoring all but the sounds of peaceful night birds. She wondered if she suddenly despised Faerydae because of her singular decision to follow the wolf. Or was it more? Did she *blame* her? No. She could not put her finger on it. To her, it seemed very apparent that the wolf had brought with her such an unrest in the group. Her beautiful raven haired Faerydae, could she possibly come to despise her? After all, she really did not know Faerydae all that well, time was not on their side. Perhaps their relationship was doomed to fade and die no matter what.

Alalia felt a tear slide down her cheek, and she wiped it away with a hushed sniffle. She smiled then. Because she did know Faerydae. She knew her better than she knew herself. Her soaring wild raven. Faerydae's hair was now much longer than Alalia's, almost reaching her elbows in thick wavy tresses. Faerydae beheld such a beautiful mixture of femininity and masculinity. If there was ever another person whom could claim Alalia's stony heart, it surely was Faerydae Nóvalie.

35

'What do you see, Temperance?' Faerydae called.

Temperance had haltered ahead of them all, her orange fur dancing in the afternoon wind. She stood like a statue. Alalia was riding on top of Lolanthie and meandering through the trunks of fat trees by the group's side, keeping her distance from everybody.

'The edge of the woods,' Temperance called back to Faerydae.

Faerydae squinted into the distance of shadows beyond Temperance's form. Light peeked in through small gaps in cross-hatched branches. But it surely couldn't be true.

'No,' Faerydae heard herself mumbling as her legs started to run. 'It can't be.'

Faerydae flicked twigs out of her way as she broke through the thatching of weak branches between herself and the light beyond. When she crawled through the barricade, she stood tall and stared at the open scene before her. A cold breeze brought with it the never-ending smell of rain. Alalia was at another weak spot in the wall of demented trees barricading her inside the shadows, tearing at them to set herself free. Lolanthie barged through the mass and Alalia appeared behind him, stroking her hair as the wind pushed it back from her flushed face.

So beautiful, Faerydae thought as she watched Alalia's features soften with a fragile smile. *So perfect. So broken. An angel with a shattered halo.*

'Well,' Temperance's clandestine voice came from behind Faerydae. '*One* of the edges of the woods, at least,' she corrected. 'This is actually the farthest away from the real edge as you could get.'

'What?' Faerydae turned to look at the creature with a deepening grimace.

'Don't worry though,' the wolf added quickly. 'This is the only way to be sure you'll get home. See, look, it's the ocean, just below those hills, on the other side of the cliffs. Can't you hear it?'

Faerydae could feel herself shaking her head, unable to speak.

'You said that we were to be returned straight home!' Alalia growled, approaching the orange animal with a murderous glare. 'So, where have you brought us?'

Grassy slopes extended from the small hill they stood atop and continued into the soggy nether region beyond. It was a totally barren world of soggy hills and frazzled grassland. There were no trees, no flowers, no people. There was only a small white cottage on one of the shallow hilltops about a mile away. In the paddock that lingered before the cottage, a tiny crop was growing in haphazard rows. The vegetation was tall. Through the haze of rain, Alalia saw corn stalks.

'If you'll listen!' Temperance insisted. 'Just listen to that ocean, what did I say? The coastline follows right along this ridge of hills. *Do-doo-do-doo-doo,*' her paw made the action of walking, as she reminisced about the path she would often take. 'And then there is but a small venture through the woods again until the Northern Province border. It is the closest thing to a map that you can get: *follow the coast*. It is the only thing that can't move.'

The sky laughed at the group with such unending drools of rain, hiding their tears if they had the energy to shed any. Lolanthie shook his muddy body with a quivering grunt.

'Is that your home?' Faerydae asked, pointing her finger at the little two-storey cottage.

'It is,' Temperance remarked gladly. 'And it is *so* wonderful to have visitors such as yourselves stay over for the night–'

'Now we're staying the night?' Alalia wailed, her anger rising again. Faerydae felt sickened by the girl's voice, wanting to distance herself from the redhead all over again.

'Ugh, is that all you ever do?!' Faerydae shouted suddenly. 'Just complain about everything? At least Temperance has a plan – what have you ever had?'

'The way I recall it,' Alalia said, 'is that I offered to help you out of the goodness of my heart. And have only continued to do so this whole time. To save you from your mess of a life. You would be nothing without me, still sitting in your boat with your stupid mother!'

Faerydae lunged at the Alalia and punched her square across her lip where the cut she had received from Eggnorphixeus was still healing under a scab. Alalia returned the favour with a kick against Faerydae's stomach, making her groan. They tussled on the muddy grass until they rolled down the hill in a jumble of limbs. Lolanthie plodded after them, as he always did.

'I hate you!' Alalia screamed at Faerydae. 'I don't know why I would have ever wanted to help you! You're useless! You don't even know what you want, what you're looking for, you just float along thinking everything will be handed to you!'

'Says you–' Faerydae pushed Alalia back to the ground from where she had risen to her knees. 'You lead people on and don't give a damn about anybody but yourself! I thought I loved you! From the first moment I saw you, you were the only person who had ever made me feel alive–'

'Well now look at us,' Alalia laughed. 'We're the two most messed up people in the world and we're not even good for each other. I should have left you to die in that wizard's house. I don't need this–'

Faerydae screamed and dove for Alalia again. 'You don't need anybody, do you! You're just so perfect! Nobody would deserve you, would they?'

Temperance's claws slid between the two girls and wedged them apart from one another before either of them could draw any more blood. Alalia rubbed her lip and Faerydae rolled her sleeves, noticing dirty scrapes across her skin from small stones and sticks in the grass. They both breathed deeply. A minute passed, and their anger simmered away slightly.

'Now, now, girls,' Temperance said. 'Let's not get cranky with one another. I think we are all a little tired, a little hungry, and could use a comfy chair. Come along.'

Temperance walked towards the house and, as she did so, Faerydae and Alalia shared a silent stare. It was a stare that acknowledged a tentative darkness developing between them, an unsure expanse of space that had grown. Thorns developing within the gaps. There was a familiarity in each other's eyes, and a recollection that they had been incredibly close, incredibly quickly. But things had since changed. *What had changed? Why was this happening?*

Faerydae averted her eyes to the wolf's hind and dawdled after Temperance with a weary stride.

'We have to get home,' Alalia said to Faerydae's back. Faerydae stopped. She turned and eyed Alalia again who stared up at the sky, crying softly. 'I can see what is happening, don't you? The woods are trying to keep us here, Faerydae. We will not survive this.' She walked closer, sincerity dripping from her in water droplets. 'I can promise you that.'

Faerydae turned back away. 'I do love you,' she said over her shoulder. 'And although I cannot bear to look at you right now, I hope that will be enough.'

Alalia blinked the rain away. She forced the words out. 'I love you too.'

They embarked across the slippery grass and into the cornfield in tandem.

The corn was tall, dominant, and smelt of damp rot underneath the crunch of old husks. The girls carved their way through the thick of the crop with Lolanthie trampling a rigid path ahead of them. Temperance, way ahead, appeared not to care about Lolanthie's hooves crunching through her field.

Faerydae found the narrow stalks to be claustrophobic. And the dozens upon dozens of pumpkin-headed scarecrow people that began to appear did not help. The people were dressed up in leather coats and hats, gliding tall above the pasture on wooden beams. Cold air moaned and made the scarepeople sway. Birds flew overhead, but they did not dare land upon a field with so many stalkers.

The tilting sand and whinstone cottage finally appeared ahead of them, almost within reach. Stretching aside the front door the crumbling rock wall of a small cemetery lay haphazardly in shambles. It was filled with dozens upon dozens of cross-shaped placards and caged burial sites. A wooden sign was nailed to one of the posts at the front. It read, through the mist: Cemetery of Temperance's Hall, you shall all live again.

Alalia veered to the side when they passed it, avoiding the area as best she could. Faerydae did too, for some reason. The cemetery – *as all cemeteries are* – was spooky. Temperance was sitting beside the corner of the crumbling rock wall, muttering at the gravestone nearest to her; a huge granite stone labelled: *Morgoa, the first to ever enter the hill.* Faerydae wondered if Morgoa might have been Temperance's favourite grave of all, a wolven family member of hers from a better time, one whom perhaps she was closer to than her other relatives. Whoever Morgoa was, it seemed they were talking about something very important.

'Temperance?' Faerydae called. 'Are you alright?'

The girls circled around the wolf, keeping their distance as Temperance persisted to mumble incoherently; her eyes shut to the world. 'Home at last… legs cramped… Almost there though… So close–'

'Temperance!' Alalia shouted.

The wolf immediately turned around, her green eyes flittering open. She bit her tongue slightly at seeing the two girls standing so close to one another, to her, but forced a smile.

'Sorry,' she said. 'Please excuse me. I – I see that you two have ceased your fighting, that is good.'

'Yes.' Alalia started for the door to the cottage. 'Now, can we please just get inside? It's freezing out here.'

Temperance rose to her paws. 'Go on then. Yes. Yes. In we all go.'

'A cemetery,' Faerydae stated as they walked. 'That is a peculiar thing to don the entrance to your home.'

'This cemetery *is* my home; it is my *family*. My extended family.'

'Your scarecrows are almost like works of art,' Faerydae added. 'So detailed.'

'They keep the birds away. They keep everything away.' The wolf seemed to make a pointed end to any thoughts of conversation at that.

Alalia walked up the rickety steps to the wooden porch and opened the front door. The door's screeching hinges echoed inside the apparently empty household and Faerydae went inside after Alalia. There were objects littered around the small rooms. Normal things. A stool. A vase. Curtains. A table. What else did a lonely wolf need in a house all to herself? The kitchen was nice enough, but held an uneasy emptiness. At the very least, it was warm and out of the weather. Faerydae teetered her fingers against a strung-up collection of herbs and wildflowers dangling above her head like icicles. Alalia preferred to hover by the wall as Temperance paced before them both.

'I shall make us some supper. The pair of you should rest up,' she said. 'Oh, my sweet angels, you must be exhausted!'

She ushered the girls into a pokey living room then, where they sat around an empty fire pit. Temperance urged them to sit and get comfortable as she fluffed each of their pillows. They didn't say a word when she proceeded to pull soft woollen blankets over their bodies with her teeth. Despite themselves, the girls were quick to grow weary. And as her eyes blinked with heaviness, Faerydae pictured the orange beast Temperance struggling to make a pot of tea using only her teeth for a tool. Temperance was a capable creature though – an *inspiringly* capable creature. And so she let herself settle into a peaceful doze.

Two cups of herbal tea had appeared before them, when Faerydae and Alalia woke simultaneously. Flower shoots and seeds swam around the purple-coloured liquid, which smelt of lavender and pine. Faerydae sipped the hot liquid in silence. The wolf had silently stoked the fire pit as well; flames now sizzled and popped in a comforting rhythm. Faerydae yawned. The girls regarded one another from

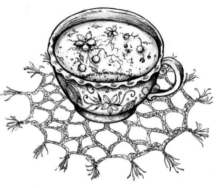

across the room. Alalia, expressionless, drank from her own tea.

Temperance soon came upon the girls with a grandmotherly smile, her whiskers twitching with inquisition. Alalia flinched as the wolf passively entered the room, meandering past them to sit on a cushy armchair where she curled up gracefully.

'Thank you for lighting the fire,' Faerydae said. 'And for making the tea.'

'Not a problem,' Temperance replied, then turned to look at Alalia. 'Did you rest well?'

'Indeed,' the girl spoke. 'It was strange, to sleep in such comforting surroundings again.'

Temperance furrowed her brow then.

'Your horse,' she started. He is looking rather thin is he not? Perhaps the trip has begun to take a toll on him, Alalia?'

'Lolanthie?' Alalia replied. 'No one has ever referred to him as thin. He has not stopped grazing since we've been out here.'

'A horse that size needs a lot to eat though, dear,' Temperance said. 'Think about your horse, dear. He needs lucerne. Oats. Barley. Would you like some lucerne? I have some if you ask nicely. '

'Huh.' Alalia's eyes were lolling about in her head, and she found herself nodding. 'That does sound lovely.'

'Excellent.' Temperance beamed. 'You must think of these things, you really must. Lest he truly begin to *suffer.*'

'I… I didn't even think of him.'

'Oh, *yes,*' Temperance nodded. 'He needs it, he does.'

He needs it, Alalia agreed. Temperance smiled.

'Come with me, dear,' said the wolf. 'Finish your tea.'

Alalia finished her tea in one outrageous gulp and then stood to follow the strutting creature out of the room.

Faerydae felt her breath slide into the deeper depths of her stomach and settle there like a pile of sludge. Alalia looked at her quickly before they left the room, but Faerydae said nothing. She was frozen in place, physically frozen where she sat on the velvet armchair. There was a sort of screaming sound inside of her mind, a voice, possibly her own, possibly Lume, wanting to tell her something. But what? What could possibly be said in that moment, everything being so… normal? There was no threat. There was nothing alarming here. But why did she feel so utterly terrified in the pit of her stomach. She tried to blink her eyes out of their trans, but she could not look away from the swirls of blossoms and flower shoots in her tea. Something needed to shatter the tranquillity in the room. There was an evil going unnoticed here. The silence had to be broken. Faerydae wanted to call out, to scream.

Oh no, thought Faerydae. *This is wrong. No, no, no. It's* **wrong.**

Her breath grew raspy, strained. Her eyes were completely unblinking now, growing glassy and bloodshot because she simply could not move them. She needed to scream, to cry, or move, or something. She couldn't do anything. She was frozen, *cursed* somehow, subtly, at some point. But how? In the tea? No, Alalia had had that too. Then when? Faerydae thought hard. Just moments before, of course – when the wolf glanced at her and winked like that. She'd turned Alalia against her. It was so obvious to Faerydae in that moment. It was not the woods at all – Temperance was the one breaking them apart, one tether at a time, until they became strangers.

Alalia's footfalls grew distant. Where *were* they going?

***

Temperance moved without haste. Alalia glanced over her shoulder, looking at the empty doorway to the room they had just left.

Faerydae was not following them. Was that odd, why would she? Perhaps Alalia was overreacting. Settle down, she told herself as she watched Temperance's feet pad over the ground. The wolf turned to the left, leading Alalia down a hallway now, beneath the stairs where a blue door sat at the end of the narrow expanse. The blue door beheld a mosaic glass window on its topmost half, which framed the view of the sky above. A door to the sky. Alalia cringed, wondering why she was still following the wolf. She didn't like this. She didn't like that door. But her legs were walking on their own. Where *was* Faerydae?

***

Faerydae was clenching her teeth so tightly that she could hear one of them cracking within her gum. The cup of tea, still in her hand, was shaking within her fragile grip. Tears were streaming down her face as she tried so hard to manipulate her own body into motion.But she could not move further than a quiver. Her face turned red and her eyes bulged. Tears dripped off of her chin and snaked down her neck as she gasped in what little air she could. More tears muffled her groans. *Alalia*, she cried. Her throat tightened and her veins bulged. *ALALIA!*

Temperance unlatched the blue door and let it swing open. Alalia stared at the void before her, motionless. A frigid wind tore down the hallway in a spiral, rattling picture frames and other items hanging from the hallway walls. The wind was loud. It was melting her, talking to her, telling her to *run*. Alalia could feel her fingertips coming to life, she could hear the world again, not just feel the haunting green eyes of Temperance upon her that had been locked in her mind's eye. The silence had been broken, it was too windy in the house now. Alalia shook her head into motion. But as soon as she did so, Temperance lunged for her throat without heed. Alalia stumbled aside, avoiding her by sheer luck. One thought instantly filled Alalia's mind then. Evil. Evil. Evil. She had always known it. The wolf was Evil!

Temperance returned for a second attempt, latching onto Alalia's leg successfully this time with her ferocious set of jaws. She skidded her over to the doorway as the girl kicked and clawed at the floor.

'You cannot escape this, child,' the wolf snapped. 'You are going out the window.'

The world expanded beyond, a foggy ocean shoreline some distance below, crashing against rock. The sun was setting now, and the ocean glimmered. Feeble raindrops floated on the high wind and made gentle patters on the roof above.

Temperance thrust Alalia through the opening without a second thought. The girl seemed to hover for a moment before she began to fall.

***

'*By the will of the omens, I free you from your cage! Desterrar!*' Lume growled, sounding like a tiny devil seated atop Faerydae's shoulder, guiding her towards freedom. '*I am the will. I am the power we possess. I am all. Desterrar.*'

Faerydae broke out of her statuesque shell with a gasp of air. She crumpled to the ground, her head hitting the wood with so much force that everything went black for a moment.

'ALALIA!' Faerydae screamed, climbing to her feet and running. She ran into the hallway. Her breath would not keep up with her as she saw the looming void into the sky. 'WHAT HAVE YOU DONE!' she screamed at Temperance who hunched before the doorway in a chastened cower.

Faerydae charged without pause, using the wall for balance as the howling wind tore a mirror from its place on the wall. Faerydae scooped the half shattered glass up along her advance and bounded for Temperance like an uncaged bear. The wind was so loud and strong that it attempted to push her back. The whole house was shaking against its gusto. Faerydae would not yield to it though. She torpedoed through the air and smashed the mirror against the wolf's head with a shriek. The mirror shattered, glass shards flew everywhere, deep into Temperance's face and eyes, into Faerydae's hands, out of the doorway too, raining over Alalia's head.

Faeydae glared through the doorway.

Alalia was hovering just outside the door, floating upon the waves of air surrounding her, her eyes glowing a brighter blue than ever before. She looked as if she were going to murder the next thing that irritated her. Fortunately, it was not Faerydae for once.

Temperance had crumpled against the wall. She screamed as her shredded head bled all over the place from the deep gashes the glass had left behind. Faerydae crawled towards her. She hammered the glass shards further into Temperance's head with her hands. There was a jagged shard poking out of Temperance's eye, making Faerydae swoon with nausea. Temperance dragged herself along the floor until she was underneath a sideboard along the hallway, where she proceeded to pick the glass out of her scalp.

Faerydae turned back to the doorway.

Alalia's hair appeared to be pulsating in the wind now, like a furious crown of snakes. The girl was blind to everything. She was a pure mass of energy and hate. It was the magic, unfurling inside of the girl and trying to get out, to be unleashed once and for all.

'Alalia!' Faerydae called to her, reaching a hand through the doorway. 'Alalia, take my hand. Please! You have to control it!'

'The world will burn!' Alalia's laboured voice spat. 'Nothing will live. Everything will taste fire—'

'This is not you, Alalia!' Faerydae said. 'It's not. I love you, Alalia. I know that you are a kind person. Just take my hand.'

Faerydae sprawled her body along the slippery, blood-soaked floor. She reached. Alalia hovered towards her, almost in a thoughtless daze. Faerydae's arms snaked tightly around her waist when she was close enough, and then pulled her weightless form inside the house. Alalia's blue dress turned red from the blood off of Faerydae's hands. Alalia screamed as she lay on top of Faerydae's chest; it was a painful sound, an empty pitiless sound. Faerydae hugged her tighter still.

'It's okay,' Faerydae said through sobs. 'You're stronger than it.'

Temperance was moaning behind them as well, attempting to crawl further away and to safety. Faerydae rolled over and pulled Alalia up to standing. They just had to run, that was all. They would run and leave this place forever.

But something truly bizarre happened then. Bizarre *even* in the Winding Woods.

Temperance crawled out from underneath the sideboard and turned back to look at them. Smiling. She shook her head. The embedded glass flittered out of her skin and into the walls like droplets of water. Temperance's fur was ruffled with stress, but a manic expression of pleasure crept across her swollen and bloodied face. She stood. Up onto her two skinny hind legs. Then she began to *grow*. Her appearance started to *change*.

Her ankles snapped and popped into place as they thickened and formed hairy red knee joints. Her paws expanded into long gnarled fingers at the end of two solid arms . Her horrid face shattered in on itself with a grinding of splintery bones. The fur fell away from her body and onto the floor in matted clumps. Her face was revealed anew, almost human. *Almost*. She was a mutation, caught halfway between beast and woman.

'Blast!' Temperance cursed. 'Oh well, at least I have my own legs back.' She laughed, titillated from the sensation of her claws against her hairless cheeks.

'N-no,' Faerydae stuttered in disbelief.

Alalia squeezed Faerydae's hand so tightly that the girl's fingers might have fallen off and squirmed away like slugs. Then her grip suddenly released and she pushed Faerydae to the side. The redhead thrust her arms affront her face where a sudden draught of air and electricity pummelled into Temperance's chest, pushing her backwards. But Temperance retorted the attack with her own outstretched hands, appearing to shield herself, digging her still clawed feet into the floorboards for balance. Alalia attempted to force the energy further against her, but the woman would not budge.

Alalia threw her hands to one side and a collection of stones in the building's wall, behind the olde wallpaper, came crashing into Temperance's body. The stones shattered against the creature's head and crumbled, deterring her slightly.

Faerydae ran from the sidelines and threw herself into Temperance. It took the beast off guard, and the pair tumbled over the glass-covered floor again. Alalia ran for the same attack, but Temperance easily flung both of the girls off of her. Faerydae landed nearest the stairs landing, a clear line to the front door. Alalia pointed from the ground.

'Go!' the redhead screamed.

'Not without you!' Faerydae assured and ran to her where she lay slightly caught beneath Temperance's legs. She pried her free and up by her side with sheer determination. They ran together, towards the door, the corn field, the woods.

Temperance crawled across the floor, far more hurt than she would have imagined of such unassuming little girls. Her gouged eye made it hard for her to see the adolescents as they ran. But she picked up a piece of jagged glass and hurled it at any object she could imagine. Temperance heard somebody scream. *Faerydae* – she'd stuck her like a little pig. But not in the chest or back. *Only an arm.* Temperance squinted. It had slowed the girl down for just a moment.

Temperance found her feet, by which time the girls were already fumbling out the front door. The wolf-woman could feel her prize slipping through her fingers, just like a runny potion.

***

Another western storm started to thunder down from the sky when Alalia leapt atop Lolanthie's back in one impressive manoeuvre. She reached down for Faerydae amid Lolanthie's jerking eagerness to run. Faerydae's arm was bleeding just below her shoulder, haemorrhaging blood onto the grass. The girl looked pale, barely conscious. Alalia struggled to hold Lolanthie as she reached for the girl again, frustration making her eyes water.

'Take my hand!' Alalia pleaded. 'Come on. Get up! Get up!'

Faerydae swayed on her feet before being knocked to the ground by Lolanthie's legs. Alalia screamed.

Temperance blew the front door from out of its frame, screaming over and over, '*Olvido! The olvido is here!*'

Alalia made to get down from the horse when she heard the sounds of moans and stomping feet coming from behind her. Her stallion reared, but Alalia knew there would be no escape if he bolted off without them. She jerked his left rein, making him twirl. The Olvido lashed down at the earth with bolts of untimely lightning and the corn swayed angrily, like a pulsating serpent.

The scarecrows of the field had climbed down from their perches. They were headed towards Alalia now, stumbling upon feet of sticks and twine, straw falling from the gaps and tears in their coats.

'Of all the Devil's creations,' Alalia whispered, staring at the trudging pumpkin army.

Temperance set the thundery sky alight with a roar as loud as the bellows of the clouds, Such a sound could not have been mortal; it entailed hellish qualities. Alalia did not know where to look anymore. Temperance's mouth hung wide open and her teeth dripped with blood – her own blood.

Faerydae moaned from the ground. 'Go,' she uttered, kicking pathetically at Lolanthie's feathery hooves.

'Lolanthie!' Alalia screamed and slapped him on the hind to stand still. He started to run instead, as the pumpkin army grew closer. His speed became so fast, so suddenly, that if Alalia jumped, she would have been trampled under his gigantic stride.

Temperance reached Faerydae's side with a limp. A colourful stream of incandescent pea soup swam through the air between them. It began to lift Faerydae into the sky.

'Get away from her!' Alalia screamed over Lolanthie's gallop.

Faerydae turned her head, watching Lolanthie from where she was floating, hovering upon a green cloud of energy. She smiled. The horse fled through the vast field so quickly, dodging the snatching scarecrows with an agile instinct. The scarecrows were *hungry*. Alalia thought daringly about jumping again, looking at the flying ground below, but the scarecrows were tailing her so closely. *A swarm.* Lolanthie refused to stop, even as she tugged at his reins. He knew better.

Faerydae took a deep breath – it was quieter up there, she noticed, in the sky. Lolanthie was struggling up the grassy hill slope, but she was floating, at rest.

I hope they find the way out of this place, Faerydae thought before she passed out. Seldom a religious girl – due to the misery of everything – Faerydae adopted a slither of faith in that moment. Dear God, I hope that my princess can find her way home.

36

The Reappearance of Wolseley's Ranch

Alalia

The horse did not stop running for some time. Alalia fell into something of a hallucination upon his back, feeling her own ghost-like feet wandering these woods alongside the stallion, running in the wind beside him. All of the energy that once filled her youthful frame had been stolen away. These woods had never been kind to her.

Through Lolanthie's ears, as the sun rose once again over the wretched woods, a familiar oversized flowerpot appeared before Alalia. It was covered in a magical haze. Alalia moaned as she attempted to sit up higher on Lolanthie's back, her neck stiff and her spine cracking. The Wolseley's ranch looked different in the fragile morning light, the redness of it was dulled to an undistinguished grey-blue. Alalia slid her torso down off of Lolanthie's coarse mane hairs and let his walking motion rock her into her own stride. Her legs were so sore and aching, her eyes red and bloodshot. It was so quiet now. She felt like a ghost. Alalia lifted her shaking hands up to her chest, which lay emptier than Faerydae's had ever been. The shivers of a loneliness she had not felt ever since…

Lolanthie's snout nudged her back, pushing her forwards and towards the Wolseley's front door.

'Alright, alright,' Alalia said, hearing her horrid voice that was crackly and dry.

She wandered towards the house. Her hand outstretched as if to to knock upon the wood when it slowly started to open itself inwards, as if repelled by her touch. The sound of it opening was soft, like the wind's hand. Alalia wondered if this was all just a horrible nightmare, that she was still asleep somewhere beside Faerydae, warm and loved.

Two green eyes came into view from out of the blackness. A set of white, milky canines followed them.

'Temperance?' Alalia spoke.

The glistening teeth and glowing eyes came closer, baring and glaring at her, and then Temperance's hairy black claw clutched the side of the doorframe, inching closer and closer towards her.

'Alalia?'

The green eyes and jaws of Temperance retreated from the sound of the voice, back into the house's shadows. Disappearing. Following after Bobbie Jo Wolseley's voice was the eruption of candlelight inside the home. The worm was slithering down the stairs.

'Alalia!' Bobbie said again as she reached the doorway to see the girl shivering in the thin rain. 'Is that you?'

Alalia fainted into Bobby's slimy hands. The poor worm quaked to hold the weight of the girl's body. Donald Wolseley appeared seconds later, wearing a nightcap, and took the adolescent from Bobbie's hold to carry her upstairs in an awkward sliming motion. He plopped her down into one of the poky bedrooms. Outside, Lolanthie kneeled down in the shelter of the flowerpot as the rain grew heavier above him. 'She's gone,' Alalia mumbled feverishly to Donald as he tucked her into bed. She started to cry again, clenching her eyes tightly shut to try and make the heartache ease. 'I let her go. I left her. I let the woods take Faerydae.'

***

Alalia hadn't woken alone for so many days now that it was strange; the only company being her own thoughts. She looked around the bedroom. Sunshine came dappled in through the window where she could see the tips of trees and birds outside.

Alalia rubbed her forehead. Her whole life came back to her then, in every heartbreaking detail and long ago moment that made her who she was. And now Faerydae was gone too. She was dead because Alalia had run away, just like she always did.

Bobbie Jo appeared slithering quietly into the little bedroom with a tray of tea. She noticed the girl sitting up in bed and grinned.

'I'm sorry,' Alalia said to her, lifting herself up further. 'I've intruded, haven't I? There's no need for you to take care of me. I'll be on my way.'

'Oh, shush,' Bobbie said, feeling the girl's head. Her squishy finger felt like a slug. 'Your fever has dissipated, which is good.'

Is it good? Alalia clenched her eyes, rubbed them vigorously. Perhaps it would be better if she did succumb to some cold quiet fever.

'I always wanted a daughter,' Bobbie Jo muttered, and Alalia trained her gaze on her. The worm placed the cup of mulchy tea on the bedside table made of roots. 'I always wanted a little thing to care for, but I was too afraid that something would happen to it, so I never did have children. Cowardly, I know.'

Alalia breathed slowly, watching the worm's expression change.

'The other girl, Faerydae,' Bobbie started. 'You said the woods took her.'

'It's all my fault. If I wasn't so... If I simply wasn't me, perhaps she might have been okay. If she'd never met me. I am poison–'

Bobbie grasped both of Alalia's hands in hers, a manoeuvre so swift and sure that it was out of character.

'Wherever she is,' Bobbie Jo said, '*whatever* she is now, you are never to go looking for her. There is no changing the way of things, what is done is done. The woods want you gone, not dead, dear. That is why they have led you back here, to us. You have to keep going.'

Alalia stared blankly. Any decision was a useless decision now. Whatever the right thing to do seemed so irrelevant and muddled-up to the point that there was no longer a clear right and wrong.

'I'm so sorry,' Alalia said. 'I never wanted to hurt anybody..'

Bobbie Jo patted her back. 'It's going to be okay again, Alalia, one day. Time moves on, you'll see. Here, have some tea.'

Alalia grabbed the cup of tea, guzzled it, then immediately spat it out all over Bobbie's face. The tea tasted like manure and rotten tomatoes.

'There, there, Alalia,' Bobbie whispered. 'Come downstairs when you are ready.'

By the time Alalia finally did come downstairs it must have been midday, though the sun had vanished behind clouds. A broom was sweeping itself across the dirty floor in the kitchen and the ladles and spoons were stirring a cauldron of pongy mulch.

Lolanthie pottered past the kitchen window, munching on odd carrots and cucumbers from the Wolseley's garden, and Bobbie turned to yell at him from where she was weeding near the pond. Alalia did not belong there. It was too nice. Too sweet. She would only destroy it if she stayed any longer. She did not know where she belonged anymore, if she ever did. Hell, maybe.

'Good morning, sleepy head,' Donald's voice came. He wandered in through the front door with his thick gloves dirty and his brow sweaty.

'Good morning... *afternoon*, sire.'

'How are you feeling?' he asked.

'I'm... I don't feel anything at all, sire.'

He nodded and sat down at the kitchen table. The worm gestured for her to sit opposite him and so Alalia slunk over to the nearest chair. She rubbed her face.

'You know,' he started carefully. 'We all must find our purpose in life.'

Alalia immediately felt like dying. She did not want to hear anything about the future, about what to do next, about purpose. The past was all that counted as far as she could see.

'Hear me out,' he continued. 'Take myself and Bobbie, for example. We had little purpose before. We were recluses in Wilburry, working in the underground mines because the world did not want us – the world doesn't seem to want many people. But now look at us. We were recruited to protect one of the most precious things known to man. We were *chosen*, over all else.' He took her hand. 'What is *your* purpose, Alalia? Wandering into danger, asking for trouble? It is only a cry for help, is it not? The woods have guided you back to us now, so I will do what I can to council you. Because we all have a choice, you know. We can all decide who we will be.'

'I think that choice was made for me a long time ago,' Alalia mumbled. 'I suppose I have just been fighting it this whole time. I need to give in. Bobbie was right, I have to keep moving, leave this place. Forget everything that happened here.'

'Don't forget,' Donald sighed, stroking her cheek and pushing a red curl behind her ear. 'Learn. But indeed, move on.'

He waited a moment and then left her alone again. Alone with herself.

'I would prefer to forget.'

Three distinct thuds drifted out of the basement then. Alalia turned to stare at the ominous door under the stairs, remembering the first time she'd heard it and dismissed it so easily. But what *were* these worms hiding? She watched the door for a moment longer, waiting for something to call her closer. When two more thuds came, Alalia stood up and looked around the kitchen. She *was* alone. Just her and her mind. Her bad, poisonous mind.

She walked to the basement door and turned the knob to find that it was undoubtably locked. *No bother.* Alalia closed her eyes, holding her hand over the golden knob, chanting, *Desbloquear, abierto, Déjame entrar. Desbloquear.*

The knob became hot and glowing for a moment, then the door sunk inwards into darkness. The smell of rot erupted out of the basement, making Alalia hold her nose until the initial wave had dispersed and the room seemed to air out somewhat. She walked down the steep stairs until they gave way to a bare dirt floor. The sound of metal, possibly shackles rattling made her look to the walls. There was literally nothing in the basement. Nothing at all. Except for a glowing object hovering in the rounded corner of the room, doused in chains. *The snail.*

Alalia approached the glowing green thing, her eyes set.

'Hello?' she said to the object. The object moved, a kind of quaking sway over air, to face her somehow. The shackles looped around and around its shell rattled and thumped against the dirt wall. Alalia crouched down and walked closer. She outreached a hand towards the snail's shell. It was about the size of a pumpkin, coarse and swirling around hypnotically towards its lumpy green core.

'*Do not,*' its hissing voice whispered into the air as Alalia made contact. '*I am not yours; I am nobodies…*'

Alalia stroked it. 'Your name is *Terra*, isn't it? The omen of the soil?'

Sparkling light flittered towards the opening of its shell where two faint beams of light seemed to create eyes and then a mouth. *'Who are you?'* It asked.

'I...' Alalia looked at her hands, her skin, the blood on her dress. 'I am Alalia Miseria,' she said.

'Miseria?' the object repeated. *'The Family... You finally found me.'*

'I can take you away from here,' Alalia said. 'I can set you free, let you express your true nature. You'll be able to see your brothers and sisters again. Would you like that, Terra?'

The snail made a breathing sound, its eyes blinking like little glowing rocks. *'Take me to **my** family.'*

Alalia peeked towards the door at the top of the stairs. She looked back at Terra and then grabbed hold of the metal chains encircling it. Alalia held her breath, squeezing tightly. The shackles became hot and glowing, just like the doorknob had done, until they exploded in a fiery shattering light. The sound was loud, like an explosion. Alalia looked back up at the door, but nobody had come for her yet. She scooped the snail shell into her hands, letting the metal chains fall around her. Her legs shook as she ran back up the stairs.

The kitchen was still empty when she reappeared from underground. Alalia glanced around the room anxiously, hastening herself through the front door with the snail held tightly between her arms. Where were the worms? If they truly were supposed to be guarding the omen, then they were doing a questionable job. The basement was possibly more soundproof proof than it had seemed, buried deep below the soil. Lolanthie stared at her when she appeared in the front garden. Bobbie Jo was still weeding, oblivious. The little worm glanced up and saw Alalia in the doorway. She went to wave before noticing what the girl held between her dirt-stained hands. They stared at one another. Bobbie blinked in confusion. Another beat of uncertainty gave Alalia enough time to vault on top of an unsuspecting Lolnathie. The horse reared and neighed as Bobbie Jo rose to her full stature, screaming, 'No! No, please!'

The worm thrust her arms in front of her pink chest and the water in the pond that she stood beside started to swarm into the air. It grouped into a wavelike formation, hurtling towards Alalia in a swirling mass.

Lolanthie fled as the water started to morph into the motion of a horde of scuttling bugs. Donald slithered around the side of the flower pot. He gasped in surprise. Alalia steered Lolanthie around him and towards the shadows of the woods, ducking stray bug droplets that had already reached her.

'NO!' Donald screamed. 'NO! Bring it back! This is not who you are – you are not a thief!'

Lolanthie disappeared into the trees and the swarm of bug-water fell to the grass, unable to penetrate the wooded landscape as a powerful collective. Bobbie wailed as the water rushed around her, no longer beholding any magical quality.

Alalia kicked Lolanthie onwards, knowing somehow that the woods would guide her home if they had any sense. She clenched her teeth, letting her body flow into the rhythm of Lolanthie's frantic gallop. She forced the snail between her legs to try and stop it from jerking around or cracking. The redhead's eyes were set on the road ahead. She tried not to think about the worms left behind, about Faerydae, about anything. Only what lay within her eyeline. Trees. Shadows. Magic. It was too painful, she decided, to feel or think of anything else. She knew what she had to do; to follow a mission was a simple thing, a mindless thing.

'This is who I have always been,' she said. 'I am a Miseria.'

37

Thine Dear Temperance

Faerydae

Temperance trudged down to the dungeon below her kitchen and dropped Faerydae's unconscious body inside one of three empty cells. She rubbed her hands together, wondering if she had forgotten anything. Oh – yes. How silly. She locked the front bars with a little key from around her neck and nodded, pleased. The woman could hear her own laboured breathing as she let the key slide back against her bosom.

She pulled up a stool and eased down onto it, examining the cuts down her arms and stomach where she was still losing so much blood. Her one clear eye glowed green as she sat there like a puddle of wasted skin and bones. Slowly, just slowly, the cuts began closing themselves up, knitting themselves back together like a quilt; an invisible hand pulled the needle and thread. Her broken rib hinged itself back onto the rest of the cage, and her damaged skull weeded out the remaining glass shards.

She quickly grew weary from such magic and let her shoulders slump. Her left eye was too far gone, it could not be saved.

Temperance glanced down at Faerydae again, so small, lying all crumpled up on the cell floor in a heap. *What was she, about thirteen now?* Temperance noticed the wounds in the girl's hands and legs. Temperance cringed at herself before weaving a little more magic for the child too. It had to be done.

When she was finished, she said, 'I hate you, Faerydae Nóvalie.'

And she continued waiting on the stool, holding her hands together, for the next hour or so, until her curse wore off of young Faerydae.

In the girl's pocket, little did the woman know, Lume was urging himself to remain quiet and not obliterate the woman right there were she sat. For she would meet her end soon enough.

When Faerydae eventually came to sit up, she moved like a resurrected corpse, stiff and slow

She observed what surrounded her now, the three heavy walls of wet slate and a wall of rusty narrow bars at the front, enclosing her inside like an animal. It smelt of disease in there, and the cold stone ground was so hard. A light lingered on the other side of the bars that, as Faerydae crawled closer towards it, she saw was a lantern held by Temperance. The woman placed the lantern beside her bare feet.

Faerydae wiped her runny nose and noticed that her hands were clean, healed over and only scarred now. Had Lume healed her? No. He wouldn't have risked it. She could sense him sitting silent and safe inside of her pocket. Temperance had not yet uncovered his beauteousness nor claimed him for herself.

Faerydae curled her fingers around the bars and looked out at Temperance. The woman had lost all of her wolf-like features now. She was fully human. Her body was short and squat, yet powerful, possibly due to the way she held herself. Broad shoulders made her capable. She wore a tattered cloak with layers of raggedly brown and navy gowns underneath, held together by an old rope. Her bare feet were covered in dirt, so too were the huge bunions near her toes, and underneath her overgrown nails.

'Do you know who I am?' Temperance asked. She gritted her teeth.

'Should I?' Faerydae replied. 'You are not just a murderous wood dweller who wants to sell me to the king?'

'If only.'

Temperance laughed, a genuine state of bemusement overcoming her. She pulled out a cigar and lit it.

'Euphraxia,' Temperance started, then puffed out a drag of smoke as Faerydae's expression of anger fell away. 'Euphraxia Nóvalie, she is my little sister.'

Faerydae felt weak at the sound of her mama's name, paused. 'You're lying.'

'Am I? *Why* would I lie though, Faerydae Nóvalie?'

'I don't know. Because you're insane.'

'Okay,' Temperance leaned forward. 'How about this one: I stole your heart.'

Faerydae sunk down to the ground, still holding the cell bars for support. 'That is *impossible...* Eggnorphixeus said... A woman of the woods–'

The lady chuckled. 'That is me, *some* of the time. I am a shapeshifter. A daemon, little niece.'

A constant dripping of water became apparent in Faerydae's ears. The cell was damp. She wondered if she was going to die down there.

'You're lying,' Faerydae repeated. 'There is no way I could have just bumped into you, of all the people in the woods – of all the *creatures.*'

'Oh, it was no coincidence,' Temperance said. 'I have been watching you for years.' She took another long drag from her cigar and breathed it out after a moment.

'Nelix Causer?' she said next. 'Heard of her? Your grandmother. A whore with big tits and a knack for seduction. No?'

'No.'

'Well,' the woman sighed. 'You need to get to know your family better, Miss Nóvalie. Your grandfather, Bremmer, he was a decent enough man before he met Nelix. I was their first child, see. But I was born out of wedlock. And, can you believe, *I* was the one cursed for their infidelity.' She shook her head. 'My parents tried to drown me the day I was born, you know.' She curled her top lip. 'They left me to die, not knowing of course that a dagger through the chest was the only way to kill a daemon. Ironic, isn't it, Miss Faerydae? I can only die by a dagger through the heart, and you were born without even the chance to protect your own heart... So many *coincidences*, as you say.'

'Yes, coincidences,' Faerydae mumbled. 'Is that why I am the way I am, my heart surviving outside of me? Am I a daemon too?'

'You, my dear,' Temperance whispered. 'Are a monster of my own creation... *The Curse of Vile Luck...*' She grinned. 'It killed your stupid father; it got rid of your grandparents. Yes, it made you a daemon. In the end though, everything winds back to your dear, perfect mother. But she is not so perfect anymore, is she?'

'You did it all?' Faerydae had never considered that one source had been the culprit behind all of her family's tragedies. 'You killed my father... My grandparents.' Faerydae felt her eyes becoming hot. She felt so small in the dark dripping cell.

'Of course,' Temperance said. 'Your mother was the daughter Nelix and Bremmer had always wanted, after I was disposed of and left to die. I cursed your mother though, dear, an important distinction; I did not curse you. Don't give yourself that much credit. You were merely a pawn, little niece.'

They were silent for some time, letting everything sink in possibly.

Then Temperance started again. 'It was my very first curse, you know, the one I put on your mother. It was a darn good curse at that. Magic likes forgotten things, forgotten people, and unspeakable emotions like jealousy. That curse was tricky and interesting.'

She started to stutter incoherently, much like she had done with Morgoa. Wandering around inside her own head, trying to understand all of her emotions by herself. It must have been a scary place: her mind.

'I... I don't know what it is,' Temperance forced the words, on the verge of snatching at the answers but finding them still just too far out of reach. 'I don't know *why*. But I need you, Faerydae. I need you to perish for me. I need to see you cry, little girl. Because there are pieces of me, inside my soul, that hurt whenever I breath. I see you and I smile. I think of how much you can suffer for me. And it makes me feel better for a little while.'

Faerydae felt the tears fall down her cheeks, but now did not feel sad enough to be producing them. Not sad at all. This was a different kind of crying. She considered that she was terribly afraid. She must have been, afraid of what was to come next possibly.

Temperance was crying as well now. But she was smiling too. It messed with Faerydae's aching head as she reflected upon the origins of her existence, how she had been sewn together by evil.

Here she and Temperance sat. Where they were always going to end up, she supposed.

Faerydae thought briefly about Alalia too, missing her courage, then stared out through the bars at her auntie. *This is my auntie*, she thought. *We are all family, here in these woods.*

'Do you hate being so full of dark magic, Auntie?'

'Magic is not dark or light,' Temperance replied without much interest. 'Magic is just an idea. Look inside yourself and it'll be there, in those emotions that you try to hide, those hidden qualities that you don't like about yourself. It's there.'

'So,' Faerydae mumbled. 'If ever there was a person who was evil to the entire world, but kind deep, deep down, the magic would live within the goodness?'

Temperance didn't really know if it was possible for magic to live in the good parts of a person. Temperance did not know herself that well. She did not *like* herself enough to get to know, and she did not like anybody else, for that matter. The world had cast her aside.

'Is my heart in this house?' Faerydae asked next.

The daemon teetered her fingertips together. 'Listen closely to the walls.'

Faerydae looked up at the ceiling of the dungeon. There was a faint beating if she turned her mind to finding it. Her heart called to her with a song of solace. And in that very tune, Faerydae understood that everything Temperance had said was the truth.

'You are pure evil,' Faerydae spoke. 'You are a murderer. But you kept my heart safe for all of these years that have passed. Why would you do that?... Dear Auntie, did you sing to it? Did you *sing* to my heart at night?'

'One does not sing to something they do not care for,' she spat. 'Singing is... well, only angels sing, I suppose.'

'ANGELS!' Faerydae burst out laughing.

'Stop that,' Temperance ordered.

Faerydae twirled around her cell, singing: *Angels! Angels! Faerydae's an angel!*

Temperance suddenly charged at the bars of the cell, growling, and Faerydae squealed in fright, crashing down to her knees. She scurried away to the far side of the cell. Temperance displayed her sharp teeth and paced before the bars, tapping each of them with her fingernail.

'You are to be my servant. You will do what I ask of you. You will grow here in these awful woods until you forget who you once were. You will not smile; you will be miserable. That is your story. That is my story too. That is how it will all end.'

Temperance returned to standing still beside the stool and lantern. She waggled her finger at the two objects until they packed themselves away in the shelving behind her, beneath the uneven rock stairs. The lantern blew itself out too. Faerydae watched as Temperance went up the stairs and closed the door behind her. The sound of a heavy crank sealed the girl in the eternal solitude of darkness.

38

Faerydae had a nightmare that lonely first night, about the devil. There were several people in her dream, but the devil was portrayed by one person she had not expected it to be. Temperance stood in a nest of flames, grinning and laughing in that sad way of hers. Alalia was there too, standing like a silent corn stalk at midnight, angelic in the dreamscape. A looming darkness was creeping through and around all of them like a fog.

Lume was in her hands – they must have been *her* hands, but they were on fire. She, herself, was encircled in an entire ball of orange flames, with a curling forked tail looping around the air behind her. Her burning feet were hairy and clawed, and she could feel the presence of the long horns in her forehead.

The devil. She was the devil.

'*We have ended up in hell,*' Lume sighed. '*But that does not mean all is doomed. Those who are gathered here mark your enemies, Flea. You are an enemy to yourself. But a daemon is not inherently bad; it is only a word, Flea. A devil does not have to reside in Hell. And a daemon does not have to feel cursed. There is such a fine line between good and bad.*'

Alalia started floating in Faerydae's peripheral vision. She was holding onto something within her hands. Faerydae's heart. The organ sat inside a jar like a little creature, beating placidly.

'*You can't let her have your heart, Flea,*' Lume said. '*Now that you know what you are. You have to hide it. Nobody can ever hold it again.*'

'Alalia would not hurt me.'

'*Angels don't have to reside in heaven either, Faerydae. A halo. Horns. Nothing is ever what it seem*s.'

'Am I going to die here, Lume?' Faerydae asked, 'here' being either the hellish prison of her dream, or the real one she remained in indefinitely.

'*You only need to worry about one thing now: escape. You have to escape this place and steal back your heart. There are bigger things at work in the outside world that you will need to tend to soon enough.*'

Faerydae stared at the triangle of people around her. And then the entire dreamworld began burning to the ground in a bright inferno. None of them moved from where they stood, and none of them burned with it.

39

A week passed. Faerydae's black hair had grown so long in that time that she'd started to trip over it when she mopped the floorboards of Temperance's house clean. She used the the blunt prongs of the gardening fork to make it shoulder length once more.

On the first day, Temperance had made the girl a set of clothes out of old rags sewn together and a coat made from a hessian sack. She wanted Faerydae to feel owned. But the week had been a mundane one, and Faerydae remained ignorant to most of the mind games Temperance played in her own power struggle.

At the morning crow-call and at the dusk-time bell, Temperance and Faerydae would eat their meals together at the dining table, both at separate ends. They rarely spoke. Sometimes Temperance remarked about the laborious work from the day and the continuation of the never-ending harvest. Faerydae would never do her jobs well enough, and Temperance would make sure to say it. 'Oh Ferrihead, don't make me punish you. Don't force my hand, sweet girl.' And Faerydae would say, 'I'm sorry, Auntie. Everything is just so new.'

Every night, Faerydae crept out from where she slept, either down in the dungeons or on the lounge room floor if it was too cold to breathe down there, and she played around with Temperance's potion ingredients or the cauldron above the firepit. Lume warned her off of such things, among other blasphemous remarks about their predicament, but Faerydae could not shun her own dark curiosity. She recited phrases that Temperance used for enchantments. Though Faerydae could not yet grasp how to cast spells, levitate, transform, heal, or anything of that nature that could assist her in any way, she considered that her potions might have their desired effect. She made a sleeping potion and fed it to herself one night, but it was hard to tell if it worked. Lume assured her it had not.

Whenever the girl attempted to brighten the sour gem's mood with plans of escape, he shut her imaginations down without much effort – she was hopeless enough without his assistance. This was curious to Faerydae. Lume believed that all would be well in its own good time, in its own strange way. But she had never thought him a patient thing. Faerydae struggled to understand his varying viewpoints, and could only try to accept her new way of existence, playing the part of a pitiless slave to her deranged Auntie.

Another two weeks came and went before Faerydae suddenly realised something as she was working in the field on an unusually sunny day, free from rain for the first time. Her birthday had passed. As she recalled it, though never as well as one should, it arrived every year, midwinter. *And it surely was that time again.* At some point, when she was lost in the woods possibly, it had been her fourteenth birthday. *Fourteen years,* she reminisced, pushing her straw hat up off her brow.

'*Each year has only brought you more and more good fortune, Flea,*' Lume teased. '*It frankly amazes me how adept you are at troublemaking…*' His voice trailed off into the background as Faerydae placed fourteen corn kernels on the ground and then blew them away, letting them plod into a messy bunch of golden boulders. Sand sprayed up into Faerydae's eyes and nose, making her cough. She sputtered and stood up straight. Her head poked out from the thick of corn stems and she peered around.

The cur-sed hoard of pumpkin-headed scarecrows greeted her, literally, surrounding her quite completely in the field. There were so many that it was absolutely petrifying to even consider trying to escape this place, but Faerydae was not afraid of the creatures anymore. True, they were under the command of Auntie Temperance, which meant that they could 'turn evil' with the snap of her fingers, but they were rarely needed for such things. Mostly, they did what scarecrows do best, and kept the birds away – they kept Faerydae company too. Faerydae had had many conversations with the scarecrow people over the past weeks. Their stories were quite fascinating if one had the patience to listen. Though they did often forget certain parts, being only vegetables after all, the fact that they could talk and move was already a miracle, so to tell stories was only a bonus.

Some of them recalled their past lives and reminisced about the days before having met their doom at the house on the hill. Their stories were often tainted by a fake happiness though, due to their Loyalty Bond. *Oh, those were good days,* they would say, *but* these *days, in the field with the madame, these are the best days.* In reality, each of their imprisonments had been uniquely horrifying and nightmarish. Temperance would often poison them first, skin them, then bury their bodies in the Binding Cemetery, to let her Living Loyalty curse work its magic. After assembling a new scarecrow, Temperance would wrap the coat of skin around them, and the thing would come to life.

Every scarecrow had been warned off of talking to Faerydae. But they somehow could not help themselves. She was so strange and new to them.

Faerydae told the scarecrows that she'd had no life at all before arriving there, that she had been lost and confused forever, and couldn't remember much of her past now. The scarecrows liked the young girl despite themselves, but there was always a separation that remained – them being so dreadfully cursed things and Faerydae's job… *being what it was*: she was often ordered to cull off the oldest of the vegetable people. It was hard; they were like friends to her, just like the voice in her head that told her one day she would be able to escape. *Lume.* She knew the scarecrows would betray her simply if asked to though, and that was the difference between her two types of friends.

Faerydae walked down the row of corn stalks with a huge basket made of woven reeds. Her bare feet dug into the soil, it was cool, slightly damp and smelt sweet. She flicked her black hair behind her ears and went along plonking an unending number of corn cobs into her basket, singing a tune of her own creation.

'Oh, the cornfield glows,
As the cold wind blows,
And the breaths of time pass bye.
My Auntie knows of the horror she bestows.
The woods that wind and wind.'

'No singing, girl. The madame will hear you.'

Faerydae faltered in her rhythm. She turned. It was Morgoa, the oldest of all the scarepeople, and possibly Temperance's favourite, if she cared at all for any of them.

'And why should that stop me, Morgoa? After all, I'll have you know that I have recently turned fourteen. I will be celebrating the event today; it's as good a day as any.'

'Don't talk to it!' Lume hissed at Faerydae, despising the pumpkin creatures considerably more than most other creatures they had come across in the woods.

'Birthday?' Morgoa nodded her giant head. 'Yes. The passing of time. The growing of age towards a restful death. I remember *birthdays*.'

Faerydae smiled, noticing the morbid rot infiltrating Morgoa's soft body. Morgoa was so old that Faerydae dreaded the impending necessity for her culling. But Temperance never gave the order for some reason, for some sentimental reason. Perhaps it was because Morgoa was the first wandering stranger that had ever knocked on Temperance's door, and the first person that she had ever murdered for doing so.

'Happy breathday, sweet child,' said the old scarecrow.

'Breathday?' Faerydae asked. 'Yes. My *breathday*. The day I first breathed. I do wonder whether there is ever a rhyme or reason to life and death.'

As Faerydae moved through the field, the rest of the scarepeople blessed her with breathday wishes. She thanked them all as she harvested the corn at their dangling straw feet. As peaceful as the day seemed so far, the girl knew she had no time to dawdle. She had been told to complete the entire righthand side of the field by midday.

The golden corn flew into her basket as she sang her song, and the scarecrows helped her by picking at the cobs around them and tossing them her way.

There was no rain at all today, not even a fine mist, which Temperance sometimes called *froalla*. The ocean rumbled in the great beyond, a place over the hill and below the cliff where Faerydae had never wandered to.

When she reached the farthest corner of the field, on top of the hill, a mild breeze ruffled Faerydae's hair as she collected the last corn cobs. The air reminded Faerydae of another time. *Some* other time. Back when she did not know of the magic all around her.

Faerydae looked in at the dark woods. She knew she had come from within hem, from another world, but could not really remember the journey itself. There were numerous black holes forming inside her mind. Moments vanished and forgotten about. She reminisced a lot about her past, trying to recall what it had been like. But Temperance was slowly stealing it all away from her.

'*Pssst! Faerydae!*'

Faerydae flinched slightly. A cob fell from her basket and into the dirt at her feet. Water droplets that were trapped inside the cob's cocoon leaves splashed up onto her beige leggings and colourful patchwork coat that she was sure had swatches of human skin in some parts. She shivered. Her heart was pounding – she could hear it crying from inside the house, throwing a tantrum as it often did when Faerydae got a little fright. Faerydae had learnt that her heart reacted to many things, just as another whole human would. It could scream and cry and even hum songs.

Faerydae turned to look at a scarecrow sitting lifeless beside her. This was a part of the pasture that Faerydae rarely ever tended to, so the motionless scarecrow was terribly neglected and mouldy. It had no name that she knew of. The pumpkin man was wearing a thick trench coat and top hat, which Faerydae stroked with her fingertips. The creature remained silent. It appeared unaffected by Temperance's curse. Faerydae turned back to her basket.

'*Psst,* you there.'

Faerydae glared back at the lonesome scarecrow and watched its head. She did not break eye contact until she saw it move just slightly.

'You!' Faerydae pointed. 'You *are* alive.'

The scarecrow looked side to side. 'Yes, I live, Faerydae–'

'It is *master* to you, scarecrow.'

He bowed his head. 'Yes, yes, of course. My apologies.'

'*Brute,*' Lume mumbled.

Faerydae examined the stammering scarecrow who appeared intact apart from the deterioration caused by the elements way up here. 'I've not spoken to you before, good scarecrow. What is your name?'

'Alberick,' it said. 'My name was Alberick when I was alive.'

'Well,' Faerydae said. 'Alberick. What is it you want to talk about? I am always here to serve the good watchers of this field.'

'I am not a watcher.'

Faerydae frowned. 'No?'

'No.' He sighed. 'The curse is powerful, but it cannot control me. I have lived so far from the cemetery for so long… *too* long. You do not need to serve me, young lady. I know how much you too have suffered at the hand of Temperance.'

Faerydae smiled lightly and attempted to chuckle. 'I have not suffered as much as you think.'

'*Shut up, Flea,*' Lume screeched from his pocket. '*Stop encouraging it.*'

Faerydae grumbled before standing silent.

'You have suffered,' Alberick went on. 'More than you remember. Your omen cares for you, so I am surprised that he has not reminded you of your past.'

'My omen?' Faerydae frowned. 'You mean Lume? You can hear him?'

'Yes.'

Lume laughed. '*Congratulations, Mister Pumpkin Man, you can hear me. And you have already offended me.*'

'It isn't hard,' Faerydae muttered.

'*I have not reminded Faerydae of that which is best forgotten,*' Lume finished.

Faerydae stepped forwards, leaning into the pumpkin man. 'Yeah, so why should I listen to you instead? You could be a spy. One of *hers*.'

'I only long to go home,' Alberick said. 'You wish for home, and I wish for it as well. I have dreams Faerydae, is that normal? I imagine how wonderful it would be to return to Dainmerry. Before I was lost, it was my home. I had a family. Before I found myself here, owned by a daemon. Dainmerry sits amongst the shadows of the Winding Wood, the only true township within this forsaken land.'

'You want to return to a town of shadows?' Faerydae asked.

'*Crazy*,' Lume agreed. '*Off his nut. Or, in this case, off his pumpkin.*'

'Surely you remember something other than being lost and forgotten?' Alberick asked the girl.

Faerydae frowned. 'That is a funny thing to say, Scarecrow. I suppose… I just can't remember.'

Alberick waved a hand. 'You are more cursed than me.'

Faerydae found herself irritated that she could not recount main themes from her childhood in order to throw them in the scarecrow's face. There were pieces, *fragments*. She remembered the old ship. She remembered the tiny puddle-troll, that flat-headed fiend. She remembered finding Lume.

'Why would I bother leaving the woods, Alberick?' she asked, then extended the question to all. 'Lume?'

Lume was silent.

'I have been here for a long time,' Alberick spoke, leaning in and whispering. He held Faerydae's shoulder, encircled her hand, gesturing to the sliced-up moon-shaped scars upon her palms. 'I was watching closely, the day you came here with the wolf. Don't you remember Faerydae? You were not alone.'

'I wasn't?' she asked. 'No… I wasn't. Of course I wasn't. There was a horse. And. And another girl was with me.' She winced. 'We had come into the woods looking for my heart. But we got lost. We killed the wizard. Met two giant worms. We crossed paths with a wolf.'

Alberick nodded, drawing a stick figure in the dirt with his long wheat finger. First, he drew Faerydae, then the horse, then the other girl with short curls.

'What was her name?' Faerydae asked him. 'What *was* it?' She strained her mind, trying to pull the answer from a lake of thoughts. 'Alalia!' It suddenly projected out of her stomach like vomit.

'Alalia,' Alberick agreed. 'Yes, that was the girl's name. She was your friend Faerydae.'

'Alalia,' Lume added to the conversation. *'She was the one who led you into this mess.'*

Faerydae crouched down and gently hovered her hand over the stick figure illustration of Alalia, as if she might be able to grasp something, remember something more.

'I cannot believe I had forgotten you, Alalia,' Faerydae spoke. 'It would be selfish to drag her back into my life now. She escaped me. She was lucky.'

The scarecrow patted her back. 'There is hope in love though, Faerydae. Love can be found again. If you find home, you can find love.'

'You are trying to inspire me to do something,' Faerydae said as she rose to standing again. 'Do you have a plan?'

'There is no plan,' Alberick admitted. 'I only have hope. I just do not know if you have the guts for it.'

'For what?'

'Killing her, of course,' Alberick said. 'Temperance. For *us*. Getting rid of the daemon will save us both. It is the only way to go home.'

Faerydae stared at Alberick as the morose words fell from his pumpkin lips. 'Kill my own auntie?'

She imagined driving a knife into Temperance's chest, into her black heart, and leaving her to rot in the isolation of a rainy haze. Such a fate would be fitting, considering how much pain Temperance Nóvalie had caused Faerydae in her lifetime.

'You can grant me a safe passage out of the crop?' Faerydae asked softly. 'If I kill her, you can get me out of the field even while the curse bids you to do otherwise?'

'My will is stronger than the other scarecrows. I am a younger pumpkin. I promise that your passage shall be safe.'

Faerydae had no time to consider it, before the voice of Temperance burst into the air seemingly right behind her.

'Ferrihead! Finish up with that corn!'

Faerydae flinched and twirled around in a swooping leap. Temperance hovered way back down in the cottage doorway, watching Faerydae closely with her one green eye. Faerydae clutched her chest, hearing her heart racing like a rabbit's from inside the upstairs study of the cottage.

'You must go,' Alberick said.

Faerydae picked up her basket of corn and immediately started back for the house, stumbling down the crackling vegetation covering the hill. Alberick began to moan and wail behind her, stuck where he was, bound tightly around his post.

'I may watch these hills forever,' he sang. 'I will watch this field until my head falls off and I am as forgotten as this whole horrible place. Filled with that endless hiding darkness.'

Faerydae glanced back at the scarecrow.

'Don't listen to him, Flea,' Lume said. *'You have enough to worry yourself with other than that creature's fate.'*

40

Faerydae scrubbed the kitchen floorboards for the rest of the afternoon. The soapy water turned brown as the wooden boards began to shine. The thick brush hypnotised Faerydae as it went back and forth across the floor.

Sunlight that shone through the frosty kitchen windows was growing less and less as the dark smog of eve crept into the household.

'*For the last time,*' Lume grumbled. '*It was for your own good. I thought it was better for you to forget about Alalia.*'

Faerydae dropped the brush back into her bucket. 'I don't believe you.'

She rose to her feet and went to the kitchen bench, pulling a chopping board her way and rolling over a warty pumpkin.

'*I do not really care if you believe me,*' Lume replied. '*I simply do what needs to be done.*'

'You're selfish,' Faerydae mumbled as she drew forth a huge shimmering cleaver. 'I deserved to know what I had forgotten. It was a curse. I thought you were my friend.'

Faerydae diced the pumpkin into chunks and boiled it down to a pulp by which time it was utter blackness outside the kitchen window. The soup bubbled thickly, making a glurping sound intermittently as it simmered. The pumpkin's ripe age and intelligence injected a sweet nutty flavour to the soup. Faerydae wondered if dreams tasted like that too. She sprinkled some wildflowers and rock salt on top.

Her ears soon pricked at the sound of her Auntie's heavy footfalls creeping down the stairs.

'Is supper ready, girl?' Temperance called, moving into the kitchen and taking a thumping seat at the table. She rubbed her shrouded blind eye and Faerydae made sure not to stare at the disfigured socket.

'Yes, here we are, Auntie,' Faerydae chirped. 'Fresh pumpkin soup. Made from *Orion*. The poor creature was past it.'

Faerydae balanced two chunky ceramic bowls of soup and a loaf of buttered sourdough over to the table on her forearms. She liked to think she was a skilled servant as she bowed and placed one bowl before her Auntie. Temperance grimaced, unconvinced. All was silent as they sat together once again. There was a faint dappling of rain on the foggy windows, but it was not loud enough to lighten the tension in the room. Faerydae knew the clear skies would not last long. Temperance started on her soup before Faerydae slurped hers up insatiably too, dipping her bread until it was a piece of soggy dough.

'You finished all your chores today?' Temperance asked and Faerydae nodded, wiping her chin.

'Yes, Auntie. All.'

Temperance peered down at the kitchen floorboards and inhaled a big dripping spoonful of pumpkin brains. She raised an eyebrow.

'The floor sparkles, Ferrihead,' she agreed. 'But you took longer in the field than necessary. There will be punishment for that, tardy girl. I have grave concerns for you, such a daydreamer.'

'Yes,' Faerydae said with a sigh. 'That sounds like something Mama would say. You two are very alike in many ways… You know, it has just come to my attention that my fourteenth birthday has recently passed.'

'So?' Temperance leaned back in her chair. 'Why would you want to remember such a horrible day?'

Faerydae looked through her, eyes glazed. 'It distracted me, that's all,' she spat.

Temperance nodded. 'Oh, come here, poor Ferrihead; you are so easily distracted. Come to your auntie.'

Faerydae waited a moment before standing rigidly. She strutted around the table and hovered beside Temperance's chair, feeling the presence of the woman's breath, hearing the sound of her throat swallowing more soup. She eased down onto Temperance's plump lap, holding her body tensely. Temperance stroked Faerydae's hair, just like Euphraxia had used to do, in the same careless manner. Temperance's nails caught on numerous knots and entangled grass seeds that she tugged at harshly to pull free. Faerydae cringed.

'We do not celebrate breathdays, Ferrihead,' Temperance whispered. 'I do not celebrate mine and nobody else should celebrate theirs. Being born is no testament to you.'

Faerydae did not say anything as her auntie's eye glared into hers, deeply but without much emotion. Temperance crooked her finger, gesturing Faerydae in closer. Faerydae leant slowly into her Auntie's grip before the woman planted a wet kiss on her cheek. It was a kiss that communicated so much more than words ever could: do as I say, and I shall love you. Temperance did not let go, burning the mark into Faerydae's cheek. *Fear me, my pet. I own your life; I can do what I want with it. I can chuck you away or ruin you or burn you or hold you. I can even* care *for you If I want, but I can also kill you – remember that. I hope you haven't forgotten all that.*

Faerydae pulled away after too long. She stumbled to her feet and retreated back to her seat uneasily, disturbed enough to cry. She touched her cheek.

'I was thinking,' the girl said suddenly. 'We should take a trip into the woods. Tonight. To find some basil sprigs together. I know you need more for your potion. It might be… good to do.'

'Why, Ferrihead?' Temperance laughed. 'I do not wish for your company on a foraging trip. And I would never go into the woods at night when I have a choice.'

Faerydae nodded.

They kept eating in silence.

Moments later, Faerydae leapt up to standing and took her empty, licked-clean bowl back to the bench.

'I think the soup needs rosemary,' she said. 'Would you like another bowl, Auntie? – I'll go get some.'

Temperance grumbled. 'I–'

Faerydae raced outside towards the bushes beneath the windowsill before Temperance could stop her, closing the front door behind herself. She leant down into a ball beside the hedged rosemary bushes, out of sight from the window, and cried a little.

'Alberick was right,' she whimpered to Lume. 'I haven't got the guts for it.'

Lume sighed. '*Oh, Flea. You have no idea what is inside of you.*'

Faerydae heard a distant moaning and immediately assumed that it was Alberick, still weeping in the field. She looked up and tried to spy him through the dark. His silhouette was fogged over by thin raindrops, but she believed she could just make him out, unmoving and distant. He was silent. The sound was coming from above her.

Faerydae stood and looked up at the study's dim window that sat slightly ajar, letting in the eerie night wind and releasing a fragile glow of light. It was her heart who was wailing. It was sad to be locked away from her. It wanted freedom. *Faerydae* wanted freedom.

'But I don't *want* to kill her,' Faerydae said, both to Lume and to her heart, which both seemed like akin forces to her now. 'I don't want to be a murderer just like her. I will end up the same if I do. I will end up empty, so full of magic that I need to feed off of other's suffering.'

'*You already are a murderer though,*' Lume replied. '*You killed the wizard, didn't you? You have killed scarecrows; they were people too. Murder is the only way to survive in these woods. Don't you remember, the wizard told you that? It's you or her.*'

Before Faerydae could organise her mind, the front door came crashing back open. Temperance loomed inside, looking down on Faerydae with a snarl. She glanced at the rosemary bush, still imagining that the girl might have truly been gathering sprigs to improve the soup, but there was nothing in Faerydae's hands.

'What are you doing out here?' Temperance asked. 'What are you up to?'

Faerydae breathed deeply. She waited, not replying. She watched her auntie so closely, looking her straight in the eye. It seemed that Temperance realised what horrifying thoughts were rushing through the girl's mind in that moment, and the tension instantaneously heightened between their bodies. Up above, the heart was still wailing gently, and Temperance finally noticed it. She looked up to the open window just as the heart began to scream, seemingly at her, for daring to look up. It wailed, then screamed louder still, attempting to break its glass jar apart by sheer will. Faerydae could not ignore it anymore.

Her eyes darkened, became set and sure. Something became clear to her then. She was ready to set her heart – herself – free.

Tick. Tick. Two seconds, two heartbeats, passed with so much trepidation that it felt like hours.

Faerydae lunged at Temperance, pummelling the old lady to the ground, not fully invested in whatever she had planned to do. Temperance growled as Faerydae grappled to keep her auntie's hands under control, failing miserably. The woman slapped Faerydae across the head so that she went tumbling the other way. Faerydae scuttled quickly to her feet and retreated inside the cottage.

She ran into the kitchen where the leftover pumpkin soup was still boiling upon the stove. Faerydae gasped in fuelled breaths as Temperance followed her through the doorway into the kitchen in a sudden frenzy. With the old lady nearly upon her, Faerydae gripped the handles of the huge pot of soup and hurled it at her auntie's head. The soup steamed its way through the air and splashed over Temperance's thin hair, her neck and face, and onto the floor. The woman screamed, skidding across the wet floor, and seemed to melt underneath the orange goo. Bubbles from the soup made it look as if Temperance's skin was bursting at the seams.

Faerydae grabbed a hold of the pumpkin cleaver, wedged within the slimy chopping block. *Could she bear it though?* Faerydae couldn't even hold the cleaver without trembling. *Ain't got the guts for it, Ferrihead! Ain't got the talent!* It didn't matter if she had the guts though, because the cleaver was stuck in the block of wood with the tenacity of glue. Faerydae jiggled it back and forth while her Auntie stumbled closer, her face a sticky film. Temperance's good eye was burned to a red blister by veggie juice. She reached unknowingly and started to claw at Faerydae's chest and throat.

'Little bitch! Little whore!' Temperance howled. 'You horrible child! Don't you know I *own* you!'

Faerydae held her off as best she could manage. The cleaver wobbled around but did not come loose as the woman started punching and scratching blindly. Faerydae moaned through the attacks. She ducked and then gave Temperance an almighty shove that forced them both to the soup-covered floor. A rattling sound echoed through their groans; the clamouring of the cleaver dislodging and falling, narrowly missing Faerydae's head. She gulped.

Meanwhile, Temperance's nails were growing into long black hooks. Her face was becoming furry and orange, and long fangs were emerging from under her lips. She rammed her claws into Faerydae's stomach, drawing blood, twisting her grip around. She pinned Faerydae on the ground, enclosing her body in a cage of strong limbs. Faerydae reached for the slippery handle of the cleaver as Temperance flailed and growled wildly. Savage lines formed down Faerydae's face; her Auntie's claws left five streaks like bloody tears. The girl screamed and her heart screamed back at her.

'Stop!' Faerydae cried. 'Please, stop!'

Temperance was going to kill her with her bare hands. She would make it slow; she would make it count.

'Please, Auntie!' Faerydae continued. 'Don't!'

Her auntie squeezed Faerydae's windpipe shut, and Faerydae looked up at her, begging her not to force her into doing what had to be done. Temperance was too far gone though to see into Faerydae's pleading eyes. Rage had consumed her body; magic had lit her figure up in a flaming green haze. The old woman was already dead inside. Nothing could bring her back from that brink, not even the gift of a fragile kind of love.

Lume... Faerydae pleaded in her mind. *Lume, I can't do it, you have to help me... please. I can't... won't.*

He crackled into life, struggling with himself, only saying one regrettable phrase. *'You need to do this, Flea.'*

Faerydae felt her steady grip on the cleaver's handle; she'd been holding onto it for a while now. The blade shimmered, clean, except for a few chunks of pumpkin goo. Faerydae's lonely heart sang and Alberick, although unseen, was listening for his call to action. The other scarecrows were already rising.

Faerydae hacked the cleaver deep into Temperance's chest, where there was only blackness feeding life into her heart.

At the sensation of the wound, the look in Temperance's eye changed to relief. She crumpled slowly to the floor, like a closing flower, and Faerydae scurried out from under her falling mass. Temperance gasped in and out, a raspy sound coming from within her gargling throat. The cleaver was too deep for healing now; the damage could not be undone by any realm of magic.

Faerydae lifted her auntie's head into her lap and stroked the daemon's tired old features.

'I feel light,' Temperance said, becoming timid as the cut in her chest started to bleed profusely. 'I feel like I am floating. I'm emptying out; everything is leaving me.'

Tears streamed down Faerydae's blood-covered face. 'I know Auntie. It's okay. It's okay. It will a be over soon.'

'Yes, I think so.' A sentimental pause. 'You are a terrifying girl, Faerydae. Such a *devious* girl. You scare me to death.'

The woman's head flopped sideways against Faerydae's bleeding legs. Faerydae could not bring herself to hug her Auntie then, as she died in her embrace, but she held her for a little while longer at least.

As the last breath fell from the deamon's lips, the house that she had ruled wept in agony for her. The green light surrounding Temperance's body glowed brighter and wickeder as it roared into waves that rippled like a serpent. The scarecrows outside moaned. The wind howled. It was a symphony of anguish.

The fire beneath the cauldron, which Faerydae had lit only half an hour ago, also wailed and sighed at the death of the madame. It stretched into ghoulish flames that began to dive out of the pit and reach for Faerydae. Faerydae dropped Temperance's body and rolled to the side. She jumped behind the separating kitchen wall to avoid the attacking flame hands. Fire coughed onto the ground surrounding Temperance. The fire then grabbed onto the floorboards and hemp rug in the loungeroom. Faerydae shrieked. Soon, the whole house would be alight.

Smoke quickly enveloped the air. Before the fire completely consumed Temperance's body, Faerydae grabbed the key around the old lady's neck and pulled it free. She stumbled out of the kitchen and hung onto the stairway rail ascending from the lounge room. She looked ahead to the smoke-filled landing above. Her little heart was calling out for her, a whimsical song. *Find me. Save me. Take me with you. Never let me go.*

The smoke filled the air so palpably. When Faerydae reached the second floor she collapsed, trying to catch her breath upon her haunches. She peered back down towards Temperance's body, could only see her legs from there, consumed by flames and sizzling. It smelt like burning flesh in the house.

The doorway to the study was ahead of Faerydae. She stood up groggily and fumbled with the key as she moved down the hall. She leant against the door and rattled the knob just to check that it was definitely locked. She slid the key into the little hole and there was a click as it unlocked the mechanism.

She kneed the door inwards. Smoke splashed inside with her. The room was lit in moonlight that sailed in through the open window. It smelt awful in there despite the fresh air clearing a path through the smoke. It was like old rot and cold leather. Threaded cotton and dried blood were strewn all over the place, and swatches of hessian patches lay in piles. There was a chair below the window, where Temperance sometimes used to sit and sew, and there was a desk with an old sewing wheel in the middle. At the very edge of that desk – below the window with the view of the marching scarecrows below – was Faerydae's long-lost heart. Waiting for her.

41

Her heart smiled by way of a warm rosy glow. It was pleased to see her, Faerydae could tell. The pink organ bobbled around in a glass jar filled with water. It was just sitting there, so simply. Swimming, naked and veiny, and beating away as it somehow kept her alive.

There was a label on top of the jar's lid, as if it might have been possible to mistake the heart for something else, it said: Friday's heart.

Friday? Faerydae's lip curled into a slight grin. Almost. Not quite.

'Hello there, my olde friend.' Faerydae picked the jar up, feeling its considerate weight. Smoke began to refill her nostrils again. She'd not even noticed that it had become so dense up there, climbing the stairs and entombing her in an ashy smog.

Her heart bobbled as she ran down the flaming staircase, gagging, eyes shut. Temperance was charred quite completely now, a black statue. Faerydae sprinted past her, through the flames and to the front door. Her feet were burned into hard shells as she ran, and she had not even a spare second to look back at her auntie one last time, before she left the house forever.

42

Scarecrows swarmed the front of the cottage. Faerydae emerged from the flames of the porch with her heart beating upon her bosom. She looked around frantically for Alberick. Many of the pumpkin creatures had caught on fire by now, and the flames had also taken to the cornfield with ravenous delight. There were no clouds brewing in the sky; the moon swirled like a milky pool above the rising smoke.

'Alberick!' Faerydae called out as the fiery pumpkins stomped towards her, moaning hungrily.

Their wispy hands reached out like demented corpses, surrounding her in a line of fiery vegetable bodies. The girl stumbled backwards, back towards the burning house that was crumbling under the sheer heat of the fire. Morgoa emerged at the front of the mass, her hands outstretched in desperation.

'You killed the madame, Faerydae!' she screamed. 'Murderer! Murderer!'

Faerydae watched helplessly as Morgoa's legs caught fire and disintegrated slowly out from under her as she walked.

'Alberick!' Faerydae screamed again.

Morgoa kept coming, the leader of the pack, the oldest of all the scarecrows. She reached for Faerydae whilst she became shorter and shorter. Faerydae curled up on the ground in a cocoon, holding her heart tight as the scarecrow pack swarmed in on her. Kill me, she thought. *I tried. At least, I tried. At least, the woods never became me.* Morgoa hissed. She stumbled closer. Alberick suddenly appeared behind the imposing wall of flames. He looked like a daemon rising from the pits of hell, a new shadowy monster for Faerydae to conquer. But he was no monster.

He smashed Morgoa's head into a thousand pieces, right in front of Faerydae's eyes. His long legs craned over the fire in an arachnid-like leap, dispersing the smoke for a moment. Lanky legs landed gently beside Faerydae, as if Alberick's body was a featherweight.

The scarecrow flailed the post that had once strung him up like a puppet; it was now just a blunt object that he used to smoosh pumpkin heads into paste. Vegetable brains spattered all over Faerydae, absentmindedly reminding her of when she had killed Eggnorphixeus.

'Quickly Faerydae, we must make for the woods!' Alberick boomed as he swatted one of the scarecrow's heads like a fly. Faerydae nodded.

They ran.

Through the flaming cornfield and into the searing heat of the fire: a traitorous scarecrow and murderous niece. Together, they felt unstoppable. They ran until they reached the end of the cornfield. The trees rose up in a wall of darkness. The scarecrow waited beside Faerydae as she teetered a foot between the verge of fire and shadow. Which was better? Faerydae looked back at her auntie's home, where her heart had been hidden away all this time, where her life, and her family's life, had been changed forever. Years from now, the cornfield would be only a field of grass, and Temperance's home would be covered in vines and sand from the faraway dunes, her body buried beneath time.

Faerydae turned and looked back into the darkness ahead. She grabbed a hold of Alberick's coarse wheaten hand.

'To better things,' she assured him with a hopeful grin. And together they stepped into that familiar hiding darkness cast by the tenacious Winding Woods.

43

The Wayward Meriel Tree

The sounds of the screaming scarecrows and the crumbling cottage quickly disappeared. Alberick and Faerydae, with her heart held tight, pushed on through the moonlit silence of night. Destruction was now behind them, but unknowable dangers lingered ahead. Faerydae knew this all too well. She stared into the water of her heart's glass jar, watching the little organ closely. It seemed so fragile; life was easy to lose.

Alberick stalked along beside her in his shadowy monstrous way. The cold in the air between them was so crisp that it was like a smell, and the moon above was so bright that it was almost like a sharp sound.

'I am finally free,' Alberick kept saying under his breath. 'Fourteen years I have been there on that hillside.'

Faerydae grimaced, in one instance feeling the sting of her wounds and the weakness in her stride. A deep breath kept her moving. The girl felt overcome. She knew the woods would not be kinder to her merely because she had struggled so much already. It frightened her to wonder how much more she could handle. You are strong, Faerydae thought, or perhaps Lume, or even her heart, was trying to convince her. You really are. You won't be afraid of the woods because you already know them.

'I can't believe I killed her…' Faerydae spoke. 'I drove a cleaver into her chest. *Me*.'

'It had to be done. And there was nobody else to do it, Faerydae.'

'*He's more intelligible than he looks*,' admitted Lume, before returning to contented silence.

Faerydae wondered what Alberick, a creature of mere stuffing and vegetable might be afraid of in here, if anything. His long legs floated along as if they walked with the gesture of the wind. He would have been freakish to anybody else, Faerydae, however, felt she had become accustomed to such frightful things. Though she'd seldom seen the scarecrows move about freely, she had imagined they would look just as dreamy as this.

Faerydae grunted and came to a sudden stop, putting her heart onto the dirt road. She leant down with a sudden feeling of nausea in her stomach. Her feet were swollen and charred and her body, whether it was still bleeding or had since stopped, was soaked in blood. Her face was ravaged. She needed to try to heal herself, like Temperance sometimes did.

'What is it?' Alberick asked her.

'I need lavender sprigs and daisy milk,' she groaned. 'How am I going to find what I need in this place, at midnight no less?'

She slumped in on herself, gripping her arms around her stomach. Alberick scratched his orange chin. What an inconvenience, he thought, to have problems of the living flesh in this moment. He reached up towards his brain and pushed his hand inside the black gap that was his mouth.

There was a moment of silence whilst he felt around in there, creating

a faint rattling, as if sifting through shelves. Faerydae frowned. Alberick drew his long arm out again, revealing a huge bunch of herbs and wildflowers in his hand. They popped out of his mouth like a plug. The huge bunch settled into a bulbous circle that Alberick offered to Faerydae with a bow.

'My secret,' he said and held a finger to his lips. 'They were my shield against Temperance. Their strong scent and regenerative properties helped prevent the curse from rotting my mind. I suppose they kept me *sane*. I no longer need them anymore; how fitting that they should be of use to you now.'

Faerydae took the bouquet from him and said, 'My hero. I guess I'd better try and make this potion work then, if I'm going to use something so precious. Where else is magic more present than on a murderous eve lost in a forgotten place? Magic is flowing everywhere in here.'

She knelt down and smooshed the daisies in her hand until they were a white paste. Once she'd smothered her wounds with the stinging white liquid, she rubbed lavender shoots over the top and they stung even more. She spoke some words like, 'heal thee, heal thee, and I swear I will serve thee,' giving the message to the darkness. Nothing happened for a while. Faerydae closed her eyes and started thinking about how good she would soon feel, about how, when she could walk again, she would battle her way out of the woods and kill anything that tried to stop her. The magic liked those thoughts; it felt tickled by the notion. It relished those such thoughts that nobody admitted they had. It liked to hide in them. The magic curled up inside Faerydae's mind and fulfilled her wish.

When she opened her eyes again, her potion had started to work. Faerydae watched the magic with incredulous wonderment. Her wounds stitched themselves together right before her eyes, and her burnt feet turned into calloused scars. Even the slashes across her face she could feel repairing and becoming the memory of a wound.

After the potion had absorbed, Faerydae rose to her new feet and grabbed the happy glowing heart from off of the ground. Alberick, who had not predicted the girl's potion to work with such obedience, stepped away as she stood tall before him.

'A daemon,' he uttered.

'Atta girl,' Lume's voice came. *'I knew you had it in you. The darkness, I mean.'*

'Let us get moving again, Alberick,' Faerydae mumbled.

After hours of guessing their way down whichever road they felt like, the pumpkin man stopped in his floating tracks. Faerydae stumbled into the faltered stride of his flimsy legs.

'This is it,' Alberick gasped.

'What is *it*?' Faerydae asked, looking around the barren road.

The scarecrow went over to a small path branching off of the main track they walked on. It was narrow, too small and windy for Faerydae to even fit.

'I came through here,' Alberick said distantly, not turning to look at her. 'This is where I lost my way, chasing after the rabbit I was hunting.'

He stared into the trees, seeing something in there that Faerydae could not.

'Alberick?' Faerydae said, watching him. 'It is so vastly overgrown down there–'

'I must leave you, Faerydae,' he cut in and Faerydae felt a sudden dread. 'This is *my* path; it will lead me back to the township I once called home.' He nodded, sure of that. 'Thank you, Master Faerydae, for your stoic courage this evening. You set me free, such a deed will not ever be forgotten.'

Faerydae looked down his new path, considering that everything was happening too fast and that too soon she would be all alone. The girl forced a smile for Alberick's sake as he kissed her hand.

'I'm glad you have found your path,' Faerydae mumbled. 'And I am not your master. I am simply your friend.'

'A friend,' he chuckled, turning to the overgrown trail and tipping his top hat. 'My home is waiting to be stumbled upon. I feel a whim of hope that I can find it, but that is all one needs, isn't it? You must find your way out of these shadows too, Faerydae. Be safe.'

'Yes…' Faerydae replied to his turned back. 'I'll try.'

Alberick moved down onto the other path with a shuffling of leaves, challenging the unwritten wood ahead. His lengthy limbs squeezed through the small opening of branches with strangeness, like he was fitting himself inside a tiny box. One hand remained behind, which he waved back and forth to say a final farewell. The girl waved too, though he would not have known it. And then he was gone.

'Be well, Good Alberick,' Faerydae whispered, wondering how long the creature might last the further away he got from Temperance's hold. She hoped he would have enough time to see those he had lost.

Just like that, she felt such an intense loneliness unlike anything she had ever felt before. But It did not frighten her. Alberick's departure was the final thread that loosened Temperance's steadfast hold on her. Everybody. *Everybody* was gone now – except Lume, of course. And yet this moment seemed to entail a sense of responsibility and independence only associated with adulthood.

'Well, little heart,' Faerydae said. 'I suppose I will have to look after you from now on. And you might look after me too. Back into the unknown.'

44

A peeking owl hooted at the Faerydae as she walked, the bird's giant eyes following her every step until she had long since passed it. Its eyes were green, just like Temperance's once were, and suddenly Faerydae felt sick again. Temperance's eyes had *once* been green. *What were they now?* Now, they were nothing; did not exist.

Faerydae knew that everything in this wood would be inquisitive of her.

As the silence became alive, and she continued ahead, Faerydae's heart beat faster and faster. The organ's light flickered on and off then dissipated and repeated that rhythm for some time. It was hard to know what the heart was feeling as it tried to communicate through luminance.

'You have a mind of your own, little heart,' Faerydae said to it.

As she looked through the murky water in the glass jar, another light source, one not radiating from the organ itself, bounced off of the warped glass and into her eyes. It was coming from the woods, in the near distance. Faerydae lowered the jar and watched the other light float about the air like a firefly, feeding warmth to the surrounding gloom as it went along. She knelt down quietly and scuttled slightly closer.

The light stopped moving and became still as Faerydae squeezed herself between the knotted branches ahead of her. The light hovered, motionless, as if it knew it were being watched. Faerydae focused her eyes in closer and the light made a rattling sound. It *turned*, capable of turning because it was actually attached to something else, something much bigger.

Faerydae let a muffled gasp escape her before thrusting her palms over her mouth. She held herself steady on her aching knees, trying not to make another sound, still gazing in horror at the thing out there.

'Run, Flea,' Lume whispered. 'Haven't you learnt not to trust anything in these woods? Run now.'

The thing had a face covered in thick chunks of bark. The coarse edges of its form were lit up in the pale glow of lantern light. *Run away, go now, before it sees you.* Faerydae shook her head.

It was a walking tree.

A lantern hung on the end of a rod attached to its topmost branches, guiding it through the dark. Its face was wooden. Its mouth was full of sappy goo and teeth of mushrooms and moss. Its eyes moved around smoothly, looking and observing, made of wood yet still glimmering with a humane wetness. With the roots below its trunk detached and uprooted from the ground, the evergreen was able to move about freely on thick, knotted legs.

Faerydae recalled that she had been told of walking trees once before: trees that walked around and feasted upon human flesh. It was those two strange farm worms. Donald and Bobbie Jo Wolseley... Everything seemed so much like a long-ago dream to her now.

She made herself smaller, hoping that the shrouding leaves overhead would conceal her. But her heart was glowing again now, it was glowing so brightly that it was almost a lantern in itself.

'*Shut that thing up*,' Lume hissed, having already dulled himself to an indistinguishable hue in his pocket. '*That organ doesn't know what's good for it.*'

Faerydae tried to sprawl her body over the top of the glass jar and dull the heart's shine. *Stop it*, she thought. Stop it now, light off. Turn down.

The walking tree knelt down with a wooden creak of its knee joints and examined a shrub by its feet. It *tsked* glumly, feeling the little plant with its twiggy fingers.

'You need new soil,' the tree said suddenly, its voice deep and somehow wooden, as if coming from the hollow of its belly. 'This just won't do. I shall be killing two birds with one stone here.'

The tree dangled its fingertips over the shrub considerately. Then, after a short moment, it simply pulled the bush out of the soil with a fizzled snap and stood back up. The shrub's frail roots swung as the tree walked slowly off through the woods again; lantern bobbing above to show the path ahead.

Faerydae let her breath go. 'It's gone.'

'*Good riddance,*' Lume mumbled. '*Meriel trees. Filth if you ask me.*'

At that, Faerydae's heart started to cry, a strange high-pitched noise that existed in the wind. Faerydae gritted her teeth and Lume swore atrociously.

'Shh! *SHHH!*' Faerydae shrilled. The heart glowed brighter, then dulled and continued to cry on in a frantic tantrum. 'What?!' Faerydae asked it. 'You like the tree? Is that it?'

The heart stopped wailing immediately. Faerydae rolled her eyes. It was like having a baby.

'We have to follow it,' Faerydae said to Lume, triggering a predictable groan and rebuttal, which she ignored.

She stalked after the tree as silently as possible, keeping her heart from screaming, at least. Faerydae wondered if her heart had always been this wilful.

The tree came to a halt after some time. Faerydae crouched down again. It placed the shrub it had collected onto the ground and then tapped its foot against the dirt, as if impatiently waiting for something to happen so that it could do other things.

Faerydae watched expectantly. The shrub started moving of its own accord, *twitching* more like. Its exposed roots crept along the ground, feeling their way until they burrowed into new dirt like gnarly hands.

'There you go,' said the tree with a smile made of mushrooms. 'That's a good number. Forty trees, thirty-two shrubs and twelve roads changed. *Oh* yes, *oh* yes.'

Something made sense to Faerydae in that instance. She could finally imagine why the Winding Woods were so inconceivable; it made perfect and confounding sense to her. The woods *literally* were changed around every night, shuffled like a deck of cards by these sorts of night trees. Plants and trails disappeared and took on new positions so that everything was different from what it once was.

How was it possible that Faerydae had never noticed this?

Faerydae's heart was glowing again. Silly thing. She looked back up at the walking tree's meticulous work, but the creature had vanished. It was impressive for a creature so heavy to have disappeared like that.

'What in the…'

There was a metallic rattling sound behind her.

'You seek the light, traveller?'

Faerydae shrieked. Birds scattered at the sudden sound of her voice. The walking tree's lantern wobbled around as Faerydae turned to see it stumbling backwards, apparently just as alarmed as she was. She climbed to her feet as her little heart went dull.

'I seek nothing from you,' Faerydae huffed in reply.

The tree looked down upon Faerydae with a stoic face. 'Is that so?' it said and glanced at her beating heart, back to her again. 'You are confident to find your own way out of these woods?'

'Perhaps not,' Faerydae admitted. 'Considering that you are the reason I've become lost within these confounded riddles in the first place.'

The tree turned its solid head to gaze upon the shadows cast by its lantern. ''Tis not so bad to remain lost.'

'Not when you have nowhere to be, I suppose.' Faerydae took a few steps backwards, ready to outrun the evergreen if she needed to. A stick snapped under her foot like a length of tight rope, leading the great tree to watch her closely.

'I am the Wayward Meriel Tree,' it said, whether Faerydae cared to hear it or not.

'*Wayward* Meriel Tree?' Faerydae asked. 'That is what you call yourself?'

'There are many Meriel trees, girl. But I am *different* from them all, somewhat more *open-minded*. You are lucky I am not like the rest, otherwise I might have devoured you up right here and now.'

'Trees do not truly eat people, do they?' Faerydae asked.

'We *can* eat people,' said the tree. 'Do not underestimate us and what we will do for the woods. But my orders are not so, not when Eggnorphixeus is so eager to collect his skulls.'

The girl's throat constricted at the mention of that horrible name, spoken so casually in conversation.

'I must also say,' the tree added. 'The king is looking for young girls about your age, and I would advise—'

'So I've been told. But do any of you actually *know* why the king wants children, or is that of little unimportance to you?'

The tree shrugged. Faerydae figured it must have been amused.

'I care not for the pursuits of men. Nor the gold that they so readily give up their souls for. No, my kind only care to keep these woods a place of fear, so as they remain forgotten, then the magic thrives.'

'A haven for darkness,' Faerydae whispered.

'*Mmmm,*' the tree groaned. 'There are forces at work that may change the way of life in here, but the shadows are a good home for magic in the meantime. That is why souls should keep away from here. So where have you come from and wish to return to? I gather you are lost from where you belong.'

'I had a home once,' Faerydae started. 'I didn't know enough about myself to appreciate it though. I guess I'm to go back there, to try and live on with all that has happened to me.'

'You came to the woods because you are a daemon though? You think you belong here instead... You wander the woods unafraid, are perhaps hollow except for the magic inside you. And you carry your heart in a jar, a curious thing to do.'

Faerydae looked down at her beating organ and picked it up off of the ground. 'I suppose so.'

'You are definitely powerful,' the tree said. 'Only those filled with magic can notice us Meriels completing our nightly duties. We are invisible to all else. A lonely life it is. This is the first time I have spoken to another soul for many breaths, actually.'

The Meriel gestured for Faerydae to follow it into the dark. She rubbed her cold nose and glanced around, deeming that she'd be no worse off to follow after the Meriel creature. After all, the wood was a maze, and this tree was the maze-maker.

'There is a wizard ruling these woods,' the Meriel explained as they walked side by side. 'A wizard by the name of Eggnorphixeus. He cast my dying soul into the bark of a Meriel tree long ago, to be one of his watchers and workers. I thought it was a blessing at first. I thought he'd saved me. But I was wrong. The Meriels change these woods around every night in the hope that lost souls will meet a fate worse than death by Eggnorphixeus' hand.'

'I am acquainted with the wizard,' Faerydae grimaced. 'But, he is... How you say... Well, dead.'

'Dead? *Possibly*,' remarked the Meriel. 'Or, perhaps, he is just taking a long sleep. A break from his hard work.'

Faerydae bit her lip. 'Work.'

The tree scratched its head. 'Such a hellish creature as Eggnorphixeus can never be stopped for good. All woodland dwellers have the same blood. *Oh yes*, it is a different set of rules in here. But stranger things are happening even *outside* of the woods nowadays... It is a great coincidence to happen upon each other, Daemon. We are both magical beings and, you see, if my oath was to be broken then my spirit would be free to leave these duties and guide you out of the woods in return. You may go and discover the world, and all of its troubles, for yourself–'

Faerydae stopped. 'In *return*?' She waggled her finger at the tree. 'I know this one well Meriel: you offer me a way out of here and I give you what you want in return, before you betray me. I have already learnt not to trust any stranger of these woods, offering me such things as a safe guide home.'

The old tree looked away from Faerydae's harsh glare. 'I cannot promise you a way out of here and I certainly cannot promise you safety. I am no monster girl, only a prisoner, just like you. But if you already have a plan of your own, then that is your decision to make. We will not bump into one another again, though.'

Prisoner.

Prisoners understood one another. Alberick was a prisoner and he had been trustworthy. After all, monsters come in all shapes and sizes, but which ones are good and bad has to be decided upon their actions. Faerydae felt the will of the woods against her. She looked back up at the tree with a desperate stare.

'What must I do to revoke your oath then?'

45

Faerydae and the Wayward Meriel stood in a clearing. Faerydae clung to her heart as the Meriel lifted its lantern from out of its high branches and placed it gently on the dirt. Faerydae, after a moment, did the same with her heart.

Lume had not spoken. He was hiding away in silence, unhappy with the turn of events. The feeling in the air was that of rising anticipation, of curiosity. The tree looked around the chosen clearing with a satisfied nod.

'If you are wilful enough with the magic inside of you,' the tree began. 'Then these words should be enough to free me from the tree's entrapment. Remember what I say, girl, and repeat the phrase back to me.'

> *'In my woods of fickle realm,*
> *Walked a lonesome tree of prickled elm.*
> *A force of good from ancient scroll*
> *To break his curse and free his soul*
> *Who's carried out thine wishes whole.'*

The tree nodded broodingly at Faerydae to repeat it.

'O-okay,' she stuttered, preparing herself. 'Okay.'

She took a deep breath and squeezed her sweaty palms together. Faerydae walked to the side of the Meriel tree and placed her hand against its harsh wooden face, imagining that it might help her connect with it. And then she repeated the sacred poem as if the words belonged to her:

'In my woods of fickle realm,
I met a lonesome tree of prickled elm.
I'm a force of good from ancient scroll
And I break his curse and free his soul
Who's carried out thine wishes whole.'

A long moment passed, and nothing happened. Faerydae let her hand fall from the tree's face. The Meriel's features saddened in a way; he looked more hopeless than Faerydae in that instant. They watched each other with bated breath, wondering what would become of the oath even if it *had* been revoked – for neither knew.

The girl bowed her head just when the Meriel suddenly fell to the earth with frightening finality. Faerydae shrieked and bent down over him, fearing that she had killed the creature altogether. A subtle haze appeared glowing over the surface of the Meriel's bark before a foggy figure sprung out of the wood with a whooshing of icy air. The translucent figure glowed with a blue aura and floated above the tree's corpse.

The spirit grinned, a mature man, slim and wide-eyed, with a curled moustache above his thin lips. He had a delicate grey over-comb and wore a cotton waistcoat of vibrant orange over his white blouse.

'Amazing!' he bellowed in a jolly voice, completely unlike the Meriel's tones. 'Oh, ho, ho, good grief! I didn't think it would work!'

He dove in and between the trees around the clearing, laughing with bewilderment. Faerydae started to laugh too, the spirit's ecstatic energy being all too infectious.

'Ooh! Ho, ho, ho!' He sang, performing midair somersaults and handstands. He walked along the high treetops and disappeared behind branches, only to reappear out from behind other ones.

The spirit flew back down and went to touch Faerydae's hand, but simply fell straight through it. He shrugged and they smiled at one another warmly. The ghost's moustache curled up tightly above two deep, tight dimples. But then he started to change. His face soured. Faerydae's heart raced as the man's face *twisted* into a dark grimace.

Faerydae took a step backwards, preparing herself for betrayal. Survival. The only two things she knew well. But it was not evil in those glowing blue eyes, it was fear.

He peered around the shadowy woods. Listening. Faerydae listened as well, until, *possibly*, she could distinguish a shuffling sound, that familiar snapping of sticks and crushing of leaves coming from all around them. It was delicate at first but grew closer in quick succession, erupting like firecrackers from nothingness. The spirit gasped.

'You must come! Quickly!' he yelled.

Faerydae grabbed her heart and followed frantically after the flying spirit above her. She glanced at the shadows at her sides as she ran, moving shadows, growing closer, and closing in on her fast.

'It's the *others*,' the ghost wailed. 'The other Meriel trees. Now that my oath is broken, they will seek to destroy me, just as I too have helped kill others who managed to escape their purgatory. If they catch us, they will kill us *all*.'

'What?!' Faerydae shrieked. 'But I can free them all!'

The ghost laughed. 'Not all Meriels seek to exist as a wandering ghost. Quickly now!'

Faerydae kept up with the agile spirit as best she could manage. Her heart bobbled around in its jar. Faerydae wondered what this ghost-man hoped to do with his existence that made him so different to all the other dutiful Meriels. But just as she had remained somewhat distanced from the scarecrow Alberick in their divergent quests, she was a stranger to the ghost as well.

They did not stop running.

Eventually, the trailing shadows became fewer and fewer, dropping away from exhaustion or loss of interest. As Faerydae grew weary, the ghost sought a hollow oak tree from the maze of woods who he seemed to know well and trusted. It was larger than any oak Faerydae had ever set her eyes upon. She felt safe under its shadow. They crept deep inside its hollow trunk and Faerydae set her heart down on the dry ground and gathering leaves. It was so silent within that wooden cocoon, and the pair did their best to keep the peace of it maintained. Legs of wood and roots passed by the hollow opening for the rest of the night.

The girl fought the urge to sleep in that lingering danger but lost the fight as the ghost kept watch over her. Lume remained, as he always did, locked away in a secluded silence. Her heart made no sound either. And they all stayed just like that, motionless, with the kindly ghost hovering at the opening of the hollow like a guardian angel.

46

When Faerydae came too, it was not yet morning, but it was not night either. It was betwixt.

'We must make haste,' the ghost's voice was saying. 'The brotherhood of Meriels have passed for now, but they shall never give up the hunt. We will be safer travelling in the early morning hours, when the Meriel's settle into the earth. But do not talk to any trees; sleeping Meriels appear the same as any other evergreen.'

Faerydae leant up to sitting and felt around in her pocket to make sure Lume was still there. He was, but he would not speak to her. Faerydae crawled out into the dangers of the open woods, seeing the icy fog in the air around the trees. Darkness sat thickly over the scene.

They started off along the ensuing road together; the ghost-man flying just overhead, keeping a look out.

'Well, miss,' he chirped, sensing Faerydae's lack of optimism, 'it is my tithe now to see you on your way. I cannot be rid of you until those little scorned feet of yours walk right on out of these woods.'

She forced a smile. Faerydae would not allow herself to believe that their escape would be so simple. The woods were too complicated, too cruel for that.

'I suppose so,' she replied. 'My home is in the North. A village called Brindille, if you know it at all.'

'I know every part of every place within these lands. And, as a matter of fact, I was actually a Brindille man myself once.'

'Really?' Faerydae asked. 'Are you to return to Brindille Village also then?'

The ghost-man raised a silencing finger to his lips, deflecting Faerydae's question. 'We should not speak of where you are heading to any further. We cannot trust these trees one little bit. They whisper too many things.'

47

The pair walked the whole day, until darkness came creeping back in. Faerydae became like a petulant child, nagging, moody, bored and tired.

They finally sheltered in the safety of another giant oak tree, hiding as best they could from the Meriels that creeped out in the moonlight and continued looking for them both. Faerydae spoke seldom, not wanting to give anything up to the listening woods. All they could do was await the safety of when they would at last be able to see the blue sky.

In the morning of the next day, the ghost-man set off even earlier than the previous. Faerydae followed him close behind, watching her feet as she went, agonising in her mind about the torturous silence. When they came to a new trail branching to the left, some hours after dawn, she perked up a little. The trail was only narrow, wide enough to put one foot in front of the other, so Faerydae pretended she was balancing on a long piece of silken hair. She spread her arms out wide and flicked the passing branches.

At the end of that trail, five more paths appeared before them. The ghost-man led Faerydae over to some wild berries and snails. She then sat down on a fallen tree trunk in the clearing and ate her berries and sucked up the snails slowly, revelling in the feeling of food inside her stomach. Spiders and beetles crept over her lap, which she watched scuttling like a river. She examined the dividing paths with her eyes, wondering if the ghost could possibly be sure that any of these roads led to the same place they once did. She tilted her head, noticing something rather odd about the path that branched off to her furthest right.

'What *is* that?' she said, standing up and pointing. 'Over there?'

The ghost tensed his hands. 'What is what?'

Faerydae walked over to the trail, staring down at the vegetation lacing the ground along the path's reach.

'They're sunflowers, I think.' Faerydae knelt down and touched the petals of one of the large blossoming plants. 'Curious that they would grow in *here*, where there is no sun at all.'

The ghost came by her side and looked down the road like looking down a long imposing tunnel. The blossoming heads of sunflowers lingered as far as he could see along the winding path, separated by a few metres each. The flowers were tall, miraculous, swinging around as if they were beckoning the travellers down their way, wanting to be followed. The breeze whistled through them.

'Sunflowers do not grow in here,' said the ghost, looking unsurely down at Faerydae. 'They must have been sewn, possibly years ago, to have grown so tall. Strange. Why would a person have planted flowers right upon the path to be walked all over?'

Faerydae shrugged and rose up to standing, still watching the swaying flowers.

'Sunshine,' she whispered, picturing the face of that girl she had lost. Alalia Riviera. How that girl's eyes had shone just like the sun. 'I think we should follow this path.'

'I don't know if that would be wise–'

'I *insist*,' Faerydae urged, suddenly possessed by the idea. 'I think somebody might have left these here for me to find.'

The ghost waited a moment, deciphering the credibility of Faerydae's intuition. He sighed before nodding. They both thrust their heads into the air then, listening to the woods. *Movement.* Leaves crackling. Movement meant danger. The ghost gestured for Faerydae to follow him and they hurried towards the entrance to the path she had chosen, where her sunflowers beckoned her inside.

'Wherever we go, we need to go now,' the ghost said. 'We *need* to keep moving.'

'This way!' Faerydae said. 'I'm sure! This is the right path.'

The sunflowers continued on down the path, becoming further and further apart with the passing hours, as if the person who had planted them had been running out of seeds or energy.

Faerydae and the ghost hiked frantically through the night, not stopping until morning light came twinkling through the trees yet again.

The trail of flowers had continued in the same manner, but now each flower was at least a mile apart.

'Lovely morning,' the ghost eventually said. 'A beautiful morning, in fact.'

'I suppose so,' Faerydae agreed groggily.

Faerydae grimaced, almost at the point of collapsing. She deemed there was no end to this road or any other for that matter; she would die walking. The ghost was smiling too cheerfully for her current mood to accept, which was not odd, he often smiled, but this smile was wider than ever. He was stopping himself from giggling.

'What's so funny?' Faerydae asked.

He said nothing but continued on his stifled snickering. Faerydae began to think he was laughing at her, that she had something on her face. But he shook his head as she tried to clean herself off with a saliva-slicked thumb. This in fact made him break out into hoots, holding his belly as he swayed in time with the snorts that followed. Faerydae could not help it, she grinned, looking the man up and down, his schoolboy laughter being so contagious.

'The edge of the Wood,' he cried, gesturing to the bright opening through the trees ahead. 'Brindille lays beyond those branches, waiting for you I'm sure. Your trail of flowers has guided you home; whomever is watching over you is surely an angel.'

And there it was.

Northern soil was almost below her feet again.

Faerydae swallowed in the dewy smell of the woods and went to the opening of trees where sunshine erupted, and the hills rolled away into the world – hills of her home province. She began to laugh too. Her heart skipped beats of exhilaration within its glass jar. The girl stared up at the ghost-man, lingering just before the rays of light beyond.

'I am sorry I ever doubted you,' she breathed. 'If I could hug your invisible body, I surely would.'

He chuckled warmly and urged her to dare a step forward. 'The Meriels shall never find you out there. Welcome back to the real world. There is enough darkness in these lands to keep us all occupied. But for now, just remember, all that has happened within these shadows is in the past, and you must leave it behind you forever.'

The girl nodded with a sober understanding of her own luck, that she had been given a second chance. 'I shall never look back, sire.'

Faerydae Nóvalie then walked out of the Winding Woods, leaving everything that had happened within those trees behind her.

48

Dear Alalia,

I hope you are well. The days have been going by steadily, as they always do.
Since you left, Mama has not been the same. She has stopped baking and
there is no longer any money coming in from the business. I am continuing
to work in Eastlea to support us.

Papa has told me of an omen that has been heard in Brindille Shire. I
suppose you will be looking for it. I don't want to impose on you, Sister, but
I have not heard from you in a while.

I am going to travel to Brindille Shire in the coming days to check in on
you, unless I hear back from this letter. I believe that an invention I have
been working on will assist you in your hunt – at least, I hope it will.

I'm worried about the events soon to unfold, Alalia. I'm afraid. People say
that you always have a choice, but this feels very much like it has only one
possible end. Stay safe, my dear, keep to the shadows.

Your brother,

Jakob. M

49

Beyond the Woods

Grass swayed like the dancing corn stalks of Temperance's field. The sun was everywhere, not a single sparse cloud could hide it away. The sky was an unending cavern of blue. The breeze truly was the best feeling Faerydae could ever explain, it almost carried her away. The elation made her want to live forever in its hold.

'*You did it,*' Lume said. '*You made it out of the Winding Woods with your life still intact – not too destroyed yet. No, not yet.*'

Faerydae knew there was something Lume wanted to say to bring her down. There was always *something*. But, graciously, he did not. She found it curious, given all the time he had spent convincing her to take him to the woods, that he did not try to escape once. She wondered, just maybe, if he felt something for her.

She stood on top of a bare grassy hill, looking out across the world of green and blue. There was a sprinkling of lights in the faraway haze, calling to her. Faerydae sized up the distant hills of Brindille Shire, wondering how long it would take her to walk back. Her legs ached so badly but she would not, *could* not, rest now.

During the quiet of another long night, a blanket of stars kept Faerydae at ease.

Her heart became heavy to carry as the hours wore on, so she swapped it between arms to keep it from weighing her down, wondering how normal people managed to lug their torsos around with such heavy organs inside them. The heart did not glow or scream or laugh out in the open world, because the magic no longer flowed through everything so vibrantly as it had done in the woods. Everything was clean out here.

At some point, Faerydae had to rest. But she was unsure how long she slept for, because she was moving again by the time the sun rose over the scattered hills ahead. Sunlight brought with it a new day filled with endless possibilities.

Faerydae reached the outskirts of Brindille by midmorning. She happened to be mumbling a Brindille folk song when the village came into view, close enough to see the names of the shops and the cobbled streets curling around.

'Home, sweet home, little Flea.'

'This place was never really my home, Lume,' said Faerydae to the gem, feeling a fragile connection to the town. 'There was but one thing that kept me tied to this dreaded village. One person. My mama.' Faerydae looked in the direction of the rocky path that she knew all too well, which lead around the village and, eventually, to the olde docklands. She would have to follow it. She would have to rediscover the dear mother she now knew so much more about. There was no choice.

As Faerydae walked, precariously slowly, thoughts of Temperance would not leave her mind. She was realising how false first impressions usually were. Temperance had been the ultimate trickster, more cunning than any other creature within the woods. Faerydae believed that the olde woman had not been as smart as she'd thought though. In fact, Temperance had been a fool, defeated by the harsh world instead of fighting against it. If Temperance had taught Faerydae anything during their time spent together, it was that every person had the power to give up, but not every person had the audacity to keep trying.

***

Small pines sprang up out of the ground at her sides, then larger ones, as Faerydae grew closer to her olde home. The rotten smell of the lagoon travelled upon the air and drifted in every direction. Under her feet, she felt the path slope gently downwards. Faerydae knew then that she was drawing near. She could see the green water through the dappling of tree trunks.

The lagoon revealed itself before her in one shocking instance, and the girl could not help but gasp. It was so very, *very* different – almost unrecognisable – to the place that she had spent her entire life in. Her childhood home, the decaying ship, was gone. Wherever it had gone *to* was a mystery, but it was no longer here. The boardwalk was gone as well, vanished from where it had once stood. And therefore, more importantly than all of those things, Faerydae's dear mother had gone along with them.

Lume let out a little gasp of his own. '*What in all Hell happened to this place?*'

Faerydae felt her head shaking in disbelief, confusion. The lagoon looked more decrepit and forgotten than it ever had before, as if a decade of tons of uplifted sand had blown in on a hurricane and buried it under itself.

'She's gone,' Faerydae said, wanting to sink into the sand. She soon did in a manner, slumping onto her back upon the damp shoreline. Crabs and seaweed soon surrounded her in a haphazard circle, claiming her as a part of the lagoon's relic.

Exhaustion truly enveloped her then, for there was nothing left for her to seek. She was home. And home had disappeared. She cried. And cried. And cried.

Faerydae lay there until nearly midday, though was tempted to remain there forever. Lume's nagging was the only thing that forced her up to sitting.

'*What do you expect, this is a land of true strangeness, after all,*' Lume was rambling. '*That is for sure. But where do you fit into all of this mess? Surely lying here won't help you find the answer to that question.*'

A sense of being stuck in the past had consumed Faerydae; she was that same helpless girl from the lagoon all over again.

'I don't belong here,' she snapped. 'I don't belong in the woods either. I am a nowhere soul.'

'*Oh no, little Flea,*' spoke Lume. 'Another *place is calling to you, an unknown place that you have never seen before. A place that holds your destiny.*'

Faerydae shrugged, bleakly dragging her fingers through the sand at her sides. Her fingers felt the edges of sharp fragments as they moved. She looked down. Mud and broken pieces of wood sifted out through her fingertips from beneath the surface of sand. Faerydae held an assortment of rubble in her palms, staring blankly at it. She recognised the flaking wood. It was the same material that had once created her ship's great bowing walls. The almost black mud that had become intertwined with sand held more secrets. She examined it closely, picking out bits and pieces as she tried to decipher a timeline of events. The sand was littered with the little pebbles that she knew came from the path] leading in and out of Brindille Village. The dirt on either side of that path had always become clayey and black whenever it rained heavily. *Olivido.*

'Someone has been here,' Faerydae stated.

Lume paused for a moment, then offered, '*Temperance?*'

Faerydae shook her head furiously, digging further through the sand around her knees, unveiling masses of ruined wood and debris. 'No, no, no,' she cried. 'Temperance *is* dead. I saw the life leave her eyes. This was somebody, some*thing*, else.'

She became hysterical, sifting through the sand with such a desperate sense of purpose. Faerydae shoved her jarred heart aside in her efforts to understand the destruction. The heart bobbled around until it settled against the side of the fallen jar.

'*Flea,*' Lume said steadily. '*You have to calm down—*'

Faerydae went to pull the gem out of her pocket and toss him alongside her heart, when a flower promptly leapt out of the unearthed chaos and wacked her square in the cheek. She yelped in shock, reeling back onto her haunches.

The flower had been smushed beneath the sand but had retained enough strength to leave a red streak across Faerydae's skin. She gawked as the light of day creeped across its leaves, making it appear to brighten in colour. The flower started to grow and unfurl before her, displaying its full beauty. It was exactly the same as the sunflowers that had led Faerydae out of the woods.

Faerydae's hands shook as she scuttled closer. 'It's another sunflower. It's *her.* Alalia is sending me messages again, Lume. She's showing me I'm not alone, that she came looking for me. That beautiful girl, she must have escaped the woods too!'

Faerydae stroked the flower. It was soft and almost pulsated with life at her touch.

'*What's that?*' Lume said. '*Look behind it.*'

At the base of the sunflower, as if having been placed there just so, sat a waterlogged piece of paper – a flyer. Faerydae unfolded the scrunched-up thing and brushed off the sand that was encrusting it. She could not believe what she was reading.

Her eyes widened, she stood, seeing the same little flyer hiding just below the sand over the whole shoreline, corners peeking up at her. Faerydae raced around the bank, collecting the flyers up into her hands. Her teeth clenched together with rage, inadvertently causing her to clench the handful of papers until the water started to strain out of them.

'Come on!' Faerydae said to Lume, snatching her heart up as she made for the track back into Brindille. Faerydae shoved a handful of soaked flyers into her pocket. 'I think there is somebody who might know where my mother is, but you're not going to like who it is.'

'*Oh dear,*' Lume mumbled. He became quiet then, perhaps pondering his extensive list of enemies.

The beautiful sunflower that was left behind started to turn grey with Faerydae's absence. It writhed, perishing so violently where it stood, until it fell to the ground, dead. More and more flyers caught on the noon breeze and fluttered up into the sky. On each, it boasted the same phrase in squid-ink calligraphy:

At Galadriel's shop of Comings and Goings,
Come in and visit the home of all things strange!

50

The village did not appear the same as it once had. Faerydae used to fear it, its people, but she had now faced far worse than the sneering glances of polished villagers. Unlike the lagoon, it looked the same as before, but there was something wrong with it. Something had set the people on edge; they looked afraid, uneasy. The breeze withheld a vile tension.

Faerydae avoided the villagers as best she could, diving down Laminton's Alley with haste. It did not take her long to find the Shop of Comings and Goings within the tangled mess of streets in Brindille. She was not afraid of the silence it beheld anymore, or the possibility of meeting strange characters on her lonesome, for she trusted herself to handle it.

Concealed within the brickwork alleyway, Galadriel's little green door sat closed. It remained so discreet, so unsuspecting, just as it had always been. It was so very tiny. Faerydae wondered if she might have grown, or if she might still be able to fit through.

'You have GOT to be kidding me, Flea!' Lume finally spoke, as if he could spit at the very sight of the ominous green door. *'Not this troll, oh deary, not again! And didn't you kill him already, ugh.'*

'It would appear not,' Faerydae started. 'Other than Alalia, this is the only person I am sure has been to the lagoon. We have to talk to him, if he'll have us. Do not worry, Lume, I won't try to sell you again.'

'I should hope not,' Lume rasped. *'I sincerely hope you would know better than that.'*

A threat. Faerydae sighed and crouched down through the small doorway, slipping inside the place where it had all begun.

Faerydae jumped as that stupid door banged shut behind her. She was not totally impervious to her memories of this place it seemed. She looked around, exploring the shop and its wonderment all over again. Mumbles sounded off from behind the purple velvet curtain after a minute. The mysterious curtain ruffled open, then closed; Galadriel was too short to be seen from Faerydae's side of the counter. He stepped up onto his pedestal and revealed himself before the girl, rising up like a toad out of its filthy swamp. Faerydae felt nauseated to meet his glowing eyes of red again. He was, even still, after every awful creature she had encountered in the woods, the *most* hideous being of all. She could hardly believe he was still kicking too, after the way she had left him. If not for the slight crook of his fat neck, Faerydae would have assumed he'd gotten away without any permanent injuries.

Galadriel cleared his cancerous lungs, looking Faerydae up and down with disinterest.

This made the girl's lips curl up at the sides. *The troll did not recognise her, the fool.* She glanced about herself, noticing her hair that was all the way down to her ribs. Of course he wouldn't recognise her. *This would make things a little more interesting,* Faerydae thought.

'Welcome to The Shop of Comings and Goings,' he said. 'My name is Galadriel, the troll of Manjarta.' Galadriel's demonic eyes veered down to settle on Faerydae's hands, more poignantly, to the object she was holding within them. Her jarred heart. Sitting tight within Faerydae's grasp, almost forgotten by herself, it had certainly caught the olde puddle-troll's attention.

'You bring forth a curious item for trade, young lady,' Galadriel gargled.

'Yes,' she agreed, nodding, tapping her fingernails upon the swirling marble of the countertop. She thought for a brief moment before continuing. 'It's a unicorn heart. I hunted the beast down myself, deep within the Winding Woods. Unicorn organs are near priceless in the Underground Markets, as I'm sure you are well aware. The heart of a unicorn is hard to come by, apothecaries and witch-doctors alike would be most interested.'

Galadriel reached a gnarled hand out and placed it on top of the jar. Faerydae released her grip, but stared deeply at him as he lifted the jar up and held it closer to his beady eyes, examining the organ carefully.

'The thing still beats,' Galadriel marvelled. 'How fascinating. It is rather small though, for a unicorn heart.' His eyes flashed with menace, wanting to be convinced.

'It was a foal, sire,' she said. 'Only young, but much more valuable still. Filled with youthful magic blood.'

'Magic?' Galadriel seemed to enjoy that word. *Oh, yes,* he thought to himself at the sound of the syllables: ma-gic. 'I am a magical creature myself, young lady. I am from Manjarta. Have you heard of Manjarta? It is a magical place; it was where I was first breathed–'

Faerydae started to laugh, unable to stop herself from doing so. 'Spare me your spiel, troll! I am not a fool and I do not care for your tales.'

Galadriel bit his thin green lips. 'Very well,' he replied. 'You want a trade, then a trade you will get. Have a look around, see if anything catches your eye.'

Faerydae looked up at the walls painted with old relics and souvenirs, biding her time.

Lume moaned impatiently. '*I hope you know what you're doing.*'

Faerydae forced herself to ignore him, to stay focused on whatever she was doing. She looked carefully across all of the items Galadriel possessed, those that he had collected over a lifetime of thievery. A small button-eyed voodoo doll came into her line of sight, sitting aboard a model horse on one of the floating shelves almost all the way up at the ceiling. *That doll,* thought Faerydae. *That surely is the same doll that belonged to my mama.* Faerydae forced her eyes to look closer, making sure that she could recognise the doll's delicate little shoes and cotton dress.

'There,' Faerydae said, banging the scuffed teal counter and pointing up at the object. 'Where did you get that doll?'

Galadriel smiled. 'You like it? It's yours–'

'No! Where did you get it, Galadriel?'

The troll was taken aback. 'Well, excuse me young lady, but it was claimed from a kingsman raid that I attended not two days ago. I didn't steal it if that is what you are suggesting.'

'Raid?' Faerydae stared through him. 'Tell me what happened, Galadriel. Where was the raid?'

Galadriel shrugged. 'The whole village was raided. That is no secret, girl, for they made no effort to hide it. As for that doll, well, all I can say is that the docklands was a place of particular interest to the kingsmen. I may have discovered it during my time with them, but a commoner like you is not privileged to know such information.'

Faerydae stifled an outburst of verbal abuse, and traced the lid of her jarred heart tantalisingly 'Would you consider trading information for, say, a worthy prize?' she asked.

'Perhaps…' Galadriel waited for a moment, then continued. 'The kingsman enquired upon my services, that's all. They needed my expertise to ascertain certain *information* at the docklands. Puddle-trolls are best at deciphering true materials from fake materials, after all. That doll was an item of interest to them. It was pointed out as an object with possible magical abilities; they believed it might have been an omen. They were wrong.'

Faerydae couldn't handle her confusion any longer, moving right on to her next accusation. She slammed the crumpled-up flyer onto Galadriel's countertop, letting sand scatter across the wood and into his little red eyes.

'What is this?' she demanded. 'And why was it left in the remains of a destroyed ship?'

The troll exhaled quickly. 'I don't know how–'

'Do not test me, troll,' Faerydae snarled, banging the counter again with clenched fists. 'Tell me the truth!'

'I merely took the opportunity to advertise my wares to a new pool of clientele,' he said defensively. 'That's all – kingsmen are wealthy folk you know! I was handing them around before they destroyed any evidence that was leftover.'

'Was there a woman there? Inside the ship?'

Galadriel grinned a sickly grin, fanning the flyer back towards Faerydae with his hand. '*No.*' And he said no more than that.

'*Liar!*' Lume hissed.

'I do BEG your pardon, miss!' Galadriel boomed. 'But if you have no *real* business here then I am going to have to ask you to leave!'

Faerydae forced her anger deep down into the pits of her stomach. 'No, just wait.' She looked around the shop once more. 'I want the doll.'

Galadriel sighed, pitying her. 'I do not want your business, young lady.'

'Please,' Faerydae urged. 'That doll for this heart.'

Her heart beat in gentle time to her words and Galadriel could not deny his fascination for the unusual item.

'Very well,' he agreed.

The troll waddled out to the shopfront, grunting with every stride. He forced a ladder out from behind the shelving, rolling it upon its two rusty wheels until it was directly below the doll. He then began his ascent.

Galadriel's legs seemed too short for the distance between the ladder's rungs, and his webbed feet made it difficult for him to even grip the wood at all, but he pretended to be well adept at such efforts. Faerydae imagined that he must be a very *old* puddle-troll by now. The things he must have seen… and done.

As he came finally to the top of the ladder with a great heaving sigh, sweating all over, Galadriel glanced warily back at the ground below him, dangling on the final rung. He looked somewhat dizzy as he waved at Faerydae. She waved back.

'*You horrible little troll,*' muttered Lume with repulse. '*I can see your past; I can hear your thoughts, your memories of thousands of years of torment. So many children. So many little girls.*'

'Settle down, Lume,' Faerydae ordered of him.

'*You cannot see what I see, Flea!*' Lume roared. '*This troll has done unforgivable things.*'

Faerydae stared at the troll way up there. 'I believe that, Lume. I surely believe that.'

'*He will die,*' Lume said next, too caught up in himself to care what Faerydae was saying back. '*We all shall die. But he, now, shall finally fall, and make this putrid world one tiny bit cleaner.*'

Lume glowed intensely, growing hot inside the girl's pocket. Faerydae blinked, feeling as if time was beginning to slow down. There was magic in the air.

Galadriel stretched for the doll with one hand, but it was just out of his arm's reach. The doll wobbled minutely from the graze of his fingers, almost cruelly, teasing him to stretch a little farther. The doll seemed to laugh as it forced him just slightly too far over the edge. But it was not the doll at all who was doing this.

'Stop, Lume,' Faerydae said, her fists clenching.

The gem did not lose his glow, only becoming hotter and hotter. '*I'm sorry, Flea,*' he said. '*I cannot stop now.*'

The troll's feet slipped out from under him, out from the ladder's wooden rungs, and into midair. Galadriel snatched viciously as his body started to fall backward. He seemed to hover motionless for a moment, almost flying – *could he fly?* – until he began to fall.

Lume roared with approval when he finally collided with the shop's steadfast floor, an explosion of blood drenching the nearby walls and the troll's precious olde antiques.

51

Galadriel lay dead at Faerydae's feet and she was not sure what to do about it. Blood was still spreading around his head and creeping deeper into the crevices of boxes and crates. The girl came to wonder why she had even come back to this awful place at all. Lume was still screaming profanities in support of the troll's death. Faerydae could not decide if she supported Lume's motives or not, but it seemed irrelevant now. And anyway, Faerydae had probed all the information out of Galadriel that she could. He was of no use to her anymore, to anyone – alive or dead.

Faerydae paced for a while, in the peaceful silence of the shop.

'*He deserved it,*' Lume gushed.

Faerydae nodded agreeably. 'Yes, I suppose he did. How I am truly becoming a product of my evil surroundings.'

She glanced up at the voodoo doll, her mama's treasured toy. Why she had wanted it in the first place perplexed Faerydae, for it was not precious nor sentimental to her, not really. *And it was certainly not the omen they were looking for.*

Galadriel had died for nothing it seemed. He had not revealed much before his untimely passing, all but a single lead. Kingsmen had destroyed her olde home and left it in ruins, that much was certain. If they had captured her mother too, then Faerydae would simply have to find them. The woman was *her* responsibility. Nobody could claim her as their own.

'We have to keep moving, Lume,' she said.

Faerydae left The Shop of Comings and Goings without remorse, only speculating on how long it would be before someone discovered the troll's corpse decaying on the oily wooden boards.

52

Faerydae was unsure where to turn to next as she stood in the cold brick alleyway.

'My mother is alive, I *know* she is,' she said, trying to convince herself, as if that was her last notion to cling to. Faerydae still had so much bursting energy and ambition, but did not know how or where to channel it anymore.

'*Your mother is not worth saving, Flea,*' Lume said. '*Some are worth saving, but some are not. She is* not.'

'You speak of my mama as if you know her,' Faerydae replied, crouching down and massaging her throbbing temples. 'But you need to accept that there are some things you cannot understand. You are just an object. She is my *mother.*'

'Do not say another stupid word!' Lume's voice came out so abusively that Faerydae fell to her side, scraping her elbows on the cobbled stones below. '*What do you think I am!*' He continued, '*Some sort of a pet?*'

'Lume!' Faerydae said. 'Calm down! I just mean–'

'*Omens, Faerydae! Have you not picked up on that peculiar word yet? It keeps surrounding you, being spoken right in front of you, but you will not listen!*'

'What do you want from me to say, Lume?' Faerydae screamed. 'You want me to praise you? Accept your every word as gospel? I don't KNOW what I'm doing anymore, isn't that clear?! If you have something to say, then, by all means, don't let me stop you, Almighty Omen!'

Faerydae threw Lume onto the road before her, looking in at his furious fiery features as they curled and glared. A moment of silence passed, everybody taking a moment to gain their bearings.

'*I've been with your family for longer than you know,*' Lume admitted, not as angry as Faerydae would have expected after being called an object and tossed to the ground. '*I knew your father, Faerydae. I knew him better than even your mother did.*'

'What…' she whispered. 'What on earth are you talking about?'

Lume stared into Faerydae's eyes regretfully, as if he wanted her to prepare herself for what he would soon say. She did.

'*Listen to me, Flea,*' Lume went on. '*When I first met you, I wanted to tell you a story, a story about Faerydae Nóvalie. Remember? But you told me that you already knew it. Well, I'm going to tell you right now that you do not. So sit there, shut up, and just listen to me…*

'*My birth was never wanted. None of the omens were. Sort of like you, I suppose.*

'*Deemed too dangerous to tame, and too unpredictable to harness, we were separated, cast away to our own separate dooms. I became stranded upon an island made of huge graphite shards and toxic waterholes, a place where nobody would ever venture, such was where I belonged. The only person who ever wanted to see me returned home was my father – or so I had thought. You see, I'd been calling out for somebody to come and save me for thousands and thousands of years before **your** father finally heard me.*

'*One thing you should know about me and my family, Faerydae, is that we long to be reunited. We want to be brought back together, no matter the consequences.*

'*Harlowe Nóvalie, your father, returned me to this land, where I felt I belonged, where mine and my siblings magic had already seeped into the soil around us. He was a good man, Flea, rest assured in that. But there was so much darkness surrounding him that he could not begin to comprehend. Even back then, sitting warm inside his pocket, I could sense a stranger's curse lingering just above Harlowe's head, waiting for its moment to take hold of him.*'

'The curse of Vile Luck,' Faerydae interjected. 'You could see that it was going to kill him. But you couldn't save him from it.'

'*No, but I didn't need to. He was not the important one.*' Lume coughed, as if he were a normal sort of creature. '*And don't interrupt me,*' he added.

'*When the girl Euphraxia came to Harlowe's ship one night, not long after my return to this land, I immediately sensed that there was more destiny within her than within him. She was the one I needed to protect.*

'*She was wise back then, cunning, but smart – and apparently obedient. She listened to me when I told her about the curse that I had sensed, how it was actually meant for her, and that it would ruin all that she cared for. I told her what to do. That there was an omen in Wilburry that was being used, secretly, to cure illnesses, curses and spells alike. Fluxo, the omen of water. It would be able to break her curse. I asked for very little in return for such information: for Euphraxia to tell me where Fluxo was being kept within the king's palace. We had a deal.*

'*I bequeathed your mother with the beauty she so desired, so that she could stand before the king without being dismissed. I gave her a beautiful silken dress to wear, a carriage of glass to ride in, I gave her the slippers too. But she did not give me what I sought in return.*'

'The slippers,' Faerydae whispered. 'The featherbone slippers that she wore to the palace, with her hair in long braids, and herself in a beautiful gown. She didn't make that up.'

'*Why do you think the king is looking for children, Faerydae?*'

She shrugged. 'Why?'

'*Because,*' Lume said. '*The king's so-called daughter who resides in his palace in Wilburry is not at all his daughter. She is a kitchen wench's orphan. A ruse. His true heir is missing – well, his truest heir. You see, the king's wife, though he would never reveal this, is barren. Could you imagine his frustration, Flea? He was not a young man even back then; he needed an heir. So, when Euphraxia arrived at his feet that day, so beautiful as I had made her, he fell in love. They spent one single night together before Euphraxia fled, empty handed of both what she had gone looking for and what I had asked for in return. She married Harlowe as soon as she discovered that she was pregnant... with you.*'

Faerydae tilted her head thoughtfully. 'Me?'

Lume smiled. '*Yes, Faerydae. You're the child everybody is looking for. You are the missing princess.*'

***

Faerydae did not know why such a reaction had overcome her, but she found herself screaming uncontrollably at the little red gem. An array of colourful language seeped out of her mouth, so vulgar and expressive that it seemed her and Lume's personalities had traded for a moment. She was mostly calling Lume a liar, among other offensive things.

'*WHY WOULD I LIE TO YOU?*' Lume demanded in return. '*It is the truth! You are a princess – the closest thing to a princess that Wilburry will ever have. Not that you look it. Imagine how shocked your real father will be, to see you standing before him without a heart. Hilariously morbid!*'

'The king has ruined thousands of lives!' Faerydae blubbered. 'I will *never* stand before him. He has killed *children*, Lume, whether intentionally or not, he was the cause of it all the same.' The girl backtracked. 'He took my mama, didn't he, Lume? That was why they raided the olde docklands, they must have found out who she was, where she lived.'

'*Most likely*,' Lume replied. '*The night she spent with the king, she left one featherbone slipper behind, which he kept as a beloved treasure always. Where was the other one? Of course, it was with your mother still. There would have been no question as to whether your mother was the king's lost lover. I also suspect that they knew she had been under the influence of an omen that night, which led them to hire Galadriel to seek out that horrid little doll. They missed the mark there though, didn't they.*' He laughed but Faerydae was miles away. Caught up in the midst of so many questions, her heart now beating insanely inside its jar, Faerydae finally stood up onto her feet.

'We have to go to Wilburry,' she stated.

'*I whole-heartedly agree*,' Lume said as she picked him up. '*We must go to Wilburry. I'll make you a deal, Flea. I'll help you get your mother back safely into your care if you agree to find the omen that she forgot. Make up for her betrayal? If you agree, we must come back with two prisoners or we won't come back with any.*'

Faerydae felt that she had no energy to argue with him, letting out a long uncertain breath. 'You said yourself that it is dangerous to reunite the omens,' she cautioned. 'I don't know enough about you or your siblings to understand the consequences you eluded to. So, if I trust you, Lume, please do not betray *me*.'

'*I would never betray a friend, Flea. Somebody who has treated me so well, we are like family, you and I,*' Lume said. '*Your father came from me when I needed him most, something my own father never did.*' Faerydae nodded and slipped him into her pocket where he seemed to enjoy residing. '*But you will discover soon enough,*' he added. '*That there are far darker forces at work than merely myself or even the dear deranged king.*'

'You can lead me to Wilburry, Lume?' Faerydae asked. 'Or, perhaps, you could make *me* a carriage of glass, give me some beautiful slippers and a lovely dress. It might be nice, you know, to relax for even a moment in comfort?'

Lume chuckled and Faerydae immediately dropped the idea. '*I need to conserve my energy for when it is needed,*' he said. '*And oh, how it will be needed soon enough. Then you'll finally see what my true nature really is.*'

Faerydae needed no more reasons to be wary of the little omen, but he enjoyed giving her yet another one.

'Fine,' she finished, and started out of the dark alleyway.

'*Take a right,*' Lume instructed.

She did. The next thing Faerydae knew, she was down on her back again, a searing pain shooting through her head and neck as she heard the distinct sounds of a horse whinnying in fright.

53

'*FLEA! FLEA!*' Faerydae could hear Lume screaming her name like a siren. '*FLEA! YOU HAVE TO HIDE ME! HIDE MEEEE!*'

The figure of a huge creature came into focus ahead of her, as Faerydae became fully conscious again. She crept one hand out along the paved road to reach for Lume where he had fallen beside her, and she replaced him inside of her coat.

The identity of the creature ahead of her soon became apparent. It was a unicorn. Its bald skin was grey and wrinkled, with blotches of white around its flanks, shoulders and neck, almost like haphazard spots. Fine fuzz dappled unevenly across its snout and legs, wiry yet frail. Its eyes beheld an eerie, empty whiteness, like fog had overcome them. A sharp horn seemed to erupt from out of the creature's skull, stretching like a fine blade almost three feet long.

A boy sat onboard the beast. He appeared reasonably short but towered over Faerydae from where she lay on the road. She leapt up to her feet and backed slowly away from the creature and its rider. At her sudden movement, the boy reached behind himself and drew forth a clunky crossbow that he aimed with precision, right at her head.

They watched one another, motionless. The boy had straight black hair, longest on top, with oily locks dangling down over his forehead like noodles, making his pointy ears look particularly huge. His eyes too looked humongous, due to the goggle-like spectacles encasing them. Over his body, he wore a rawhide jumpsuit with brown lace-up boots.

Strange sorts of inventions and trinkets clanked around from where they hung randomly off of his leather belt.

The boy gave Faerydae a precisive glare, as if he were well practiced in such confrontations, yet he seemed no older than herself.

'Don't move!' he said to her with a cavernous voice.

She didn't.

'Now what!' Lume wailed and Faerydae bit her lip. She did not have time for this, they had to keep moving if they were to have any chance of finding her mother alive.

'Who the hell are you?' Faerydae asked plainly to the boy. 'And do you mind moving out of my way.'

The boy did not lower his weapon. 'Firstly,' he said in a quant well-spoken voice. 'That is no way to speak to anybody, little girl. And secondly, you do not get to ask questions when *I'm* the one with the crossbow.'

Faerydae raised an eyebrow. 'Fair enough.'

They stared one another down for a moment longer before the boy finally lowered his garish weapon slightly. He noticed the beating heart sitting in Faerydae's hands, encased within the safety of its jar. He seemed unfazed by it, possibly even impressed.

'Do I know you?' he asked then.

Faerydae could have laughed. 'Boy, if you knew me, you would remember.'

He seemed to like that answer very much and immediately let his crossbow fall by his side with a smile. The unicorn he rode upon started to paw at the cobbled stones and he gave the beast an endearing pat on the neck. Faerydae looked over the boy's sharp features, thinking, *if ever there was a prince that might fit somewhere in my story, he would surely look like this.*

Lume gagged at the girl's thought. *'Unbelievable,'* he said with disgust.

Footsteps started to sound from up the winding road as Faerydae felt herself blushing. The boy peered over his shoulder at the approaching sound. Faerydae peered behind the unicorn too, to where the streets started to unfurl back towards Flood Lane.

So simply, there strode forth Alalia, standing tall and elegantly under the clear blue sky above.

Faerydae blubbered, her head quivering with pure bafflement.

Alalia was wearing a black gown that laced up around her full chest and plumed out widely at her ankles. A pair of dainty black heels encased her small feet. Around her head she wore a white bonnet tied up with a silky ribbon, keeping her red curls tamed beneath.

Alaia stopped short, taken aback by the sight of Faerydae too. She stared into Faerydae's eyes; an unknown expression reflected therein.

'What are *you* doing here?' was all Alalia said to Faerydae.

'Harsh,' Lume blurted.

Faerydae felt that she needed to say something in reply but was far too perplexed to know what she should *want* to say to the girl. Her mouth could not form words. *Where to begin* – that was the question.

'Good heavens,' Faerydae managed to start with. 'Alalia. How ever did you get out of the woods?'

Alalia's lips nudged slightly upwards at such a question, amused. She took one step closer towards Faerydae before scowling dramatically. 'I could ask you the same thing.'

Faerydae pursed her lips in fairness. She thumbed the lump that was Lume, sitting snug inside her patchwork coat, and muttered, 'Intuition.'

'Is that so,' Alalia said.

The redhead crossed her arms and Faerydae clasped her hands tighter around her jarred heart in response.

'Hang on, hang on.' The somewhat forgotten boy leapt down from the grey unicorn and shook his head between the two girls. 'How do you know each other? What have I missed here?' He looked to Alalia expectantly. 'Sister?'

'*Sister?*' Faerydae repeated. 'You are Alalia's brother? Jákob, isn't it?'

There was clearly much that needed to be explained to the poor boy, but it seemed Alalia was not interested in that right now.

'What are you doing here?' Alalia finally asked Faerydae, ignoring her little brother. It was the most sensible question to ask next. 'I mean, have you been looking for me? Following me?'

'Of course not,' Faerydae replied. 'How could I be? I thought you must have been looking for me.'

'I'm looking for a shop,' Alalia deflected. 'Was told it was down this way.'

'A shop?' Faerydae frowned.

Alalia only nodded. 'A shopkeeper down Flood Lane told me that if it was something unique I was looking for, to come here.' She gestured to the sign above Faerydae: Galadriel's shop of Comings and Goings.

'Oh.' Faerydae looked at the sign, then shrugged. 'I don't think Galadriel is seeing any new customers at the moment.'

Lume laughed dismally.

'We'll have to take our chances,' Alalia spoke as she gestured her brother forwards and started for the entrance to Galadriel's alleyway. 'We really must keep moving. I'm sorry, Fae–'

'What?!' Faerydae started, feeling that she'd overcome too much, been too patient with this girl whom she felt was mostly to blame for everything that had happened to her. Faerydae shuffled towards the alleyway entrance, blocking it somewhat with her body. 'You can't believe that us meeting again is a coincidence, can you? I surely don't, no BLOODY way! After everything we experienced together, you're really just going to run away again.' Faerydae searched her mind. 'You left me signs, Alalia,' she protested. 'You have been guiding me back to you this whole time. What about the sunflowers?'

Alalia stopped trying to sidestep the girl as Jákob hung back, watching what would happen next.

'Flowers?' Alalia repeated softly. 'I don't know what you mean.'

'You do!' Faerydae argued. 'You left a trail of sunflowers to guide me out of the woods. And what about at my olde home, the lagoon; you went there, didn't you? Looking to see if I had returned from the woods as well. But when you found everything destroyed like it was, you left me a sunflower just in case I ever did make it home. Tell me the truth, Alalia! You owe me that much.'

Alalia turned away, keeping her eyes on the ground so she did not dare show her true emotion.

'You tried to run away?' It was Jákob now, asking such a candid question to his sister.

'Yes,' Alalia said in a huff. 'I tried to run. And yes, I left those flowers for you Faerydae. But I was wrong to do so. I have more *important* things to focus on now. I have my own life to worry about. I am sorry, Fae. But I've finally accepted who I am, what I am destined to do. And I will not try to run from it ever again.'

Faerydae shook her head, grimacing in disbelief. 'I don't believe you.'

Alalia twirled away from them both furiously, causing the unicorn to shy and scramble backwards.

'I am SICK of everybody thinking they know me!' Alalia bellowed. 'Know what I feel and what I want! All you people ever do is end up being disappointed! What right do any of you have? Listen to me, Faerydae, and listen good: step out of my *way*, step out of my *life* and you'll be much better off for it. People just end up getting hurt when they're around me.'

Faerydae could see the pain in Alalia's eyes, her skin was tight with stress, with worry and hurt. There was an imperative longing in her gaze to be set free. Despite everything she was saying, Faerydae still felt the exact same way she always had for the girl. She felt sorry for her. She felt an obligation to make her feel the way she deserved to feel. Faerydae had always believed that Alalia deserved to be happy, to be loved and to be kept safe.

'What are you looking for in the Shop of Comings and Goings, Alalia?' Faerydae asked next. 'Believe me when I saw that nothing good awaits you in there.'

'You wouldn't understand, Faerydae,' she replied hopelessly. 'This is all far bigger than you now.'

Faerydae felt Lume's form inside her pocket again. She bit her lip. *Alalia needed to know.* Alalia *needed* to know that Faerydae knew things too.

'Are you so sure of that?' Faerydae asked. 'Just tell me what you are looking for, Alalia.'

Jákob eyed his sister closely, wondering if she would show any such trust in this stranger, or if she was playing an entirely different game. For Jákob knew his sister too well, the different sides of her that were unravelling, deteriorating, ever more since she had begun to lose herself completely. She was falling into that same hopelessness in the world's compassion as their father had.

'We...' Alalia glanced briefly at Jákob. 'We are looking for an omen. Apparently, one has been residing in this village for some time.'

'Alalia?' Jákob warned. 'We can't trust *anyone.*'

'You can trust me,' Faerydae cut in. 'You can, Alalia.' She stepped towards the redhead, reaching into her pocket. Lume was threatening Faerydae in a way she had never heard him do before. He warned her with such distinction to NOT reveal him. But Alalia's eyes were too hypnotising. She pulled him free of her coat and held him out in her hand for all to see, it was the first time she had ever shared Lume with another person before.

Alalia and Jákob both glared at the gem, searching it over with their eyes so as to try and understand its significance.

'Where did you get that?' Alalia asked, staring at Lume.

'I've had him for ages,' Faerydae stated. 'He calls himself Lume, and he is a rather devilish thing.'

'Hello, Lume,' Alalia said sweetly. She looked up and met Faerydae's wary gaze. 'You know, Faerydae, my brother rode *all* night to find me here – and it would have been a bumpy ride upon that beast, but it was an important ride–'

'Very,' Faerydae interjected. 'Whatever happened to Lolanthie?'

Jákob inhaled a quick breath at that name and held it tightly inside his chest.

'Lolanthie?' Alalia said in surprise. 'Why, that *is* Lolanthie. My father *changed* him. He can travel to places he never could before now, though

I know his transformation has been rather shocking.' She shook her head. Jákob finally exhaled his breath. 'But what I'm trying to say,' Alalia continued. 'Is that Jákob *needed* to find me, Fae. For he has built something that can recognise an omen's magical pulses in particles of the air. So many people claim to have omens, Fae, but they are rarely one of the true five. Do you mind if I let Jákob use his Ometer on this gem?'

Faerydae leaned away just a minute amount, taking Lume with her, just to show that she did not trust Alalia quite that much. It was so subtle, but Alalia recognised then that there was a tension between them not wanting to be noticed. She smiled despite herself.

'Please, Faerydae,' Alalia said. 'It is extremely important.'

Faerydae sighed, nodded agreeably.

Jákob stepped forth and approached Faerydae, lifting a small gadget out of his assortment and thrusting it towards her. Lolanthie hovered where he stood, untethered. He almost looked like he wanted so terribly to run away but dared not.

The gadget looked like some sort of a magnifying glass attached to a glowing handle, a cylindrical compartment of sorts, filled with little white orbs. Jákob moved the invention around Lume's form. Lume remained silent as he did so. The omen was angry, angrier than words could express, possibly even disappointed. *Betrayed.*

Jákob's ometer started to shudder and change colour in response to its close proximity with Lume. It was like the collection of glowing fireflies within the ometer's handle were trying to escape, to fly out and engulf Lume within their glow. They were bright red.

Alalia and her brother exchanged quizzical gazes.

'Is that a good sign?' Alalaia asked him.

Jákob itched his nose. 'Gotta be. I haven't seen the sparks swarm like this before, usually they just change colour. This object must be a true omen, the omen of fire, just like she said. Lume.'

They all stared at one another.

Alalia gripped Faerydae by her shoulders. 'Do you know what this means, Fae?'

Faerydae stepped back, holding Lume tight.

'Lume is one of the five omens I, and so many others, have been searching for,' Alalia urged, following Faerydae until she had backed right up against the coarse brick wall. 'It needs to be reunited with its brothers and sisters, Fae.' Alalia looked to Jákob who was holding Lolanthie tight again, then back to Faerydae. 'We have already acquired two other omens, Fae. Terra, the omen of the soil. He was being hidden by the Wolseley worms, deep underground, in their basement. And the omen of breath, Vida. She was hiding in the Ivory Mountains, my papa found her many years ago.' She paused, growing excited and apparently hopeful for the first time in a long time. 'If we find the rest Faerydae, they will be able to create a single omen again, just as they were when they were first breathed. My father's father's father crafted the first omen. It was formed in the clock tower of Wilburry's cathedral, by a vicar named Garwick Miseria. Jákob and I are his direct heirs, one of *us* will be able to tame the all-powerful omen, and bring magic out of the shadows. It won't have to hide any longer! Imagine that, Faerydae. People like us, we will belong. We won't have to hide anymore. Magic will exist in *every* object and *every* thought, not just those that are hidden, those that are shameful and *bad*. You can join us. We're riding back to Amaryllis tonight to deliver our findings to my papa. If you'll just give Lume to me, I can repay you.'

Faerydae frowned. 'Repay me?' she had to repeat the absurd notion.

'Of course,' Alalia implored. 'Whatever you want... Even perhaps...' She looked at Faerydae's bottled heart, on the ground beside the alleyway. 'Would you like to have your heart back, Fae? To have it safely inside of your chest? I could give you that. You know I can. I'm a wiccan, more powerful than you know.'

Faerydae's breath dropped into her stomach, feeling too heavy and too palpable to reacquire. She felt as if she'd forgotten how to breathe entirely. She could hear her beating heart thudding frantically against the glass sides of its jar. It was trying to get out of its cage, to slither back into her body. What Alalia was suggesting had been her whole life's dream; it was *everything* and the *only thing* she had *ever* wished for. And yet, she knew so surely that it was not right.

Faerydae looked down at Lume. He was still not saying a word; his quietude suggested the importance of every word that was to follow. Her hands just wanted to give the spiteful gem over to Alalia. Faerydae *knew* that Alalia was a good person, deep, deep down. Faerydae believed she truly was. But her hands still would not move of their own accord.

Alalia's teeth were beginning to clench. 'It is your choice, Fae,' she said. 'Do the right thing.'

Faerydae stared through Alalia, begging her to be more convincing than that. Lume drew closer to Alalia's clutches as Faerydae found herself starting to walk towards her.

Surely, Faerydae's whole life had been leading up to this point. That was as much as she could assume. Her story, it was drawing closer to its end. She would *finally* have her heart. Even though, it seemed she already did. *Didn't she?* For there it truly sat, right before her.

Faerydae's head was throbbing. She could not quite reach the answer when the question seemed to keep changing. *Do the right thing,* Alalia had said...

What had changed within Faerydae since recovering her organ – if anything? She had fought so hard to claim her heart back, yet it wasn't really what she had been looking for. What Faerydae had found in the woods was not her heart at all, it was herself. She now knew how strong she truly was. Her heart hadn't changed her, it couldn't, she was exactly the same despite it.

'Give Lume to me, Faerydae,' Alalia said with finality. 'And I shall give you what you have always wanted.'

'I...' Faerydae felt her palms begin to sweat. 'I can't do that Alalia. I can't. I'm sorry.'

Alalia clenched her eyes tightly shut, her entire being slumping in on itself. 'Please,' she pleaded wearily. 'Please don't make me hurt you, Faerydae. Just don't.'

'You won't hurt me,' Faerydae whispered, hoping it to be true.

'Oh, Fae,' Alalia groaned. 'You really don't know me at all.'

A wicked flash danced across Alalia's gaze. She changed so instantaneously that nobody at all could have seen her next attack coming.

Faerydae screamed as an invisible wave of energy blasted against her chest, throwing her sideways and into the brick wall halfway down the street. Lume fell from her hand and onto the cobbled stones by Lolanthie's peculiar clawed hooves.

Alalia's arms hung tensely in the air at her sides, as if she was holding some invisible force. Jákob backed away, attempting to settle Lolanthie down and not let him crush the precious omen.

'I warned you not to make me do this, Faerydae!' Alalia called down to the girl. 'But you never listen! You never do what you are told!'

Faerydae clawed herself up to her knees and scrambled back across the street towards Lume. But Alalia was moving faster. The redhead reached Lume just as Faerydae gained some traction.

Alalia snatched the gem up and held it to her face. Faerydae hovered just metres from her. She watched as Alalia examined Lume briefly. Her knees stung and her arms felt weak, but Faerydae urged herself to rise up and attack the girl she had once loved so dearly. Lume finally spoke then, in fact, every single person near heard him as clear as day.

'DO IT!' he cried. 'DO IT NOW, FLEA, OR YOU WON'T EVER GET THE CHANCE!'

Faerydae nodded. She leapt into action, tackling Alalia to the ground by wrapping her arms around the girl's torso. Alalia cried out and back-rolled onto her knees. She held Lume firm all the while, smiling at Faerydae's courage.

'You cannot win,' Alalia assured her. 'You are only common, Faerydae Nóvalie. I am a wiccan, whatever were you planning to do?'

Faerydae snarled. 'You have always underestimated me, Alalia.' She climbed shakily to her feet once more. 'But you don't really know me either. I am a *princess*! And my best friend happens to be that vulgar little gem in your hands! You will not take him from me.'

Alalia's free hand once again tensed around the air at her sides, holding the power of elusive magical particles in her grasp.

'Don't make me laugh at you, Faerydae,' Alalia warned. 'Don't make me stoop to that level, little *princess*.'

Lume began to glow just then, held tight in Alalia's other hand. He turned almost instantaneously from a pale orange to a burning hot red. Alalia's hand started to steam as he burned his way free of her hold. The redhead cried out, unable to keep her fist clenched around him, letting Lume fall towards the rigid road. But Lume did not fall far, he caught himself in midair, floating peacefully before the girl as Alalia gripped her burning hand with the other. Her face contorted in pain, but she set her sights back on the omen, snatching for him again. He hissed at her desperate hands alike a serpent.

'Get those sticky hands away me, you bitch!' He screamed and a searing sound tore across the sky.

A blazing fire burst forth from Lume's glowing core, sending Alalia flying from the flames he produced. Faerydae held her hands across her eyes so as to protect them from the intense light. The jar concealing her heart immediately shattered at the piercing sound. Faerydae felt a sharpness inside of her chest as glass cascaded over her delicate organ.

Alalia's velocity sent her tumbling almost ten metres across the road until she collided with the villa walls on the other side of the street. Lume growled viscously as he turned his attention to Faerydae.

'Let's go!' he called to her and Faerydae nodded frenziedly.

She ran to her heart where it lay in a pile of shattered glass. There was not a scratch upon the thing, but her body still ached. She knew why: she was frightened, she was *heartbroken*. Faerydae held the heart in her bare hands, feeling it beat with such a closeness, skin against skin. The heart was soft and warm, fragile and yet so powerful. With nowhere else to put it, Faerydae merely plopped the thing inside of her other coat pocket, opposite where Lume liked to sit. She turned round.

Jákob had apparently given up on Lolanthie and was running for his sister as she lay within a crumpled pile of bricks. He attempted to pry her free of the rubble, tossing pieces of brick back across the street in a frantic panic. Jákob cared for that girl more than she could ever care for him, Faerydae considered. She looked to the unicorn next. Lolanthie's hazy eyes looked through her. He hadn't yet made for his escape, he was anxiously shuffling from one foot to the other, unsure where he should flee to.

'Come on!' Faerydae said, running up to and grabbing Lume from the air. He glowed evilly within his plumes of flames, but none of them dared touch the girl as she retrieved him. Faerydae held Lume firm as she crept into Lolanthie's company, raising her hands up as a sign of kindness. 'Now, now, boy,' she said softly. 'It's me, Faerydae. You remember me boy? I don't know what they've done to you, but you're safe with me.'

She stepped closer, one foot at a time, until she was almost able to stroke his flaring nostrils.

'GET HER!' Alalia's voice sounded off in the distance. 'GET THE

OMEN, JÁKOB! PAPA WILL KILL US BOTH!' The redhead was climbing out of the bricks, seemingly unfazed by the attack.

Faerydae snatched Lolanthie's reins, with no time to soothe his fragile nerves any longer. Lolanthie reared as Faerydae scrambled her way onto his near-vertical back. Jákob raised his crossbow and kneeled upon one leg to gain balance. He aimed with one beautiful grey eye and fired just as Faerydae kicked the unicorn in his sides, sending him galloping in an instance.

The arrow made a distinct *zoom* sound as it sliced the back of Faerydae's head. It stung the girl but missed anything important. Three more arrows came her way as Faerydae steered Lolanthie up the veering street that would lead them back to Flood Lane. The arrows narrowly missed Faerydae. They missed the unicorn too, which seemed an equally imperative factor to their ultimate escape.

Following the arrows was a bombardment of mighty explosions, all of which resided from Alalia's hands. The girl was now hovering just above the road, being levitated by the sheer amount of magic that she'd called upon and was now surrounding her. She almost looked like Temperance to Faerydae now, with such anger and fury in her eyes.

Though the airy blasts ravaged the road ahead and made it difficult for Lolanthie to continue on, he did not stop running even as the crumpling stones fell out from under him. The unicorn surged to freedom in the cloud of dust that each explosion caused.

When the dust settled in front of the Miseria children, Faerydae, Lolanthie and, most importantly, the omen, were gone.

Alalia screamed in such a vile way, creating a noise unlike anything she or any creature she'd encountered had ever made. It was as if she was turning into a disgusting, ruined monster, which frightened even herself.

The girl sunk back to the street, too hollow to chase after the unicorn. There would be time enough to recover the lot of them – if Alejandro saw fit to keep either of the Miseria children alive, that was. Alalia couldn't find it in herself to even raise her head just yet, she needed time to regain her bravado. For now, it seemed, she accepted that she had failed.

Alalia had failed, *yet again*.

54

Lolanthie would not stop running for some time, Faerydae knew it all too well. She was quite acquainted with the beast. And he was still that same frightened stallion she had once known, even in such a form as this. His skeletal frame jostling beneath her body was the most uncomfortable thing Faerydae had ever experienced, but she didn't care, she was moving farther and farther away from Alalia and from Brindille, and towards her mother, wherever she might be by now.

Ultimately, Faerydae was heading to Wilburry, and she would not stop until she arrived there.

Lume knew the path to take and Lolanthie was only too willing to run faster, wherever the wind might steer him. Faerydae tucked Lume into his coat pocket, next to her heart, to keep him from falling from her hand during the incessant whiplashing of Lolanthie's stride.

'I'm so sorry, Lume,' Faerydae cried, crying for so many reasons at the one time. 'I didn't think she...'

'*It's okay, Flea,*' Lume spoke in the softest voice he had ever beheld. '*Neither of us saw it coming, my dear.*'

Lume glowed again, first orange, then a pale red, not burning hot this time but just nice. A pleasant warmth. Faerydae stared on as Lume's ambiance sparkled through the material of her coat. *So beautiful.*

Thanks to of the omen's powerful light, Lolanthie was able to see the path ahead even when the sunlight in the sky faded out completely. Faerydae cried on all the while, unable to stop herself. She'd never cried quite like this before, deemed she had never truly cried at all until now – she'd never had anything worth losing.

'*There, there,*' Lume purred. '*You are safe, little Flea. I won't let anybody hurt you. We'll get through this together. I promise.*'

The omen kept Faerydae warm as they galloped towards the infamous city of Wilburry, towards more danger than ever before . Lume's warmth and his soothing words made Faerydae feel safe as a gentle sprinkling of rain started to fall, washing away Lolanthie's hoofprints in the dirt.

Froalla.

Georgie DeLaine

END

BOOK ONE

Shawline Publishing Group Pty Ltd
www.shawlinepublishing.com.au

SHAWLINE
PUBLISHING
GROUP